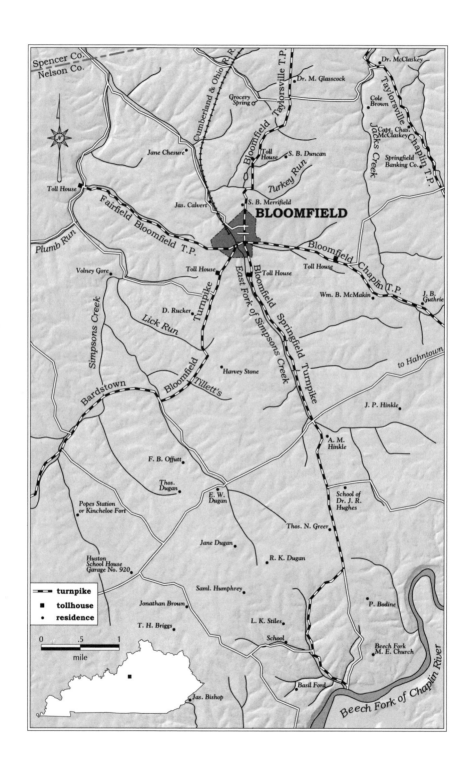

Spencer Co.
Nelson Co.

Dr. McClaskey

Dr. M. Glasscock

Cole
Brown

Grocery
Spring

Capt. Chas.
McClaskey

Jane Chesure

Toll
House

S. B. Duncan

Springfield
Banking Co.

Turkey Run

Jas. Calvert

S. B. Merrifield

BLOOMFIELD

Toll House

Bloomfield Chaplin T.P.

Plumb Run

Toll House

Toll House

Toll House

Volney Gore

Wm. B. McMakin

J. B.
Guthrie

D. Rucker

Lick Run

to Hahntown

Harvey Stone

Bardstown

Tillett's

J. P. Hinkle

A. M.
Hinkle

F. B. Offutt

Thos.
Dugan

E. W.
Dugan

School of
Dr. J. R.
Hughes

Popes Station
or Kincheloe Fort

Thos. N. Greer

Jane Dugan

R. K. Dugan

Huston
School House
Garage No. 920

Saml. Humphrey

P. Bodine

Jonathan Brown

L. K. Stiles

T. H. Briggs

School

Beech Fork
M. E. Church

══ turnpike

■ tollhouse

• residence

0   .5   1

mile

Basil Ford

Jas. Bishop

Beech Fork of Chaplin River

SUE MUNDY

Kentucky Voices

Editorial Advisory Board: Wendell Berry, Billy C. Clark, James Baker Hall, George Ella Lyon, Bobbie Ann Mason, Ed McClanahan, Gurney Norman, Mary Ann Taylor-Hall, Richard Taylor, and Frank X Walker

Buffalo Dance: The Journey of York
Frank X Walker

The Cave
Robert Penn Warren

Famous People I Have Known
Ed McClanahan

Miss America Kissed Caleb
Billy C. Clark

Sue Mundy: A Novel of the Civil War
Richard Taylor

The Total Light Process: New and Selected Poems
James Baker Hall

SUE MUNDY

A NOVEL OF THE CIVIL WAR

RICHARD TAYLOR

The University Press of Kentucky

Publication of this volume was made possible in part by a grant
from the National Endowment for the Humanities.

Published by the University Press of Kentucky
Scholarly publisher for the Commonwealth,
serving Bellarmine University, Berea College, Centre College of Kentucky,
Eastern Kentucky University, The Filson Historical Society, Georgetown College,
Kentucky Historical Society, Kentucky State University, Morehead State University,
Murray State University, Northern Kentucky University, Transylvania University,
University of Kentucky, University of Louisville, and Western Kentucky University.

Editorial and Sales Offices: The University Press of Kentucky
663 South Limestone Street, Lexington, Kentucky 40508–4008
www.kentuckypress.com

Images courtesy of Kentucky Historical Society.
Maps by Dick Gilbreath.

10 09 08 07 06   5 4 3 2 1

Library of Congress Cataloging-in-Publication Data

Taylor, Richard, 1941-
    Sue Mundy : a novel of the Civil War / by Richard Taylor.
        p. cm. — (Kentucky voices)
    ISBN-13: 978-0-8131-2423-0 (alk. paper)
    ISBN-10: 0-8131-2423-9 (alk. paper)
    1. Clarke, Marcellus Jerome, 1844-1865—Fiction. 2. United States—History
—Civil War, 1861-1865—Fiction.   I. Title.
    PS3570.A9515S84 2006
    813'.54—dc22   2006024022

Manufactured in the United States of America.

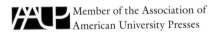

Member of the Association of
American University Presses

For my children,
Willis and Julia
and
In memory of
Philip Richard Taylor
(1978–2003)

"We are a short time here,
a long time gone."

ACKNOWLEDGMENTS

Over the nearly thirty years taken to complete this novel, many friends have given me assistance and encouragement in writing about the brief and violent career of Marcellus Jerome Clarke, whose nom de guerre was Sue Mundy. I am grateful to them.

Parts have been published both early and late, including "Logan County, 1855," "Aunt Mary Tibbs," "Cockfight," "The Pond," and "Magruder" in *The Journal of Kentucky Studies,* Volume One, Issue One, Northern Kentucky University, July 1984. "Sequestered," "Out the Newburgh Road," and "Simpsonville" appeared in volume two of the same journal, September 1985. "Logan County, 1855" was printed in *Hard Scuffle Folio '82,* Winter Edition, Nana Publications, Louisville. "Recessional: Louisville, March 15, 1865" appeared in a chapbook titled *Shackles,* Richard Taylor and George Wolfe, Frankfort Arts Foundation, 1988. More recently, David Batholomy will publish an excerpt titled "Caldwell" in *Open 24 Hours,* Brescia University, Owensboro, Kentucky. *Kentucky River,* the literary magazine at Kentucky State University, will publish an excerpt called "Home Life." "Redemption" has been accepted for publication by the *Journal of Kentucky Studies.*

Thanks to the National Endowment for the Arts for awarding a creative writing fellowship that granted me time to research and write a first draft and to Jack Shoemaker of Counterpoint for having the manuscript critiqued, giving me valuable insights when I took up the work again years later. Thanks to Kentucky State University, which awarded me a faculty research grant to travel to Washington, D.C., to dig up military records and court martial proceedings in the National Archives. Thanks, too, especially to my chairperson and friend George Shields for his support of a sabbatical during the fall semester of 2004 to research, rewrite, and complete the manuscript. Thanks to George Weick and the late David Orr (my literary godfather), who sampled the manuscript and pointed out more than one bird that wouldn't fly. Warm thanks to James Baker Hall and Jeff Worley for reading the manuscript and making many helpful suggestions. Thanks especially to my dear friend Michael Moran, who uncomplainingly combed many kinks out of the text and offered helpful medical and literary therapies relating to Jerome Clarke's evolution from the perspective of an escaped English major who now practices psychiatry. Thanks to historian Jo Fisher of Midway, who generously provided information relating to the raid on Woodburn Farm. Thanks to Harold Edwards of Perryville and Steven L. Wright of Elizabethtown, scholars both, who know more of the guerrilla war in Kentucky than can be found in books or fiction writers can imagine. Thanks to the Kentucky Historical Society, the Filson Historical Society, and Special Collections of the Margaret I. King Library at the University of Kentucky for their assistance in securing photographs. Photographers Gene Burch and Bob Lanham printed and digitally improved the photographs in this book and, in one instance, resurrected the intentionally marred photo of Sue Mundy and Mollie Thomas from nearly complete visual obscurity. And thanks to Cheryl Hoffman of Hyattsville, Maryland, for her astute copyediting. I especially am grateful to Steve Wrinn, director of the University Press of Kentucky, who, with the hardworking staff, gave me encouragement and full partnership at every stage of preparation. Finally, I am beholden to my wife, Lizz, with the assistance of Kenny Bates, for her patient technical aid to one whose computer skills remain unreconstructably antebellum.

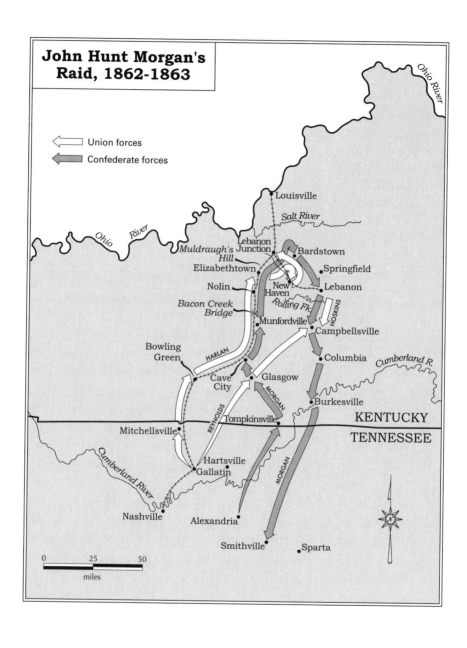

John Hunt Morgan's Raid, 1862-1863

Union forces
Confederate forces

Ohio River

Louisville
Salt River
Lebanon Junction
Muldraugh's Hill
Bardstown
Elizabethtown
Springfield
Nolin
New Haven
Lebanon
Bacon Creek Bridge
Rolling Fk.
HOSKINS
Munfordville
Campbellsville
Bowling Green
HARLAN
Columbia
Cumberland R.
Cave City
Glasgow
MORGAN
Burkesville
REYNOLDS
Tompkinsville
KENTUCKY
Mitchellsville
TENNESSEE
Cumberland River
Hartsville
Gallatin
MORGAN
Nashville
Alexandria
Smithville
Sparta

Ohio River

0   25   50
miles

SUE MUNDY

SUE MUNDY: A PORTRAIT

Several likenesses of Marcellus Jerome Clarke, aka Sue Mundy, survive him. All are daguerreotypes taken during the war years, most between 1864 and the early months of 1865. The best presents a boyish figure seated—slumped, really—on a simple chair, right leg crossed over left knee, booted ankle resting forward on the cap of the knee, too far forward for comfort, strained momentarily for the eye of posterity, obviously a pose. The impression is studied repose, the upper half relaxed, the lower self-consciously and rigidly fixed in an attitude just short of swagger. The arms, superfluous before the camera, billow slightly from the narrow shoulders (not a man's shoulders) and drop to either side, the thumb of the right hand braced against the chair seat, fingers curled under, a little tense. The jackboot extends up the shin beyond the knee, running diagonally across the lower half of the body and jutting into the foreground. Unnaturally large, it gives the overall image an exaggerated sense of depth. A blaze of intense light adheres to the buffed leather of the boot.

The face, no longer a boy's face, is fringed by shoulder-length hair, thick girl-like tresses that fall back over the shoulders. The head is surmounted by a felt hat turned up on the sides, worn high and angled downward in a graceful curve. To the right rear of the hat, dropping over the shoulder like a foxtail, is an outrageous plume. Possibly an ostrich feather, though it is dyed darker, as dark as the hat. Minus boots and mannish style of knee-crossing, the form is arguably feminine.

Features are distributed evenly over the face, the wide-set eyes focused on the camera's lens, the mouth similarly broad but down at the corners, forming a gradual arch, full underlip set firmly. The chin is prominent, high cheekbones contributing to the feminine countenance. Elusive and fluid, the expression caught is earnest and desperately resolute, yet with no malevolence, no sign of the felon, the fanatic, the sadist. Pride, yes, and latent defiance in the firmly set mouth, the thrust of the chin. The composition is the sum of its gestures. No theme is stated for us, the expression holding itself intact, obediently neutral. The overall impression is tension held in check, motion and energy disengaged, suspended temporarily like the torso of a dozing boxer. Opposing this slumbering resilience is the softer cast of the features, the warm sepia tones of the original plate, the intricately wrought curlicues and arabesque tooling of the frame whose swags form a series of buttocks or bosoms. The right eye is bleared slightly as if irritated by the photographer's artificial light, an eye resisting the inclination to blink, intent on perpetuity.

He is wearing a cavalry uniform. Cavalryman: horse-man, chevalier, cavalier, chivalry-man. The short, single-breasted, woolen jacket, called a roundabout, is studded with brass buttons unfastened in fashionable disarray, except for the topmost, which secures the plain, square, clerical collar. Without frill, ascetic, this collar contrasts sharply with the courtier's plume. While the sleeves are cut of proper length, the jacket appears ill-fitting, snug, which may account for the unbuttoned front. Probably the jacket is ready-made, sized and fitted out for the frame of a hypothetical patriot. Underneath is a vest or waistcoat and an invisible row of closely set buttons. At the neck is the hint of a chemise. The total effect of this outfit is androgynous—a young woman masquerading as a male, a male masquerading as a young woman.

On both hips ride revolvers, probably the much-favored Colt, butts forward in the style for ease and quick cross-drawing on horseback, the long barrel removed from the holster with the opposing hand, lifted less awkwardly and thrust clear in one sweeping motion. On the butt of each is a metal plate to which crescent-shaped grips are attached, modeled to fit the hand efficiently. Each handle is covered with a leather flap that buttons or snaps to the holster, a precaution when riding. Not seen is the silver crescent said to have been pinned to his hat for luck. His face seems depleted, melancholy, a little wistful but somehow familiar. What part of him is none of us, what part all of us?

PART ONE

There is something in the very air of Kentucky which makes a man soldier.

—*The Baltimore Patriot*

His appearance was striking, namely six feet in height, slender but sinewy, straight as an arrow, face smooth and full (he was not yet 21 years old) with long dark hair reaching to his shoulders; it seemed so strange, so sad to associate such resounding villainies with so seemly a form and so juvenile an actor.

—C.V.S., *New York Times,* March 16, 1865

The moral effect upon the young of the nation on the perusal of such a life as that which is here faithfully detailed, with its awfully ignominious end, can not fail to be of the most salutary kind, and dissuasives to crime will be found in its own history.

—Major Cyrus J. Wilson,
*Three Years in the Saddle:
The Life and Confession of Henry C. Magruder*

LOGAN COUNTY, 1855

Uncle Nether led the way through woods a mile from any path Jarom knew. The old man shambled like a bear, his bulk borne forward in an easy rolling motion lighter than his years. He was thick, ageless as the stump in the Tibbses' kitchen yard, his caramel-colored skin free of creases and hair, the mappings of age. Crossing the wide bottom, he led Jarom through what seemed to the boy an ocean of nettles, acres of black silt that flooded and bogged each spring like the Nile, the river in Egypt he'd read about in Woodbridge's *Modern Geography*. The ground was nearly treeless, the rises drowning most roots except for a fringe of willows and stolid sycamores along the creek and a few maples whose undersides were silver—trees that tolerated high water.

There had been a shower, and the laps of Nether's jacket raked water from the heart-shaped leaves, stems switching to one side as they passed, whipping back against Jarom's hands. Tromping a path through the nettles, Nether, rumpled collar half covering his grizzled head, seemed legless. Wading, he wore the weeds like a girdle, his arms outthrust above the stinging hairs. Jarom watched as he navigated his way toward higher ground, each step high and cautious against what he could not see. Shorter, the bucket bumping his side, Jarom could hold only one hand free. The bucket hand, pulled down by the weight, dragged dangerously over the invisible barbs, and Jarom knew he could not both escape the stings and keep the bucket. The first ones were sharp and tingling, prickling his wrist with a thousand tiny needles, telegraphing pain through the conduits of his nerves, skin puffing red. The smarting shot up his arm faster and more painful than he could keep from showing. They walked a few yards farther before Nether uttered his warning.

"Don't let those stickers take and bite you," he said. "They'll sting you till you want to cry."

7

They walked nearly a mile through the creek bottom before the nettles opened onto a mudflat, a creek bed brilliant with white stones, its banks cracked in crazy patterns. Jarom sensed they were stepping from the nettle world to the water world. He was soaked, his pants legs clinging to him like flour-meal paste, pinching and slowing him as he stepped into unhindered space. Looking up, he saw a buzzard lofting over the ridgeline, its wingtips balanced and curled under like wind rudders.

For a time they stopped while Nether studied the way, then tottered across the rocks to go at the nettles again, Jarom fighting through until they reached firmer footing on the slope that rose out of the bottom. Imitating Nether, he used the trees as handholds, pulling himself up with the help of saplings and vines. Halfway up, Nether turned, Jarom turned, to look back on the quiltwork of green filling the low ground to either side of the branch, a trail of silver ruin where they had tramped through, light pricking the tree tops, pearly spittle in the leaves. Listening, he could hear the scritching of birds and the fidget of woodlife among the trees that was as much a presence as a sound.

Jarom carried the bucket, Nether the ax. He clutched it by the neck as he had taught Jarom, hurting edge to the world. The ground as they climbed gave under layers of sodden leaves whose undersides smelled to Jarom like the cellar under his aunt's house. Where the going was steepest, Nether planted the heel of his ax in the mulch, grasping the handle as he would a staff to steady himself. Each step they took etched a path in Jarom's memory—the snapping of twigs, the bird-twitter that grew louder uphill among the sheltering oaks, specks of light that filled his vision and registered almost like sound. He followed the split seam running up Nether's back, the coat he wore dropping shapeless from the mound of shoulders like a blanket. One elbow was out, and the nap had worn from wool that was dove gray and darkened in places with colonies of stain, one mean red cocklebur riding the hem. From behind, Nether's head looked to Jarom like a spit-thistle, perfect but for an umber slab of baldness scooping down the stubble onto the bull neck. His smell was overheated rooms and bacon.

Where the ground flattened at the crest of the ridge, Nether hunkered against a sugar tree, the breath sucking into his chest in measured gasps. The sun was high now and dazzled off the rocks. Jarom could feel the globules of sweat pop as they beaded on his face, the pain in his wrist now a persistent itch. Laying the ax by, Nether worked one arm and then the other out of his jacket. His black galluses formed bands down his shirtfront, his sleeves wet with gray patties of sweat in the pit of each massive arm. He was thick about the middle, but Jarom could detect no slackness, no cables of fat. From his pocket Nether drew forth a red bandanna and wiped the beads from his forehead and the hollows of his neck. His pink tongue swiped once across his full lips. Palm over his mouth, he turned to look at Jarom sitting across from him, legs crossed Indian style. He watched as Jarom rubbed the crease in his bucket hand.

"That bucket too heavy for you?" he asked.

"Not yet it isn't," Jarom said, turning his palm down to hide it.

And that was all. After they had gone another quarter mile, Jarom, his arm now aching with every step, had to ask him how much farther.

Squatting, Nether looked into the trees ahead as if to measure the miles.

"Not much farther," he said, nodding somewhere indeterminately ahead. All Jarom could see along the ridge were outcroppings of stone and a few scraggly cedars rimmed with brush. He'd expected him to point toward the bluest feathering of trees on the farthest ridge.

"Fact," he said, "right here'll do just fine." Jarom could see him grinning for the first time. "One spot will suit as well as another when you just come down to it. It isn't the place that counts so much but what you bring to it."

"But how will I know this is the right place?" Jarom asked.

"You just will," he said. "You just will."

Carefully hanging his jacket on a limb, Nether set to work, picking up the ax and swiping at the undergrowth, cutting and piling the scrubby cedars to one side. Using the blade of the ax as a flail, he beat back the brambles, swinging the handle in low, wide arcs. Though to Jarom he seemed to make little progress, soon bush and stalk bent and broke, humbled under the punishment. In a few minutes Nether had cleared a bare spot about six feet across.

"Now fetch the bucket," he said, and Jarom brought it back to him.

Picking up a thumb-sized stick, he stirred the corncobs in their bed of honey and sorghum molasses into a lumpy mush.

"See that rotting log over there?" he said. "Bring me a slab of its bark about the size of a shovel's face."

When he was satisfied that the cobs were sopped, Nether laid the stick aside and picked up the bucket, pouring some of the thick mixings onto the bark. With the stick he worked the gummy mass until it was spread evenly over the yellowing inner bark. When he'd finished, he gave a grunt, collecting bucket, ax, and his coat from where he left it on the limb, motioning Jarom to follow.

"Now, honey," he said, "watch what comes to sweetness."

The lookout he chose lay in speckled shade, just into the trees where he and Jarom could eye the bark without drawing notice to themselves. Unlike the rocks, the shade to Jarom seemed to swim with motion. The trees formed a knit of shadow that shifted with the slightest breeze. The light riddling the dust reminded him of Uncle Beverley in his garden, his face flecking with sunlight through the basketry of his hat.

The slab was about thirty feet away. Beyond it was furrow after furrow of ridge that in the distance softened into the silver blue of sky. Jarom asked Nether what to do next.

"Hush," he said. "Keep your eyes hungry and your mouth shut, and you just might see something."

Jarom locked his eyes on the clearing with its centered bark slab. Each rock, each twig, each tuft of stubble was still as though glued in place and drying under the heavy wedge of sky. Watching, Jarom could almost feel the glare building in the rocks, the green baking out of the piled cedars. When he looked toward the rocks, he could see a fluting of heat rising off them. In the clearing was the honey on its bark platter, an amber splash in which he recognized the color of resin knots on the enormous black cherry shading the fencerow at home.

They waited over an hour before Nether nudged him, directing his eyes to the honey. Jarom didn't see anything at first but soon spotted a dark speck that flitted into the clearing, orbiting a few times before lighting on the slab. A honeybee. One of the dark natives that Nether described as "nigger bees." Diving, it feasted on the gooey cobs, a bullet springing nervously from one to the other in sticky leaps. This went on for several minutes. Then, rising perceptibly slower, almost drunkenly, the speck made a circuit above the bare spot and struck off neatly through the trees.

"This missionary," Nether said, breaking the silence, "has gone off among the Canaanites to spread the good news."

Soon, more specks darted into the clearing and flew the ritual circuit before descending on the sweetened cobs. They would feed for a while, then rise abruptly and vanish in the same direction as the first.

Before they could return, Nether hustled Jarom over to fetch the slab. Nether took it and started off through the woods, roughly in the direction of the bees. About a hundred yards in, he and Jarom came to a natural clearing next to a place where a large oak had fallen. The clearing was smaller than the first, covered with buckberries and some spindly grass. Nether deftly flattened a space with the ax, batting down the buckberries until a flyway was cleared. Again the slab was placed in the center, this time on the splintered stump of the fallen tree. More honeyed corncobs were poured onto the slab, and Nether led him to a niche in the trees, closer and not so well hidden this time.

In minutes the mixture was black with bees, each taking its fill and zipping off along the same route. As they rose from the bait, Nether carefully calculated the path of flight between the trees until he was sure his sighting was true. When Jarom asked how he meant to follow, Nether explained that the course the bees traveled was a path in the air that would lead them directly to the honey-pot, for the line from the first feeding spot to the second would form arrows that crossed. Where they met, Nether told him, they would find the hive. Facing ahead, then turning to face behind, Nether sighted until he seem satisfied.

"Halfway to honey," he said when he'd finished. "Now we know which way, we just must know how far."

To fix the distance, he paced off an imaginary line of about fifty or sixty yards, then reset the slab. Again the bees came, lifting from the honey toward the hive. Leaving Jarom to follow that line, Nether returned to the original, telling him that to find the hive they had to walk very straight. Each set off following their lines, which met about a quarter-mile away. They had crossed along another ridge to reach a dense stand of trees, mostly hickories and white oak. The branches formed a canopy through which the light leaked only in patches and daubs.

When they met, Nether told him they were in voice distance to the hive.

"I can smell 'em," he said, scanning each limb of the trees, his gray head making a slow revolution. "I can smell 'em fretting over that honey."

Finally, he nodded and pointed off to the right. Following Nether's angle of vision, Jarom saw a busyness in one of the trees. What seemed to be hundreds of specks were swarming around a fist-size hole halfway up a largish white oak at a spot where lightning or wind had lopped off a limb.

Reaching its base, Jarom heard a droning like the hum of a whipsaw cutting a hollow log. Putting his ear to the trunk, he heard a humming that resonated through comb and hollow like bows on fiddle strings. Again Nether grinned.

Though this spot was far enough from any wagon road that no one was likely to chance on it, Nether then lay formal claim. With great solemnity, he took up the ax and cut a neat X in the bark about chest high. The blond cleft was an unmistakable sign that the tree and its contents had been spoken for. It was a hunter's mark that all were bound to honor. Whose property it was on, Nether told him, made no difference. The tree and its contents would be safe until fall when Nether would return with a crosscut saw and gum. He told Jarom that he would fell the tree and cut out a section a foot or so above and below the hive. The "mother of 'em all" would be delicately removed and placed in the homemade gum. When it was moved, the swarm would follow to build a new nest, and Nether would portion out enough of the honey to see the bees through the winter. Nether took pride in his reputation as the best bee man in Logan County. Farmers called on him to transport hives and answer their bee questions. He had an eye and also what he described as a heart for bees, having located hundreds of hives without, or so he claimed, ever being stung. Though nothing out of the usual for Nether, for Jarom the hive was a first find.

Hunting with Nether, he understood later, was more than a practical application of a Greek named Euclid whom Nether had never heard of. Along those paths, through gruffness and peach grizzle, he often saw that smooth face, the dome of Nether's head yellowed and later creased like a butternut, the great jowls sloping from the nose and chin, a tired intelligence in the heavy-lidded, turtle eyes. At ten Jarom could follow a beeline though he and Nether knew that the woods were not a lesson so much as a means, that what Nether taught was method and patience, patience and pluck. How honey is rendered from honey.

WHO MY PEOPLE ARE

(from a composition book belonging to M. Jerome Clarke, 1860)

My father's people, the Clarkes, and my mother's, the Hails, came to this region of west Kentucky in the early years of the century. My grandfather Charles Clarke, of Chesterfield County, Virginia, was a soldier in the war of independence, fighting under General Horatio Gates. In 1815 he picked up and passed through the Cumberland gap into Kentucky, settling in Logan County, which later came to be Simpson County. With him he brought, in addition to his wife, his two sons, Hector (who fathered me) and Beverley, and his daughter Nancy, in whose house I later came to live.

My mother, born Mary Hail, held me in her lap and told me that my father was named for Hector, chief of the heroes of Troy in Mr. Homer's *Iliad*. Of my father, my mother said that he had fighting in his blood but no war to use it. She told my Aunt Mary Tibbs that the tragedy of his life was he'd been born too late for one war and aged too early for any of the others. She said he joined the County Militia to satisfy his love of martial exploit. They had married in the early 1820s and lived on a farm of three hundred acres where I and my brothers and sisters were born. From earliest memory, she called me Jarom, a kind of pet name that others came to call me by. My father set up as a farmer though he was not much suited to working a farm. He relied on laborers of the African race to put food on our table but mostly kept his own boots and hands unsoiled. He wore a white shirt nearly every day of his life.

After his death, which I will presently tell you about, my Aunt Nancy told me he always prized his station in life a little too much and scorned working with his hands. She told me this in hopes that I would follow the blood of the Hails, who never thought so well of themselves that they would not join those who labored in barn and field. Though no one said it, it became clear to me that my father, despite his good traits, had no head for details and was but a poor manager. He let others handle his accounts, just as he relied on others to empty his slop jar or take up his hoe. Though we were never hungry, we were never well to do. For a time he held the title of postmaster of Franklin, a job of work he took from need, not from inclination. Yet he loved all of us and saw to it we lacked no advantage it was within his means to provide. For my fifth birthday he led me out to the stable where I found an Appaloose pony, which I soon learned to ride about the farm. After I fell off him several times, my father called him Bouncer.

Aunt Nancy told me that my father's biggest passion was for the citizen army of the county militia. She said that after the threat of Indians passed it was mostly a game, a gathering more social than military in its doings. He loved the sound of drumrolls. He loved the pageantry of wars, the display of arms and uniforms, shooting matches and turkey pulls. I was proud that he rose to the rank of Brigadier General of the state militia.

My Uncle Beverley came to prominence in the public eye, not in the military but in politics. Born in Virginia in 1809, he came first to Logan County and then hauled off to Christian County. He read for the law in Lexington and soon became a candidate for a seat in the Kentucky General Assembly. Not one who knew him, it was said, was surprised when he won the election. After one term, he went to Washington City as a U.S. representative in the Congress, promoting the principles of the Democratic party. In 1855 he ran for governor of Kentucky, losing to James Morehead, a candidate then on the Know-Nothing ticket. President Buchanan soon appointed him Minister to Guatemala, but the fever raging there took him shortly after he arrived at his post.

Beverley was a particular favorite of Mary Tibbs, a relation so distant I was never sure of the tie of kinship, though I believe she is my great aunt. She favored Uncle Beverley, praising his elevated state as a source of family pride. It was she who told me that if I cut my finger the blood would run blue. I should also mention Uncle Beverley's daughter Pauline, who married an attorney of Howardsville back in old Virginia. His name is John Singleton Mosby. She left the Protestant faith and converted to the Roman Catholic Church.

I am sorry to confess that the family has at least one black sheep. Branch M. Clarke, my father's cousin, was never mentioned among the family in my hearing. He had committed a murder in the town of Madisonville, though I have not learned the particulars. His son Tandy was painted with the same stripe for a jury convicted him of robbing the mails. Although the family tried to keep it a secret, he chopped off one of his hands in the penitentiary to escape hard labor.

My mother's family, the Hails, are disciples of respectability, solid and predictable in their ways. My mother's father, John Hail, came to Kentucky from Halifax County, North Carolina in 1810. He too served in the army, fighting on the Wabash and Raisin rivers during the second war of independence. He and a group of citizens named Simpson County after one of his comrades, John Simpson, who was among those massacred by the Indians after surrendering at the River Raisin in territory that in recent years became the state of Michigan. In school we learned the battlecry "Remember the Raisin!" and my classmates would always add "And don't forget the Grape!" John Hail came home unscathed, living as a farmer and deacon for over forty years before dying late last summer of a fever that took him in his sleep. He had a reputation as a shrewd trader, owning nearly a thousand acres and a large number of African slaves. He was a county magistrate more than forty years.

Only once, he told me, did fortune bring him before the public eye. He was selected foreman of the jury that tried Samuel Houston, governor of both Tennessee and North Carolina, for fighting a duel. His opponent was General William White. Houston had said that his political opponent had not the moral character to serve the public trust. His honor offended, General White challenged him to a duel. To avoid legal difficulties, Mr. Houston accepted and the two of them fought at a farm just over the border of Kentucky and Tennessee. When they fired, General White missed his mark but himself took a ball in the groin. His wounds mended, and the two of them were said to have become friends, burying the hatchet. Though John Hail owned a good many slaves, he became in sentiment but not practice an abolitionist, refusing until he died to give up his slaves until his neighbors did.

My mother, Mary Hail Clarke, brought six of us into the world and died of pneumonia before I was five. I was the youngest of the six, with two older brothers, John and Billy, and two older sisters, and another sister, Virginia, that I never saw since she was carried off by the typhoid as an infant two years before I was born in the year 1845. My mother had a weak constitution made frailer by having so many children. Young as I was when she died, I remember her as a gentle presence. It is hard to summon her face, but she wore her hair done up around her head. There is a charcoal likeness of her made just before she married. She stands stiffly but smiling, wearing a wide straw hat with a ribbon wound about it. Her eyes stare off into the Beyond, as if she saw things the rest of us don't or heard sounds the rest of us don't hear.

When she died, my father was at sea without her. Pained by memories, he moved twenty miles away to Rabbitsville in the north of the county. He may have moved because he needed extra help for us, though my brothers and sisters have since married and set up housekeeping on their own. Or maybe he wished to start anew in a place that was new to him. He never was a man to take others to his bosom with confidences.

When he moved, others saw a need to keep me close with a woman's care. My father, not much able to do anything for himself, much less for others, did not raise a fuss when I was taken to Aunt Nancy Bradshaw's. She is the wife of William Bradshaw, the largest building contractor in Logan County. She has no children of her own. Though I lived under her roof, I visited my father on most holidays and family gatherings. This was the way of things until he took sick and died in the fall of 1855, a few weeks after Uncle Beverley lost his election and not long before my eleventh birthday. I can remember the military band at my father's burial and great swags of black crape hanging from the porch. Someone covered every mirror in the house for fear of raising spirits of the dead.

One obituary that Aunt Nancy later showed me described him as "possessing an abiding fondness for weapons, martial music, and heroic characters." The article went on to say how he belonged to all the military companies of the county, counting him always present on parade days wearing a cocked hat and plume. Another noted that he had "courage, pompous manners, and the kindest of hearts."

After the burying I had to make another adjustment. The court appointed me a legal guardian, Mr. A. G. Rhea. My father's friend since before he married, Mr. Rhea lived near Russellville. I lived with Aunt Nancy until I reached the age of thirteen when I was deemed old enough to be reunited with my larger family. In 1858, along with my brothers John and Billy, I moved to the home of Mary Tibbs. She is a widow well up in years and owns a farm of ample size known as Beech Grove. Her three great nieces, Elizabeth, Sarelda, and Sarah Lashbrook, looked after her for a time and helped her keep house. Then Elizabeth and Sarelda married my older brothers and moved not far away. Also living with us is John L. Patterson, her grand nephew or some such relation. Living in this large household with those of my blood, I no longer feel myself an orphan. As for the Hails and the Clarkes, for better, for worse, I see myself taking after the Clarkes more than the Hails. Aunt Mary Tibbs repeatedly speaks the notion that blood will tell. I do not know what to make of this, whether it is a threat or a sign of promise.

HOME LIFE

If he were asked six months before to portray those he knew in terms of mechanical contrivances, Jarom would have described Aunt Mary Tibbs as a steam engine. She seemed to him in all particulars the perfection of that vessel designed to boil water into an almost invisible vapor—steam—and force that vapor through an airtight cylinder in order to drive a piston and produce energy, the energy to be converted into mechanical force and motion. Work. As with any machine, the ultimate measures of her value were productivity, efficiency of operation, ease of maintenance, and durability.

Jarom imagined taking this engine and placing it in a kitchen. He imagined it housed in a human form of late middle years, the body as an upended boiler tapered inward slightly at the midline, quadrangular, neither bulky nor slight. If he were asked to re-create a model, he might have provided the following as specifications: Sheathe it in gingham, a modest print stippled like a guinea's back, buttoned at the neck and dropping to the very toes. Roll the sleeves to the elbows at mealtimes and freckle the forearms. Blanch them with flour or slick them with shortening scooped from the vat. Pinch the features of the face and flush them crimson from the stove heat in whatever season. Draw the hair back in an uncompromising Calvinist bun but release a few intractable wisps about the temples and bead them with droplets of righteous sweat. Tie a white apron, stiff and spotless, about the middle. Shoe the feet under the long skirts with mannish shoes.

Set the engine in motion. Supply soup spoons, fry pans, cook pots, kettles, colanders, fruit jars, a stone-china measuring cup, a biscuit cutter, butter mold, a flat-handled skimmer, cake plates, breadboard, and spatterware. Furnish a basket of garden truck fresh from the dooryard each morning before sunlight tops the upper step of the porch. Brisk and bustle. See her bending over the new kitchen range that required six men to carry, one toweled hand opening the firebox, the other chucking kindling from the apple crate, kept constantly filled. A metal hod next to it for ashes, kept constantly emptied. These are her verbs: pluck, pare, peel, hull, dice, mince, chop, slice, roll, knead, strain, mash, grate, sift, mix, measure, stir, spoon, pour, bake, parboil, simmer, fry. Serve: mutton soup, dandycake, hoecakes, mustard greens, dill, quince preserves, watercress, kitchen ketchup, corn dodgers, cabbage pickle, shoat steaks, veal.

And after every meal he witnessed her performing the ritual of resetting the table for the next—teaspoon, butter knife, china fork, salt and pepper cellars, sugar bowl, a cruet of apple vinegar steepled in the center, the whole overlaid with a cloth of starched white linen, the tabletop with its snow-covered peaks and ridges resembling a miniature Alps. True Alps if the kitchen were not so seethingly hot. Those tropics through which passed generations of White Rocks and Wyandotte, white miles of biscuits, acres of steamed greens. Her life was composed of such lists.

Wherever she was, but in the kitchen especially, her word had the force of law, and as Jarom could testify, her words were many. She was the most forceful person he had ever known, though she limited her sphere of interest to things domestic, especially the preparation of food. She affirmed by some unspoken right or title that the kitchen was her domain. This meant no pets, no children underfoot, meals served with the imagined timeliness of well-regulated trains. In her cosmology the kitchen was a continent apart, a country whose capital was the cookstove. From the time he came to live with her after the death of his father, Jarom was under her sovereignty as though he had crossed the frontier of another country—keeping the woodbox filled, seeing that the cook-fire embers never languished to the point of extinction. Chores were performed in accordance with long-established schedules. Knives were whetted the first Saturday of each month, sausage rendered on such and such a day if weather permitted, radishes, potatoes, and other plants whose edible parts grew underground planted during the dark of the moon. Though she would not scruple to wring the neck of a fryer, meat she required to be delivered to her kitchen gutted and dressed. Leisure to her was another species of waste.

"Idleness," she said so often it was a litany, "is the serpent's second head and squalor's midwife."

For Aunt Mary, life and the preparation of victuals followed two time-tested principles: utility and plenitude. Gastronomical refinement and delectation of taste were not matters she bothered herself about. Living plainly among plain people, she served plain fare. Eaters of normal girth who sat at her table looked to her puny—a minister of the Russellville Methodist church, visiting relations, the odd passerby. Once they entered her precincts, she made probing and persistent inquiries about their health, contending that their ailments were imagined, that what their constitutions lacked was nourishing food in generous portions.

Opposed to spirits in any form, she would not cook with wine and would not tolerate anything more fortified than buttermilk. Holidays and special occasions were no exception. She was also obsessed with tonics of one kind or another. She drank sassafras year-round and attributed her robust health to the pots of tea she consumed each day as well as to the eating of rhubarb, okra, and poke in season. She passed these preferences on to Jarom, insisting that he swallow what seemed like gallons of well-drawn water each day.

"Stand up straight," she would say, "or you'll go through life arched like a rainbow. Get ahold of yourself and rediscover your backbone."

Upholding one end of a conversation was not among her social skills, and she reviled gossip that so often had taken root among those of her association, in church and out. "About" and "out" she pronounced in the Tidewater way as "aboot" and "oot." A woman generous in bestowal of food, she was an inveterate borrower of wisdom, often relying on notations in the ladies' journals and books on household husbandry that prescribed ways to redirect one's moral compass. In response to an innocent observation about the weather, for example, Jarom heard her turn her response in such a way so as to drive her convictions home: "A cook in the kitchen is a shade tree in summer and a backlog in winter."

Was this, Jarom asked himself, some kind of code or riddle?

Then and after, Jarom was never sure he understood such homilies, especially the notion of her kitchen as cool when in fact, summer or winter, it was a tropical zone elevated above the temperature outdoors with something always baking. The beads of righteous sweat on his forehead never comported with her references to shade trees. What he understood was that waste in her world of efficient consumption was unforgivable, that the abuse of plenty was the moral equivalent of the Antichrist. Many evenings he'd found himself marooned at the dinner table, condemned to sit until he'd eaten his broccoli or had the opportunity to secrete it in his pocket.

But there was a slacker side to her intercourse with the world, a quality of kindness that softened the frictions of the kitchen. During the summer months she would keep demijohns of buttermilk cooling in the springhouse. When hay was being cut and raked into manageable windrows, she would serve pitchers of lemonade in the side yard under a dark latticework of maples as the men came in from the fields, hay dust like a batter on their necks, their fingers melting chill-beads from the glasses. No other drinks were as cold or as restorative as that pale liquid afloat with squeezed yellow rinds and gravelly ice chipped from blocks of winter pond stored underground in sawdust, the lemonade accompanied by platters of sweetmeats to fortify the blood.

Jarom came to know her by helping in the kitchen, not always with complete willingness. A large bowl on the table between them, they snapped beans or cored apples or peeled potatoes. When the garden hit its peak of profusion and vegetables came in by the basketful, he watched her can tomatoes, squash, okra, and similar truck. The aqua jars into which they were converted formed neat rows along the tiered shelves of her pantry. While they worked, she would tell stories and recount the family saga of settlement, the struggle of her father to wrest a living from the earth. Often she peppered her talk with references to what she always referred to as the Word of God. Jarom came to savor the hours he spent with her, unconsciously fitting his life rhythm to hers, taking her teachings as a lens through which to interpret the world. Seldom laughing, alert to any failing, she seemed derived from one or all of the prophets of old. Despite the sternness of her behavior, Jarom discovered a vein of affection beneath the crusty exterior.

She did not so much dwell on Scripture as live it, though Jarom sensed that her spirit was always more comfortable in the Old Testament than the New. And she always retained a healthy portion of heathenish superstition, convinced as she was, for example, that the cure for itching fungus between the toes was to step in fresh cow dung. She moved with nervous feet, a kind of quickstep that some would describe as clumsiness as though her limbs, her body, were, like poor servants, to be tolerated but never trusted. She took snuff in small doses but did not permit tobacco to be smoked indoors. Though she was well up in years when Jarom came to live with her, the only sign of her aging was a turkey wattle under the chin. She carried all of her receipts in her head and from May until November never appeared outside the house without a bonnet.

MOLLIE THOMAS, SUMMER 1861

The house where Jarom came to stay with Aunt Mary Tibbs and her many floating connections stood on a slight eminence surrounded by fields generally flat to rolling. The land about it sloped down on three sides and drained into a nameless creek—simply called "the creek"—that formed a horseshoe around the rear of the farm. What lay inside the hoof was mostly cleared and put in crops of wheat, Indian corn, and dark-fired tobacco or was sown in hay or dedicated to pasture. The lush bottom the generations of Tibbses reserved for crops up to where the ground softened into marsh along the branch. What lay outside the hoof was wilderness.

The house consisted of two stories of wood, built over an original log pen whose enormous stone chimneys dominated the gable ends. Against the sky the elevation stood plain and unpretentious, ample rather than severe in plainness, the side- and fanlights at the main door being the only concession to ornament. Ash and sugar trees shaded the whole of the fenced-in yard, survivals of the old woods that drew a breeze even during the hottest months. The canopies interwove so tightly that only a few varieties of grass would grow there. To the rear lay a plot of land, an acre or so, set aside for garden. It formed an axis for a cluster of outbuildings—a henhouse, toolshed, smokehouse, privies, and a small barn for implements. Jarom could seldom resist pedaling the treadle grinding wheel outside the toolshed.

To the rear of the garden grew an orchard, several rows of apple and peach trees, some planted by Aunt Mary's grandfather before the Second

War of Independence. Nether and the field hands Ralph and Sam and their families lived in three neat cabins along the edge of the orchard. Aunt Carrie, the oldest person on the place, had a cabin to herself, closer to the house and kitchen where she helped Aunt Mary when needed. To the right and halfway down a hill was the "new" stock barn and stables that Fenton Tibbs, Aunt Mary's late husband, had built two years before he died.

One Sunday afternoon when the house was full of Tibbs relations, including a dark-headed girl a year or two younger whose company Jarom wasn't willing to keep for an afternoon, he decided to disappear to the springhouse down the hillside from the house. If asked by a trusted questioner where he found sanctuary from work and the world of adults, Jarom would have answered the springhouse. It was a simple, one-room structure built of rough fieldstone with dry-stacked walls topped by a few feet of logs and a shake roof. Its floor was dirt except for the spring that flowed from under a rock shelf. Jarom searched among the fine gravels and silt for crock shards the color of bone, each with its mosaic of hair-thin cracks. The air in that place seemed cavelike, always cool and dense with humidity. He could close his eyes and imagine the grotto of the fairy stories his aunt Nancy Bradshaw had read to him. Among the rocks he lifted he found salamanders, a tribe of them, in the coolness sheathed by gravels that were fine as sand. He classified them as members of the lizard family, all tail and no trunk, their stubby legs ending in clawless toes. Like miniature hands. Bright and peppered with specks, with reddish backs that gave them a gaudy look, bracelets dropped glittering among the stones.

Life went on in layers there. High along the eaves, the dry climate of rafters, he spied the tubular nests of mud daubers. When he broke the crust of one of them, he found it stuffed with dead insects to feed the unhatched young. A cat's cradle of webs, a wheel of stretched spittle boxed into the frame, spanned the window that opened onto the humming pasture. In it Jarom noticed one wasp balled up in tinsel, a housefly marooned in the upper weave, the iridescent sheen of its armor a nasty jewel. The smell inside, stale and somehow safe, seemed most to him like the ruptured horsehair loveseat in the attic of the house.

After a time he felt the desire to wander. He left the springhouse and followed the water that spilled through a sluice in the stone wall and flowed toward the back of the farm. A few crow caws broke the stillness of the summer afternoon, the sky above him nicked with buzzards floating in lazy circuits above the fields, the tips of their great wings curling for balance.

Roughly following the stream along the hard ground above the marsh, he passed a dozen or so milk cows that grazed pasture sown in fescue and bluegrass. He passed Nell and Rio, two fat-haunched workhorses that he sometimes bribed with sugar for a ride, throwing a halter over Nell's head and slipping in the bit, then hiking himself up and going bareback. In the soggy bottom he passed the beds of watercress Aunt Mary had him pluck for salads through late spring and summer. Wading, he would yank it up in green heaps, exposing the undersides with their skein of stringy white rootlets, which smelled like moss. On another day he might search along the banks for arrowheads and bits of flint, having once found a grinding stone large as a man's fist. He could imagine the first dwellers of that place grinding cornmeal harvested from stalks in the flatland along the creek. But today he went on, entering the shade of the woods where the branch widened across large flags of stone in a series of descending shelves that dropped into falls like rough steps up the creek bed. In one place the creek flowed over the ledges into a natural pool, just deep enough for swimming when the sun drove him from the fields. John Patterson had shown him the spot first on one of their outings. But now John had other interests—mostly skirts and sweet nothings whispered to eligible young women. More often Jarom spent time with George and Easter, his play- and workmates whose parents lived in the orchard cabins and worked the fields.

Jarom followed the path of least resistance toward the pool. As he approached the overhang from the upper end, he sensed something different. He stepped into a pocket of chill air, the same unearthly cool of the springhouse, and he felt himself on the border of another world. He remembered Nether telling him that Induns, as he called them, held such spots sacred, believing there were places in the world where the spirits gathered, their expelled breath explaining the cooler air. Sounds from the upper world of sunlight and open field—cow bellow, dove call, the snapping of butterfly wings—were absorbed in the low, steady patter of creek water leaving its bed to drop on the rocks below. The surrounding walls of the overhang formed a cavity or chamber in which the water sounds resonated.

Stopping short of the edge, Jarom veered off and circled past a margin of trees and down a funnel-shaped slope matted with ferns. There was a path, and he felt the ferns brushing against his legs, half expecting to step on a sleeping snake. He was halfway down, the water sound welling in his ears, when he realized he was not alone.

There, in the shallows of the pool, water just above her white ankles, head fringed by a sparkling curtain of water, was the girl he had been studying to avoid when he left the house, Mollie Thomas.

For a moment he did not recognize her. She wore a simple, high-waisted frock, a speckled blue with a wide band about the middle. To one side on a platterlike rock at the rim of the pool she had neatly paired her stockings and pumps.

Staring into the shower of spray, water plashing into the pool and vibrating under the hollow stone shelf that curved around the falls, she did not hear him on the path. Over the centuries the falls had gradually undercut the softer minerals until the overhang in places had tumbled in, leaving thick sheets of canted stone and pockets scooped into banks of clay. Fixing on her form centered among the rocks and water, Jarom saw that everything about her was damp or wet, her skin jeweled with droplets. As he watched, he felt a slick film of moisture forming on his own arms and face.

Though he had met her earlier in the day, he met her as he would a stranger, more an object to be avoided, like a footstool in the center of the room, than a composition of flesh and senses. He had given her no more attention than he would the sun-faced clock on the landing of the stairs or the first lightning bugs in June, momentarily registering on the mind, quickly forgotten. Here, removed from the household and transported to the creek bottom, she seemed a new person, someone Jarom determined to know. Age? She might have been fourteen, and he regarded her as a child, though only a year or so separated them. He imagined her moving in the company of women, a fence of them around her like upright trees in a palisade. There were no fences here.

A full minute must have passed before she sensed that anyone was near. Her back to him, she stood perfectly still in the water. Then she turned. She did not start when she saw him. Nothing in her face, as he would remember, showed the least surprise. Slowly she raised a hand to sweep back some wisps of hair that fell across her forehead in bangs, a dark color made darker by the water, not so much a color as a texture, fine and tightly woven.

"I didn't hear you come," she said, smiling. "You must think me a fool or a simpleton standing here in the water like this."

In fact, to Jarom she seemed to belong there.

"No," he said. "No, it's all right. I come here myself. I come here all the time."

"Why aren't you off chasing horses or fooling with those boys, with George or Easter?"

This struck Jarom as more observation than question.

"So this is where you get off to when you want to be alone?" she said.

"This or a dozen other places," he told her, realizing only after he said it how silly it sounded.

Then she stepped out of the water, careful to keep her footing on the slippery rocks, her skirts still hitched slightly above her ankles. Under the water her feet had seemed foreshortened and bone white as the roots of watercress. As she raised her foot, he glimpsed a tracery of blue veins in its curvature. Spots of light played across her face and frock when she moved, the shade above deepening but strands of brightness still shimmering about her head.

Turning to one side, she sat on the stone platter to pull on her stockings and shoes. As naturally as the flow of water around them, she began to talk as if to some lifelong friend, telling Jarom things that were neither really important nor very personal.

Jarom sat down on another rock and listened as he seldom listened to anyone but John Patterson, commenting after each pause and even talking a little about himself. Above the bowl of rock and water in which they'd hidden themselves, he knew the sun had nearly dropped behind the western ridge.

They walked together up the path and across the pasture up to the house. Back at the house they sat on the porch until Mrs. Thomas, an older version of her daughter so close in appearance she might have passed for a sister, came out and scolded Mollie for missing supper and quickly sent her to bed.

In his own room Jarom rehearsed the afternoon, reconstructing it in almost perfect detail and sequence. But clearly as the sight of her fixed in his mind—down to the water skates skittering in the shallows, the clusters of gnats, the huge spiderweb they stepped through passing between some trees on the trek uphill—he couldn't remember much of what she'd said. Yet something about her, not so much her appearance as the setting in which he found her, fixed that evening in his mind, established her shape and expression as firmly as paint on canvas.

PATTERSON

Jarom was never certain how the bond with John Patterson had formed. Moving to Aunt Mary Tibbs's house in the fall of 1858, he didn't meet Patterson until midwinter, when Patterson, a distant relative, returned to Beech Grove for a long visit. Ten years Jarom's senior, Patterson had worked as a pilot on a steamboat and plied the Mississippi and its tributaries for months at a time. Water was his element. From New Orleans he would steam north to St. Louis or Louisville or farther upriver, as far as Pittsburgh. He professed that water gave him serenity, and Jarom likened him to a placid pond whose unruffled surface seemed immune from turbulence. Jarom imagined him high above the river, between belching smokestacks, his hands steady on the great wheel, eyes scanning the expanse of river before him. He was convinced that Patterson's vigil against deadheads and sandbars, against tricky currents and shoals, gave him a kind of mastery over events and confidence to control what lay before him, the power to accept what lay beyond. Drawn by his worldliness and quiet authority, Jarom regarded him as a second father before he was ever conscious of it. He idolized him. Even the name seemed to possess special qualities. When he heard it spoken, he heard the echo "father-son, father-son, father-son."

A natural learner and an apt teacher, Patterson fueled Jarom's own love of learning and curiosity about the world beyond Logan County.

He brought the same rigor to local lore, becoming an encyclopedia of its few triumphs and many failures. And Jarom took to it, thirsting for what Patterson taught him and eventually supplementing that knowledge with books. He would read whatever Patterson put before him and whatever he could borrow elsewhere. Showing Jarom a map of the county one day, an irregular rectangle that lay in the region called the Pennyroyal (pronounced *pennyrile*) whose lower quadrant formed the northern border of Tennessee, Patterson taught him the one most interesting fact about the place.

"Do you see anything irregular about the shape?" he had asked.

Studying the boundaries, Jarom found what Patterson later described as a cartographical oddity. In an otherwise straight line between the two states a nipple of land protruded into Tennessee like a bite out of a cornstick. Placing his forefinger on the spot, Patterson affirmed he'd been referring to the notch

"Do you know how it came to be there?" he had asked.

Patterson explained that the notch went back to one of the region's earliest settlers, Captain Jake Groves. For some reason—taxes, pride, maybe simple preference—Groves was disappointed to learn that the land described in his patent was located in Tennessee rather than Kentucky. The story went that he let the government surveyors know he had placed a barrel of top-grade sippin' whiskey under a blackjack tree at the southernmost tip of his holdings. If the surveyors would bend the line around it, they were welcome to consume as much of the barrel as they wanted. They would. And they did.

Patterson taught Jarom that sinks and caves as well as "lost rivers" honeycombed the county's level to gently rolling land, channels and streams that surfaced here and there but flowed underground for miles. Jarom visualized the subsurface of the county as a huge piece of Swiss cheese riddled with pockets through which hidden rivers flowed. Jarom saw Patterson himself as an expanse of hidden rivers through which facts flowed. Jarom learned, for example, that Simpson County contained one hundred eleven thousand nine hundred forty-eight acres, that wheat, corn, oats, and tobacco were its chief crops, that it was as ideally suited for grazing livestock as it had been for bison several generations earlier.

In the deep woods in the back of the Tibbs farm, Patterson taught

Jarom the grammar of trees: the peeling scrolls of the sycamore, the intricate and somehow oriental lobes of the locust leaf, the mittened hand of the sassafras. In the silt flats along the creek, Jarom studied the language of prints—possums, muskrats, coons, deer, even once a bear. Patterson showed him which bank offered the best clay for molding marbles. Along the creek Jarom had his first lesson in the art of idleness. Sometimes he waded whole afternoons, overturning rocks to snatch at crawfish that scuttled off in clouds of yellow underwater smoke. When the changing seasons made it too chilly to strip and swim, he waded, soaking himself in the construction of dams and bridges. He would take up terrapins and box turtles, confining them in a wood box from which they would mysteriously disappear by morning. In the fall he and Patterson hunted squirrels with the old muzzle-loader that had belonged to Fenton Tibbs, traipsing through a field of frost to the hollow where they scanned the bare limbs for movement, any silhouette against the dawn sky. Under the largest walnut, Jarom learned to hull nuts, smashing the green pulp with a wooden mallet, the stains yellowing his hands for weeks. Jarom added these things to his store of knowledge about bees.

The woods became his second home, the place where he could be himself, dreaming or dawdling out of earshot of the house. Nature became for him a great library, trees and rocks the monuments of some vast outdoor museum. Sometimes he brought his books. In the natural seat carved out of rock over the eons, he spent long afternoons reading *The Hunters of Kentucky* and Swift's *Gulliver's Travels*.

Jarom soon learned that Patterson would hold forth about anything or anyone but himself. From Mary Tibbs he learned what few particulars he knew about Patterson himself. Born in 1835, Patterson had lost both parents, to cholera or one of the other scourges that periodically swept the upper South. Like Jarom, he had been brought up by aunts and uncles. As a young man, he'd clerked in country stores and bummed around the villages and hamlets of western Kentucky. For a few months he lived near Louisville in Jefferson County, working on a farm belonging to a Dr. Standiford. But he was too restless and venturesome to stay fixed on farming. After a round of various odd jobs, he found a berth in the river trade, drawn to water, he once confessed, because it kept him in motion. With a head for figures and an intelligence suited to reading spaces as well as charts, he made an excellent pilot. Towns with their randomness and unfocused complexities he came to despise, seldom exploring them beyond their wharves and warehouses, always within earshot of the lapping waters. A nomad by inclination, he enlisted among the cozy fraternity of rivermen and misfits that constituted the river's floating brotherhood. Had he stayed and the war not intruded, he probably would have become a captain. When the fighting broke out in '61, he held a responsible job as assistant engineer aboard the steamboat *Peytona*, making a weekly run between Louisville and New Orleans.

Patterson harbored no love of slaveholders. He would not expect anyone to do for him what he could do for himself. Servants he saw not as aids but hindrances to his own freedom, encumbrances to be fed and clothed and cared for. Having a servant, he said, is like having a dog and doing your own barking. Footloose, he regarded dependents of any kind as impediments, which is why, Jarom told himself, Patterson had no wife, no children, no roof he called his own.

To the surprise of those who thought they knew him, he got caught up in the war fever and decided to quit the river and become a private soldier in the Army of Southern Independence. Patterson told Jarom that the *Peytona* later went on to run the blockade that closed Southern ports and was not heard of again.

Jarom and he became reacquainted when Patterson came back to Logan County for a short visit before enlisting. He had the courtesy to inform Mary Tibbs in person of his plans, feeling that because she was his closest surviving kin he needed her blessing, however reluctant she might be to bestow it.

By then, Jarom lived at nearby Crow's Pond with his older brother John and John's wife, Elizabeth, who was a relation of Patterson and Mary Tibbs. His other brother, William, had married Elizabeth's sister Sarelda Lashbrook, and for a time Jarom himself had a crush on the third Lashbrook sister, Sarah. His older brothers answered the call to arms and marched off within weeks of enlisting. Jarom initially tried to join them but was told that, like the tobacco in its bed, he was too green in the leaf. Hearing the news of Patterson's intent to enlist, Jarom felt a sudden urge to follow him. At fifteen, he stood nearly six feet and could easily pass for sixteen, the minimum age for legal enlistment. When Elizabeth got wind of his intentions, she told Mary Tibbs, who immediately summoned Jarom to Beech Grove. He went, and she tried to dissuade him. He would be foolish, the gist of her argument went, to lose his life before he'd started living it. But Jarom had made his mind up, and she could not get through to him, especially when he argued that John Patterson would be there to keep him out of harm's way and advise him at every turn. The best she could extract from Jarom was a promise to speak with her again before signing the ledger of enlistment.

To gain ground on Mary Tibbs, Jarom carried his cause to Patterson, steadily rasping away at Patterson's reluctance to buck his blood relation. Patterson balked at first, reluctant for Jarom to join for all the same reasons plus a few of his own, namely, the responsibility of keeping Jarom alive and safe. As an inveterate loner, he had no desire to nursemaid a youth who would divert his energy and concentration from the enemy. As Mary Tibbs had, he tried to stall him, not directly assaulting Jarom's essential premise but postponing it, asking to him to put off joining for a year or two.

The stratagem bore no fruit. For every objection, Jarom had a justification or counterargument, for every negative an alternative proposal. "Everyone knows this war won't last," he said. "It'll be over in a few months at most, and we'll be the losers if we don't act now."

Jarom adopted irritation as his method, pestering Patterson until Patterson saw no way out and no way to silence him. Conceding that Jarom had enough size to pass the age requirement and could enlist on his own without anyone's consent, Patterson gradually crumbled and gave in, conditioning Jarom's signing up with him on Aunt Mary's blessing—the securing of which would be no small feat.

So the venue changed and Jarom's pleading with Mary Tibbs started again. All of one day he tried with no success to persuade her. The second day he convinced her that it was better for him to go one day with Patterson than the next with strangers. They both knew that if she'd been adamant in her disapproval, he would not have disobeyed her. But she faltered.

"You remember that old gum tree to the side of the house?" she asked. "Remember when that wind storm nearly blew it over, tore up its roots? We loved that old tree, but all of us knew there was no putting it back. It was either cut it down or let it fall."

Accepting the inevitable, she finally agreed that Jarom had a better chance of survival under Patterson's protective wing than running off on his own hook.

"Even the blind bird," she said, "by nature must try its wings, and who are we to bind it to the nest? I just pray that your wings bear you up and at least one of your eyes opens before you hit something or something hits you."

Then he had only to persuade his sweetheart, Mollie, who over a period of weeks had become his confidante, someone whose company he sought at every opportunity—at church, on errands, on weekend visits. A few days passed before he could arrange to see her. When he broke the news, she had no arsenal of arguments to fight his going. Hers was the rhetoric of the heart, not the courtroom, not the pulpit. Instead of putting forth her misgivings, she burst out crying, weeping until Jarom, much affected, felt himself on the verge of tears. When she raised questions about his age, he said God would forgive him for telling a "gray untruth."

"But *lying*?" she said.

"If the Lord has put up with Yankees all this time," he said, "I guess he can forgive me a little stretching my birthday."

"What if you're hurt?" she came back. "What if you're wounded? What," she paused for emphasis, "if you are killed?"

He asked if she would rather live with one who wore a yellow feather, who, should he survive, could no longer keep company with himself or others. She admitted she wouldn't but equally insisted she couldn't bear the thought of him lying wounded on some far-off battleground.

Jarom assured her that Patterson would be along to see no harm came to him. He said he could never be happy if he let others down, if he failed to shoulder his share of the burden. If he was not actually aflame to join the Confederacy, she could see that he was kindled.

For a time he himself faltered, uncertain how he could live not seeing her whenever he took a notion to. For her part, Mollie had grace and good sense enough to accept what she couldn't prevent. She knew she would lose him if she stood in his path as an obstacle. Jarom believed she'd convinced herself that going was the only way he could prove himself to her.

All that was left to do was seek out the recruiter and take the irrevocable step. About that time, Patterson reminded him that his father had chosen a military name for him, for his unused first name, often presented simply as M., was Marcellus, "one devoted to Ares, the Greek god of war whom the Romans called Mars." According to Patterson, it derived from the Roman general Marcellus, whose specialty was cavalry tactics.

DONELSON

Early in September 1861, within a month of Jarom's enlistment, General Simon Bolivar Buckner had taken command of the troops at Camp Burnett near Clarksville in Tennessee and appointed Major Rice E. Graves to form an artillery unit. At the time Jarom and Patterson were assigned to an infantry company under a Captain Ingram. The central command soon transferred his company to the light artillery. All accompanied General Buckner to Bowling Green, Kentucky, where they helped build an earthenworks fort as part of the chain of defenses designed to protect western Tennessee. A few days after they arrived, the general issued an order for the locks at Rochester on the Green River to be blown up. Major Graves, formerly a cadet at West Point and a native of nearby Owensboro, selected Jarom and Patterson as part of the demolition squad. At Rochester Jarom won his first commendation when he made a suggestion about where to place the powder charge used to blow up the locks. On the strength of this showing, Major Graves gave Jarom several special assignments, some of them taking him and Patterson behind enemy lines in the counties to the north.

During that winter Jarom and Patterson temporarily separated when Graves sent Jarom to Nelson and Marion counties as a spy. Patterson told him that being chosen did him honor because commanders as a rule selected only their shrewdest and most reliable men for such duties.

When not away on special assignments, Jarom worked with Patterson and his messmates building and strengthening the fort, an undertaking central to the Confederate plan of defense. For weeks he and Patterson dug trenches, heaping dirt in earthworks until Buckner ordered the army to Fort Donelson when it became clear that Union general Ulysses S.

Grant planned to attack there. The defenses weren't complete when word came that Grant had deployed the advance of his army.

The sky to which Jarom opened his eyes shone dull as one of the pewter dishes leaning upright on Aunt Mary Tibbs's mantel back in Logan County. The light pried through cracks in the dugout's wattles and laid bands along the opposite wall where he could hear Patterson's breath coming steady and untroubled. The weather had turned bitter cold. Though unseasonably warm air had blown up from the Gulf for three days in cruel mimicry of spring, overnight the temperature dropped to the teens, and the rain that fell during the night turned to sleet. Jarom felt the arctic bite on his skin as he propped himself on one elbow and watched the wispy threads of Patterson's breath. Outside he could hear the first rustlings of the camp: low voices, a ding of metal, and the whickering of an artillery horse hobbled somewhere behind their battery. Farther off came the cawing of a crow in one of the barren cornfields west of their positions where thousands of men rose from their pallets of straw as a wedge of morning light cracked the ridge and began to eat at the shadows.

An unfamiliar sound like a mechanical churn, a chaffing of driven metal that came from below in regular measures, brought Jarom to clarity. Its mechanical regularity reminded him of something he might hear in a millworks. Tying his stiff brogans, he stepped outside to the parapet, from which he could look down on the Cumberland. Timbered bluffs cut to the nearly invisible river, which gouged a wound in the landscape like a view of the Alps he'd seen in a book of travels. Hung with swatches of fog, the river bent and narrowed until sucked into the folds of west Tennessee. Two inches of snow had fallen, and dark bristles of trees poked out of slopes otherwise flawlessly white. A grainy pall hung over the valley, a wintry haze the texture of dirty wool. Already, the snow under his feet loosened to slush.

Patterson came out wrapped in a blanket, clapping his arms to shake off the cold. Jarom watched him turn his attention as someone farther down the line shouted, "Ironclads, ironclads!"

Through the haze at the bend of the river Jarom could make out what appeared to be a shallow barge surmounted by a sardine tin. The sides of the tin slanted inward, giving it the shape of a capless pyramid. As it huffed into view, he saw hatched portals along one side from which little sticks protruded. Atop the tin, two dark stems spouted black billows of coal smoke. At the bow he made out a pin-size pole from which hung a fluttering rag.

They watched what Patterson described an "ugly contrivance" make progress against the current until it swelled to the size of a thumbnail. Jarom immediately thought of their unfinished defenses. Trees had been cut down along both sides of the river and towed to a point about nine hundred yards below the water batteries. Anchors and iron weights were chained to their roots and lower trunks to form a kind of submerged forest. But recent rains had so raised the river that their tangled limbs offered no threat to any boat whose draft was sufficiently shallow. When the boat approached within a quarter mile, its three bow guns rattled the silence, spitting flames and little collars of smoke. Two of the shots bounced harmlessly off the hillside above one of the water batteries. A third fell into the river fifty or sixty yards offshore. Where it hit, the brown surface puckered and swelled, spewing a geyser of white into the air.

Though he'd never seen an ironclad, Jarom had heard stories of those who had escaped the surrender at Fort Henry on the Tennessee. Rumor had it that General Tilghman gave up because he believed such boats unsinkable. Instead of piercing their thick armor, shells ricocheted off the canted sides. Jarom knew how pitifully weak their own defenses were. For three days and two nights they had dug rifle pits but had completed only a third when they sighted the first bluecoats.

He also knew that General Buckner had met all night with his senior generals, Pillow and Floyd, to decide how their combined force of fifteen thousand men should be deployed. He himself saw Donelson not so much as a fortress as a crimp in the landscape with a few advantages, namely, a high bluff commanding a view of the Cumberland River. The earthenwork fort, enclosing about fifteen acres, had only three pieces, an eight-inch siege howitzer and two nine-pounders, most of the artillery being concentrated in the shore batteries at the base of the hill so as to sweep the river at the waterline. Generals Pillow and Bushrod Johnson deployed to protect their rear between Indian Creek and the landing near a little cluster of buildings named Dover. General Buckner's line, including Graves's battery, formed just to the rear of the fort overlooking a maze of gullies and a swamp between Indian and Hickman creeks.

As the contraption advanced into the cleft shadow of the ridge, it came within range of the nearest batteries, yet there had been no return fire. Emboldened, the ironclad moved still closer, firing a cannonade of seven loads, none of them doing any visible damage to the emplacements on shore. Their concussions clapped against Jarom's ears and formed a protracted drone that buried itself finally in the immensity of the woods. To the ironclad's crew, peering through gunports and slits in the metal, the fortifications must have seemed deserted. Five minutes after the tenth shot, the boat submitted to the current and drifted downstream out of sight.

"I can tell you what they're up to," Patterson said. "They're trying to draw our fire."

With his camp knife Jarom was splitting the last of a pone of cornbread that had been their chief sustenance for three days.

"They want to home in on where our emplacements are," Patterson said, "but Buckner's too smart to be taken in. He's held off firing so as not to give away the placement of our guns."

By two that afternoon the gunboats were back, and this time Jarom counted four ironclads and two armored gunboats as they rounded the bend. The fog had lifted, affording a clear view of the ridges. From nearly a half mile away they began to shell the bluffs, probing the slopes in calculated grids in the manner of bird dogs canvassing sections of a field to scare up quail.

But this time when the boats steamed to within four hundred yards, the gunners in the lower batteries loosed their first salvo, firing low across the pewter-smooth surface of the water. Jarom could feel the tremors under his feet. Graves ordered them to their guns and Jarom looked down on the gunboats. Because the waters of the river had risen so high, the lower batteries had the advantage of firing even lower across the water. The shells kissing across the surface reminded him of skipping stones across the farm pond but for their force of impact, which resembled a huge hammer. For about ten minutes, the parties traded salvos.

At one point Jarom saw a shell splinter a flagstaff above one of the emplacements. A stick man in gray dashed from behind the embrasure to fetch the flag. Ignoring the storm that broke above his head, he trotted back to the breastworks and hopped over. In a few moments he was back, clambering over with the flag on a new staff. After planting it firmly, he jogged almost casually back to safety. Still watching, Jarom then saw the Stars and Stripes shot away from between the twin stacks of one of the gunboats. Another stick man, blue this time, ran onto the deck to refasten it.

Jarom had never witnessed such an extravagant display. He had an image of a son of one of the stick men asking his mother how his father came to die in the Great War of the Rebellion. "Planting a rag on a stick in the earth," the widow might truthfully say. After mess Jarom shared an account of this absurdity with Patterson. His senior thought a minute. "Whatever we lack in food," he said, "in shoes, in bullets, cooks, and quartermasters, numbskull generals on whatever side always manage to supply more than enough ignorance to go round."

About midafteroon the gunboats announced their return with more firing. The racket of their guns hurt Jarom's ears, the blasts drowning out the gunnery officers who shouted their puny commands. Shells smacked the armor of the ironclads with loud whangs, the raw sound a blacksmith's hammer makes against a naked anvil. Though he and the rest of the crew stood safely above the main fighting, Jarom fought the impulse to cover his head with his hands and hunker in the pit. Major Graves, no more than three years his senior, calmly propped his elbows on the breastworks and watched the spectacle through his glass, studiously making notations in his notebook as though in a classroom. At one point he commented to no one in particular that the closest ironclad, the *St. Louis*, had taken fifty hits.

Jarom could see that the pilothouse had been wrecked and that its steering seemed disengaged, for it floundered about until the current hauled it back downstream, floating broadside. The *Louisville*, a floating snuffbox, had also been hit, hanging sullenly for a time before drifting in silence beyond the range of the shore batteries. Standing by what he began to think of as his own cylinder of destruction as it cooled, Jarom cupped his hands along its barrel for warmth, as did his gunmates. That an instrument that served up mechanical death could also nurture and preserve was an idea he puzzled over. Following the others, he stamped his feet to shake off the cold, a practice that Patterson, making light of adversity, dubbed the snow waltz.

For Jarom, this was his first time under fire, the first time he became conscious that others sighted along the barrels of their weapons to loose hot metal at him. They intended to pierce his organs and end his life or seriously impede his ability to live it. From this distance he felt oddly detached, aware of the spectacle though not a part of it, absolved from bloodletting. Viewed from above, the action meant no more to him than a dispute in miniature he'd come on once in the woods, battalions of red and black ants swarming over an earthen mound, tiny formations and remote casualties in a silence that belied what must have been an epic struggle of the insect family. When the nearest ironclad drifted too far for a decent hit, Graves ordered them to withhold their fire. Unharmed, feeling harmless, Jarom awarded himself the honorific title, Inspector of Mayhem. Their would-be slayers, distanced by hillside and limits of sight, took on the appearance of featureless midgets, revealing themselves only in glimpses through wads of smoke.

Jarom and Patterson had enlisted in the Confederate army at Russellville, the seat of Logan County, less than six months previously. Though they did not actually muster in until August, Patterson, ever the historian, reminded Jarom that the enlistment day was Bastille Day, a time when an oppressed people rose to throw off the shackles of an unreasoning monarchy. Louis XVI was a hereditary king, he said, in many ways no worse than Lincoln, who threatened to enchain the people of his own country, a despot to beat all despots.

They were recuited by a Captain Morris from Henderson, an ardent secessionist who, they learned in passing, had clerked in a hardware store before the war. Smartly got up in a knee-length coat with a double row of buttons that tapered down his torso, Morris canvassed towns and villages in the borderland, recruiting dozens of young men from farms and village streets, from churchyards and shops, leading his volunteers to Tennessee as a kind of human harvest. Morris gave them a small travel allowance for the distance of a hundred and five miles to the place of rendezvous at

Camp Burnett. Walking and hitching rides on farmers' wagons for three days, Jarom and Patterson reported for duty on August 25 and mustered into Company B, Fourth Kentucky Infantry, of the First Kentucky Brigade. The date was firmly fixed in Jarom's memory because it marked his sixteenth birthday. Walking back to camp, Patterson picked up a buckeye under a roadside tree and passed it to him as though conferring a gift.

"The buckeye," he said solemnly, "is one of the first trees to leaf in spring, the first to lose its leaves in fall. Long as you carry this buckeye in your pocket, it will bring you good luck. My father told me this as his father told him. Keep this in your pocket for luck, as I tell you."

Charmed and buoyed by the sense that this mystical connection might in some way protect him, Jarom put the shiny sphere in his pocket and kept it as he would a letter from home or the piece of music he kept folded in an oilcloth packet among his belongings.

The music was the score of a ballad named "Lillibulero." He found it after his father's death, while rummaging among some receipts and legal-looking documents in the tall desk in which his father had kept his papers. Jarom had been attracted by the musical notes, which looked to him like a procession of tiny banners moving along a straight but rutted roadway. The banners reminded him of his father, resplendent in his militia uniform on muster days. To an eleven-year-old the sheet of music was a memento, a keepsake that brought his father back to him each time he saw it. Above the score was an engraving of three sailing ships cannonading a fort from which puffs of smoke returned the compliment. He didn't know what the images meant, but the scene brought back the image of his father in his gaudy uniform. For some reason he could not explain, he found the word "Lillibulero" alluring, and he loved to repeat it to himself. Was it a place, a person, a saying, as Patterson had mentioned, in the ancient tongue of the Irish? He included the score among the few personal things he packed to take with him when his father died and Nancy Bradshaw had come to clear up her brother's affairs and see to his belongings. Since that day he'd carried it in his kit everywhere he went, its mystery a tonic. Its unheard melody carried a sense of excitement and possibility, and he came to associate it not so much with war as with the prospect of open ground and promise of a future.

If he later had to cite reasons for joining the Confederate army, he could not say he'd been seduced by the rhetoric of recruiters like Morris or by the editorial tocsin of the Russellville newspaper to defend Southern honor and self-determination against immigrant hordes and Unionist usurpers. Nor by any desire to defend the institution of slavery. Patriotism was not an answer. Nor had he felt, like Patterson, a lust for adventure that took him away from home. Nor could he say that he enlisted to protect those he loved since they all seemed perfectly able to protect themselves. Except for his older brothers and sisters—all of whom had married and started their own families—the elder generation of his family had pretty much died out. His grandparents on both sides all were dead. No, he joined simply because Patterson had.

Next day the ironclads reappeared, but Buckner had other uses for the Fourth Kentucky. A relatively untried but confident general named Grant had made several attempts to attack their rear, and skirmishing went on until midafternoon. Behind the breastworks, their gun primed but unfired, Jarom and Patterson tried to evaluate the battle by the density and direction of the firing of others. The rifle reports sounded in the distance like a sheet being ripped to pieces a little at a time, little stitches that sometimes heightened to a crescendo. Sometimes, storms of artillery deafened them, walls of timber and a pall of grayness obscuring their view. Fire from the gunboats worked up faintly through the hollows and a bulwark of trees. Jarom imagined the generals, men whose vision was no less limited, trying to get the gist of the fighting. Sightlines, even from the high ground, were obstructed, and sound had a way of deceiving among the gullies and hills that cut the slopes into isolated pockets. An officer ensconced in one of these crevices might not know over the spine of wilderness and rocky divides whether his troops scrapped for survival or had routed their enemies. Patterson gave these distortions the name of "sound shadows." Feeling isolated, apart from things, neither Jarom nor Patterson could see a single swatch of blue.

Patterson found what comfort he could against the earthen backfill of the emplacement. Jarom was eyeing the thread of river when word arrived that General Buckner had ordered the Fourth Kentucky to secure a patch of scraggly woods above Indian Creek from which enemy skirmishers were firing enfilade across the bottom into the trenches. Colonel Hanson, a burly man on a dappled, low-centered horse, formed his regiment into a battle line and marched down the ravine and up toward the trees from which the firing came. Borrowing some binoculars, Jarom brought the ragged woodline into focus, spotting clusters of cottony smoke from the discharge of muskets and even a few spits of flame.

He watched Hanson dismount within thirty yards of the trees as his line, uneven now and considerably thinned, penetrated the timber. Without pausing, Hanson pushed the still invisible bluecoats deeper into the gray tangle of upright limbs. For a moment he remained visible as he followed his stick men into the woods, which seemed to suck them into a maw of wilderness from which they would return transformed, if they returned at all. As he scanned the bands of smoke that hung across the treeline, he could reckon the battle's changing locus by sound until whatever it was that swallowed the men lapsed into near silence. A few pitiful stragglers staggered downhill as if in a swoon, many of them hobbling from wounds. Jarom turned to Patterson, who'd been watching too but without benefit of magnification.

"It's the one who stays out of it," he said, "that sees the most of a fight."

Seeing the wounded and imagining the dead who must be piling up in the shelter of the woods, Jarom understood Patterson's irony.

Then word came back to the ridge that Hanson and his men had lost their way, that somewhere during the intensity of firing they'd lost their bearings and were now in danger of being captured or annihilated in the darkness. Rice Graves, first to sense the danger, had asked the dozen or so men about him if anyone would volunteer to act as a runner to find Hanson and guide his men back to their lines. Jarom glanced at Patterson, who was signaling with his eyes not to go, but Jarom stepped forward and said he would try.

"There's a good boy," Graves said, not much more than a boy himself.

Stripping off his heavy jacket and emptying his pockets, Jarom felt a quickening and simultaneously a sinking somewhere in the hollows of his chest, a feeling he remembered from the time when at nine or ten he'd thrown his leg over a balky horse, knowing he couldn't control it. To throw him, it veered suddenly into the orchard, dragging him through a scourge of low-lying limbs that raked across his back and gouged his face as he hugged the saddleless horse about the neck. Someone working in the barn had spied him and managed to drive the frenzied horse into a fence corner, grabbing the bridle and pulling him off to safety. That feeling of crashing through the stubby gauntlet of apple limbs he felt now, a sensation that constricted the air in his lungs and fired his body with exhilaration and fear.

As Jarom stooped instinctively to top the parapet, Graves handed him his navy pistol, a heavy affair known for its inaccuracy and tendency to misfire. It offered Jarom more assurance than actual protection in the face of what he knew, and didn't know, was before him.

And then he was off, climbing over the parapet with the river to his back and starting to descend the bluff on the opposite side. The slope was steep and broken with outcroppings of rock and stumps from the trees felled for the defenses, the footing uncertain. In the failing light the landscape replicated the seared gray he'd seen in daguerreotypes glued in his mother's family album. The images of trees resembled those in the album, blurred and slightly out of focus, the way he imagined they might look to a nearsighted person who'd lost his glasses. Working his way through the long shadows as the sun dropped over the western ridge, he entered a ravine. Thick with snarls of honeysuckle, dry vines tangled in skeins tore at his feet and made the going slow. In summer he knew it would be a place of serpents, but now it became the domain of snappings and cracks, a place to stumble and fall. Though he saw discarded haversacks and a rifle with a shattered stock, he saw not one of his kind, living or dead, until he crossed to a converging gully that opened onto a wide valley.

Scrabbling over the rocks, he encountered the first corpse he'd ever seen outside a coffin wherein the deceased had been properly fitted out, hands closed in some sanitized posture of repose. The dead man lay sprawled on his back as if napping after a family picnic or resting at noon after scything in a field. His right knee was raised, his right forearm rested across his stomach, his left stretched outward open-palmed, as if to expose itself to some imaginary sun. Death had closed his eyes; briary dark hair formed a wreath about his head. His woolen coat was pulled open midway up the chest, but nowhere could Jarom see the slightest sign of a wound. Though he didn't recognize the face, he would lay a wager that the dead man, a private soldier, belonged to the Fourth Kentucky.

He moved on, sensing time and light against him now. As he came into the scrubby flatlands, he found more dead strewn like heaps of scattered laundry.

Passing along the base of the ridge, he followed a tricky path between the barely visible ridgeline and the edge of a slough that backed up from the river. Ridges hemmed in the pale and meager sky. He located the fighting by the pop of musketry. As he moved toward it, he expected at any instant to be fired on, maybe by his own troops. The shooting took on patterns of single reports punctuated by explosive sputters that resonated in the hollows. As the light failed, the firing slackened, and someone not twenty feet away rose out of the sedge and challenged him.

Jarom told him his name and unit, uncertain whether the challenger was friend or foe. The boy, shivering in what looked like his mother's paisley shawl, led him by huddles of men resting along the hard ground. They found Colonel Hanson hunched under a tree talking to two of his surviving officers. He was a low-built man, blocky and muscular as a butcher, his face stubbled and drawn. When Jarom identified himself and said that Major Graves instructed him to lead the colonel back to their lines, Hanson cracked a smile.

He told Jarom he'd become disoriented, that in the excitement of the attack he'd been carried along much farther than he'd planned to go.

"All these hills look pretty damn much alike," he said, "especially after we'd climbed three of four. First thing we know, we got turned around, and here we are at suppertime not daring to light a fire. We're scattered all to hell in these woods between this ridge and the next."

Jarom said he knew the way back.

"But can you guide us in the dark?"

Jarom said that he could, adding that the route they'd follow would keep them mostly shielded from fire.

"But how can we move without firing a torch?"

"We'll feel our way," Jarom said, projecting a confidence he wasn't sure he could keep.

This pacified Colonel Hanson, who passed an order to collect as many of the outliers as they could to quit this place forever. He ordered the men to stick close, each to follow the man ahead of him. He made provision for litters to carry those wounded who couldn't move by their own power. As much as the terrain permitted, he put out flankers to probe the darkness and prevent an ambush. Jarom leading, they snaked along the slough and by the edge of the woods, then into the ravine back to their lines, feeling their way until the landscape seemed more familiar. At one point Jarom heard enemy pickets and spotted a huge fire along a fringe of woods. Around it they could make out figures seated on the ground, their bodies angling toward warmth. Though these men easily could have been taken or killed, Hanson had no more heart for fighting, and they crept past the fire. Along the way they found six wounded men—four of their own, two of the enemy's. When they crossed the embrasure into their line again, Graves shook Jarom's hand and promised to make a full report to General Buckner. At formation the next morning Buckner, a serious man whose long mustaches extended across his face like wings, called Jarom to the head of the ranks and commended him before the company for acts of exemplary valor. Groggy, in his mind still threading his way in the darkness along the slope, Jarom stepped back into the ranks, wanting nothing more than sleep.

From that moment of triumph when Jarom felt he'd earned the respect he craved, things took a turn for the worse. The Fourth Kentucky had lost sixteen men on February 13, but another enemy, the weather, deployed its forces for an assault the next morning. By dark the temperature had dropped to ten degrees, freezing the water in Jarom's canteen. Water seeping into the rifle pits hardened to ice so that moving even a few feet became a triumph of ingenuity. During the night several of the wounded, including two who had not been lost in the valley after nightfall, froze where they lay. Dozens suffered from frostbite. There was nowhere to send them, neither hospital nor cubicle of warmth in a farmhouse, because Grant, flushed with his victory at Fort Henry, had surrounded their fortification. A chain of ironclads forestalled evacuation along or across the river.

Jarom and Patterson hunkered in their dugout, getting up to fuel the fire and stomping their shoes against the frozen ground to keep their blood circulating. Jarom could feel the cold pry its way through his underclothes, the flannel vest he'd scavenged on the field, his woolen jacket, the blanket in which he shivered. The cold knifed through to the bone, where it established little outposts of numbness in his toes and fingertips. Worse, that night the order came down not to build fires, inside the huts or out, since sharpshooters had been posted along the edge of the woods, dropping anyone who stood out against the ridgeline. There was little to do except huddle under the flimsy shelter while the generals devised some means to sever the noose that threatened to strangle them.

In the morning, orders came that they would attack to the rear of the river to open a way for a retreat to Nashville. At half past six, before light had filtered down to the frozen backwaters, Bushrod Johnson led his men out of the gullies to attack Grant's right wing. He aimed, as Graves surmised, to run a sweep of the Wynn's Ferry road, the one remaining route of escape to Nashville. Attacking at dawn, Johnson caught the federals off guard. After what reports later described as a "brisk little scrap," the enemy line folded in on itself. Elated, Bushrod Johnson bragged to his superiors that he'd "busted 'em up and scattered 'em from hell to breakfast." An hour later, Buckner punched a hole in the federals' left wing, pushing it far enough that the Wynn's Ferry road could be held open for several hours, long enough for most of the army to escape.

Rice Graves, returning with orders, instructed the battery to direct its guns beyond the point along the road where the Second Kentucky had made its attack. Jarom and the others wheeled the nine-pounder around to a position where its dark muzzle aligned with a tongue of trees beyond the advance on the ferry road. From his nest above the low ground Jarom watched the even ranks of the Second Kentucky, three rows of them. The pale morning sun caught the gray of their backs and glinted from whatever metal was exposed. They marched in perfect order two hundred yards across a field toward Grant's army secreted in the woods. He watched as the line seemed to buckle under the first fire, ranks closing in perfect order to fill the gaps where those in front went down. Jarom expected the command to return fire, but Hanson held back as his first rank approached the timber, their battle flag clearly visible in the smudges of smoke rising from the brush along the woodline. The troops did not return fire until they came within forty yards of the woods. Then they rushed into the dark mesh of trees, where the firing grew more intense.

From a distance, the din reminded Jarom of a bonfire crackling through meshes of sticks. Looking back along the route at their march, Jarom saw a spoor of dead and wounded soldiers, a straggler or two trailing off toward the high ground in the cautious and crouching way of skulkers and survivors.

Graves gave commands to fire the nine-pounder. Touched off, the muzzle erupted with a deafening blast; the jolt of the barrel as it recoiled called for constant alertness lest it break an arm or knock the wind from their lungs. Jarom's part was to ram home the charge, stepping out from the bore after setting the charge and ball, packing the powder and shot for maximum compression. As he raised the rammer time after time, he devised a kind of rhythm that made the movements of the crew steps an elaborate dance of precision and elegance in which each partner, like a practiced waltzer, grew accustomed to the others' cues and gestures.

Moving from gun to gun, Graves personally directed the fire, sometimes elevating or lowering the muzzle to sight along a more favorable line, sometimes igniting the fuse himself. Hatless, he zipped about giving orders, his look of intense concentration setting a tone of high seriousness they all adopted in firing. Flushed red as a pepper, he ordered the crews to land shells twenty yards into the woods, then forty yards, then sixty, following the invisible foe as it presumably pulled back under the advance. His prompts were not so much visual as auditory, possessing as he did an uncanny sense of where the shot would most lethally fall. After a time, he ordered the crews to change their charges to canister and grape, elevating or lowering the fire wherever he imagined blue clusters. The firing raked blindly into the woods as hail might perforate the leaves of a tree. When the gun came to rest, Jarom and his gunmates again cupped their hands along its curvature for warmth.

Even before Hanson's men entered the woods, the firing transformed the verticals to wreckage, reminding Jarom of a timber stand he'd once seen after a bouncing tornado had touched down. Trees in one small area had been felled as though struck by a giant mallet, a few feet from those that stood perfectly intact. Along the fringes of the woods, few trees remained unbroken and whole. Where fire had been most concentrated, the ground resembled a hayfield through which a swath had been mowed, not cut but bludgeoned as with a dull scythe that battered and bent everything it couldn't cut. But among the mangled trees lay humans. The advance ground everything in its path to splinters, the dead lying in ragged windrows. Despite his ability to detach himself from what appeared so remote and minute, despite the abstract quality of so wide a panorama, the spectacle left Jarom shaking. He felt a constriction in his throat and an uneasiness in his bowels that made him think he would vomit.

During the early moments when those defending the woods clashed with those entering, a sober young man named Estin Polk was reassigned to swab the bore of Jarom's nine-pounder. He was a native of Warren County, and Jarom knew the family name and even had talked with him about acquaintances they had in common. Polk's people were farmers, owning a boundary of poor land in the knobby region of the county. He told Jarom his parents were poor, never had a stone. He told him that though there was no public school in his section, when he could he had attended a nearby academy where he had learned his letters and received his call to enter the Baptist ministry. Pious and shy among his comrades, he had been stuck with the moniker of Parson Polk, a name he accepted with a semblance of pride. Jarom had asked why he did not strike back at the scoffers.

"Such men we call Hellfire Christians," he'd said. "When the ground starts shaking and the ground opens to reveal the burning pit, they are first to drag themselves forward for absolution. When the pit closes, they will go back to their unrepentant ways. I am not the Word. I am only the bringer of His Word."

After each discharge of their piece, Estin Polk was assigned to swab out the leavings of the shot to prevent debris from accumulating and causing the muzzle to explode. Closest to the cannon's eruptions, he had dark rings around his eyes and complained to Jarom after several detonations that the smoke shortened his breath. Patterson, no friend to religion, ragged him without stint, gibing him about getting singed if he drew too close to what he now called "the devil's trumpet."

Jarom thought Polk was decent enough and held no strong opinion on the existence of a deity, never having given the matter much thought. Though religion was a fever with Polk, he kept accounts of his spiritual struggles to himself. From what Jarom observed, Polk did not hang about and gossip with his messmates. He kept pretty much to himself except on

Sunday afternoons when he conducted a kind of Bible society. Other days he spent his free time with his nose in the Testaments, a batch of bound sermons, or one of the American Tract Society pocketbooks that circulated around the camp. No exhorter to salvation, he delighted in quietly poring over Scripture and practicing unstinting good works.

"He'll read that Bible to tatters," Patterson said.

Because many in the regiment lacked skills to put pen to paper, Polk often took down their messages home. To his credit, though never known to sample strong drink or utter a profane word, he neither scorned nor scolded those who did. No ranter, he ministered by example. At camp meetings, it was said that he was prayerful and when the need arose would willingly act as chaplain and read words over the wounded or dead. His favorite hymns, he once mentioned to Jarom, were "On Jordan's Stormy Banks I Stand" and "There Is a Fountain Filled with Blood."

On the slavery question he held strong views. "The Southern Confederacy," he declared to Jarom, "must humble itself, must renounce slavery and seek genuine spiritual redemption among Christ's company through individuals leading the Christian life." Jarom decided that Estin for his own peace of mind could countenance no middle ground. Estin, Jarom believed, knew that his stance on slavery was scorned by fire-eaters in the regiment, but he was tolerated because he performed his duties as a soldier with the same diligence and efficiency as his ministry, his work contributing to loosing storms of shot upon his fellow mortals. He had never skipped a roll call or complained about rations of tainted pork and inedible bread as the others did. Whenever Jarom saw him about camp or at his post, he was clean-shaven, having scraped his jaw with a straight razor and whatever softener he could concoct to cure the whiskers—precious portions of hand soap or even dollops of lard. Jarom attributed this obsession with cleanliness to a desire not to encounter his Maker looking less than his best.

Estin's death raised more questions about the nature of the divine than ever his preachments did. During the cannonade, as he rammed a charge down the muzzle, his head and back exposed through the embrasure, he was struck in the nape of the neck by what Rice Graves later reckoned was a spent bullet.

"It was as though God had tapped him," Patterson said, "wanting to get his attention."

This freak shot descended out of the sky almost providentially and thumped against his upper spine, scarcely penetrating the skin but killing him instantly. Without a sound he reeled and dropped to his knees in a parody of prayer, pitching against the gun carriage and almost into Jarom's lap. The bullet had traveled so slowly that it might have been dodged had he seen it coming. Examining him, Rice Graves found a raspberry bruise at the base of his brainpan, the head nodded to one side abnormally.

"The rain surely doesn't trouble itself much," Patterson said, "about who it falls on."

He and Jarom eased the body off to a place where they wouldn't have to see him until they laid him in the common pit dug for the ones who had fallen that day. There was no time for words at his burial.

Despite Hanson's temporary success in rolling up the road, it was General Pillow's attack that finally opened a route to evacuate the fort.

Overrunning General McClernand's encampment, Pillow captured six guns and put two thousand federals out of the battle. Since the defenders of Donelson had no food to feed the prisoners, Pillow had paroled them, exacting a pledge not to take up arms again under penalty of being shot if captured. All the ground within the immediate vicinity of Jarom's battery was under Confederate control again, and the federals had not had sufficient time to organize a counterattack. Jarom noted that even the wind seemed to cooperate, trees in the distance along the road coming to view again as smoke was swept from the hillside. An acrid smell of burning sulfur had worked its way into Jarom's clothes and blankets, inflaming his eyes. All the cannoneers appeared tearful.

Though the stage was set to wedge the Confederate defenders between Grant and Nashville, the opportunity dissipated as quickly as the smoke when Pillow inexplicably ordered a retreat, this at a time when everyone was anxious, as Patterson put it, to fly the coop. It was common knowledge among everyone in the army that Grant was receiving reinforcements by the hour and that the strength of the Confederate army was declining, with no realistic hope of any relief. It was also clear to everyone except the generals that the opportunity to break the ring must be seized before it too was lost. Soon, everyone heard Pillow's order. Perplexed, angry, they knew that on that single decision rested the chances of winning or losing the campaign—the whole game, as Patterson said.

Buckner, a scrapper less concerned with caution than honor, protested the order, but Floyd, a politician who had no military experience, went along with Pillow, an act his troops regarded as amounting to rank cowardice. As Jarom interpreted it, in one almost treasonous stroke the defenders of Donelson without a fight had forfeited everything they'd gained, and giving up under any circumstances went against his grain. So, without any cost in blood, Grant's eager newcomers quickly retook the ground they had lost, placing his troops in a suitable posture to attack at first light. In less than an hour, the mood of jubilation of the army turned to gloom. Colonel Hanson, who had made deliverance possible, cupped his face in his hands and cried.

"'The privates win the fights,'" Patterson said, quoting the old saw, "'and the generals lose the battles.'"

As if anything could be worse, the generals who had bungled the victory with their decision to surrender withdrew themselves from humiliation by deserting during the night. Before absconding, General Floyd said he feared surrender because he might be hanged as a traitor, having served as secretary of war under President Buchanan. This had the effect of raising the suspicion that he was indeed still in the employ of the government and thus welcomed the chance to give up fifteen thousand armed rebels. At the very least, Floyd had suffered a loss of nerve. Both Floyd and Pillow protested that they feared what might happen if they fell into Union hands. What they really feared, according to Patterson, was becoming the first Confederate generals of the war to surrender their troops. They might be jailed, they might be hanged. Taking a few of his Virginia regiments with him, Floyd escaped on a steamboat still at its berth by the riverfront. Leaving less conspicuously, Pillow simply rowed across the Cumberland in a skiff under cover of night.

That left Buckner, the man who by rights and talent should originally have been senior commander, to negotiate a surrender he'd never wanted to make. The story passed through the ranks that before giving up the army, he had sent a message to Grant, his friend from West Point, asking terms of surrender. Grant, out to make a reputation, replied that the terms were immediate and unconditional surrender as he proposed to attack immediately. So much for friendship. Buckner was left with no recourse but to hoist white flags above the rifle pits on February 12, 1862. With this act he surrendered over twelve thousand men and forty guns, all irreplaceable. Great stores of provisions stockpiled for the winter, which he had refused to destroy, also fell into federal hands.

Jarom, soon to be a prisoner, felt some encouragement in the act of one little-known commander, Nathan Bedford Forrest. Stating simply that he had no stomach for surrender and that he hadn't come up from Hernando, Mississippi, to be placed in captivity, he escaped sometime during the night, leading his ragtag cavalry through swamps that rose to the skirts of their saddles. Jarom and his comrades found themselves with no choice but to swallow a bitter pill. Their captors split those who surrendered into two groups—one made up of officers, the other of enlisted men. Officers were sent to Camp Chase in Ohio, the rest, including Jarom and Patterson, to Camp Morton near Indianapolis, farther north than Jarom had ever been. Boarding a captured steamboat named the *Dr. Kane*, Jarom and a boatload of other private soldiers floated down the Cumberland to the Ohio and upriver to the Falls at Louisville, then traveled by train and later marched overland to Camp Morton.

To the day, Jarom had enlisted five and a half months previously. Safe in his pocket, he still carried the buckeye that Patterson found under a tree and gave him the day he enlisted, its hull split into halves, a knob of wonder that reminded Jarom of the walnut patina on the three-footed table in Mary Tibbs's parlor, placed next to her rocker with the back of arrows. Still holding its luster, it was now disfigured by an ugly crack, an uneven fissure that marred the burnished shell and shaped in Jarom's mind a token of the world's imperfection and changeability. When he showed it to Patterson, his friend said it represented the failed Confederacy, shiny on the surface but split all to pieces inside.

Among the belongings the guards allowed him to keep was an ambrotype of Mollie and himself, one they posed for in a studio in Springfield. He also held on to the folded-up sheet of music. Despite its encasement in oilcloth, it was beginning to show signs of wear. Jarom opened it and showed it again to Patterson, asking him what he made of it. Patterson had no ready answer but said he reckoned the tune and the lyrics were

Irish, probably related to the strong political divisions between Protestants and Catholics during one of the Catholic uprisings at the time of the Glorious Revolution toward the end of the seventeenth century. Patterson had Jarom read all twelve stanzas to him, each ending with a refrain that was largely a repetition of the song's title, with the addition of some nonsense syllables: "Lil-li-bur-ler-o bul-len-a-la Lero-o ler-o, Lil-li-bur-ler-o, Lil-li-bur-ler-o bul-len-a-la o ler-o ler-o, lil-li-bur-ler-o lil-li-burler-o bul-len-a-la."

Though he couldn't fathom the song's content, Jarom loved to repeat the words aloud, especially what he called the chorus, though he had no idea what they signified, what tune they were married to. Musically illiterate, he knew only that the melody had a fast tempo because of the notation at the beginning of the score that read "Briskly." So he imagined some of the bravura of the drinking songs he'd heard, though he could not construct a specific tune for it since neither he nor Patterson could convert the notes and clefs into melody. The song consisted of twelve two-line stanzas, not one of which made complete sense to either Patterson or himself:

Ho, brother Teague, dost hear the decree?
Lilliburlero bullenala
That we shall have a new deputy,
[REFRAIN]
Ho! by my shoul it is the Talbot,
And he shall cut all the English throat;

Tho,' by my shoul, the English do praat,
The law's on their side, and Creish knows what.

But, if dispence do come from the Pope,
We'll hang Magna Charta and themselves in a rope,

And the good Talbot is made a lord,
And he with brave lads is coming aboard,

Who all in France have taken a sware,
They that will have no Protestant heir.

O, but why does he stay behind?
Ho! by my shoul, 'tis a Protestant wind.

Now Tyrconnel is come ashore,
and we have commissions gillore;

And he that will not go to mass
Shall turn out, and look like an ass.

Now, now the hereticks all go down
by Creish and St Patrick, the nation's our own.

There was an old prophecy found in a bog,
'Ireland shall be ruled by an ass and a dog.'

And now this prophecy is come to pass,
For Talbot's the dog, and James is the ass.

Patterson admitted that Talbot was a cipher to him, but James may
have been James II, the Catholic king replaced at death with a Protestant one, much to the displeasure of Catholic Ireland. Whatever the
words meant, Jarom felt a special need to preserve the sheet as a relic
whose mysteries might someday be explained to him. He could see some
connection with strife, with the war that rived the country. But politics meant little to him, and he could not name a single member of the
Confederate government beyond Jeff Davis. Though the names and personalities in the song meant nothing to him, he could detect an obscure
inner coherence. The words became an incantation, a kind of talisman
or charm, something he could carry with him as protection and safe
conduct through the end of the war. In some vague way these indecipherable words and notes represented a prospect of the future, a road
toward some desirable destination. To Jarom, they tokened a prophecy
of well-being and hope at present unreadable, a message encoded in
events that lay before him.

~~~~~~~~~~~~~~~~~~~~

CAMP MORTON

For the first time in his life Jarom found himself with more time than he had things to do. Prison bored him. Discipline loosened to almost complete laxity because for some unfathomable reason almost all of the officers at the prison had been transferred elsewhere. The chief authority became the guards themselves, most of them green in the game of lock and key. Much of the surplus time the inmates spent yarning in the mess or barracks, and Jarom often sat in, more to listen than to speak while others prattled about their families or bragged about the virtues and comeliness of their sweethearts. He longed for books and newspapers, but there were no books, no papers.

The more he heard, the more Mollie came to dominate his thoughts. He tried at first to summon her in his imagination. He created a neutral space in which they were the sole occupants, a picnic, a parlor, a walk on the farthest feather of ridgeland. He saw her look up smiling in the kitchen, her arms blanched with flour. He saw her outside feeding the chickens, broadcasting handfuls of golden corn from her pouched apron. On Sundays he saw her got up for Methodism, prim and bonneted, wearing pink ribbons and a matching sash in the spring morning. Sometimes while he lay on his pallet, there came dark moments when he saw her flirting at socials, dancing or sparking with strangers.

Though Patterson carried in his pack a pair of scissors to trim hair, Jarom let his grow. It grew dark in long tresses that he tucked in the crevice behind his ear, swept back over his neck. At first he thought long hair made him appear more manly, but then as it inched down over his ears and his back he realized it gave him the aspect of a young woman, especially when he began to shave off the stubble that sprouted on his chin and about his mouth. Though Patterson and others cultivated mustaches, he took pains to scrape off every facial hair, only half conscious of the results until some of his messmates began to call him Young Miss. When he borrowed Patterson's rust-stippled mirror to pull the pocket razor over his high cheeks, he began for the first time to think of himself as handsome, almost pretty.

One evening around the fire one of his messmates, a joker with a streak of meanness, tried to get a rise out of him, saying he bet Young

Miss didn't have a sweetheart. When Jarom owned that he did, the giber tried to provoke him, saying that if he did he should have proof certain, a letter perhaps.

"I can do you one better," Jarom said. "I have a likeness that she gave me."

A little reluctantly, Jarom tendered to the man, whose name was Evans, a *carte de visite* that Mollie had given him, an image of her standing in a camera studio flanked by an Ionic column on which stood a vase of plucked flowers. She was sitting bare-armed in a print dress whose pattern formed a constellation of intricate geometries, her hands crossed on her lap, more child than woman, about fifteen. She stared straight into the lens, dark tresses, resembling his own, to her shoulders, a part line dead center like a cleft above her broad forehead, a beaded necklace at the base of her neck. Playfully defiant, her eyes caught the light, locked on the cameraman's lens as though he had dared her not to stir. He looked at it, but not so often because it seemed lifeless and cold, a study in inertness. It did not match her corporeal self, her flurries of nervous motion.

Studying it a few moments, Evans passed it on to the next man, and around the circle it went until it came to a bully named Crow. For no good reason Crow snatched it up and tossed it into the fire, too fast for Jarom to pull it out. He watched helplessly as the heat first smudged then curled the backing, the flames consuming her image, reducing it to charred wisps. Crow, still wrapped in his blanket, snickered and smirked at him across the fire.

Uttering a kind of half-scream, Jarom hopped to his feet and leapt across the fire. He tackled Crow's midsection, landing with such force that the man had no time to react, surprised and too much encumbered to put up much resistance as Jarom's weight fell against his chest. Jarom tore into him with his fists. Crow thrashed about in his blanket as Jarom pummeled him, unable to free his arms to get in a swing of his own. Evans, who must have felt some responsibility, pulled the two of them apart, and that was the end of it. Crow wiped the blood from his mouth, cursed the Ruler of Heaven once or twice, and rolled over in his blanket.

Reporting this incident to Patterson, Jarom said that hitting the bastard had done him some good, had done both of them some good.

"When I saw that picture aflame," he said, "I knew I could fight the bastard into next week."

He rubbed his skinned knuckles, one of them gashed from striking a tooth. They throbbed so persistently he believed he must have broken something. After that evening, Jarom kept mostly to himself. Crow scowled now and then but kept his distance, a dog once bitten. Afterward, at other evening assemblies around the fire, no one questioned or made light of his feelings for Mollie Thomas, though Crow and some others now addressed him, behind his back, as Sweet Missy.

ESCAPE

Chafing under weeks of confinement, his freedom hampered, Patterson organized his cellmates in a plan to escape, the object being to rejoin their comrades in Tennessee. Some hygiene-minded authority at the prison had ordered daily sorties to the river, rotating the bathers cell by cell so that in a week everyone had at least one dip in the water. The routine in which prisoners marched beyond the brick walls seemed made to order. Jules George of the Second Louisiana and Ben Coleman from Jellico, Tennessee, joined the conspiracy. Coleman stood a giant, an oversized farmer who looked capable of lifting a sutler's wagon. Following Patterson's lead, the four of them plotted a scenario of escape when it came their time to bathe.

On that sultry afternoon four guards, led by a self-important corporal named Heinzman, marched the four captives through the prison gate past a guard tower. The crenellations of this roofless tower reminded Jarom of a Gothic castle he'd seen engraved in one of his uncle's books. Slogging in the heat, they turned off the county road onto a wooded lane that twisted around a rugged hillside to the river, a sluggish stream that in Kentucky Jarom would have called a creek. When he saw it, Patterson disdainfully declared it a piddlin' branch, a ditch, with just enough water barely to wet their heels. At the waterside, the four of them stripped off their tattered uniforms while the guards lounged in the shade of an enormous sycamore whose white roots formed a snarl maybe twenty feet from the water.

As he waded into waist-high water, Jarom felt a band of coolness beneath the heated surface. Across it, the late afternoon sun laid down a blinding sheen. When the four of them reached midstream, they went through the motions of scrubbing themselves, sharing two bars of rough lye soap Heinzman tossed out to them. Jarom noticed that against the muddy yellow of the water their upper bodies had a greenish tint, the unshorn hair plastered to their noggins, enlarging their features as their head sizes seemed to shrink.

Acting on cue, Jules George began to pick a fight with Patterson, slapping a handful of water into his face and reaching out his long white arm to dunk him. Patterson took up the challenge by thrashing about in the water and cursing George as a goddamned spittle head. From the left, Ben Coleman joined the fracas, diving underwater and pulling George's legs from under him. The guards, their rifles leaning against the base of the sycamore, looked up from their game of cards, mildly amused and only vaguely interested. "Let these yokels drown themselves" seemed to be the prevailing sentiment. Sprawling in the shade of the scabby white limbs, they soon turned back to their card hands, taking this rambunctiousness in stride. What started as horseplay in the river quickly escalated into a free-for-all, the four prisoners kicking and throwing punches in the water.

This new sport soon caught the guards' notice, and each began to yell for his favorite, egging him on. The guards were too green or indifferent to see that each punch and counterpunch was feigned, the commotion in the White River all performance. "All juice and no pickle," as Patterson later put it.

"Go get him, George," Corporal Heinzman cried. "Grab him round the neck and dunk him good."

Slowly, the guards entered into the spirit of things, whooping and cheering the fighters on, one or two of them rising and coming closer, leaving their arms where they rested against the tree. They hollered for a while, gibing and rooting, even doing a pantomime of exchanged punches. Soon bored, they returned to the complexities of their game, all but ignoring the horseplay in the river as if to say, "If these damn rebels want to maim themselves, who are we to hinder them?"

Jarom, seeing his chance, dived underwater and swam ten or so yards downstream, surfacing in a little stand of scrub willows close to the bank. As he cupped his hands into fins and pulled, he prayed that the guards for a few moments would imagine four where now they saw only three. He glimpsed Patterson upstream, thrashing about, trying to break George's hammerlock. Coleman was yawping to one side, jockeying about in the shallow water and acting as referee. Grabbing one of the willow branches, Jarom pulled himself out of the shallows, almost slipping on the slimy beard of a rock as he crouched on dry ground. He paused a few seconds before starting his sprint toward the guns, as close to him now as to the unsuspecting guards. Looking up from their cards, the one facing in his direction must have been astonished to see a naked man with intense eyes rushing toward the tree. Quickly undeceived, he started to hoist himself up to meet the threat. Reaching the guns a step or two ahead of him, Jarom grabbed the weapon closest to hand and trained it on his chest.

"Back off or lay dead," he said.

The man stood stock-still, dazed, so close Jarom could feel the warmth of his breath, close enough, he realized with some alarm, to twist the barrel from his grasp. The others were on their feet now but hung back in bafflement as the enormity of the ruse began to dawn on them. For a few seconds, the man at the end of his rifle barrel glared at him perplexed, a clean-cut boy, Jarom surmised, from one of the small towns that honeycombed Indiana. His enemy took a step backward and raised his hands, still confused, not able to grasp in summation what had happened: the flailing fists, the yelping in the water, this strange turn of fate in which he and his comrades found themselves duped.

Jarom stood the four of them down while the bathers emerged from the water fresh from their serious frolic. In just seconds the features on Heinzman's face passed from amazement to alarm to defiance.

"You can't do this," he said. "You can't just pick up and walk two hundred miles of country where you have no friends. You'll never make it back to wherever you came from."

"I can," Patterson said, as he stepped closer, dripping. "I can, I have, and I will."

Saying this, he took up one of the rifles and directed its business end toward the speaker's chest, a move that stifled further conversation.

"Now strip," said Patterson, "unless you can tell me which one of you has a mother that wants to bury a son?"

They stripped off shoes and tunics and dusty trousers, their castoff clothing forming a blue heap in the clearing. George rolled their clothes into a bundle, shoes tucked inside, and secured it with the broad belts, which had spangled brass buckles embossed with the letters US.

As the guards stripped, Ben Coleman gathered up the guns and began chucking them into the river, all but the one Jarom still held. Everyone looked on entranced as the new Springfields, still slicked in government oil, seemed to pan on the surface a moment before sinking into the murk. Jules George made a pack of their prison clothes, weighted them with a flat stone, and then tossed them into the deepest part of the river. Shadows lengthening on the water gave reminders of the time.

Jarom kept his gun directed at the guards as the others waded out into the water, the heap of contraband clothes raised like a trophy over Patterson's head. They rose on the far bank, dressing again in the discarded uniforms, as their former keepers felt sufficiently emboldened to bellow complaints before beginning the humiliating trek back to their barracks, bare-bummed and barefooted.

Watching them move away in a style between wariness and panic, Coleman whooped in triumph. Swinging his elbows in little arcs, he began a shuffle that evolved into a kind of low country jig. Whirling, he vowed that he never tasted a wine so sweet as liberty, then raised a shrill rebel yell that sent the guards packing, white hams in the rushes.

NEWBURGH

Weighing their chances of escape, Jarom and the others decided to split up, George and Coleman going one way, Jarom and Patterson another. They clasped hands and wished each other luck, vowing to call a reunion when the war was won, then slipped into the dusk of Indiana. Hiking most of the night, Jarom and Patterson put up for a few hours under a corncrib. They stole some clothes from a Negro's cabin and traveled as near as they could reckon southwest. They passed through fields and along back roads some of the next day and most of the night, sleeping again toward morning in a dilapidated barn far off the road. They ate what they could forage, raiding gardens and grain sheds, once eating themselves sick in an orchard whose limbs sagged with green apples. Occasionally, they met strangers on the road from whom they cautiously asked directions.

Toward morning on the third day they came to the Ohio, a broad brown stripe of water a mile across on whose far shore they could see a fringe of trees and bits of what they knew were roofs. Fearing capture by one of the federal gunboats that chugged along the river, they waited until dark, stealing a fisherman's skiff they'd found tied to a cottonwood tree in a backwater slough.

They crossed without incident, Jarom feeling each stroke of the oars that Patterson dipped in the swill of dark water as bringing him a yard or two closer to freedom he'd never valued so greatly. Though they heard voices and saw lights of a packet, they managed to cross without being observed, putting in at a place on shore where no lights were visible among the dark curtain of trees.

Outside Henderson they overtook a local boy leading a foundered mare. Barefoot, he stepped as gingerly as the mare, whose shambling reminded Jarom of a wounded man he'd seen slogging up the slope at Donelson, too tired, too drained to know or care about his destination. Hailed, the boy, maybe fourteen, stopped and turned around, his toes fidgeting in the dust as the two of them approached.

"Hallo," said Patterson, "can you tell me which town we're coming to?"

"Henderson," the boy said.

"Are there Yankees about?"

The boy gave him a knowing look, not sure of his allegiance, and said noncommittally that he'd heard some had set up camp on the road just east of the town and that home guards were patrolling all the roads at night.

Patterson asked if he knew whether there was anyone about who sang rebel songs.

The boy looked puzzled, then calculating. "There may be, there may be not. Who wants to know?"

After professions of allegiance to the Southern cause, Patterson persuaded him of their loyalties and that they had just set foot on the soil of Old Kentucky after escaping from a federal prison. He said they were tired in the extreme, as famished as songbirds after a snow, and needed a place to lay up where they didn't have to worry about being boated back across the river, where their former captors had determined to even scores.

That persuaded the boy, no taller than a hoe handle and nearly as lean. He said he reckoned he could direct them to a Southern man who would be sympathetic to their predicament. He gave them directions to a certain farmhouse up the road about a mile and parted company, his sorry specimen of a field horse limping off behind.

The Southern man, whose name was Johnson and whose two sons served under Braxton Bragg in Tennessee, welcomed them into his modest clapboard house, which covered a double-pen cabin. His tongue-tied wife fed them chicken and cornbread while her husband listened avidly to the details of their escape. Satisfied with their loyalties, he then led them to a camp near the river where he introduced them to Captain Adam R. Johnson, in the vicinity of Henderson recruiting cavalry to form a squadron called the Breckinridge Guards.

A Henderson native who had emigrated to Texas and started a ranch, Johnson was slight of build and, as Patterson put it, close to the ground. Jarom estimated that he stood about five-five or -six, his most conspicuous feature a cascading mustache that hung in twin tails badly in need of cropping. Jarom imagined him at table, constantly swiping at the buttermilk and crumbs from the drooping ends that engulfed his mouth and nested on his chin. Whether naturally disposed or trained with wax, its tips extended wider than his face, like whiskers on a cat, as if to warn him about places too narrow to back out of. Patterson later commented that they must have served him well because he too had been at Donelson and had been among the lucky few who slipped into the darkness with Forrest the morning before the surrender. Jarom quickly understood that Johnson's daring escape owed more to pluck than darkness.

In the morning Jarom learned that their joining brought the number of Breckinridge Guards, counting their commander, to twenty-seven. The camp, situated in the low end of a cow pasture, consisted of a field tent and a mess wagon. All of the recruits slept under the stars, rolled in whatever they could improvise to shield them from chill night air and the inevitable dew. After a breakfast of johnnycake and a flitch of bacon, Johnson called them together in a powwow. From the same boy Jarom and Patterson had met on the road, Johnson had learned that Henderson's garrison, consisting of eighty men, had withdrawn to Louisville to reinforce that city's defenders against a threatened attack by John Hunt Morgan.

Johnson informed the company, most of them young men from that locality, that they would eat supper in Henderson and sleep, for that night at least, indoors. Since they lacked several horses of mounting everyone, Jarom and Patterson each had to ride double. Decamping, the band simply rode into the sleepy little river town and sought out the mayor, an accommodating man who offered no resistance. Johnson, with some awkwardness, accepted without a shot the surrender of his hometown. In the street he afterwards shook hands with old schoolmates, friends he hadn't seen since he'd gone west. Jarom looked on as one of his new comrades in arms unfolded a flag and disappeared into the courthouse, emerging on a balcony to affix the stars and bars to what probably was a broom handle.

Jarom's experience that euphoria is always brief was borne out later that afternoon. Across the river stood Henderson's sister town of Newburgh, whose warm relations with Henderson had been strained, then ruptured, by the war. Johnson didn't have to be told that Evansville, just north of Newburgh, garrisoned federal troops. Hearing that Henderson had been taken, the garrison's commander had dispatched a gunboat, on its way to snip any stem of rebellion found in Henderson.

"Events are as fickle as weather in March," Patterson said, quoting what Jarom recognized as one of Mary Tibbs's folksy sayings.

That afternoon an envoy from Newburgh rowed over the river with a flag of truce lashed to the bow. He carried the message that Henderson would be shelled post haste if the offending flag was not immediately removed from the cupola of the courthouse. Intuiting the ultimatum more as a show of bravado than statement of intent, Johnson temporized and managed to stall the man until dark. He then reclaimed the flag and left town, not wishing to lose local goodwill in testing the resolve of whatever yahoos were on the gunboat, which continued to hover menacingly midstream. For his new campsite Johnson chose a farm a few miles outside of town belonging to a man named Soaper.

If the federals seemed well apprised of what went on in Henderson, information flowed in both directions. From undisclosed sources, Johnson learned that Newburgh contained a large cache of arms and ammunition issued by the state of Indiana to arm its home guard and protect the Hoosier state's southern shores against imagined hordes of ravening graycoats massed to the south. Not one to miss an opportunity, Johnson assembled his twenty-six men and told them the Southern Confederacy needed those armaments and that he proposed to fetch them over the river. When he asked how many he could count on to help him, everyone nodded in the affirmative.

Located on a lane that led to what had been a small landing, the Soaper farm provided an ideal spot from which to launch the boats needed to carry the war across the river to Indiana. Johnson, familiar with Newburgh since childhood, described it as a little two-penny river town. It had grown up around a cluster of sheds and storehouses on a rise above some pilings and plank walkways that served as a dock. From what Johnson understood, a two-story building close by the landing housed the guns. Asked how many Union soldiers guarded them, Johnson said only some local home guards who would rather smell bacon than tussle. The place, as he reckoned, had no troops because it had no strategic value, though a detachment of home guards under a Colonel Bethel had been assigned to protect the guns. By coincidence, Bethel, an entrepreneur, owned the building in which the arms were stored.

Somewhere Johnson picked up a recent edition of the *Evansville Journal,* boasting that the citizenry of Indiana would not allow its sovereignty to be compromised for even a moment and that Hoosier fields and valleys would remain inviolate forever. Reading this statement aloud to Jarom and the others, he tossed it to the ground and spiked it with the tapered heel of his western boot.

"Let's put 'em to the test," he said.

Next morning Jarom and the other members of Johnson's little army assembled on the river bank in plain sight of Newburgh, some buildings and a steeple or two appearing dimly through a screen of trees. Johnson produced an ancient telescope through which he surveyed the shoreline and pointed out the building whose bricks shown salmon pink in the early light.

"When we cross," he said, "we will be treading up to our buttocks on gunpowder. The merest spark will destroy us all, the merest show of cowardice or indecision."

"We're with you, captain," said his young lieutenant, Robert Martin. "Tell us what you have in mind."

Smoothing a place in the dust with his hands, Johnson scratched in the river, Newburgh, Henderson, the Green River ferry, and a building he referred to as the arsenal.

"We'll split off into two groups," he said. "First, I'll cross the river with two men and take the storehouse. We will hold it until the rest of you, led by Martin, can cross by ferry, create some kind of diversion, and march the half mile or so from the ferry to join us. If Martin meets any opposition, we will create our own distraction by setting fire to the shingle-roofed building between us. Once we are joined, we will load the arms and row them back to Henderson. Martin's men will stay at the storehouse until we safely reach the Kentucky shore."

In the face of questions, he stressed speed and secrecy essential to the plan's success because the telegraph connected Newburgh to Evansville, where the federals had gunboats and a large force of regular soldiers.

"Success," he said, "depends on our playing out a hand of bluff. Since this war started, we've always needed to seem more than we are."

In answer to the question how to expand twenty-seven men into an army, he outlined a trick or two about how to magnify their numbers. First, he ordered those with horses to bring them out of the trees at the appropriate time to make as big a display as possible. He directed Jarom and Patterson, whom he knew had some experience with artillery, to improvise two counterfeit cannons, using whatever materials they could locate in town.

They strode off down the main street to see what could be improvised. From a nearby blacksmith's shop, Martin helped them scavenge two pairs of old wagon wheels still attached to their axles. Wheeling them to an exposed position in plain sight of Newburgh, he had several men lash a sizable log to one of the axles. To the other he fixed two sections of stovepipe requisitioned from a dry goods and hardware business farther down Henderson's main commercial street.

"Add a stretch of water and two parts fear," Johnson said, "and a dollop of imagination, and our army is equipped with artillery."

Jarom felt low when Johnson told him and Patterson to stay behind and man the imaginary guns.

Once the plan had been rehearsed to everyone's satisfaction, Johnson, Frank Owen, and Felix Eakins pushed off for Newburgh in the same stolen skiff that Jarom and Patterson had used a few days before. None of them wore uniforms, largely, Jarom learned, because only Johnson owned one. It being mid-July, the weather was sultry, and the river seemed more a lake, wide and placid. The mist had not fully lifted, and a grayish-blue haze hung along the Indiana shore. Jarom and Patterson stationed themselves by their makeshift artillery and settled in for a long wait.

From what he later learned from Frank Owen, a twenty-year-old with residual freckles whose father had determined he would be a typesetter, the three of them hid their weapons in the bottom of the skiff. If spotted, they hoped to pass for fishermen or sightseers. While Jarom and Patterson played their passive roles as cannoneers, Martin with eighteen or nineteen men went upriver and commandeered the ferry, a crude affair that resembled a floating corral.

Johnson crossed without mishap and boldly tied up to the dock without meeting a dockhand or any of the loafers who lie about such places. Arming themselves, the three of them went directly to the warehouse, which stood open and unguarded, where they barricaded the doors and shuttered the windows before settling down to wait for Martin. Since it was nearly noon, they assumed that most of the townspeople would be sitting down to dinner at home or the town's one eatery, a rooming house next to the livery.

Johnson felt assured that things were going as planned until, glancing up the street, he saw five or six men dash into the hotel several doors from the boarding house. Telling Eakins and Owen to keep a lookout, that trouble was brewing, he picked up his two-barrel shotgun and walked casually up the street as a citizen might on an errand to post a letter or pay an account at the grocer's.

"My purpose," Johnson put it later as he patted his sidearm, "was to reason with them in terms they would understand."

During his walk up the street, he spotted a man in one of the upper windows of a clapboard house holding a large cartridge box. When the fellow realized Johnson had seen him, he stepped back out of sight. Clearly, someone had alerted the town and at least some of the citizens had organized to fight. Not a child, not a woman, had been seen.

A large structure with three stories, the hotel was the most prominent building in Newburgh. As offhandedly as any guest, Johnson walked up the steps to the verandah. Without breaking stride, as Owen noted, he pushed through the large double doors that opened onto the small lobby, which consisted of a counter, a registry desk, and a few chairs. Now it contained sixty or seventy citizens armed with every description of weapon, from squirrel rifles and new Enfields to antique swords as well as a saber or two, pistols of every variety, and even a pitchfork. A few of those to the front carried their firearms cocked and presented, close enough, as Johnson put it, to tickle his chin. Johnson knew he had either to bluff his way out of this predicament or surrender. A mighty hubbub arose in the room, so he had to yell to be heard.

Pushing the rifles aside with his double-bore shotgun, he brusquely ordered the assembly to hold their fire, promising that if those present surrendered their arms, his men would harm neither them nor the town. His problem was that none of his men was yet visible. Johnson said he felt a tremor pass through the company like an electrical current. Some tense moments passed before all of them, like a congregation acting in unison to rise for a hymn or kneel in prayer, put down their arms. There followed a great clanking of metal as weapons clacked against the poplar floor. Relieved to a degree appreciated only by reprieved criminals and high-stakes gamblers, Johnson waved his shotgun like a baton to back them to the walls and into the corridor, ordering them to keep so silent they could hear their grandsires whispering from the grave.

Just as he thought the pendulum had swung in his favor, a large man dressed in an officer's uniform burst into the room from a rear door, a horse pistol in his hand.

"What's the meaning of this?" the man demanded.

Of course, Johnson immediately identified the stranger confronting him as Colonel Bethel, a hefty, athletic man in his forties whose every action, he later said, bespoke confidence and decisiveness.

"What are you doing with my guns?" he asked as a proprietor might speak to an interloper.

The room went silent.

Spotting Johnson, the shotgun swinging like a dial on a pressure gauge to stop on his buttoned chest, Bethel shouldered his way toward the front of the room, the company parting and closing in his wake like a puddle passed through by a wheel.

"Advance another step," Johnson said, "and you will step into eternity on a load of buckshot."

Bethel stopped. Speechless, defiant, he glared at Johnson. Recovering after a few moments, he said he couldn't speak for the others but that for himself he would never surrender. Just then there came a commotion from the front of the room, and someone announced that a body of armed men were entering the hotel. Jarom shared Johnson's relief when he saw six or seven of his little band parading into the room, weapons at the ready.

Acting as though this had been his plan all along, Johnson sent one of his men and one of Bethel's to fetch the muster roll so Johnson could parole Bethel's men and put them out of contention.

The rest had been easy. Martin had left the hotel to see to the loading of the captured rifles onto two commissary wagons that he'd found behind the livery. This completed, he sent them upstream to the ferry so they could be transported across the river. Just as they were exiting town, word came that two hundred and fifty home guards from Evansville were approaching in an attitude of attack.

Johnson was forced to play his last card. He declared to Bethel that he knew the guardsmen were close and that if his men were fired on he would shell the town to rubble, blast it so completely that not one stone would stand upon another. Bethel, understandably flummoxed, said he saw no cannon and demanded that Johnson show him where they were positioned. Johnson marched him to a little rise by the storehouse, handed him the collapsible telescope, and pointed across the river, inviting him to see for himself. Bethel raised the telescope to his eye and scanned the Kentucky shore, the upraised cylinder hesitating when it came to

Jarom and Patterson's battery. He lowered the glass and looked to his storehouse, large and closest to the water. The tension broke when he asked Johnson for permission to send runners to call off the attack, a request Johnson readily granted.

As was later related to Jarom, by that time the cargo of guns was halfway across the Ohio. He and Patterson could see his comrades waving and dancing about the ferry. Saluting Bethel, Johnson returned to his skiff and took his place in the stern as Eakins and Owen, already at the oars, churned their way toward Kentucky. When they reached mid-channel, Johnson later said he noticed a dust cloud outside the town, marking the arrival of troops from Evansville. Before they touched shore, he beheld the storehouse and banks of the river aswarm with soldiers.

Looking downriver, he spied billows of smoke from a gunboat that was closing fast. From the shore Jarom and Patterson heard shots fired, though by mistake, he later learned, and not at either him or Johnson. In the excitement back at Newburgh the guardsmen had shot two of their fellow citizens by accident. For the benefit of anyone that might be watching, Jarom and Patterson performed the motions of loading and sighting their cannon, then stepping aside as though awaiting orders to level the toy town across the river with their make-believe guns. Fearing that they might be seen through a powerful lens, they kept somber expressions during the masquerade but broke into a fit of laughing when Johnson completed the crossing safely.

While Martin and the other men unloaded the ferry, a gunboat hove into view, its decks bristling with soldiers. The ferry had been steered downriver two miles to a long peninsula between the Ohio and Green Rivers where the latter emptied into the main stream. When it became clear that their play guns had outlived their usefulness, Jarom and Patterson abandoned them and tramped out to rejoin their jubilant comrades. Johnson quickly saw the tactical danger of the gunboats unloading troops up the Green River, for the river had to be crossed to move the guns south. He sent Patterson, Frank Owen, Jarom, and a young man named Jack Thompson to come with him to the mouth of the river.

Borrowing horses, Jarom and Patterson followed Johnson, who made a dash along a farm lane to the mouth of the river, approaching it just as a gunboat and transport nosed into the shade line of the Green. Heavily wooded, the peninsula made an ideal spot for an ambush. The colonel sent Patterson and Owen to a patch of willow scrub and brush across the river near the point. Leaving their horses tethered in the trees, Patterson and Owen swam the backwaters and took positions at the designated spot. The colonel, Jarom, and Thompson found cover fifty or so yards upriver in a stand of water maples just a few feet from the water.

As they made their way through the trees, Johnson explained that he proposed to create another diversion, calling it "a trick these people never learn." From among the maples, fist-thick saplings full of suckers, they could see the gunboat along the narrow channel, its deck only yards away. When it approached so close Jarom could count the rivets on the metal slabs beside the cannon ports, he and Thompson started firing.

With the first shots, the pilot ducked his head, as did several venturesome souls who had stepped onto the deck to watch for drift and deadheads. After the firing commenced, the pilot immediately reversed the engine and backed the boat into the Ohio, where it joined the troop transport, which was a mill of confusion. Someone was shouting orders and the men had nowhere to take cover except behind the ironclad, which came chugging to their deliverance. Before it reached the point, Patterson and Owen commenced yelling and shooting their carbines, trying to create the impression that a regiment lay in ambush, rebels spoiling for a fray. Hovering near the middle of the wider water, the gunboat shelled the point for two hours, long after Thompson and Patterson had strode off upstream to help transport the plunder across the Green.

Jarom, a month later, came across a tattered *Louisville Times* that described the incident as a great sensation, exaggerating the facts sufficiently to locate Henderson and Newburgh on the larger map of the war. Newburgh, he read, enjoyed the distinction of becoming the first town captured north of Mason and Dixon's line. Later, Adam Johnson told him the *London Times* devoted a disproportionate amount of print in accounting for the capture of the great tobacco port of Henderson. The writer, someone who'd probably never set foot in North America, described it as an important town in Ohio—someone had his geography wrong—and its capture as a significant triumph for the South. In both the Northern and Southern press the event took on the grandeur of epic. More immediately, enlistments in the Breckinridge Guards increased dramatically as local youths vied to enlist, seduced by the old prospects of excitement and glory.

For Jarom and Patterson as well as many others, Newburgh became a defining event. Bethel was humiliated and Johnson promoted to colonel. Jarom and Patterson became members of the Tenth Kentucky Cavalry, the entity that the Breckinridge Guards was absorbed into, and the Tenth Kentucky was in turn annexed into Morgan's Brigade at Hartsville, Tennessee. Jarom later learned that tobacco marketed at Henderson that season fetched a higher price than ordinary tobacco elsewhere and, even more amusing, that Colonel Adam R. Johnson had picked up the sobriquet "Stovepipe Johnson."

ALVINA LOCKE

Heading south—Johnson's order being to move in small groups—Jarom and Frank almost passed Patterson without seeing him, Patterson practicing his penchant for scouting ahead on his own. With the help of others, they would later try to reconstruct what had happened. Though they had not heard them, shots had obviously been fired. Either Patterson was too far ahead for them to hear, or sound shadow had deceived them again. They were in rugged, hilly terrain in which sound had a way of straying, sucked up in a ridge or foliage or burrowing into valleys or draws. A cannon blast less than a mile away might simply be swallowed by a cushion of hills or dissipated in recesses or densities of air that hung in certain valleys. Science Jarom had no mind for, and he willingly resigned himself to the growing sum of the world's mysteries, large and small, he would never fathom: the fact that the earth under his feet was part of a speeding rotation, that life on the planet was much older than church elders were likely to acknowledge, that an infant might be born with six toes, that the stones about him held the remains of creatures that had swum in a sea covering most of Kentucky. He acknowledged to himself that beneath the world of observable cause and effect there existed a murky realm alive with mysteries and subtleties cut too finely for him to understand, and what Patterson called sound shadow was one of them.

Whatever the cause, neither he nor Owen heard the shots whose thunderings would normally have carried at least a mile. As he had done dozens of times, Patterson had left them, saying he would scout a little ways ahead and meet them up the road. Not meeting him, Jarom supposed him to be waiting somewhere ahead, maybe at a hospitable farmstead where some trusting householder served him sumptuous foods and opened his barn to provide provender for his horse. Patterson would not detour from the main road without leaving a note on a fencepost or a token of some kind, a rag tied to a limb or a teepee of sticks. Of that Jarom was sure. He could not remember crossroads of any dimension at which Patterson would have felt the need to indicate a change of direction. The road before him wound a bit but was generally southerly in its intention. Still there was no trace of him, and Jarom felt a rasp of worry, a vague but perceptible sense that things weren't right.

Then ahead of them was a rider, a woman they surmised from the side-saddle style of sitting the horse. As she drew closer on a smoky gray mare, he could see her frailness, limbs long and nearly meatless, her bony frame covered by the sheerest knitting of flesh, what skin there was exposed as fragile and translucent as old parchment. She frantically worked a willow switch across the mare's ample rump to little effect, for the mare seemed to be as intent on dawdling as she was on hastening its pace. When Jarom and Owen came close enough to hear her, she drew up in the center of the road as though afraid the two of them would simply pass her by.

"Can either of you show me a doctor?" she asked, her voice high pitched and shrill, her question preceded by no acknowledgment, no greeting.

Jarom saw blotches of what appeared to be bloodstains tracking down her frock, a gray-print gingham buttoned from ankles to throat. He thought at first she'd been injured and wanted medical aid. Jarom asked what the matter was and what they could do.

"Praise God," the woman said, spewing forth what had happened in a cascade of desperation.

Alvina Locke lived with her sister Sabina not too far back the way she had come. She was a widow—Jarom estimated she was in her sixties, and the way she spoke indicated she'd been brought up genteel—and lived there with only her maiden sister to keep her company. She had been outside parceling corn to the chickens, her sister inside baking bread, when they heard a spatter of shots close by that broke the stillness of the afternoon. According to her account, a cover of trees stood between their house and the road. She and Sabina had let it grow over as protection against designing strangers and the tramps who filled the roads these days.

When they heard firing, they took refuge in the root cellar behind the house, a stone cubicle dug into the hillside, closed off from the world by a battened door. Inside, they sat on some upended crocks, the space darker than a cow's stomach. Having forgotten both lamp and candle, they waited, keeping tally of the shots they heard. Seventeen fired in rapid succession. The sister, Sabina, said they sounded like corn popping under a tin lid. After the shooting stopped, they sat quiet for a full minute, then heard a single shot, the last and somewhat louder. It sang in their ears and died off slowly.

They waited a full quarter hour until they were satisfied the firing had stopped. Opening the cellar door, they heard what seemed to be a troop of riders passing in the lane, the sounds of multiple hooves clapping on hardpan. They shut themselves in again. They waited long after the clatter died, then reopened the cellar door and crept cautiously along an overgrown fenceline that ran parallel to the road. They followed it toward where the shots had been fired until Sabina tripped over a body in field grass that was high as their heads. Her scream summoned Alvina, who took Sabina's arm to help her to her feet. Then Alvina saw what she described as a destiny of flies buzzing about a destroyed face, lifeblood thick as jelly caked over a hideous wound. Certain that all breath had left that tenement of flesh, they'd improvised a prayer, and Sabina had gone in decency to fetch a coverlet from the house.

Fretting while she was gone, Alvina noticed several tiny bubbles rising from the nucleus of the face where the nose had been. A bubble would appear and swell like a fragile balloon before noiselessly popping. As she watched, she first believed that the corpse was simply sloughing off its spirit or that the organs had constricted in death and somehow exhaled as the body closed down province by province. When the bubbles persisted in a slow simmer like stew over a steady fire, Alvina finally convinced herself that life had not passed from the body. His chest, like a leaky bellows, rose and fell ever so slightly.

Shouting for Sabina, she cradled the man's head in her lap and tore some cloth from her underthings. She dampened the cloth with spittle and carefully wiped the crust of blood to clear a channel so air could pass more freely. By the time Sabina returned with a horse blanket, his breathing seemed steadier, less faltering. When they edged him onto the blanket and tried to raise it, the weight was too much for them. They had come to an impasse. With no male help on the farm and no near neighbors, they had to rely on the closest farmhouse nearly two miles away, and harnessing the horse and hitching it to the old buggy would take too long. Alvina had determined to saddle the buggy mare and ride for help, hoping to meet someone on the road, when Sabina came up with a solution. Wrapping the man in the blanket, she devised a means for the two of them to drag the deadweight to the house.

This maneuver took the better part of an hour to go less than forty yards, their greatest worry that the rough handling would finish him. When they bumped him up the porch stairs and across the threshold into the house and discovered he was still breathing, they were mildly surprised and greatly relieved. They said another prayer. Then it dawned on them that they must care for him until help could be summoned, or he would die. In the stuffy parlor with its needlework and shelves of bric-a-brac, they laid him out on their only couch, a settee really, not long enough to accommodate the ropy calves and feet but fortunately armless. Removing his boots, they improvised by lifting his lower extremities onto a caned chair. Sabina, racking her memory of sickbeds and visits from the doctor, brought a pan of water and tore some sheets for a compress to stanch any bleeding aggravated by the move. Blood sopped the bosom of her dress and dried the color of chestnut; her sleeves were tracked with darkening flecks. Sabina had the better touch for nursing, so Alvina went out to coax the buggy mare with a carrot, caught her, and cinched the saddle to go for help. Setting off to fetch the doctor, who was miles away and might or mightn't be at home and might or mightn't be willing to come, she met Jarom and Frank Owen instead.

Jarom found Patterson stretched out on a daybed in the parlor, his socked feet protruding under a beautiful quilt of the Lone Star pattern. One eye had been shot away; the other was intact but apparently sightless. What had been the straight edge of his nose had a ravine excavated by the bullet. When Sabina raised the compress, he saw the mess of the nose and forehead, a broad mulberry swipe across them like jam smeared on with a butter knife. His high leather boots, still spurred, stood side by side on the filigreed carpet.

Though no one said it, Jarom knew they were considering that Patterson could not last more than an hour or two at best. He was pitiful to see, the topography of the face ravaged beyond recognition, a sorry imitation of the face Jarom had known as intimately as his own. Swollen with hurt, his features took on the crudeness of a carved potato. A turban of bandages was swathed around the head, and Jarom wanted to believe that the ruin before him was not Patterson but an impostor, some stranger who had stolen Patterson's boots with their peculiar olive tint and replicated the cracked leather of his belt. The size and general shape belonged to Patterson, but he had deflated like one of the gas balloons the Yankees sent up to study the disposition of their troops. The arms and legs were sapped of vigor, the color drained from his skin. Jarom had to force himself to acknowledge that what lay broken on the couch was John Patterson, the man who had trotted so confidently into the afternoon two hours earlier. He remembered his feeling of disquiet at Patterson's absence and persuaded himself that at the moment of his shooting some mystical means, maybe something electrical, had telegraphed the news to him—so close had they bonded.

In the kitchen the sisters told Jarom and Owen what they knew. When they mentioned hearing a final shot after a spate of firing, Jarom fit the pieces into a speculation about what happened. This last shot did the injury, and almost certainly it had been fired after Patterson had become a prisoner. The pistol had been discharged so close that particles of black powder were embedded like metal filings in the wound and adjacent skin. It singed off the hair on the right side of the head, confirming that the pistol had been only inches away when discharged. When it occurred to Jarom that Patterson had been shot after putting down his weapons, he couldn't understand it, could not explain to himself how one human being could do this to another.

Excusing himself, he stepped out onto the porch. At nearly dusk, the air still hung oppressively hot, listless, stagnant as the low water in the farm pond they had passed along the road. The katydids had begun their parliament in the old trees that backed up on an overgrown orchard. From the plantain stems the first wave of fireflies rose into the near dark. Several swifts dodged above the line of the shake roof, each jag in their flight thinning the insect population of the world.

He thought back to 1858 when he'd first met Patterson, who had returned to the farm for one of his visits. After New Year's, Patterson had taken him to a cockfight in a neighboring county. He'd heard about cockfights all his life but never seen one. They entered a common stock barn, six or eight stalls to either side of an earthen walkway. The central part had formed a crude circle or pit. Its circumference had been striped with lime, less a boundary for those inside the ring than those outside it. A large company of farmers had gathered, most from the neighborhood but a few like themselves from beyond.

They also found an assortment of vagabonds and touts who followed the roosters. The bet takers stuck gaudy feathers in their hat brims, recording their wagers on chits and pocket-sized ledgers in script that resembled the scratchings of domesticated chickens. All the onlookers were men and boys, some hanging on their fathers' pants legs. Most were past middle age, slack men, a little stooped, wearing old clothes in which they appeared to have shrunk. Under lanterns that hung along the rafters, their faces had a coppery cast that reminded him of dried tobacco. All were hatted.

Other fights had occurred before they'd arrived, for to one side of the door someone had set a barrel into which dead and dying birds had been thrown. In the pit an old Negro man spread sand from a bucket, raking the packed ground with a switch broom to smooth it for the next fight. Into his gunnysack the man swept wads of white fluff and plucked feathers. Much of the barn, as Jarom recalled, had been in shadow. He remembered it lacked heat of any kind; he was so cold Patterson had given him his scarf to wind about his neck. Amidst so much stamping of feet and rubbing of hands, Jarom wondered why these men had not stayed home in front of their woodstoves. A few drank, drawing swigs from bottles and flasks tucked into their pockets. Despite the cold, the space seemed filled with good humor—the age-old defense of the miserable—and Patterson took a swig from a bottle proffered by a farmer standing beside him, a man with eyes nearly lost in a thicket of eyebrows. Patterson carefully showed his manners by thanking him and making a joke or two.

From a loft above the pit on three sides feet dangled, most of them shod in cheap brogans, though Jarom could remember one pair of polished knee-length boots. The smell of raw whiskey mixed with hay rot and the reek of fresh manure. Then above the din someone raised a hullabaloo that sounded like a henhouse under siege, a stream of squalls and mindless cluckings answered with a cockcrow—four guttural notes exploding from the throat, perfectly accented on the third. Stomping their feet, grumbling, the company began to lose patience.

Patterson asked the bearded man when the next fight would start. The old man thrust a finger toward the stall across the ring. "Soon's that pokeslow fixes a knife to that bird is when," he'd said, sputtering little bits of tobacco.

Jarom looked over in the stall to their rear and saw a man and a boy crouching. The boy held a rust-colored gamecock and stroked its breast while the man tied gaffs to the nubs of its spurs. Patterson explained that gaffs were gently curved lancets of steel maybe two inches long. Jarom locked in memory the look of them, their edges, honed and deadly looking, prickling with light. Patterson served as Jarom's interpreter as, one after the other, the man wound an invisible thread around the horny legs to fasten the gaffs. When he finished each one, he would bite off the excess thread and deftly knot it to the hock, carefully cutting the string ends with a pen knife.

Jarom remembered gawking at the rooster, which was surprisingly small. Its coat was a mixture of reds and golds with a full cushion of tailfeathers. Patterson described its tail as a gracefully crooked upright that spilled behind like a fountain.

Patterson pointed out that the rooster's comb was missing. "Trimmed off," Patterson said, making a snipping motion with two fingers. The same, he said, with the spurs and wattles. The gamesters called the practice dubbing.

"Why cut him?" Jarom had asked.

"Cocking," Patterson said, "is sport only for those who watch. For the cock it's a contest to survive—spike and dodge, dodge and spike.

Throw two roosters in a ring and blood comes. Get the other fellow before he gets you."

"But why the comb?"

"Because," he said, "the comb makes a ready target and bleeds easily. Peck at the comb and the bird might be blinded or bleed to death before the fight has really started."

As with everything, Patterson seemed to know all there was to know. He had witnessed cockfights up and down the river, many on the decks of whatever steamer he was working on.

Together they had watched the cock, its nervous head cupped tenderly in the boy's hand. At the crown where the comb should have been Jarom saw a pink scab. Patterson explained that serious breeders held certain superstitions. Birds could be trimmed only when the moon was in Pisces, for old-timers believed that birds not trimmed during the sign of the Feet would bleed to death. He also said that fighting did not begin until November, when cocks came into full feather, having molted their old plumage during the summer months.

Some commotion sounded, and from another stall came an eagle-faced man with thick mustachios. He looked vaguely kin to the birds he handled, his brows like feathers, his nose forming a beak between close-set eyes. As Jarom remembered, he carried a blondish-gray cock whose pupils shone tomato red. The bird-man's stepping into the ring as challenger had been the signal for preliminaries to begin. Patterson had alerted Jarom to watch the stages as part of an elaborate ritual—"spar and gambit," Patterson called it. The defender started with a mock bow as the first man, alone then, walked, half strutted, to the center of the ring. With outstretched arms, he raised the rust bird above his head with a yell that caused the bird to flap its wings as though to fly. The second man followed on cue, stepping to the center and holding his own bird up for inspection. A flurry of bet making followed as the feather hats registered amounts and odds shouted across the ring. The crowd pressed in, forming a natural corral about the ring, feet scrupulously up to, on, but never crossing the white stripe.

Cradling their birds, the handlers began to pace about as if they would spar, the birds resting complacently in their arms. Patterson commented that the rusty bird was a high flier, a cock whose torso sat high off the ground and whose long legs gave the impression of agility and speed. "Splendid" was the word that came to Jarom to describe how he looked. The feathers smoothed down about the body in a reddish sheen, the wings appeared slickish as though they'd been dipped in oil. In the wavering light of the barn, his back glowed with an eerie iridescence. By contrast, the gray bird had been low stationed, almost squat. Though both weighed nearly the same, the gray looked stouter, more powerful. Patterson described him as a "stayer."

Because they'd so unsettled him, Jarom could still recall the murmurs and grumblings of impatience as the tension mounted.

"Let blood! Let blood!" someone behind him shouted.

"Go git him, fox!" another began yelling. "Go git him, fox. Go on, go git him now."

Still cradling their birds, one hand grasping the legs just above the gaffs, the other clutching the neck, the handlers talked each other around the ring. They gradually closed distance until the roosters' beaks came within pecking range, only inches apart. Patterson told him regulars called this phase of the contest the "tease." Watching, Jarom noticed a change as the cocks' hackles rose and their necks spread like half-opened parasols. He could tell now they were tense and threatening, their necks crooked like feathered snakes, each poised to strike. The handlers continued to flirt in an outlandish waltz, leading and closing, then drawing back, circling the ring until both birds ruffled their feathers, spoiling to fight.

On signal, the handlers pitched them to the clay floor and nimbly stepped clear. Loosed, the roosters rushed together in high hops, their legs thrusting forward so the gaffs could be used to advantage, the tiny blades snicking and flashing in a blur, their wings beating furiously, snapping and spitting like flags in a storm. Spreading their wings, they leapt at each other, their legs, a burnt orange, making fanlike arcs and razory swipes. Four feet up in midair they clashed, necks still arched, the wings pummeling to gain height and keep balance, both of them lost in a squall of motion. Time after time they dropped, only to spring up again, needling with the gaffs, fanning slow blizzards of pinfeathers and down.

At first, everyone hushed in wonder, awed by the fury of the attack. But after a few clashes the novelty began to pale, and each hit produced a heathenish clamor. Inches from Jarom's ear, Patterson began to root for the gray bird, his face flushed, the veins in his neck bulging like strained cords. In that closed space Jarom could feel a tension swelling for release as the fight moved toward climax. For a moment he imagined himself in the ring with the swiping gaffs, probing for the spot that would still the frenzied wings, soothe the shrillness into some semblance of calm. Impatient for the kill.

Then the rust bird went down with a gaff in his back.

"Git at him," someone shouted. "Go for the heart!"

"Handle!" someone yelled from the other side of the ring. "Handle now!"

Both owners reentered the ring and carefully separated the birds, the rust bird's owner delicately removing the gray bird's gaff from the upper back just behind the wings. Where the gaff had stuck, the feathers were bloodied, stain already spreading in sticky crimson blotches.

But the fight wasn't over. Again the handlers set the birds eight feet apart, and again they danced and maneuvered, slower this time, the rusty bird sluggish, Jarom guessed, from loss of his life's blood. Moving in for the kill, the gray bird pounced on the rust, which in one inspired instant, reflexively threw up a gaff, catching the gray's soft underside. The shock of the blow knocked the gray cock off his feet, and someone urged the rust bird to show some steel.

Dazed, the dying gray cock tipped to one side, his head on the hay-strewn floor of the barn, a ribbon of blood stringing from his beak. Someone pronounced him a goner, a dead one for sure. Tipsy, unsure of his footing, the gray bird rose. Before he could right himself, the rust was on him, yellow bill hammering, pecking and treading him into the clay.

Feeling a nudge on his back, Jarom turned to look behind him. When he faced the ring again, the gray bird lay in a slick of blood, beak open, throat stretching and gasping for breath. Patterson told him this was called "rattling," an indication a lung had been punctured. Now the rust bird was standing in triumph, his orange back caped with blood. Following the established etiquette, his owner lifted him from the ring. As the winners crowed, the bird nuzzled against his owner's chest. The loser next stepped in to pick up his bird. The wings drew in on themselves, tight against a body that seemed depleted, shriveled in defeat. The blood dried on the wings in dark splinters. The pale legs looked brittle as twigs; both eyes were miraculously still open.

As Jarom remembered it, the fight from start to finish took less than three minutes. It opened and closed with the old black ringman, who now spread sand on the floor and raked it for the next fight. Jarom had a vision of the floor as a brief ledger on which the ringman smoothed over the scratches and scrawlings that recorded the fight, leaving as little trace as the clouds his breath formed on the bluff at Fort Donelson. The lanterns after the fight seemed dimmer, and for the first time that night he felt an abiding chill. Patterson, he remembered, had picked up one of the sickles and handed it to him as a souvenir—a long, curved tail feather. Settling their bets, the winners and losers puffed little fists of vapor that blended into shadow and rose to the ridgepole of the barn. As Jarom began again to think of armies, he remembered that neither he nor Patterson had any inclination to stay for a second fight, had no need even to say so.

Somewhere at the base of his ribs Jarom felt an abiding void, a fluttering lightness that wouldn't settle, that combination of glut and emptiness one feels in the moment before vomiting. He forced himself to swallow, considering that this Patterson was not his Patterson. Blind, an invalid, probably addled in his mind, he would, if his wounds mended, walk out his days with a stick. He would never mount a horse again, never pilot a boat. He would be obliged to rely on the charity of others to pilot *him*.

Jarom reeled back his mind to the history of changes in the way they understood each other, the inventory of things Patterson had taught him to see and understand that Patterson himself would no longer see. He remembered the poet of old who knew life as a movement through darkness into a brightly lit hall and into darkness again. For Patterson and for himself, he realized, the room was too narrow, the room too soon dark. He had an image of the continuous night that Patterson would endure for the balance of his days. The path that his life ran would be lightless, illuminated only by what light shone from within.

The longer he stood on the porch in that failing light the more he sensed some powerful feeling that welled up from some dark aquifer within, a surge of rage that rose from the cavity in his chest in a mixture of hatred and helplessness. He wanted to strike back, to kill the man who had fired the shot, a man whose name he would probably never know. There being no specific object or being to which he could attach his hate, he felt frustrated and hurt. He conjured ways in which he would take out his frustration and pain on the heads of his enemies, known and unknown.

Over the farm's expanse of darkened fields and leafed trees he imagined a colossal flood, a tide roiling over the lowlands. In the near fields he envisioned battered cornstalks and drowned calves, the loosened palings of fences that had been swept over by some irresistible force with origins unknown, destination unknowable. Like water. He came to see water as a metaphor for the force he was beginning to recognize as malevolence. Like flooding waters, it ran blind and limitless, taking on definition only by the levels it could sink to, the reservoirs in which it could pool. He imagined the flatlands ravaged, a wake of ruin and decimation where the torrents had passed. Unlike fire, water would not consume itself but grow in volume and momentum as it surged. Like water, the god this force would worship lacked discrimination or loyalty to anything human. It defined itself only by motion.

Back in the room, over Patterson's nearly lifeless form, Jarom studied Patterson's ravaged face, his bandaged eyes, the blue splinters of pistol burns on exposed cheek.

"Can you hear me?" he whispered.

No response.

"I will find him," he swore, not so much to Patterson as to himself. "I will find him. I will the pay these devils back in specie." Then he conferred with the gentle sisters and discussed what to do if Patterson died, what to do if he survived. In either case, he asked them to contact Mary Tibbs, and knew they would, one way or another.

"By the way," he asked before acting on an imperative to move on, "what county are we in?"

"Union," Alvina said.

PORTER

Jarom didn't learn the particulars of Patterson's shooting until some months later. Whenever he came upon prisoners, he quizzed them, asking where they called home and whether they or anyone they knew had been at Newburgh. Outside Bardstown he finally happened on a man named Porter, who admitted he lived near Newburgh. Garrisoned at Evansville, he hadn't been at Newburgh during Johnson's raid, but he had been a member of the party that Bethel organized the next day to chase down the culprits.

Within a few hours of Johnson's snatching the guns, Porter said, Bethel's pursuit crossed the river in one of the available transports, horses and all. Bethel led Porter's bunch in person, most of the party consisting of home guards whom Johnson had captured and paroled. Still smarting from the humiliation of being taken by chicanery, they rode out to redeem themselves. Promising he would not be harmed, Jarom persuaded Porter to give an account of what happened to see if it confirmed what he had already pieced together.

Bethel, quickly assembling his men, had crossed the river at Henderson in hopes of cutting Johnson off before he could slip farther south. It amused Jarom to hear that Bethel's party, as it paraded through town, suffered much taunting, mostly about stovepipes. Meeting riders on the road, Bethel asked all he met if they had seen other riders, but he got little help from the locals, who all, as Porter put it, sang rebel songs. Bethel made little headway until he hired a man named Windrup, who claimed intimate knowledge of the back roads. Porter said he had come jogging up to them, a worried-looking man astride a piebald mare with feral eyes and welts on its rump.

"From the look of that mare," he said, "you knew you couldn't trust him, a man that would treat an animal like that." Porter said this looking Jarom in the eye, and Jarom would have bet a loaded Colt that he had heard an accurate appraisal of the man.

Bethel asked him which way they should go, and Windrup said they should get on the nearest back road heading south. "Minnows," he said, "you'll find in branches or creeks but never rivers."

Jarom asked Porter to describe Windrup, wanting enough particulars to pick him out in a crowd. Porter weighed this as if he were reconstructing a portrait from memory.

"He was scrawny," he said finally, "and dried up, kindly like a prune, you might say. His face was all socket and knob, skin the color of overcooked turkey, stretched tight over the bone and pitted with smallpox. He'd curled the brim of his hat into tiny scrolls. His face was rough ground, all gulched and furrowed. His eyes were flat and dark as shale. He was a man of dark countenance, even darker under the stiff felt hat he wore low on his head."

"Is there anything else?"

"He rode so low on his mount," Porter said, "that his spurs raked seeds from the roadside grass. He could read signs, the merest stirring of dust or hoof scuff on the road. He made up for these skills in his deficiencies of speech, mostly the language of grunts and nods. He claimed to be a resident of Webster County in the sovereign state of Kentucky, but from the wear on him he was by all appearances a vagabond."

"All right, then," Jarom said, changing directions. "Tell me with as much detail as you can what happened."

"Riding several horse lengths ahead, Windrup sighted the rider first. Just north of a little town called Slaughtersville, we rounded a bend and Windrup shouted back to us, 'Hey, look up the road there.' About eighty yards ahead sat a man on horseback. Spotting us about the same time, he reined up and sidled off into some trees. From their shade he stood up in the stirrups to determine whether we were friend or foe. After a little he must have been satisfied, for he waved his hat, dropped in the saddle, and came on in a confident canter. Even from that distance he looked to be smiling.

"At half the distance, about forty yards off, he drew in his reins and stopped, maybe realizing his mistake. The head of his horse flinched, wrenched by his motion. Then his horse, a sorrel, cocked and twisted his head as if to cushion the shock. Coming to a standstill, the rider looked about for cover. There was none, only an expanse of pasture enclosed by a rail fence, a steep slope of brooms edge on the other. He lacked time or distance enough to turn around, a chance to break and run. Close as we were, he knew and we knew we could easily have chased or shot him down.

"So what does he do? He had no choice but to give himself over—or so we thought until he hunched down jockey-style over the sorrel's neck, pulled down his hat, and took the reins in his teeth. He set spur to her flanks and came dash at us, a pistol in each hand, the devil for mischief. We stood by in unbelief and wonder. When he'd closed half the distance between us, he leveled a pistol to either side of the sorrel's head and tried to shoot his way through. And nearly did. Balls started singing by our heads, the firing so close we shuddered and ducked as we saw the hammers fall."

"Was there anyone hit?" Jarom asked.

"No," Porter said, "but it wasn't for lack of trying. After the first shots, no one needed to ask us to get clear of him. Windrup, already firing back, peeled off to one side of the pitching horses, trying to get a clear shot. One or two of the boys in the rear turned tail to get back down the road as if to have a head start on a race they knew they'd lose. The rest of us drew and tried to bring our pistols to bear, but by this time he'd come amongst us, barging and bullying that wild-eyed sorrel through, working both pistols. It was the shots that started the commotion. The whole spectacle seemed to be happening somewhere far off, mouths shouting sounds that didn't reach my ears, horse eyes and flashing metal taking on a presence of their own. One or two cooler heads got off a shot before he closed with us, but the most of us just hugged our horses and tried to stand clear as you might in a wagon stalled on a track with a train of cars bearing down on you.

"As he passed, I caught a glimpse of the mustache and the desperate eyes. In all the confusion some of our riders fell or were knocked off their horses. One of them, a young buck named Hollis, whose father I know, snagged the madman's bridle just as the sorrel broadsided Windrup's little mare. Though both kept their saddles, the collision slowed the madman long enough for Hollis to get a purchase on the sorrel. Using his weight to advantage, Hollis jerked the bridle so the muzzle wrenched back against its chest. That was enough to break its stride, though the legs kept churning until the other horses pressed in to close the gap. Hollis then managed to snatch one of the Colts, someone from the left side knocking the other from his hand.

"Seeing the game was up, the madman came to his senses and simply stopped. He sat there a moment, his chest heaving. Then he shrugged and looked speechlessly at each of us, giving each the same woebegone look."

"What made you think he was mad?" Jarom asked. "Even a lunatic will fight for his life."

Porter didn't choose to answer, though Jarom noted that afterward he exercised some discretion and stopped using the word "madman."

"Before the dust could settle," he went on, "before any of us could read his purpose, up rode Windrup. Not taking his eyes from the prisoner's, he coolly laid the long barrel against the man's cheek as familiar as a brother—a taunt I was thinking—and pulled the trigger. Down came the hammer. There was a snap and a flash, the clap of the explosion ruffling the air between us, a hot gust slamming against me but most directly against the rider, who was knocked from the saddle and thrown into the lane under the hooves of my spooked mare.

"She skittered to one side, and everything was jumbled by the close thunder of the shot. Windrup froze with the upright revolver in his hand. I remember sweat gleaming from one of the horse's rumps, which I first thought was blood. Men on horseback were pinwheeling about the riderless sorrel. When the smoke cleared and the ringing gentled in my ears, the rider lay sprawled there on the road, intact and perfectly whole at one end, a ruin at the other. Blood was streaming from a terrible wound in his face and pooling in the dust. Even from where I sat, it was clear the ball had creased his upper right cheek, blasted at least one eye out, and wrecked the bridge of his nose. White splinters of bone poked out of the skin like drumsticks on a Sunday chicken."

Porter held off a bit. Jarom could see the sweat beading on his forehead and the eyes losing their focus.

"You heard enough?" he asked.

"Go on," Jarom said. "Let's hear it all."

"Without uttering a word, Windrup holstered his pistol and motioned to Hollis, who was still gaping at the nasty face. Hollis at the boots, Windrup under the shoulders, together they lifted the body and heaved it over the fence as casually as you would toss a sack of grain onto a wagon. As Windrup climbed back on his little mare, we saw a track of blood down the front of his checked jacket. He said not a word but made a kind of clucking sound in his cheek. Someone took the sorrel in tow, and we were gone."

When Porter finished, Jarom felt a wave of relief. He couldn't speak. Then it was Porter's turn.

"Why are you so interested in this?"

"He was my brother," Jarom said.

Porter went pale. Scrabbling for excuses, he said none of them believed for a minute that Windrup would shoot but that even if they'd known, they hadn't time or means to stop him. Porter went on to say that afterward someone wanted to shoot Windrup but that Bethel had said what was done was done and they'd best forget about it, that they had other fish to fry.

"Was Windrup reported?" Jarom asked.

Bethel said Windrup wasn't even in the army and that they couldn't order him. He also said that most of the men were still het up about Newburgh, that some of them believed the man had it coming.

Jarom had heard enough. He first had an inclination to shoot Porter and balance the scales a bit, at least even some scores. After all, he had been there and might have stopped Windrup. He seemed decent enough but also worried about what he'd said, probably wondering whether he'd said anything to set Jarom off—the man's own brother. Jarom guessed Porter's age to be mid- to late thirties; he was a decent enough man with some education, from the way he spoke. Still, though he seemed civil enough now, why didn't he do something more then? The account put him back on that dry expanse of road. Again he imagined Patterson sprawled in the roadway and felt his blood rise. Porter could see it too, for he stepped back, anticipating, Jarom believed, that he was about to be shot in much the same way Patterson had been.

Jarom's oath came back to him, but he knew he could not pull the trigger—at least not on Porter. Shooting him now would put Jarom on a level with Windrup. What would Patterson say? Something like, "You don't burn the forest to remove a cankered tree." Porter, he decided, was simply the man who saw it and felt bad about it now but had done nothing when doing something would have counted.

Over the next months Jarom ventured out on his own in an effort to locate Windrup, even crossing the river against his better judgment in hopes of finding him. Jarom would meet someone who had news of him but was never able to close the distance or to find out precisely where he lived, though he reckoned it was somewhere in southern Indiana, probably near Evansville. The man was elusive as smoke.

BACK TO OLD KENTUCKY

When General John Hunt Morgan entered a room or rode by on his blooded mare, Black Bess, people straightened themselves and took notice. Standing six feet tall, he was compactly built and weighed, Jarom estimated, about a hundred eighty-five pounds. He moved with the assurance of one on whom the world had conferred its bounty, a man who not only merited attention but implicitly demanded it. Jarom understood how uttering commands for him had long been an easy matter. Morgan had owned a large hemp factory and a woolen mill where dozens depended on his good offices to keep bread on the table. In Jarom's experience such persons claimed command as a birthright. Morgan moved with a natural grace said to have resulted from a lifetime of dancing and riding. His precisely trimmed goatee and his tendency to assume picturesque poses gave him an imperial air, as though he'd stepped out of Van Dyck's portrait of Charles I hunting, an engraving Jarom had admired in one of Aunt Nancy Bradshaw's *Godey's* magazines. Van Dyck suited him, for though the general's manners seemed relaxed, he aped the grand style of the Cavaliers, who were cavaliers more in the sense of courtly manner than equestrian skills.

Usually, when Jarom caught a glimpse of him, he had one brim of his hat pinned to the block to reinforce the impression of devil-may-care. His gray eyes were close set, giving him in the right light a cross-eyed appearance, the hair thinning to form two deep scallops behind the temples. This hair loss may have been hastened by the appeal he had for the ladies, who would walk up to him with a pair of scissors and, usually with his permission, clip off a bit as a souvenir.

Morgan fascinated Jarom the way that novelty invites comparison, not so much because he wanted to be like Morgan but because Morgan was so unlike himself. As the general strolled about the camp during lulls between scouts and raids, Jarom studied his manner and behavior. He learned that despite his outward show of ease and confidence, at times he brooded, gave himself over to sulks, being quick to withdraw when the currents did not flow his way. He noted that Morgan was always in motion, often without discernible purpose but going, doing, always initiating some weighty enterprise, or seeming to. In quieter moments he displayed a vein of melancholy, the tonic of all romantics, owing probably, Jarom thought, to the death of his first wife, Rebecca. She had been described to him as a delicate flower that bloomed, faded, and died just at the time her husband, certain that war was imminent, came into full flower. Jarom doubted that Morgan truly loved her, for he heard that the young Morgan spent most of his time in the company of men, especially with the Lexington Rifles, the company of neighbors and local bloods who rechristened themselves the Second Kentucky Cavalry when the war began. Though Morgan seemed charged with a special quality of magnetism, Jarom felt drawn to him largely by a quality he could name only as buoyancy.

His association with Morgan had begun when Adam R. Johnson's Tenth Kentucky Cavalry attached itself to Morgan's brigade in northern Tennessee after the sensational raid on Hartsville, Kentucky, in early December of 1862. In that venture, over which much was made in the papers, Morgan captured two artillery pieces, two thousand prisoners, and several wagonloads of desperately needed boots and shoes. A few days later, President Davis himself arrived by a train of cars from Chattanooga and congratulated the intrepid Colonel Morgan, a man who brought morale-building good news. Davis, savvy about the value of rewarding vigor and derring-do, lost little time in promoting him to brigadier general. Standing in a file of men who had gathered at the track siding, Jarom caught a glimpse of the president's sober profile as he wheeled by on his way to review General Bragg's veterans. They had lost some of their brio and many of their bravest since Bragg had returned with his army from a bumbling offensive into Kentucky that ended at the battle of Perryville in October of 1862.

A week later, camp gossip circulated that Morgan had married his sweetheart, Martha Ready, in a ceremony conducted by a fellow general, Leonidas Polk, who also happened to be an Episcopal bishop. Four days before Christmas of 1862, after a short honeymoon, Morgan assembled his brigade, which numbered seventeen hundred men, and marched north, Jarom eagerly among them. He crossed the Cumberland River into Kentucky at a piddly little place called Sandy Shoals, near Tompkinsville in Monroe County. Still brooding about Patterson being left in the Locke sisters' care until Mary Tibbs could fetch him, Jarom felt heartened to touch his feet on home ground with a chance to damage those who had damaged him.

When Morgan led his serpentine column into Kentucky, cheering moved along the line, the same bravado and brashness of boys who had skipped Sunday school or tipped a lowing cow. Morgan staged a homecoming for these sons of old Kentucky, and they cantered with the zeal of crusaders reclaiming the Holy Land from the infidels.

The friction began just south of Glasgow on the Louisville Pike when scouts ahead of the column brushed aside a small band of federals and overtook an enormous sutler's wagon drawn by twenty magnificent Percherons. Its destination had been Glasgow, where the enterprising sutler intended to offer Christmas delicacies to the garrison encamped south of town. Instead, Morgan's riders forced him to play Santa Claus, distributing gifts from the wagon's interior until it emptied. Jarom hadn't seen such largesse since he had enlisted: hams, corn, crackers, molasses, and candies among the foodstuffs; overcoats, shoes, and a plentiful supply of smoking and chewing tobacco, even snuff, among the dry goods. He snagged some tobacco, having experimented with smoking his own rolled cigarettes.

He and Frank Owen stuffed themselves with chunks of ham and slices of raisin bread they'd whittled from round loaves with their camp knives. At the bottom of a trunk he found a fine pair of buckskin gloves lined with lamb's wool. He slept with them on that night when they bivouacked five miles below Glasgow, the county seat of about five hundred, which Jarom remembered visiting with his aunt Nancy Bradshaw's husband on construction business. The cold penetrated once they stopped, but it did not keep either him or Owen from caroling with the others around a huge bonfire, enjoying the spoils of war and drinking brandy for toasts made to Morgan and the liberation of Kentucky. Morgan's scouts rode to the outskirts of Glasgow, reporting that the place seemed glum and cheerless, without decoration in the face of an attack the citizens expected at first light. Jarom and Owen rolled up in their blankets inside an unheated brick tannery, their horses snuffling a few feet away and stamping the earthen floor to ward off the cold.

Cradling his head in the crook of his saddle, Jarom stared up at the heavens through a jagged hole in the roof. The constellations reminded him of the patterns on the rug in Alvina Locke's parlor. He could see Patterson on the daybed, his head swathed in bandages. The skin of his face appeared peeled and pink as hams on the scraped hog he had helped butcher at the Tibbs farm. He imagined a Patterson of the future, his muscles slacking with inactivity, a cane in his hand as he begged on the streets of some nameless city. The life he would live seemed as bare and rooted as the bony oak whose limbs scraped against the split shakes on the roof of the barn, a sound he heard until reveille next morning.

For weeks he'd felt a numbness unrelieved by what went on around him. Any reference to Patterson—a word, a memory, something they had done together, places they had been, someone who favored him or walked with his step—stabbed him with hopeless grief. He recognized Patterson's nose on the face of a stranger, his posture on a passerby. He knew that he would spend the balance of his life enduring these painful pricks. Absent a cure, he knew that immersion in events, in a cause, in sheer busyness gave a temporary reprieve from the kind of sulk that would finally sink a mourner into despair. He wanted to live for Patterson, as a kind of unpaid substitute, to see what Patterson couldn't see, do what he couldn't do.

Next morning, as he, Owen, and several of the others crouched around a fire roasting sutler bacon skewered on sticks, they discussed the report that Thomas Quirk, Morgan's chief scout, had been shot twice in the head during a fracas with a federal patrol his men had blundered on along the road. Rather than seek out the surgeon, Quirk hobbled back to camp with a neckerchief tied about his head.

"A cranium built in County Kerry, Ireland," he said, "and toughened by shillelaghs can surely withstand mere bullets."

Later, the darkening clouds suddenly loosed a downpour that mired the roads, sending yellow gushets along the ditches on either side. A persistent murmur of complaint flowed among the horsemen as the water soaked their blankets and coarse woolen tunics that smelled rank as pond mud. Drenched, exhausted, Jarom felt relieved that they had bypassed Glasgow, this being no weather in which to fight. As he lay burrowed in a wet haystack, he was plagued by the picture of his enemies, neat rows of them, lying smug and dry in their barrack beds several miles away.

The world that he awoke to next morning seemed a world returned to its base element of water. Everything lay sodden, the frozen ground around the camp pocked with iced puddles that made even the simplest maneuver chancy. The leather of their saddles, pinched and stiffened, creaked when they mounted and set off again. Someone passed the word to swaddle their firearms with blankets so as to be in firing order. Before that could be done, the blankets, saturated and sheathed with ice, had to thaw before an open fire.

Morgan intended to cut the Union line of supply from Louisville to the armies farther south. Sitting on a wet log by the smoldering fire, Jarom for the first time heard their destination, two wooden railroad trestles at a great timbered dome in the landscape called Muldraugh's Hill, about thirty-five miles south of Louisville. Destroy those trestles and they would cut off the lifeline of winter supplies for much of Kentucky and the lower South, paralyzing Rosecrans's army in Tennessee until the Confederate army could be refitted after the losses at Forts Henry and Donelson and a half-dozen other battles.

Late on Christmas Day Jarom heard that at a place called Bear Wallow outside Cave City the advance of Morgan's brigade flushed a covey of skirmishers in a fight that lasted ten minutes. The sounds of battle came to him like raindrops plopping on a dry roof, a rain of distant fire deadly to those on whom it fell.

The weather turned dry but stayed bitter cold. In midafternoon they came to Green River, a silvery band winding between palisades of stripped timber on each steep bank. Quirk and his scouts found a passable ford, and the hooves of Jarom's horse, Rattler, minced the shattered ice in water that rose to the horse's knees. When Morgan ordered them to cross four abreast, Jarom's rank edged down the embankment, which, by the time Jarom reached it, had become a hashwork of mud. With prodding, Rattler waded into the water, quivering as the current cut into his flanks. Jarom instinctively raised his boots from the stirrups in a vain effort to keep dry. When he looked back, the crossing resembled a long funeral cortege. He could hear only cracklings of ice and a clacking of hooves as the horses clambered up the frozen bank on the far side, their bony faces glazed in sullen shock. From the higher ground on the other side, Jarom turned again in the saddle to check the progress of the crossers. The column extended along the road like a stricken caterpillar—one long, fat, braid of muscle nearly paralyzed by cold. That night they camped at a little rail stop called Upton, and again rain fell. Jarom came down with a cold, as had many of the others. The rain, unrelenting and chill, needled through his blanket and clothes with little pricks of ice that seemed to puddle at some low spot in his bones.

In the morning, somber and depressed, he rode with a squad that Morgan detailed to tear up some track and fire the bridge at Bacon's Creek. Given spud bars and crowbars brought specially for the purpose, Jarom and Owen pitched in with the others, prizing up rails and the sleepers on which they rode. Together they stacked the ties into pyramids and, by the hardest, struck a fire. Tom Hines, a specialist in this line, showed the company how to use heat to soften rails so they could be bent around trees. Some wag gave the twisted rails the name "Morgan's neckties," though they put Jarom more in mind of pretzels cast in metal. As a further affront to the Union war effort, others chopped or pulled down some nearby telegraph poles, wrapping the wires around trees and tossing other rolls of the tangled strands into a nearby creek. Tiring as it was, Jarom took satisfaction in the work, knowing he had helped to unravel the cords that connected Rosecrans to the North. He also witnessed the work of "Lightning" Ellsworth, a genius at tapping the wires and confounding the federals with false reports of Morgan's whereabouts.

Later, resting, it came to him that what he loved most about wilderness was its pristine order in which nothing, nothing at all, seemed out of place, in which little or nothing had been altered by the instruments of man. The woods untouched comprised an assemblage of the various and the random, everything at home. Those downed poles and twisted rails, his memories of the carnage on the slopes at Donelson, reminded him that this war, any war, came down to an organized effort to disassemble things—whether railways, bridges, landscapes, or bodies—to render them useless, disarticulate. And the bent rails, the wounded and dead he'd seen, became a part of his interior landscape, a ravaged place containing desolated valleys and bloodied streams, people and things deprived of vital purpose, deprived of their functions.

Later that afternoon they joined the party attacking a blockhouse built to protect a bridge over the Nolin River. After a brief show of resistance, the garrison surrendered, and Jarom assisted in firing the bridge and two blockhouses that had failed to protect it, witnessing the largest fire he'd ever seen. Its blaze turned night into day, throwing spits of flame high into the chill air, galaxies of sparks that popped in the mizzling rain.

Next morning the temperature dropped to the twenties, and he awoke to a sky as colorless as pond ice, the first such sky since leaving Tennessee. He chose to interpret it as an omen of good fortune to follow. They advanced steadily north through a country of low hummocks and swells that graduated to hills rising ever higher and steeper. Some, protruding from land that tended toward flatness, reminded him of an engraving he'd seen of humps on a camel. Along the road Morgan's advance met a party of three riders from Elizabethtown, the seat of Hardin County. They advanced under a flag of truce. Incredibly, they presented the demand of a Colonel Smith for Morgan to surrender the army into the colonel's custody. Morgan informed the messenger, a brash and callow lieutenant, that he had been mistaken about the condition and the intentions of Morgan's command. He then issued his own counterultimatum, namely, that Smith immediately surrender Elizabethtown's garrison. A quarter-hour later, the colonel replied that as an officer of the United States he had been schooled to fight, not to surrender.

Creating a command post on a knoll six hundred yards south of the town whose church spires rose above an arbor of shade trees, Morgan personally directed the fire of the four Parrot guns they had brought along for just such an enterprise. Basil Duke, Morgan's brother-in-law and second in command, deployed his brigade to the right of the track leading into town, and William Breckinridge—a cousin of the former vice president—formed his men to the left. Jarom heard that Adam Johnson had been offered this command but for some reason had declined it. Jarom and Owen, who was complaining of a toothache, took their positions with Breckinridge's unit, learning later that they were to stand by with the reserve.

From the hill where they gathered as observers Jarom had a spectacular view of the attack. A Parrot that had been wheeled onto the road shattered the stillness, sending a shot into one of three brick warehouses where the defenders took refuge. From the heights Baylor Palmer let loose with the other three, shells punching dark holes through brick walls like pins through paper. A bugle signaled the attack. In a wave of gray, the Ninth Kentucky dashed from sheltering trees toward the buildings, drawing the fire of federal sharpshooters scattered in houses along the town's fringes. Running across an open field, Stoner's men reached the walls of a warehouse and proceeded to batter down the doors with their rifle butts.

After several minutes Jarom spied a stream of bluecoats pouring out of the building, hands over their heads. But as Stoner's men disarmed them, they received fire from a building, which Jarom surmised to be a retail business by the sign across its facade. Three stories high, it had two rows of upper windows and other apertures ideal for firing into the street. Atop it, he spotted a fluttering Stars and Stripes. Jarom assumed it must be where the federals had formed their headquarters. Next to it was a neatly trimmed brick building whose spire identified it as a church.

Duke had two of Palmer's six-pounders wheeled forward to root out the defenders. At the same time, he placed another howitzer behind the railroad embankment, facing the rear of the building, where there were no windows. With great precision Corbett's gunners poked holes in the building's blind side while Palmer's shot point-blank at the front. But flushing out the defenders was not easy. After each shot Jarom could see a dozen or so bluecoats rush from the building to snipe at the cannoneers. This continued until Breckinridge moved up a company on either flank of the Ninth Kentucky and laid down fire that persuaded the defenders to stay indoors. Though no one expected them to hold out much longer, someone foolishly ordered a direct assault. The gray line marched forward, exposed to fire on the side of the building honeycombed with windows. Jarom saw eight or ten of the attackers fall before someone had sense enough to order a withdrawal. Finally, a white flag waved at one of the second-story windows, and the garrison surrendered. Jarom saw Colonel Smith deliver his sword to Morgan, who accepted it without comment. Among the spoils were some Enfield rifles, which Jarom recognized as the finest firearms on either side at that stage of the war. As for the prisoners for whom a score of graycoats had died, Morgan held them only a few hours before paroling them.

That night the column moved south again, camping near Bear Wallow. The name held for Jarom a strange fascination, and he wondered what it must be like to see a bear wallow. He imagined great balls of fur with feral eyes that glowed in the night, paws the width of a flat broom that could swat rival mammals senseless. He saw great balls of matted fur caked with dust or mud that offered some protection from the mists of insects that must follow them during the temperate months as they did his own species. He wondered about what prompted some early settler or wanderer who came upon such a place, a dust bowl perhaps, or a place where salt permeated the soil, to name the spot, giving it lifetime that would last longer than the bears that had at one time found comfort there.

After firing three more bridges the next morning and tearing up several miles of track north and south of Elizabethtown, all before noon, scouts confirmed what Jarom and others anticipated—that a pursuit had formed and was bearing down on the cavalcade. Quirk reported that John Marshall Harlan, a fellow Kentuckian, was snapping at Morgan's heels, hoping to intercept the main force before it reached Muldraugh's Hill, the most vulnerable point on the rail line between Louisville and Nashville. Though no alien horses appeared and no one placed bets, Jarom knew that all of them had committed to a race.

Rattler, his buff coat turned a somber gray, was nearly exhausted when the column passed through a deep cut about five miles north of Elizabethtown. Hearing a great commotion ahead of him, Jarom learned that Quirk's scouts had sighted the trestles. Men to the front raised huzzahs and waved their arms in celebration. Several bolted ahead as though to clinch the race and declare Morgan the winner.

When they reached the top of the next rise, Jarom looked out over a vast expanse of furrowed ridges that stretched as far as he could see. On either side of the largest he spied two trestleworks, fabrications of matchsticks over three hundred yards long and sixty or eighty yards high, which towered above the valleys. Rails cut across the top of the rise between the steep slopes and a prickly knoll of timber like the carefully combed part dividing a head of hair. The hill itself, bristling with shorn trees, resembled an oversized pin cushion. At either end of the trestles he could make out earthworks and artillery emplacements. At the southern and northern ends substantial blockhouses covered the approaches. According to Quirk's intelligence, the Seventy-first Indiana had been reinforced by two companies of the Twenty-seventh Illinois. He also learned that the emplacements contained no cannon.

Morgan immediately called a powwow and again split the force into two wings. Encircling the trestles, again he used Palmer's battery to press his argument with the iron logic of shot and ball. Through the fork of a buckeye tree on an adjoining ridge, Jarom watched the gun crews spew a storm of shot that dented and chipped and chewed the blockhouses to ruin, some shots ploughing gullies in the earthen mounds heaped to protect them. The concussions of the cannonade sent tremors he could feel through his boot soles. This studious procedure of igniting powder to propel hardened bits of the planet, it came home to him as never before, was a crude but effective means of extinguishing life, an even more effective instrument of indiscriminate maiming. He remembered the broken bodies he'd seen at Donelson, the terrible canal in Patterson's face. For what? For one government to impose its will on another, giving up its young as payment to assure its enforcement, a resulting back and forth of spilt blood, severed limbs, ruptured vitals, sightless eyes, fractured lives. To justify the mayhem, those in command provided flags and martial music to soften the barbarism, appeals to honor and duty to steel those who survived for the next onslaught. And he acknowledged himself a part of it. Though he had not knowingly snuffed out another life, not yet, he knew that he would, if not today, then tomorrow or some day in the weeks to come.

For an hour he watched the bombardment until the defenders, their resolve flagging, waved a white pennant, and several hundred more troops surrendered themselves into their enemy's keeping. Miraculously, this time neither side lost a single man. Whatever demon exacted his toll in lives and shattered bodies had breached the protocols of ravagement and waste, though probably not without an injunction from below to make it up next time. In the aftermath, when the last projectile buried its thunder in the hollows of the hills, Jarom saw Morgan in his businesslike way giving instructions to Duke and several other officers, directing them to parole prisoners, distribute the captured arms and foodstuffs, and designate a special unit to fire the trestles.

Jarom marveled at the efficiency of those chosen to demolish the great mesh of wood that made up the trestles. As he and hundreds of others, both friend and foe, looked on, the fire starters dragged fallen limbs and branches from the woods and piled them around the base of the elaborate timber trestlework. Jarom thought of Mary Tibbs fashioning little cabins of tinder in her cookstove to cook sausage for breakfast. The workers stacked limbs against the foundation at thirty-yard intervals, starting at the proximate center and extending four or five piles in either direction. They doused each pile with coal oil carried nearly two hundred miles specially for the purpose. For several minutes, they allowed it to saturate the pith before other men with torches touched off each pile, the flames fluttering and slowly licking themselves to an unimaginable brightness as the fire began its long ascent up the vertical trusses. When the wood caught, it crackled like gunshots as resins trapped inside ignited and sooty black smoke plumed through the gorge, billowy serpents, the air filling with the noxious stink of burning creosote.

After the cheering stopped, Jarom and a blanketed multitude watching from the heights looked down on the arc of light for three hours as the flames consumed a vast forest of struts and trusses on each span. Even the prisoners stood by in wonder as the timbers charred and twisted to spidery wisps before collapsing into the valley, striking the frozen ground in an eruption of sparks. Jarom mused that the rising smoke must have been visible to John Marshall Harlan, certifying to all the outcome of the race.

But Harlan seemed unwilling to concede. Before the fire petered out, Jarom heard shots ahead and learned that Harlan's cavalry had caught up with the southbound column at a ford on Rolling Fork just south of Bardstown. As Jarom prodded Rattler into freezing water that fortunately did not rise about the horse's fetlocks, he saw flashes from Harlan's cavalry, whose troopers had dismounted and taken cover behind piles of driftwood that had accumulated upstream. A great confusion of horses thrashed about in the river as Jarom and others rushed across the exposed space and broke for the screen of trees south of the water. Duke and the rear guard, with help from Palmer's artillery, which unlimbered on the safe side of the water, held the advance long enough for everyone else to cross.

Then word came that Duke had been hit by some shell fragments and was believed dead. Thomas Quirk, Jarom learned later, carried him unconscious to the nearest farmhouse where he impressed a carriage, stuffed it with mattresses, and drove to Bardstown in search of a doctor. Next morning Duke miraculously reappeared, swathed in bandages like a Hindu, but alive. Under a heap of blankets he lounged in the buggy on a bed of feathers. The fragment tore out a chunk of skin and bone behind his right ear but hadn't injured his brain, another wonder of survival.

Leaving the rail line, Morgan turned south through Bardstown and Lebanon, rushing to prevent his pursuers from getting between him and Tennessee. In this second race Jarom knew the finish line to be the Cumberland River. If they could reach it first, Harlan would be unable to cut them off.

What Morgan had not reckoned on was changeable weather. Late in the afternoon of December 30 the skies unleashed a snowstorm, a blinding swill of cascading snow that covered the roads and everything it touched. After midnight the snow turned to icy rain, encasing Rattler in a glacial sheath. The cold razored through Jarom's new fur-lined gloves so that they might as well have been cotton. He petitioned the invisible gods that presided over armies, asking them what misbehavior merited this punishment. Because the pursuit had not slowed, those pursued could not pause to build fires and shelter themselves from the nipping wind. Jarom felt his fingers and toes going numb. When he tried to dismount to pee, he found his boots frozen to his stirrups. He had to beat them with the butt of his carbine to prize them loose.

That night was the worst he could remember. Icicles formed on Rattler's mane. Owen had daggers of ice protruding from his nostrils, the same ice that froze the mucus in Rattler's nasal cavities, giving him the appearance of having tusks belonging to some hulking creature arrived from the first age of mammals. The shards crystallized in beards and mustaches like mean teeth, giving everyone an aspect of ghoulishness. Jarom's eyelashes froze. To fight the cold, he pulled out his knife and cut a hole in his blanket to form a crude poncho, draping the excess over Rattler as best he could. Where his calves rubbed against Rattler's flanks, wherever hide touched skin, he felt a primal heat that mammals must have shared in the first ancient cuddling of man and beast for mutual survival. They rode through the night. The driving sleet bit into Jarom's hands and gnawed his skin raw. Along the way men periodically dismounted to stomp circulation back into their frostbitten feet and clap lifeblood back into their hands.

On New Year's Eve, after almost thirty-six hours in the saddle with only two brief stops for rest, the column halted in Campbellsville, where foragers discovered a large commissary. Since no one had eaten a solid meal for over two days, the men fell on this godsend, forgetting discipline and rank in the press to restore heat to their bodies. Finding a large cauldron used to scald hogs, someone made a stew, throwing in chunks of meat, whole onions, unskinned potatoes, hardtack called worm castles, and tins of sardines, from whose label a Neptune with trident grinned. Taking shelter with others in a barn, Jarom stuffed himself and then burrowed into a heap of men who spooned themselves together for warmth, waking the next day to an even colder first day of 1863. He thought nothing of the fact that those with whom he bundled were males, though he would have preferred an ample woman, a pretty one.

That afternoon as they rode over a bleak landscape of stubbled fields and wooded ridges, the faintest sound of distant thunder jolted Jarom from his stupor. He looked up at the cloudless sky, its color the dull gray of stoneware. He did not learn until days later that they'd heard a cannonade nearly seventy-five miles away as Bragg challenged Rosecrans at Stone's River. Two days later they crossed the Cumberland to safety. Tom Hines worked up a report of the damage they had wrought and shared it with the men: thirty-five miles of wrecked track, including three depots and two thousand two hundred ninety feet of bridging. Prisoners in the sum of eighteen hundred seventy-seven had been captured in addition to huge stores of much-needed rations and ammunition. They had broken, at least temporarily, the vital linkage between Louisville and Nashville. Frank Owen, a punster in the style of famed Louisville newspaper editor George D. Prentice, made a joke of it.

"Now, for a change," he said, "the feds'll go unfed."

FURLOUGH

A week after what became known as the Christmas Raid, Jarom felt an irresistible pull toward home, at least toward Mollie Thomas. Though he had sent and received several letters, he hadn't seen her for the better part of two years. Exploiting whatever goodwill he had accrued for his service, he asked for permission to visit his family in not-too-distant Logan County. To his surprise, he was granted the week he needed. But instead of returning to Nancy Bradshaw or Mary Tibbs, headstrong, he took out for Nelson County, twice the distance he had proposed and triple the risk. At the time, he felt the lie was a small price to pay for the reward of seeing Mollie. Though he had no way of contacting her beforehand and no assurance she would be there when he arrived, he resolved to make a try. But if careful, if lucky, if fast, he might be able to see her face and return intact in time for duty.

So it was that in the second week of Old Christmas in early 1863, Jarom set eyes on Mollie for the first time since enlisting. The weather had turned snapping cold after a few almost balmy days, and on the way he had a mishap, which he later read as an ill omen. When he crossed the platter of ice that covered Green River, Rattler, on whom he increasingly relied, lost his footing as he clambered up the bank, pitching both of them onto the pleated ground, whose frozen ridges drew blood from Jarom's knee. Feeling himself toppling, his weight shifting, he was able to escape greater injury by cushioning the fall with his arms so that he scuffed his hands and thigh along the ice. They seared with pain.

But Rattler got the worst of it. In falling he broke the crown of one of his long anterior teeth, gashing his nether lip. His legs splayed, and Jarom had to tug and push the horse against the bank before the animal gained enough traction to stand up. But no bones had been broken so far as Jarom could see. A spoor of hashed-up ground recorded the mishap. Rattler's hooves, useless on ice, chiseled white grooves that etched his struggles in a flurry of swirls and gouges. For the remainder of the ride they shared their suffering, Jarom catching an awful cold that burrowed into his chest and did not loosen its grip for weeks. At times he felt that a wing of the federal army had invaded his lungs, driving tent stakes and making a drill ground of his chest.

He was feeling a little better when he reached the Thomas farm just at dark after two and a half days' ride. The trees to either side of the house stood thinner than he remembered them. The wind raked some upper limbs against the eaves, making the sound of a dry pen against paper. Someone had drawn the curtains on the parlor windows, but a light shone in one upstairs. After unsaddling Rattler in the barn and helping himself to some hay for the famished horse, he cut back toward the darkened rear of the house, taking a shortcut through what remained of a vegetable garden where he tangled his feet in a snarl of vines, some balls of shriveled squash still clinging to the stems. Another omen.

The moon reflected light enough for him to see his blue shadow as he crossed the yard and rapped on the back door, loud enough to be heard but not urgent or menacing. Mrs. Thomas, an oil lamp in her hand, stepped back as she opened the door. As he entered the lean-to kitchen, Jarom felt a wave of brightness and warmth. Mrs. Thomas studied him a moment before the corners of her mouth smiled in recognition.

"Well, praise glory!" she said. "It's you. When I heard the knock, I said to myself, well, here's another poor refugee come for potluck and some lazy time by my stove."

Pulling him inside, she made a fuss, taking his muddy surtout and prodding him to the parlor where Mollie had just risen from the settee in the firelit room, a pile of knitting on the lap stool beside her.

Mollie hesitated slightly. Then she recognized him and summoned a smile. She smiled again and took a step or two toward him. Her hair was pinned back on the nape of her neck in a way he hadn't seen it. Her skin seemed paler, and the shawl over her shoulders made her look frailer than she was. She stood five foot, two inches and, nearly sixteen, seemed on the verge of womanhood but still mostly child. As he took her hand almost formally, he felt a chill, certain that either she was sick or recovering from sickness. He compared her face with the one fixed in memory. The skin around her eyes seemed drawn, the face less playful, somehow more knowing, her expression coming into alignment with the world.

She said she was so glad to see him, and that she had no notion of where he'd been, whether he was well or wounded, whole or in parts. She said she was certain he would tell her about all that. But for now she was happy to see him standing before her alive and entire.

"I'm well enough," he told her, "but I've been places I couldn't describe to you. You don't look well yourself."

"I've been down with the influenza, but Mama says I'm nearly back to normal."

This explained the pallor. Jarom remembered the old joke about one messmate inquiring about his comrade's recovery: "Is he back to normal?" he asked. "No sir," said the other, "but he's back to himself." And that was enough for Jarom. She was, he decided, both herself and not herself. Something in the green eyes, in the pressure of her hand, told him she was not the same person he had left so many months ago.

After what seemed only a few seconds Mrs. Thomas came into the room, still smiling. She carried a plate of warmed-over biscuits from which little spouts of steam rose. She told him that Mr. Thomas was off to the east fighting with the Army of Northern Virginia. As Jarom helped himself, she asked a few polite questions about the fighting, especially rumors that the war would be over by summer. Jarom gave her the expected brave words and improvised weak answers. The truth was he couldn't imagine the war, at least his war, ending at all, so he said something about having come too far to back off now and let the matter die a natural death. She said she had made up a bed for him in the spare room at the top of the stairs. Then she left the room again, not before asking Jarom if he wanted some buttermilk. Jarom thanked her and said he'd had enough, thank you, and he heard her going up the hall toward the kitchen, located in the lean-to addition at the rear of the house.

Before he could begin to speak his heart to Mollie, Mrs. Thomas came back with her knitting basket, seating herself by the fire. She stayed, Jarom decided, part as sentinel, part as curious listener and retailer of news. He imagined she must be very lonely and worried sick over the fitness of her husband, a man in his forties, to withstand the rigors of hard rations and exposure to the elements, not to mention the possibility of being shot or blown to pieces.

Jarom hadn't noticed the three gold bands she wore on her wrists until they started clicking as her flashing needles began to punctuate the conversation. Asked what she was knitting, she said a pair of socks for her husband with a double heel in anticipation of hard wear. She said she would trust them in a parcel to the mails and pray they reached him in

Virginia. But Jarom also suspected that now she knitted them for him, the surer hands, the surer feet. It would be like her not to tell him until satisfied they would suit. He would know in the morning. She sat off to herself and pretended to be oblivious, but over the clicking of the gold bands Jarom knew she latched onto every word.

Mollie, as if anticipating what her mother wanted to know, asked a spate of questions about the war—where he had been and what he was doing, the words strangely animated coming out of the tired face. Jarom answered as vaguely as he could, describing how he had become separated from Morgan's command and had been weeks unsuccessfully trying to rejoin it. He explained that once he was back in Kentucky he found it difficult to get back to Tennessee. Federals or self-appointed regulators nested on every hilltop, guarded every ford and crossroads. The limited Confederate presence consisted of a few irregular units banded together more for survival than initiative. The needlework would stop as Mrs. Thomas took in the more vital pieces of information.

As for the fighting, he referred to one or two skirmishes, downplaying the danger. He tried to give the impression that he spent most of his time in camp, far removed from the actual fighting. He said he had hankered to be in uniform again with the remnants of Morgan's mounted infantry, manning his battery and waiting out the end of the war when he could come honorably home.

Mollie, ignorant of what he'd seen and done, kept coming back to risks, asking how he'd managed to keep out of harm's way, whether he'd found enough to eat, whether he'd pinched himself in what she'd called "tight places." Jarom sensed that the question she could never quite bring herself to ask was whether he had another sweetheart. She seemed less concerned with what he'd done than with what might be done to him if wounded or captured.

What attracted him to her most, he suspected, was her innocence, her insulation from the war. Armies were massed and closing in on what remained of the Confederacy in the east and a few concentrations of defense in the west. Scattered episodes of violence occurred daily in almost every county of the state. Not yet sixteen, unfamiliar with war except for what she'd picked up in gossip from neighbors or gleaned from newspapers, she was an island of purity, undefiled by politics and mayhem.

Sometimes Jarom thought he was drawn to her more for what she wasn't than for what she was.

What kept her alive in his thoughts? He had no ready answer. But over the months he had found himself obsessed with her, the notion of someone whose existence was not touched by the death and carnage he had witnessed all around him. After much pondering he suspected his own desire for escape fueled the romance, his desire to protect someone who needed protecting. At times he felt more like an older brother than a lover. She was petite, her figure slight under the billowing skirts, her breasts more gesture than swell. She came to represent for him all that he himself was not—innocent, expectant, genuinely sanguine about the prospect of a long and promising life.

In moments of revelation, he confessed to himself that his fixing on her stemmed in part from the things he had watched dissolve in his life. He likened the loss to a block of salt he had carried to the pasture for Mary Tibbs. The first few times he saw it, he found it cubed and white, but over the weeks its edges rounded, the squared planes scalloped from the pink tongues that would eventually lick it down to nothing.

He could not tell her about his bitterness over Patterson's blinding, about his resolve to kill all his enemies he could, so he told one sweet lie after another. While she eagerly described the future she imagined, he estimated the chances of seeing her again or his odds of surviving the war, the Confederacy obviously losing ground. In his brightest moments, he saw the two of them in a clean, high-ceilinged house, surrounded by rough but tillable fields, a team of draft horses standing in harness. He peopled this dream with sons and at least one daughter. When he couldn't visualize himself as a turner of earth, he created a variation in which they would move to town where he would clerk in a store, later start a business of his own. What kind he couldn't imagine. Even the details of the house he would build would not reduce to particulars, the image of it founded on incidental details—clumps of bridal-wreath spirea and rosebushes, a wide porch, big trees in whose shade they would have picnics. What varieties of trees he didn't know. The plan of the house, its dimensions, even its building material, he could not envision.

Mrs. Thomas finally rose from her knitting and announced that she must get to bed. As she put the snicking needles into her sewing basket, the room went awkwardly still. She excused herself, wishing Jarom a snug sleep in his featherbed and commenting about not having to take his repose this night on the cold, hard ground. She gave her daughter a knowing look, half admonition, half indulgence, then excused herself. She stuck her head in the door a few moments later, as though she'd forgotten something.

"Mr. Clarke must be pretty well played out," she said to Mollie from the doorway. "Don't keep him up too long."

They heard her reach the landing before Jarom began to speak his heart, knowing Mollie would be expected to leave in a few minutes.

"There're times," he told her, "when I try to imagine what you are doing. Sometimes you're sewing or reading a book. Other times you're collecting eggs in the henhouse or just sitting under the tall elm out front."

He stifled the impulse to confide that even if he survived the war, things would never be the same, and that everyone, even those who had never been in earshot of a rifle, carried wounds that would never mend completely. He realized now that the most lasting wounds were never visible, drew no blood. Patterson carried both visible and invisible wounds, and no one could give him back his view of the yard or let him select for himself what color socks he would wear. Jarom couldn't bring himself to mention the reality that both of them understood at some level—that the South teetered, trying to keep its feet in a fight it could never win, its vitality eroding in the way that salt block had melted to a cube no larger than a butter mold, a snuffbox, a button of bone.

He changed the subject, asking about her mother's health, how she managed on the farm. She told him how hard it had been for her mother to take on her father's chores in addition to her own—seeing that the stock were fed, the corn picked, shocked, and shucked, the horses shod and trimmed, and keeping up with the random demands of mending fence or rehanging a gate, patching the roof of the henhouse, replacing a wagon wheel. She had helped her mother, she said, as much as she could.

He took her hand. As the two of them sat staring into the fire and wondering what would happen next, Jarom suddenly sensed this might be the last time he would see her. He wanted to prolong the moment, at least to memorize everything as it was: the plaid shawl across the narrow shoulders, the light as it shone on her forehead, the steadiness of her pale green eyes, the color of the underside of the leaf on the water maple. One forefinger unconsciously twirled and untwirled a piece of fringe on the shawl. The other hand, which Jarom's covered, curled over the knob of the chair arm. The smallest crease in her skirt seemed crucial to record, every nod and gesture, even the marbling of veins on the underside of her wrist. Knowing what he knew, he wanted this night to last. He wanted to commit her every breath and movement to some ledger in his mind that he could thumb through to restore the instant, recover each word. He would have been content to sit the night studying her across the hearth as she dozed.

"If I don't go upstairs," she said about half past eleven, "she will come down."

He took her hand again, feeling the warmth restored in her fingers, seeing some color in her cheeks now. As she stood up to move toward the doorway to the hall, he stepped toward her. For a moment she kept her stride, then stopped abruptly. She started to say something when he cupped her chin and drew her close, her swishing skirts resolving themselves after the legs stopped moving. He felt the upper half of her body melt into his. Her hair smelled faintly of smoke, a scent of woodiness he knew he would remember. Before kissing her, he felt her warm breath on his cheek, the small breasts appling into his chest. Though he knew what he knew, he promised he would come back. She looked him in the eye, then floated up the stairs, turning for an instant to glance at him over her shoulder as she turned the landing.

Next morning when she came down for breakfast, Jarom felt the invisible screen erected between them again. Mrs. Thomas, dressed in clothes she would not ordinarily have worn anywhere but church, flitted in and out, pouring something that tasted vaguely like coffee and asking nervous questions to break the silences. She hovered over them, protective and smothering. When the sun broke through the grayness, he could not put off going any longer. He bundled up again and made his way across the frost-hardened yard to the barn where he saddled Rattler, breaking ice in the water trough so he could drink.

He stopped at the house only long enough to thank Mrs. Thomas, who presented him with a thick new pair of gray woolen socks, the thickest he'd ever seen. He could imagine the snug feel of them in his boots. He thanked her and she went inside, leaving Mollie on the porch, the shawl clasped tightly at her throat. He could still see her waving, one hand clasping the shawl, one raised in a gesture of farewell, as he twisted back in the saddle, Rattler's clip-clops erasing whatever it was she shouted. As he rode the rest of that morning, he carried the image of her in that high-ceilinged room, light playing across her face, bright eyes rising from the fire.

DOLDRUMS

Safely returned from Nelson County, Jarom settled into life at the other end of the dipper, a long period of inactivity while Morgan waited for the thermometer to inch its way into spring. He wrote some letters to his relations in Kentucky and received two back, one from Mary Tibbs, one from Mollie. As winter dragged into late February, he discovered himself, as Patterson so aptly said, low in his mind. At odd times during the day Patterson would appear to him unbidden, a blindfold over his eyes, a crooked stick in his hand. One day, commenting on his hair, which Jarom had let grow long—perhaps because Patterson had been his barber—an effeminate young blade named Ira Crune played up to him and asked him if he wanted to take a walk some evening. Perplexed and caught off guard, Jarom quickly spurned him. Crune responded by getting huffy and calling him a tease.

For recreation he played faro and learned the fundamentals of five- and seven-card stud with Owen and several other messmates, holed up in one of the perpetually cold oilcloth shelters. He read whatever came to hand, old Nashville papers, an occasional *Harper's* with its abbreviated and often biased accounts of battles to the east of them in Virginia. He read and reread a dog-eared copy of Mr. Dickens's *Great Expectations.* Drawn to the orphaned Pip, he had a fascinated repulsion for Miss Havisham, who because of being jilted on her wedding day, felt cheated in life and hated all men. When he read that she stopped all the clocks on the hour of her betrayal, he felt a perverse kinship with her. Hadn't his own expectations been betrayed in that pistol flash along the road near Slaughtersville? For weeks he simply went through the most frugal and cursory motions of survival. He ate sad rations, he slept, he drilled, he wrote, he took walks and did his time on picket duty. He played stud poker with a deck from which several cards were missing and read the omission as another metaphor for his life's emerging pattern.

In the early spring of that year, 1863, someone received in the mail a copy of a book titled *Raids and Romance of Morgan and His Men*, written by a Bluegrass bluestocking named Sally Rochester Ford. For a week around the campfire Tom Hines read it aloud to anyone who would listen. To Jarom's thinking, the book demonstrated beyond dispute that Mrs. Ford had not been among the horsemen at Muldraugh's Hill or skirmished with Harlan's cavalry. She depicted Morgan as a gray knight, high minded and honor bound, a man who could do no wrong. His men had consecrated themselves to a cause that included a courtly code, gratuitous risk-taking, and grand gestures. Listening with the others, he found it syrupy and artificial. Though familiar with most of the names given its characters, he wasn't attuned to the personalities she'd given them. The book had all the qualities needed to fuel the illusions of the loyal ladies who read it, sparing them from stinks, the rancid meat, the gore of a field hospital, the fear with which any soldier in either army slept and woke. She depicted John Morgan as an Ivanhoe who surrounded himself with champions of virtue and manly prowess. She peopled her cast of villains with caricatures of abolitionists, turncoats, defeatists, skulkers, and unleashed tyrants. She inseminated her plot with impossible feats, abductions, and daring rescues—Sir Walter Scott transferred to the American heartland and his characters given names that any American reader would recognize. Her account of Morgan's forays, Jarom concluded, amounted to a flattering diversion, her account of the December raid a romantic journey down roads neither he nor she had ever traveled.

THE GREAT RAID

In late June, Morgan moved what he called his mounted infantry north again, this time on a raid that extended to Ohio and Indiana. Toward

Bardstown and north toward Brandenburg, where they crossed into Ohio, they rode for a short time without challenge through country flush in full summer, hay fields up to their waists, corn tasseling, fat cattle clumping under great shade trees. With great good luck Quirk and his scouts captured two steamboats and used them to ferry horses and men across the gray expanse of the Ohio.

Reining Rattler in, Jarom stared into the rising mist for a view of the far bank, the steamy shreds drawn into coves and pockets along the Indiana shore. At first all he could see of the alien place he had escaped were several chartreuse fields rising to the darker treeline on the bluffs. That world had soft edges, blue wings of vapor clinging to the riverbanks. In the bottoms, patches of corn scalloped into slopes and rose to bluffs too steep for tillage, now pasturage. He could make out a few humps like terrapins that he knew to be haystacks from a first cutting. Three-quarters of the way up, a wall of fieldstone ran roughly parallel to the base of the hill. Behind it he saw ranks of sticklike figures he remembered from Donelson, their rifles like bristles on some slithering beast behind a stack of rocks. One longer stick held a limp scrap of cloth. Off to one side stood a fieldpiece from whose mouth spurted fire and a collar of black smoke, the hollow boom rolling down the hillside, through a screen of white-topped sycamores, and across the swollen river, the sound heard an instant before it clapped against his ears. Off to the right a bouquet of white rose from the water, ruffling the swell with a bull's-eye of widening concentric rings. From the Kentucky shore came the bark of one of Palmer's Parrots, lifting several bushels of Indiana and promoting a general scramble to the rear.

The squadron disembarked and formed quickly into mounted columns. Once ashore, they met no resistance until they reached Corydon, where defenders threw up a barricade across the road. Morgan gave orders, and Jarom saw a body of men sweep toward the barricade, driving the defenders into houses along the route. As they advanced, he counted eight of the cavalry dead and estimated thirty wounded. Incensed, Morgan turned his foragers loose on the business district to liberate what they wanted from the shops and store windows.

Astride Rattler, Jarom watched as troopers lugged out sacks of fresh bread, cheese, butter, preserves, canned peaches, berries, and bottles of wine cordial—commodities they had not seen or tasted in months. Several filled their canteens with buttermilk, which formed a white foam around their mouths when they drank. Dismounting, he joined some men carving a beef from someone's larder. He helped himself, making a sandwich of cold roast, and took some swigs of cider from an earthenware jug making the rounds. The jubilation ended when Tom Hines, having located the telegraph office, arrived with news that Lee had retreated after a battle fought near a town in Pennsylvania called Gettysburg. He also brought news that a pursuit had formed outside Corydon, making it necessary to move eastward toward the town of Salem.

After they routed a party of home guards at Salem, Jarom rode down a side street with John Carrico, an older married man who replaced Estin Polk as rammer in Jarom's old battery. Bells from several churches clanged the age-old signal of alarm. Pointing up the street, Carrico leaned over to get Jarom's attention.

"What do you suppose that rascal up there is trying to do?" he asked.

Jarom at first saw no one but a bonneted woman in full skirts shuffling into the shadow of a porch. Farther up the street, he spied two men trying to bridle a skittish horse. Beyond them, the street seemed deserted.

"I don't see anyone but those men with the horse," he said.

"No," said Carrico, "I mean by that big tree over there," pointing again.

Now Jarom saw him, a wiry man in a blue vest coming out of the smithy's next to what appeared to be a public stable. He jogged up one side of the street, balancing an extended shovel before him in an effort not to drop an orange coal the size of a cantaloupe.

"Let's see what he's about," Jarom shouted back, and the two of them set off at a canter up the street.

They saw Blue Vest turn and regard them, stopping for a few moments like some inveterate idler caught with a work implement in his hand. Jarom knew something was amiss when Blue Vest hastened his step and looked back over his shoulder while Jarom and Carrico closed the distance between them. Once, as he looked, the man stumbled and nearly fell, the shovel still miraculously balanced in his hands. Quickly recovering, he started a kind of awkward scooting so as not to lose his balance, the shovel before him as though it carried something precious.

"Stop, you!" Carrico shouted, as they approached within twenty yards of him. "I command you to stop!"

The man kept running.

"Drop that shovel and stop," Carrico shouted, "or I'll shoot you as you run." Jarom looked over and saw that he'd raised the hammer, sighting on the man's back.

Abruptly, the runner stopped, the shovel with its glowing cantaloupe still extended. He stood before them panting, an athletic-looking boy about Jarom's age with long dark hair slicked back over his ears. His chest heaved, but his face held the composure of the righteous as Jarom imagined them, martyrs extending their arms for the nails, their necks for the noose.

"Where you off to in such a rush?" Carrico said casually, his right hand with the pistol in it resting on the pommel of his saddle.

"I was trying to get home," Blue Vest said, shrugging and glancing up the street where Jarom could see the cupola of the courthouse on a shaded green.

Jarom and Carrico remained unconvinced.

"Why the fire?" Carrico asked.

No answer.

Suddenly, what the man was up to dawned on Jarom.

"Hold him till I get back," he said to Carrico.

Neatly rotating Rattler, he spurred up the street toward the courthouse about sixty or seventy yards away. On the shaded lawn four or five citizens stooped over some sort of contraption. Bells still clanged, and Jarom heard more shots fired farther down the street. In the confusion, the men didn't spot Jarom until he'd closed with them, only several horse lengths away. Too late, two of them broke toward the courthouse door. Two others, a lanky man in dusty jeans and a pudgy man, his head bald and smooth as a white onion, threw up their hands.

"Don't shoot us, mister," said the pudgy man, "don't shoot." His dark suit suggested an official of some kind, a judge or maybe someone employed at a bank.

Between them, buffed and shining, perched a miniature brass swivel, a cannon so small it might be taken for a toy or a salesman's model. Mounted on a stone pedestal, it could swing on its axis in any direction. At a glance Jarom saw it was charged and pointed in the direction from which he'd just come.

"It's ceremonial," the pudgy man said by way of apology, "used only on holidays and celebrations." He had the look of a man who lied and knew others knew it.

"What day are we celebrating?" Jarom shot back.

Again, no answer. His lanky comrade, who had found his courage but not his voice, glared at Jarom now, his eyes fixed on the dark eyelet of the leveled pistol. Using his pistol as a baton, Jarom waved the two of them away from the swivel.

Jarom yelled back to Carrico, jogging up the street with some other riders, their pistols held handy over their heads. They reined in, climbing off their huffing horses to admire the swivel, which, despite its age and probable origins aboard some antique vessel in times equally uncertain, seemed capable of firing. Carrico, who had an aptitude for things mechanical, began to dismantle the swivel from its carriage, removing the tapered muzzle from atop the stone pedestal. Someone else went off with the lanky prisoner for tools, and in minutes the three of them hoisted and lashed the swivel across the saddle on Rattler's back. When Jarom presented it to Adam Johnson later that day, Johnson congratulated him and made a lame jest about collecting stovepipes.

After having the horses fed and cared for, Morgan ordered the telegraph lines cut and the railroad depot burned as well as a bridge over the nearby Blue River, to slow pursuit. He then discreetly disappeared while both brigades methodically plundered the town. Jarom, who had previously witnessed lawlessness only on a modest scale, looked on as troopers broke into buildings and removed valuables as frightened storekeepers stood helplessly by. Jarom interpreted the plundering as the natural climax of frustration and fear that preyed on the men, in part owing to the intensely hot weather and in part to the brandy and other spirits found on store shelves and in the local tavern.

Carrico brought a demijohn of homemade wine fetched from someone's cellar and offered Jarom a taste. Grasping the large bottle with both hands, he upended it and clenched his lips for a tentative sip. It reminded him of fruit juice with an edge, its scent reminiscent of blackberries, neither sweet nor sour but strangely fortified. Taking several swigs as the wickered bottle made its rounds, he began to feel a little dizzy. After several more swallows, he felt tipsy, experiencing a lightness as though the blood had drained from his head to pulse against the skin of his cheeks and forehead.

After a time he felt an agreeable giddiness as though he'd been stone-struck in the head, but painlessly. He eased down against a tree and laughed at everything that was said, having trouble following the dips and swervings of the talk, which seemed vaguely to center on who would win the war. When several of the topers got up and began rummaging about a sundries and dry goods store, he joined them, tossing things around until they'd wrecked the place.

A list of the culprits could be compiled by inspecting them as they rode. One man in Duke's brigade traveled with seven pairs of ice skates about his neck. Another ladened himself with sleigh bells, great leather belts of bells the size of a two-bit piece, which an officer made him discard because they announced the column's whereabouts for some distance in all directions. A corporal in his company accumulated the most plunder, items packed in his saddle roll and strung from his pommel. Jarom speculated that Stickyfingers had equipped himself to host a banquet in the field or set up a sundries shop. Jarom ran an inkless inventory of the items attached to the corporal's person or fixed to his kit: a large chafing dish, a medium-sized Dutch clock, a green glass decanter with glasses to match, a bag of horn buttons, bolts of calico, and a cage with three canaries. When quizzed about the canaries, the corporal had a ready answer.

"They give me a sense of well-being," he said, "a feeling of tranquility."

After two days and some gentle persuasion from his messmates, the rescuer of birds left the sole survivor with a Christian lady at a farmhouse along the road.

Jarom brought off a pair of binoculars he thought would help him sight artillery or at least spot trouble coming. On a whim he also picked up a piece of china that reminded him of his aunt's Sunday dinners. The pink rose heads, turned in symmetrical patterns and connected to pale stems and stylized vines, gave him a sense of permanency and order in a world that seemed to lack both. He wrapped it carefully in his blanket.

Each time he looked at it he saw Aunt Mary in her kitchen serving him slices of baked ham or a breast of chicken. He carried it successfully for days until one night he opened the folds and found it broken into five pieces. Even then, he couldn't throw the fragments away.

RECROSSING THE RIVER

Jarom could remember all the particulars of the last time he saw Hunt Morgan before enemy cavalry captured the great man. The general was sitting comfortably on the gallery of a crossroads store where troopers stopped to fill their canteens at the well. Though everyone in his command knew that his old enemy Colonel Frank Wolford of the First Kentucky Cavalry had joined the pursuit, he seemed relaxed and good humored. He had opened his tailored wool jacket and pulled off his boots. His forehead and nose shone tomato red from the summer sun that beat down on them all. Except for the uniform, he might have been a local farmer escaping the heat for a few minutes while the storekeeper filled his grocery order.

Adam Johnson joined him for a few minutes and later reported the conversation to Jarom. Morgan, nothing if not a gentleman, first asked Johnson to sit down and rest. Johnson pulled over a chair, though nervous apprehension harried him and fed his anxiety about whether they could recross the river before Frank Wolford attacked in force. After hearing his concerns, Morgan thanked him and gave assurances that his worries were groundless.

"By this time tomorrow," Morgan said, "we'll all be secure on Southern soil. The river is only twenty-five miles away and no one, not even Frank Wolford, is close enough to stop us."

Johnson admitted that he could only shrug and accept the general's assessment when he actually wanted to wail in exasperation. Others had told him that nothing could penetrate the general's shield of self-confidence, and now he believed it.

Johnson had small satisfaction when he reached the ford to find the shallow bars covered with high water from heavy rains upstream, the ford itself guarded by a ragtag band of ad hoc militia with supporting artillery.

That night while Jarom and several other pickets sat under some trees by the road listening to crickets and the pained sonatas of tree frogs, they heard an indefinite rustling in the woods, the slightest interruption of what might have been the creaking of leather and the collective weight of multiple hooves muffled in the leaf fall, the slightest break in the natural rhythms, more felt than heard. As they listened, he thought he heard the dinging of metal on metal, a horse snorting, once even a distant voice. Someone fetched the captain, who sent word back to Morgan that enemy cavalry were bearing down on them.

The captain directed Jarom and the others to hide themselves along the road and hold fire until they heard a shot from his pistol. When the first riders appeared as shapeless shadows in the darkened road maybe thirty yards away, the captain fired. The roadway erupted with jets of fire, and flashes spit back and forth in the darkness. Jarom raised his Colt, aimed it toward the flashes, and tripped the hammer, the concussion lifting his barrel with each shot. He fired until he emptied both his revolvers. He heard agonized screams on the road, proof certain that some of the men and horses had fallen. Like pranksters caught in some feat of vandal stealth, the mass of riders turned back and raced down the road in a jumble of men and horses.

Jarom woke next morning in the perfect stillness of dawn. Around him, tentless, slept hundreds of blanketed forms, a few stirring in the half-light. Someone was coughing, and a crow cawed in the river bottom. Rolling up his blanket and securing it on Rattler's back, he stood on the bluff and looked out across the river where he made out the dim outline of ridges, a gray succession of furrow and hump in what he knew must be Virginia. The camp stirred now, and some musicians, as if divining the moment's serenity, began strumming sentimental tunes on their stolen guitars. Someone took up a fiddle, and a hundred voices began singing a popular song that Jarom recognized as "Juanita," followed by a patriotic rendering of "My Old Kentucky Home."

A crackling of gunfire interrupted "The Hills of Tennessee," and Jarom rushed to take his place in the battle line he knew would be forming. Clapping the saddle on Rattler's back, he hitched himself up by the stirrup and followed others down the bluff to the flats near the river. At midriver he saw a shallow-draft sternwheeler, artillery pieces protruding from makeshift armor strapped to its sides, twin stacks rising through the threads of river mist. As the vapors lifted, the boat started tossing shells on the encampment, now full of scampering men. At the same time, the cavalry they had routed the night before advanced on the rear of the column. Duke and his men rode back to hold them off while Morgan and the main body took to the water, forcing their reluctant horses to swim. Morgan himself had crossed halfway when, apparently deeming the effort futile, he turned back to lead those not in the water north in search of another crossing.

Prodding Rattler down the bank, Jarom hit the water. The unexpected coldness sent a shock through his arms and legs that left him gasping. Ahead, he could make out Adam Johnson hanging around the neck of his Texas-bred stallion, water up to their necks so that they seemed bodiless survivors of some beneficent guillotine that left the heads with life yet in them. Jarom winced as he felt the water stab through his clothes and settle in his crotch and upper thighs. Upriver, beyond Buffington Island, he could see several spouts of smoke rising ominously above the river. More gunboats. To his left, a man in a wide-brimmed hat, hugging the neck of a stolen Norman horse that struggled to keep its nose above the swell of water, shouted that he couldn't swim. His hat had been dunked and clearly he'd lost his gear in the current.

"Hold on!" Jarom shouted, as he heeled Rattler in the flanks to steer toward him, reining him to the left. "Hold on! I'm coming."

This assurance did not visibly soothe the panic in the rider's eyes. Jarom interpreted his expression as *I-am-drowning, I-am-drowning.* The rider clasped his arms in a death hold around the horse's neck, the big horse itself choking and beginning to fail.

"Let go the neck!" Jarom shouted as he closed the distance between them. "Grab hold of the saddle," he said more calmly. "Let your horse do the swimming."

But the heavy Norman draft horse, already succumbing, turned on its side and barged into Rattler, nearly dragging the four of them under. Jarom envisioned them all being sucked into the roiling waters, his bleached white remains eventually washing up on one of the piles of drift that collected along the riverbank, his clacking bones lashed by the reins to Rattler, whose once muscular haunches had slackened to a ghost of their former shape.

The rider, a stranger to Jarom, gave him an imploring look, a wordless but emphatic plea for deliverance. Sliding off Rattler's downriver flank, Jarom grabbed the cantle of the drowning man's saddle and paddled alongside, coaxing Rattler and palming the water with one hand, as he slowly towed the three of them—the larger horse, the terrified rider, and Jarom himself—toward the Virginia shore. In that welter of struggling forms, distracted by booming gunboats, by shouts of the wounded and drowning, Jarom fixed on the fringe of shorn trees that marked a return to the solid element on which men and horses were condemned and blessed to tread.

A few yards short of the bank, Jarom felt his feet touch bottom. Seconds later, he sensed a shifting of weight as both horses found their footing again and heaved upward almost involuntarily, trembling, dripping, spent. Unsnarling the reins, Jarom led them out onto a sandbar. Exhausted, resisting the clinging weight of water in his clothes, he lugged the waterlogged rider up the bank. Hopelessly distraught, the big man, bearded and burly, scared out of his wits, moaned senselessly. Water ran from the ringlets of his beard as he slowly woke to the prospect of redemption.

"Father, Son, and Holy Ghost," he said, "I'm saved." He focused on Jarom, his deliverer. "There's no denyin' I owe you my life. Thank you, thank God."

When the man made it to his feet, Jarom asked him to take the horses to a copse of scraggly willows a ways from the river. As he turned back toward the water, he saw other horses rising out of the Ohio, shaking their backs with great spasms of relief, their mane-drenched heads swinging from side to side as their hooves found purchase on the bank, reentering a world all their instincts told them they had lost. Now Morgan's command was divided, one on temporarily safe ground, the other racing to find another crossing. Looking back toward the land of the Buckeyes, Jarom saw a vista of bobbing heads, black lumps protruding across the river's gray expanse. Someone rowed out in a fisherman's skiff to pull in those still reachable. Others waded into the shallows to drag the weak ones to safety. At the moment when Jarom felt most relieved, it occurred to him that all of them—those under the trees, those still in the water, those marooned on the Ohio shore—had survived one danger only to face others, and he tasked himself to drag in as many as he could. He knew the soldier's greatest fear of confronting peril alone.

Feeling a desperate energy, he fished out more of those floundering in the water, expecting any second that the gunboats dropping shells on the Ohio shore would turn their guns toward Virginia. Adam Johnson, heedless of any harm, stood perched on a sandbar. As those that survived the water crawled and scrabbled up the embankment, he ordered each, rider or walker, to rendezvous a quarter mile inland beyond the shells of the gunners. In the confusion, Jarom couldn't understand Johnson's gestures and mouthings, but Jarom knew he would be shouting.

Jarom remounted, looking back over the river. He knew that most of those who hadn't made the crossing likely would soon be prisoners— Duke, Morgan, and Thomas Quirk among the hundreds taken with the prized horse-drawn guns. He knew that most of those in the water were drowned men, their sodden remains being swept off by the current to resurface in some backwater or eddy, nameless, graveless, the features that might identify them bloated and chafed beyond knowing. The multitude of hats floating on the surface of the river brought him low. He had at first mistaken them from a distance for swimmers; they reminded him now of stepping stones, then drifting grave markers. He could see dozens, but he knew to multiply those dozens to hundreds he couldn't count. He felt a desperate need to inventory his own small store of belongings, some of it certainly at the bottom of the river. As soon as he could, he dismounted and unrolled his blanket, opening the oilcloth packet that contained the shards of china plate and the folded sheet of music, which had a few wet blotches but remained otherwise undamaged. He felt the lucky buckeye in his pocket.

CYNTHIANA

In May 1864, Jarom accompanied his comrades on the march to Saltville, Virginia, where Morgan assumed command of the Department of Southwest Virginia. After being forced to divide his forces on the so-called Great Raid, the general had managed to evade Union cavalry for another week before being captured while trying to cross the river at West Point, Ohio. After several months in captivity, he had escaped from the Ohio State Penitentiary. Morgan had ordered his reorganized forces to Wytheville, Virginia, to fend off an attack from Union forces that penetrated from Kentucky through the Cumberland Gap, the passageway between mountains through which Daniel Boone and the first settlers entered Kentucky.

On May 11 at Wytheville, Jarom and others found some citizens, amateurs, trying to maneuver an old six-pounder that belonged to the town. When Morgan took charge of the gun and called for volunteers to man it, Jarom and a man named Davis stepped forward. The episode was the closest Jarom had come to meeting Morgan, who stood by to direct the fire. Their eyes met as Morgan looked on while Jarom and the others wheeled the gun into service.

"Good work, son," the general said, redirecting his attention to what lay ahead. Jarom felt himself swell with pride, imagining that the addition of the cannon might change the battle.

By summer Jarom found himself among more remnants of Morgan's command that reassembled at Abingdon, Virginia. By some miracle of goodwill and necessity, Morgan was still in good graces with his superiors. The South badly needed a symbol of boldness and invincibility in the face of losses in almost every department, and Morgan fit the description. The Confederacy was being bled to incapacity by casualties that were irreplaceable and a will to fight that was showing signs of strain. Morgan's escape seemed a miracle, a tonic for flagging spirits. Several hundred of those outmaneuvered at Buffington Island, a quarter of the men who set out at the beginning of July nearly a year earlier, had been killed or captured.

The losses compelled a reorganization, and Jarom and Frank Owen, who also nearly drowned crossing the Ohio, were reassigned to Captain James Cantrill's company of Major Cassell's Second Battalion, a muster of men that contained the core of the "Old Guard," the veterans who had survived raids, skirmishes, substandard food, and camp diseases. Two other regiments were made up mostly of replacements, many of them eager recruits from the hills of East Tennessee, which was largely loyalist. To Jarom, the replacements seemed a sorry lot: inexperienced, green, many without guns and horses, some without shoes or decent clothes. Like the diminished trees that replaced the forest giants, this timber lacked the stature and growth of the originals. The numbers might increase but not the quality of what had been lost.

Rumor had reached Morgan in late spring that the Union army occupying his hometown of Lexington possessed hundreds of horses, some of them blooded thoroughbreds from the heart of Kentucky horse country. The press to provide his men with mounts justified his drawing his troops from the defense of southwestern Virginia and making another foray into his home state, this one to Lexington. Jarom couldn't understand how losing a quarter of his command on the last raid had magnified Morgan's stature in the press and drawn so many recruits. Eight hundred men seemed willing to walk two hundred fifty miles with the prospect of fighting for him and capturing a horse along the way.

As for himself, though he had misgivings about the general's patience to form and execute a plan, he didn't doubt Morgan's pluck or determination. The weather was fine, the trees full-leafed, the pastures lush enough for a first cutting of hay, though with fewer men to cut it. Despite the neglect he saw on several farms, he felt he had entered a land where God purposed to create an ideal against which to compare the places on which He had frowned, the barren and rocky places, the dry and the sterile. Tobacco had been set, and wide fields of corn would soon be tasseling. Few regions of the state or country could match the Bluegrass as a breadbasket to provision an army.

To reach this replica of Eden, the column passed through a land in which God in the guise of sightseer had opted for spectacle over plenty. The landscape paralleled His displeasure at earthly offenses, both real and imagined. The rugged landscape through which they passed represented what a newcomer, seeking to read Providence by its shadows, might construct if the Maker had swept all the scourings from the Bluegrass to this corner of the commonwealth. To get to Eden, they had to pass through a desolate mountainous country in which everything seemed canted, inhospitable to all but a few species of beasts. Jarom likened it to entering the kingdom of the rock, the unscalable cliff, the dried-up creek bed.

Morgan chose this uninviting and unpopulated route through a pass in the crenellated wall of mountains as an entryway, the long column passing through Pound Gap. Atop one of the foothills that rose out of the lowlands, Jarom mapped the topography of narrow valleys, steep ravines with their inevitable rills, and dense wilderness that sprang up wherever a pinch of soil formed to sheathe the stone. Rattler, though acclimated to hardship, strained in such terrain, his hooves seeking solid footing among the scatter of rocks that lay along the route, as though sown by some malevolent strewer who declared man his sworn enemy. If the four-leggeds found the way hard, those who proceeded by shank's mare, especially the shoeless, suffered a greater penalty. Their scrapes and lacerations left records of blood among the flags of rock.

Such rough ground took its toll on the riders too. Passing through this harsh country, Jarom felt a chafing against his thighs that pinched and rashed him until he rode saddlesore. The constant rasp of Rattler's rocking and swervings along the path wore the skin of his inner thigh raw. Critically in need of reshoeing, Rattler himself seemed in a desperate state, but he plodded on, clopping one hoof in front of the other.

When they came to open country, Jarom felt he had been repatriated to a land of the living, a sweet domain of broad farms and villages. Citizens gathered along the roads sometimes waved. They seemed well fed and secure in their lives, at least as secure as the defenseless could be as rebels passed through their dooryards bent on unseating established authority. Passing beyond a country of knobs and hummocks covered with dense thickets and cedar stands, they encountered more farms tucked into coves and hollows, a more gracious country of gentle rolls and swells. The great clumps of wild roses blooming along the road put Jarom in mind of Beech Grove, where they spouted in white fountains along the fencerows.

The cavalcade reached the outer rim of the inner Bluegrass without mishap. Passing a field overgrown with blackberries whose white blossoms betokened a season of plenty, Jarom felt a sudden pang of homesickness after nearly a year outside his native state. He thought of John Patterson tutoring himself to live with a cane in a world deprived of blooming and the pleasurable architecture of trees. Passing through rolling pastureland and by well-kept farms, he imagined Mary Tibbs performing her daily chores, twisting the neck of a chicken, tending her kitchen garden, patching an old quilt. Mollie Thomas he saw, bonneted and well fed, relaxing in a lawn chair near the Thomas grape arbor.

Jarom and every man in the formation knew the Confederate States of America had all but lost the war in the West and things weren't going well in the East, though only a few confirmed pessimists would certify the final outcome. His messmates contracted in their relations to the world, hardened themselves—some bitter about the loss of friends, some pining for family, some despairing of ever crossing their own doorstep again. Still, they retained pride in their leaders and a will to carry the fight to their enemies' strongholds.

"The devil take those who don't believe we can chew 'em up and swallow 'em," Frank Owen said, "or at least chase them back to wherever the hell they come from."

The next opportunity to chase came at Mount Sterling, the last of the mountain counties on the fringe of the Bluegrass, a transitional terrain that partook of both. At the outskirts the column deployed to attack a tent camp of slumbering federals. Unlike the encampments of Morgan and his men, this bivouac had an air of permanency, laid out like candles stacked in a gift box, a grid of canvas cubes that held a pleasing and tempting symmetry.

Taken by surprise at breakfast time, the startled defenders quickly surrendered after Duke's cavalry enveloped the camp and closed off every means of escape. Jarom captured a portly cook in his shirtsleeves standing with a larded skillet in his hand, a study in bafflement. Jarom next came upon a host of his comrades, who, with little ceremony, helped themselves to their enemies' breakfast, sitting at their enemies' camp tables, eating off captured plates with captured utensils. Hungry, he bolted down most of a rasher of bacon and fresh-baked bread, drinking his first cup of coffee in six months, a great tin cup of it sweetened with lumps of genuine sugar. Afterward, the troops marched into Mount Sterling's business district, where officers looked the other way when the looting began. Towns, even sympathetic towns, had become both commissary and quartermaster to the desperate and needy.

Ashamed to be associated with an army reduced to larceny, Jarom held back. In his own moral primer he made a distinction between depriving his fellow Kentuckians of property and depriving their enemy of theirs in Indiana or Ohio. He stuck on a fine legal distinction between stealing and liberating. Wherever Morgan now went, his men left a wake of dry goods, pieces of furniture, and other household utensils strewn in the street. The same citizens who had welcomed Morgan's troopers a year ago now stood by in fear and wonder, believers who had seen lapses of discipline degenerate into outright thievery. Some were kin to men in Morgan's command, cousins and aunts and in-laws, even siblings. No longer able to scoop off the cream, Morgan in desperation had filled his depleted ranks with anyone willing to sign a ledger. He conceded that many of them, unrepentant scoundrels and rank opportunists, lacked any principle of restraint or decency. Jarom wanted no part of it.

When the column arrived at Lexington, thirty or so miles to the west, Morgan didn't find the rumored five thousand horses. Though Morgan took the town with little resistance and destroyed some government property, in the end Jarom felt fortunate to come away uncaptured and unharmed. After Morgan dispatched men to burn the warehouses and train depot, the dawn sky glowed so intensely that many Lexingtonians, awaking to find another flag over their city, believed that Morgan had ordered the whole downtown torched. Jarom heard the fire bells ringing as the Lexington Volunteer Fire Department came to extinguish the flames as best they could.

"Fact is," said Frank Owen, "this is the same department that citizen Morgan served in fulfilling his civil duty before the war. Now he's putting 'em to the test, starting fires, not putting 'em out."

Jarom picked up a report that one of the local banks had been robbed. In the horse department Morgan managed to acquire about a thousand mounts, much to the relief of those still walking. Many were thoroughbreds, fine sleek horses whose tinkering Creator seemed to have put together with elegance and speed foremost in His specifications. One of these specimens was the famous Skedaddle, a filly taken from Ashland, the home of the late Senator Henry Clay, who, though deceased, remained Lexington's most persuasive claim to prominence.

During the turmoil that ensued, Morgan was said to have visited Hopemont, his family home two blocks north of Main Street. While riding alone in the neighborhood of the college, he'd been spotted by a federal patrol. Chased up the street in which he had played as a boy, he sought refuge at Hopemont and rode his horse up the front steps and through the wide double doors, his sudden disappearance baffling his pursuers.

In defiance of caution and the dictates of good sense, Morgan, when he departed Lexington, struck out northwest along the pike that led to Cynthiana. His staff and others, who often tried to second-guess him, anticipated that he would move southeast and swing back toward Virginia. As Jarom now understood the erratic actions of the man who governed his fate and that of a thousand others, unpredictability was Morgan's greatest virtue, his greatest fault. Morgan at times seemed less motivated by strategies derived from maps or sage counsel than by whim, as if he asked himself, which is the boldest course, which the way that will most exhibit my pluck and foil my enemies?

The farms that they passed, ample and well tended, showed few signs of privation, often having a manicured look that showed less the diligent fruits of husbandry than the presence of slaves who could be impressed for any task between the seasons of planting and harvest. Fields of tobacco exploded into green, and there were stands of shoulder-high hemp and tidy ranks of sweet corn, which reminded Jarom of the neat troop formations he'd seen in artists' renderings of battles in *Harper's Weekly* but nowhere else. The rolling landscape matched his mental image of Canaan, the land promised to Moses, where rich soil, abundant rain, and palmy weather combined to make crops thrive.

Rattler perked up when he smelled the cloying sweetness of honeysuckle that covered the embankment along one stretch of lane. Trumpet vines twined around the uprights of a rail fence, their blooms a gaudy reddish orange. Jarom remembered that Patterson had aptly called this roadside growth devil's trumpet. Where the wood fence ended, native limestone walls began, an artful stacking that bespoke permanence and care. Herds of shorthorns and Herefords congregated under the native trees, leafy spreads of bur oak and blue ash that had shaded similar congresses of buffalo.

Marching all night, the advance riders of Morgan's men reached Cynthiana at dawn. The little town of eight hundred lay profoundly still, not a dog barking. According to Frank Owen, a man named Harris founded the town, naming it after his two daughters, Cynthia and Anna, and naming the larger entity of county after himself. Cynthiana typified the country towns that formed a constellation radiating from Lexington, and Owen, reared in neighboring Bourbon County, described it as insular and sleepy, idyllic. Situated on the South Fork of the Licking River, its trim brick buildings and covered bridge gave it the look of a place untouched by war. Jarom spotted two steeples poking up from the treetops and the cupola of what must been the Harrison County courthouse.

Quirk reported that the federal troops stationed at the town had set up camp in the flats near the covered bridge marking its western approach. Bennett ordered Jarom and those about him to dismount and tether their horses; the attack was to take place on foot. Jarom slid off Rattler into a meadow whose grass slicked his boots and pants legs with dew. He could hear a dove cooing nearby, and a mist still hung over the river bottom, giving the blurred buildings and trees across the river a nappy edge that defied definition—similar, he thought, to the unfocused movement of pounding hooves or the gyrating wings of hummingbirds. Vague forms rose around him in the grass, and he could make them out as cows, standing nearby still as porcelain figurines, their only motion a measured raising and bending of heads. He heard the friction of their teeth in a subtle chawing that broke the stillness, and he could imagine the ruminant, oddly circular movement of their jaws, the knobby heads extended in dumb concentration.

Just before the attack a cock crowed. Then he and a hundred others charged on foot through the adjacent wheatfield to hit the encampment. The first fire came from pickets, alerted, Jarom guessed, by footfalls rustling among the sheaves. They fired a second time and pulled back, and Jarom heard at least one bullet as it ratcheted its way through the leaves of the tree behind him. And then he could see the camp, the ordered rows of quadrangular white tents, as it suddenly came alive with motion. The sudden stirring reminded him of the anthill he and one of his aunt's hands, a boy named Easter, kicked over one summer day as they roamed the woods. They had watched, fascinated, as their prodding feet sent ants scurrying. After several minutes, the volume of fire increased as the defending federals rallied from their initial confusion and swung around to form a line of battle.

Then Morgan commenced his mounted charge on the far side of

the encampment, and the ragged blue line began to cave in on itself, shrinking to a protective but steadily eroding core. Though the belts of mist made sighting uncertain, Jarom believed he dropped one of the marksmen picking targets from behind a pile of railroad ties. Seeing the rifleman sink out of sight gave him a queasy feeling, knowing he had killed or injured someone not much different from himself beyond the tint of his uniform. The soldier part of him felt elated; another part, remembering Patterson in his pitiful state, was unaccountably shamed. His command disarmed and assembled the prisoners in sullen clusters. And Morgan, triumphant but knowing pursuers to be near, prepared to leave Cynthiana.

Then, to the north of town someone sighted a thin ribbon of blue at the crest of a ridge. As he watched, Jarom witnessed the ribbon unravel into several strands, the strands into units of cavalry deploying for an attack. Morgan, not one to lose his head in a crisis, coolly deployed his own regiments, improvising almost spontaneously an effective fighting plan. As the first riders spilled down on his men, Morgan put his simple stratagem to the test. While one regiment remained dismounted and laid down harassing fire, Jarom's regiment, still on horseback, circled to the rear, using the wooded terrain and the town itself to screen their movements.

Halfway across the open ground, the advance of blue riders faltered like a boxing arm that had reached the limits of its thrust and, feeling the restraint of ball in socket, retracted. Those closest must have flinched in wonderment and fear as they heard the high keening that marked the Kentucky variant of the rebel yell. It came from behind them where Jarom and two hundred riders sprinted along a railroad ditch before fanning into the open field in a movement that neatly folded the Union rear. Though he had emptied his Colt at the fleeing Union cavalry, he doubted he had hit any of the riders. But others had. Under the force of the charge, they scattered like flushed quail. Looking back across a field of wheat that had been mashed to stubble, Jarom saw a blue litter of Union dead and wounded, several pained horses whinnying in agony, riderless, one downed sorrel struggling to rise in the snarl of its own reins.

Turning, he saw Morgan canter up the frazzled line of gray, directing fire and savoring each rent in the federal line. When a white flag went up,

Jarom looked up as Morgan, with his escort of Quirk and several officers, pranced over on his blooded mare to accept the sword of General Edward Hobson, a man who had chased him across Ohio and Indiana, now humiliated. Rigged out in a fancy uniform, Hobson reminded Jarom of a pigeon, a great puffed breast with spindly legs, a fitful manner, a mien swollen with self-importance.

"There's a man," Frank Owen quipped, "has more buttons than sense."

But Hobson, more fox than pigeon, proved him wrong. The general shrewdly pretended to have the authority to exchange prisoners belonging to Morgan's command for himself, his staff, and the six hundred volunteers he had brought down from Cincinnati. Anxious to recover men he could ill afford to lose, Morgan tried to come to terms with him, but Hobson only played him along, and the two dickered for four hours before exhaustion forced them to break off.

Unable to agree on terms for an exchange, Morgan at last said he needed to sleep on the matter, certain that by morning he would have thought out a solution to the impasse. Believing no Union soldier closer than a two-day march, he gave orders to camp for the night. Jarom and the others unrolled their blankets and prepared to bed down, some sleeping in salvaged tents of their prisoners. Bone-tired as he must have been, Morgan seemed in no hurry for his day of triumph to end. Jarom saw him, obviously pleased with himself, strolling from cookfire to cookfire making small talk, smiling at jokes, and passing kind words. He wore a jaunty getup, a snappy vest over a clean, white linen shirt, cavalry pantaloons, and boots burnished the color of a walnut table leg. After a victory came the usual revelry, and the feasting and singing did not end until after midnight. Jarom, still leery of strong drink, stuffed some bits of wadding in his ears and did his best to sleep on the damp ground.

Feeling indulgent, Morgan next morning permitted his men to have a leisurely breakfast—a critical mistake. As Jarom hunkered by the cookfire eating some contraband eggs, someone shouted that the camp was being attacked. At first Jarom saw no one, and he hoped the warning was a practical joke. Then a hush fell over the encampment as a faint rumbling rose from the far side of Cynthiana. A minute later the first attackers crested the ridge. Off to the left on a rise near the rail track another mass of blue riders assembled, the metal of their muzzles and belt buckles glinting in the wide band of light at the horizon. For a moment Jarom felt dazed as though under the spell of some drug that robbed him of his senses. In the next instant he saw riders roll down the ridge in rivulets that turned to torrents, a flood sweeping through camp before any of the men could horse themselves.

Grabbing his carbine from his saddle holster, Jarom ran to the nearest tree, drawing a bead on the closest rider, a big man waving a horse pistol. As he drew the trigger taut, something wrenched the carbine from his hands. He felt a terrific blow in the heel of his right hand. Only the spasm of pain shooting up his forearm told him he had been shot, a stunning sensation like the sear of iron heated to a glow. Looking down, he saw that something, a minie ball, he realized, had gouged out the fatty underside of his hand. The fact that he could still flex his fingers told him no bones had been shattered. He glanced at the splintered stock of the carbine that lay at his feet, then noticed that he was bleeding. He drew out his bandanna, remembering Aunt Mary's injunction that no gentleman ever be caught without a handkerchief. Using his left hand and clenching one end with his teeth, he wrapped it around the gouge and managed to tie it tightly, knowing the pressure would help stanch the flow of blood, ease the throbbing.

Pandemonium engulfed him. The main wave of the attack went halfway up an adjoining ridge where he could see a flimsy line of defense giving way under a tide of men and horses. Closer, men around him ran helter-skelter, other men on horseback trying to shoot or chase them down. Rattler, shot or captured or fleeing for his life, was nowhere in sight. Through the din of shot and shouting, his eye lighted on a cut where a small branch flowed into the Licking. Jumping over the embankment, he found a trickle of olive-colored water smothered in weeds and scrub willow. Wading to the inlet, he tied both ends of his neckerchief to a stick and twisted until the bleeding stopped.

In an instant of self-appraisal he realized he had lost his weapons, his pistol belt still with his blanket, the carbine lying useless thirty yards away. Raising his head above the cut, he saw darting figures, a few of his comrades with hands raised skyward already being herded to the rear. Whinnying hysterically, a horse with a bloodied rump struggled to regain its feet and run, a sign to Jarom from whatever deity presided over battles that he should take flight.

Cupping his right wrist with his good hand, he slid down the bank and tiptoed through the tepid water, trying to keep his footing on the slickish stones. Sticking close to the near bank, he worked his way up-stream over shelves of lichen-splotched rock to an overgrown fencerow along a ridge running parallel to the Licking. Now fifty or sixty yards from the river, he followed the fenceline until he reached a small clearing scooped out of the encompassing woods. Moving along its edge within a fringe of sumac and horseweed, he circled toward a mesh of wilderness so dense no horse could readily follow.

The sting in his hand was a throbbing now. If pain were a sound, its utterance would have been a loud and persistent scream. Cradling his hand, he started running as he imagined fugitives in defeat had always run, intent only on distancing themselves from the probing swords of the victors, from the hooves of whatever carried them. He ran until he could hear only the vaguest popping, his shirt drenched with sweat, his chest heaving from an exertion he knew he couldn't sustain. Only then did he feel that he had outdistanced the men who wanted to kill him.

Resting under a giant tulip tree, he listened. Over his own labored breath he began to detect sounds in the woods around him, a thrashing through the underbrush and once a banging of tin. Back toward the river he could hear distant shouting, the firing muffled now and less frequent. The attack must have been a complete rout because he heard no concentrated fire to indicate Morgan had made a stand or paused to cover the retreat.

Against the skyline he glimpsed something in motion, highlighted among the stand of verticals, the subtlest alteration of light, as though something had passed between the periphery of his eye and the light's source. Watching, he could gradually detect figures, dozens of men ducking through the woods, a few, like himself, hobbling from wounds. From one of the bull sessions with Patterson and his comrades around the campfire, he remembered the joke about the hearts of some soldiers pumping rabbit blood.

"Rabbit blood," Patterson had said, "is the ungovernable impulse to run at the slightest threat of danger."

Once he saw two men making their way together, but most who came within his seeing went as solitaries on their own hook. Taking to the woods again, this time he spotted a group of a half dozen or so moving purposefully through the undergrowth. As Jarom stepped out from cover, the leader merely nodded, and he joined them, strangers and brothers, as did others while the day wore on into late afternoon. By evening there were over twenty in the party, all of them horseless, without food, most without weapons. They shared, it became evident to Jarom, an unspoken desire to elude whatever lay over the next ridge and make it back to Abingdon. Make it back they did, except for the two hundred fifty or so killed or captured. Or those who had simply had enough and quit.

Feeling the absence of Rattler, Jarom hoped that the buff stallion had survived the fighting and was somewhere feeding on golden corn, whether federal or Confederate he didn't care, so long as his loyal trailmate survived.

GREENEVILLE

As Jarom would remember it, though he did not see the death of John Hunt Morgan at first hand, he was close enough to hear the shot that widowed Morgan's new wife. He saw him for the last time the morning before the general's death, September 3, 1864, a few miles outside of Greeneville, Tennessee, where Morgan planned to spend the night. Jarom's company, detached from its artillery, had been chosen to ride as the advance because several of the men knew the back roads through the country.

Late in the morning Morgan notified Captain Cantrell that he, the general, would ride at the head of the column, a practice not often advised because of the risk of being bushwhacked by ridge runners or enemy sharpshooters, especially by the discriminating—those who had a penchant for identifying and shooting officers. But Morgan, as evidenced in his choice of careers, his craving for excitement, gave little thought to self-preservation. Nor did he shrink from public sight, notwithstanding his imposing figure and the telltale plume that made him a tempting target. Knowing that clans of bushwhackers populated the hills, Cantrell sent one of his lieutenants to warn the general to stay to the rear—time wasted.

"A general rides at the head of his army," Morgan said. And that was the end of it.

Jarom heard this story and for the remainder of the day fully expected to hear from some cove or fastness the rifle crack that would tumble the general. When he was a child, his father, placing Jarom in a chair next to his own in the parlor, read him *Plutarch's Lives* and *The Iliad*. Though he regarded superstition as the scripture of the cave or cradle, Jarom minded the admonitions of antiquity—how fatal it was, for example, for humans to flout the will of the gods, to tempt them with an assertion of human will, no matter how heroic. "It's the raised nail that feels the hammer," his father said then. Morgan was brazen, was brash, traits that were not insurable.

Before the lieutenant could take his place again in the column, General Morgan showed up astride a magnificent chestnut sorrel named Sir Oliver, a gift from a well-wisher to reward his escape from the Ohio State Penitentiary. Raising his hat in salute, the general passed Jarom, who was riding a skewbald mare named Nancy, going down the open road at a brisk canter. With perfect carriage he went bouncing by, so in tune with the stallion that he seemed some natural appendage. When Captain Cantrell again protested, Morgan dismissed him with a wave of his braided arm.

"I don't apprehend any harm from the enemy just now, Captain. Besides, it doesn't take me long to tire of breathing your dust."

"But, General," said Cantrell.

"But me no buts, Captain, I mean to ride at the head of my men if it kills me."

Hearing this, Jarom suppressed the wish that someone would drop the man from his saddle. Such snootiness tempted the gods. Instead, as the general clopped past, he joined a tremendous cheer that followed him along the column like fire passing along a succession of match heads. Jarom saw such bravado as an omen, later reflecting that this was the last time many of the men would see Morgan alive.

Their destination was Greeneville, a modest assembly of houses and buildings centered on a courthouse square located on the Virginia and Tennessee Railroad. Adding to Jarom's sense of something ominous in the air was the fact that Greeneville was the hometown of the state's military governor, Andrew Johnson, now Lincoln's vice-presidential running mate in the pending election. Tennesseans in Morgan's command, especially East Tennesseans, despised Johnson. Assigned to another brigade, Jarom's regiment set up camp on the Jonesboro road northeast of town. The general personally ordered Cantrell to place his battery on a high hill a few hundred yards from town. Cantrell chose the position well, for from the heights overlooking the street an approaching force could be ushered to oblivion. Jarom knew that Colonel Bradford's Tennesseans camped on the Bulls Gap road at the other end of town and that Giltner had posted his brigade on the Rogersville Road but spread out his men to cover several others on the right flank.

As Jarom later learned, Morgan planned to camp at Greeneville for the night and throw his force against General Gillem's defenses at Bulls Gap in the morning. By two thirty that afternoon all the units had been deployed, all the approaches to Greeneville, so far as anyone knew, were protected. From his perch on the hill where the battery had been positioned, Jarom swiveled his binoculars over the town, the enlarged radii lighting on street corners, windows, the house in which he knew Morgan would be sleeping that night. He trained his lenses on a group of men in the yard behind the house, fixing on the general. Morgan bent over his camp table, studying a map and conferring with two or three of his officers under a tall locust whose canopy showed the first rust of fall. Even his critics owned that Morgan had an uncanny feel for terrain—an instinctive eye for the easiest route or the most defensible position—in the way a good farmer had an intuition for weather. But his antennae had no reading for impending danger. Jarom could imagine Morgan, dipper in hand, oblivious, strolling for a sip of water into the half-dark of a springhouse full of writhing snakes. Such was the loyalty of those who served him that they would have unquestioningly followed, even after they discovered the writhing forms.

The next morning a letter from Aunt Mary Tibbs, dated three months earlier, caught up with him as he oiled and cleaned his pistols with a kit he had bought for a pile of Confederate scrip from a sutler who set up store for a couple of days outside camp. She wrote that everyone in the family was well but that Nether had died of old age—no one knew how old—and had been buried next to his long-dead wife. He lay, appropriately, Jarom thought, near his true love—his bee gums, set up in a stand of locusts on a ridge that overlooked the square miles of woods from which he had harvested his honey. According to her account, the old man simply rose one morning, said he wasn't feeling well, and lay dead by noon. Jarom called up his face as it had been nearly a decade ago, an old man never more at home than in wilderness, a person comfortable in his world as, increasingly, Jarom wasn't in his. Whenever he heard the droning of bees or tasted honey, he felt Nether's presence. Jarom imagined him trekking through some celestial woods, his eyes lifted toward the airways, his ears pricked to detect the telltale hum.

Patterson, his aunt wrote, had gone to stay the winter with relations, a cousin and his family, near Hopkinsville. He talked of finding a place of his own, one where he would not be anyone's burden. The surgeon had sewn up his face, but where the bridge of his nose had been was a cleft that made strangers stare. He seemed, she wrote, some better, on his feet and able to hobble about, tapping his way with a cane. But, sadly, he did not seem to her to have anywhere to go, no destination toward which to direct his feet. After he toppled her favorite vase and upset some dishes, she had to put everything breakable away in the cupboard. She bought him some spectacles with dark glass in them, but he refused to wear them, insisting that he appear to the world as he was—*just as I am*, he had insisted, parodying the old hymn.

Though Patterson often seemed dispirited and out of sorts, occasional zephyrs of warmth kept her hopeful. He told her he longed for spring, when he could sit outside and listen to birds warbling, feel the wind against his skin. One day he even asked her to read from a recent novel, *The Mill on the Floss*, by the British author George Eliot, who, he insisted, was really a woman. Mary Tibbs protested that it couldn't be so, that she'd never in her days heard tell of a woman named George.

But mostly he just moped about, spending whole afternoons sitting wordless at the window he could not see out of, as if he could imagine the scenes that passed there, as a sleeper might construct a world populated by ghosts and invisible beings. She said that for some reason seeing flecks of sunlight on his pants leg had made her cry. Reading *Harper's* to him, she skipped articles that made any reference to battles, but it was battles he wanted to hear about, knowing the war was going badly. Patterson constantly asked after Jarom, but she had little to report. She confessed that she at first felt relief when he left for Hopkinsville but now fretted about him, wondering whether he received enough attention, enough of the right things to eat, enough sympathy if he was blue. She convinced herself she could alter his mood by making him his favorite dish, sweet potato pie.

The weather, typical of upper Tennessee in early September, hung stultifyingly hot and muggy, the air so laden with moisture that people wore as well as breathed it, waves of heat visibly fluting from the dust of the street. Even the crows in flight seemed sluggish, as though accoutered with weights. Merely walking caused horses to work up a lather, and a shawl of mustard-colored dust hung over the road. Patches of chicory, their open florets showing pale cobalt, grew along its shoulders. Chicory had a tint unlike anything else Jarom had seen in nature; where it had spread, whole fields vibrated with a silvery shimmer. Other colors seemed dry and lackluster like leaves of the black locust, spotted with rust. Everything felt overripe to Jarom, oppressively still. The weal where the bullet had hit his hand had nearly healed, leaving only a ghost of proud skin on the heel. Though his fingers sometimes stiffened, the flesh had knitted itself, through nature's help, whole. Well enough for him to hold and fire his pistol without impediment.

Jarom judged from the slant of afternoon light as they reached town that the hour was about four. After unfolding and buttoning his canvas to Frank Owens's to form shelter for the night, Jarom stripped off his shirt and stretched out in some shade at the crest of the hill, eyeing the twitches of sunlight that poked patterns into the shade. On one elbow, for a time he watched the shadows inch across rock formations on an adjoining hill until they turned soot gray. Never completely loosening his body in repose, he worried about the ominous feel of things, the vulnerability one senses in an open space with unseen eyes watching.

Mollie came to him in a waking dream. The two of them were posing for a likeness in a photographer's studio. She held in her lap, bundled in a quilt, their firstborn—a son. She was smiling at him, her arms cradling the tiny head, barely visible in folds that formed a wreath. As the shadows deepened, he lay there until he heard the bell for supper, accompanied by a stream of lumpy storm clouds from the east, rolling in from the Smokies. Everyone around the mess seemed in a better humor, as if the rain they knew was coming would restore them all.

Two days later, he learned in detail how Morgan spent his last hours before Death paid his call the next morning. In his customary quest for comfort, the general had gone into Greeneville to spend the night. He selected a large brick house used as a sleepover by officers in both armies. It belonged to Mrs. Catherine Williams, the mother of sons in both armies, two Confederate, one Union, so men from both armies felt equally welcome. Since one of the two sons in gray served as a major on Morgan's staff, the invitation came as expectation rather than request. Mrs. Williams's conscience, whether bowing to the sentiments of her neighbors or the greater weight of allegiances in her own family, quietly favored the South. But her daughter-in-law, Lucy Williams, made no secret that her hopes lay with the Union army in which her husband, Joseph, held a commission as an officer.

Three stories high, the house occupied most of a block and fronted on a side street near the main-traveled road. In back was a formal garden with roses in bloom. A grape arbor and a hedge of boxwoods ran along the borders, backed by a high plank fence for privacy. Taking advantage of the house's size, three junior officers shared bedrooms on the second floor, down the hall from Morgan's. Around four thirty, Mrs. Williams showed the general to his room, where he removed his boots and stretched out for a nap.

Lucy, characterized as stern-faced and affecting a masculine manner, didn't show up for dinner. When asked about Lucy's absence, her mother made excuses, explaining that her daughter had taken the buggy out to the family farm to fetch some watermelons for the guests. But she hadn't returned, and those who made enquiries after Morgan's death claimed that she rode eighteen miles to General Gillem's camp. There she reported Morgan's whereabouts and those of his men. She pointed out that most of his command bivouacked some distance away along the arteries into town.

After dinner that evening, the general called for Sir Oliver and rode out to inspect each of the camps. Those close to him later reported that he seemed tired, acting fitful and restless, unusually worried about security, as if he had a premonition of something amiss. About eleven o'clock he sent his aides out to check the pickets again, and several interpreted this as another omen of trouble to come. He turned in after midnight, shortly before the thunderstorm, forming all day, descended on the valley. At one in the morning he rose and thoughtfully ordered the house guards to come in from the downpour.

At that time Gillem's column must have been groping toward Greeneville under cover of the storm, using flashes of lightning to guide the men along paths that skirted the picket posts. The rain fell until early morning. About four o'clock one of Morgan's aides awakened him. The general asked if it was still raining, and the aide replied that it had let up a little. Morgan asked him to inform the staff that orders to march at daylight had been changed. Instead, they would move out of town at seven, giving the men time to dry their guns and have a warm breakfast. He then went back to bed.

Unannounced, at dawn a troop of blue riders dashed into town, heading straight for the Williams house. They surrounded the entire block before most of Morgan's men, inside and out, could rouse themselves. On the hill, as he remembered it later, Jarom became aware of the attack when he heard a rumbling like thunder that wasn't thunder. He confirmed his misgivings when gunfire crackled in the distance and steadily moved closer. Then someone shouted the alarm. Some of Morgan's guards jumped on their horses bareback to escape, and others, running for cover, returned fire. Morgan and several members of his staff bolted out of the house toward the stable before scattering. Accompanied by one or two others, Morgan crawled under the only building on the block that did not belong to the Williamses, a Presbyterian church. He attempted to hide because he knew the sentiment among his enemies that he should be shot on sight. There being no clear means of escape, one of the officers with him under the church suggested they barricade themselves in the house to give his outlying troops time to come to their rescue.

"It's no use," Morgan said, "the boys cannot get here in time. This I do know—the Yankees will never take me prisoner again. They'll shoot me first."

Feeling compelled to act, he and three men ran across the yard to the hotel facing Main Street. Hiding in the cellar, he sent Major Gasset to the front of the hotel to scout the street, just as a troop of Union cavalry rode up the alley running behind the hotel. Seeing his opportunity, the major hopped on a stray horse and made his escape, leaving Morgan trapped in the hotel basement. To avoid being cornered there, Morgan and his two remaining companions dived under some grapevines.

When a man in a jeans jacket rode up to the garden fence, Morgan, mistaking him for one of his command, stood up. The rider shouted for him to surrender. After Morgan ignored him, the man in the jeans jacket aimed his long horse pistol and fired.

"Oh, God!" Morgan yelled and threw up his arms, his body pitching forward, falling into some of the grapevines.

The bullet, it was later determined, entered his back inside the left shoulder blade, pierced the heart, and exited through the left side of the chest.

Though Jarom did not see the body until late the next day, he heard that at the time of his death the general wore an old blue overcoat, a pair of parlor slippers, blue trousers, and a fancy white shirt with blue polka dots. Pinned to his shirt was his theretofore lucky Masonic pin. When his murderers discovered that they had downed "the Thunderbolt of the Confederacy," they tore through the fence palings, tossed the body across a horse, and paraded their trophy through the streets.

By the time Colonel Smith ordered Jarom's and the other batteries to shell the cavalry in the streets around the Williams house, Morgan lay dead. Commanding four guns in the battery, Jarom rushed the crews over to charge the pieces. Moments before they fired, Jarom heard a great shout erupt in the street, but he had no idea at the time what it signified. Through his glass he could see cavalry milling around the block containing the residence. His first shot arched high over the town and dropped north of the Williams house, striking what appeared to be a church on the corner across the street. This scattered the cavalry. The second landed short in a vacant lot.

Adjusting the elevations, Jarom placed several shots close to the house, but after the first few minutes the streets had all but emptied, leaving few discernible targets. Through the haze hanging over the rooftops Jarom caught glimpses of bluecoats, a careening horse, and stick men scurrying here and there. Only when Colonel Smith ordered a charge did

Jarom and the rest of the gun crew realize that a second party of raiders had reinforced the first. As a consequence, the initial, almost spontaneous counterattack had been easily thrown back. As combined Union infantry and cavalry assembled to march on Jarom's hill, Graves, arriving, ordered the battery to limber its gun and retreat to Jonesboro.

When Jarom and his comrades got the news, no one could accept Morgan's death. Jarom had seen him only a few hours before, radiant and confident. Then, despite his mixed feelings about the general, he had stayed the impulse to approach and introduce himself, to tell Morgan how much he and the others admired him. A better occasion, he was certain, would present itself. When Jarom first received word, he wanted to believe someone had made an error, that someone had misreported, that someone else had been shot, that Morgan had been captured again, or at the worst, that he was lying somewhere wounded. Dead did not seem possible to him, to any of them. The men under him, some with him since '61, regarded him as a god, exempt from the laws that splintered organs and laid hundreds down in shallow ditches or under trees whose bark had been riven to pulpy shreds.

Though Jarom scarcely knew the man and always felt awkward in his presence, Morgan's death left him stricken with profound guilt. When Morgan exposed himself at the head of the column, Jarom had wished him ill, and this thought haunted him now as the wish fulfilled itself. Morgan wasn't simply someone all of them took orders from and whose peccadilloes and lapses they tolerated or overlooked. For Jarom, Morgan was an emblem of his best self, a father whose approval he and the others fought to win. Most devastating, he felt he had lost a part of himself. As the fact of the general's death took hold, a second wave of guilt passed over him—and, he suspected, many others. How had they failed him? Had the general been shot trying to surrender? If it had not stormed. If someone had checked to see that all of the points of entry were covered. If someone had been suspicious. If someone had stayed awake.

When Jarom saw the corpse, he could no longer deny the fact of Morgan's passing. Jarom saw the body first lying long and pale in a wagon bed, blood on the muddy nightshirt; the second Morgan lay in dress uniform in a polished coffin under a weight of fresh flowers. Jarom knew that something of himself went with him, though he had no name for it; was it spirit, an appetite for life, a will to victory? Or were these qualities he imputed to Morgan because he wished to believe them so? No one serving under Morgan, he knew, would be the same. Nor would the world, which now seemed drained, frayed, lusterless. He did realize finally that it was not the deflated anatomy under the bursting grapes that he mourned for, the bundle of slack flesh thrown over a horse and paraded through the streets, but himself.

Later, after some reflection, he felt more ambivalent about the life and death of John Hunt Morgan, not love but a combination of attraction and repulsion, the same feelings he had toward the father he'd scarcely known. Both had been distant but looming and prominent in their authority. Both, in a sense, played war—more show than substance, more charade than somber calculation and commitment. Yet, these understandings didn't exempt him from feeling the inescapable letdown and vacancy of loss. Another monument, a tarnished monument, had been extracted from the landscape of his life.

When he wrapped himself in his blanket again that night, Jarom couldn't sleep as he tried to reconstruct Morgan's face. He could call up his lanky build, the way the braided hat sat on his head, the triangulation formed by his mustache and goatee, but he couldn't bring back the expressive face, the intensity of the eyes. He knew only that something vital had been lost, someone whose life had affected his, and would still. Instead, he saw Patterson's face uninjured, a pallid smile holding across the now smooth terrain of cheek and bone, light playing across the mouth and eyes, irresistibly alive, irresistibly human. As he lay on the damp ground, the face migrated to Tennessee, to Greeneville, this time wreathed in smoke, a dozen brute horses deviled and staggering under their human freight, stomping clumsily among the vines and bed of irises. *Orphan,* he said to himself, the word coming up unsummoned, orphaned for the last time from his last father.

Before dusk the next day Jarom received orders to return to Kentucky as a courier. He was to bring out men there who had been engaged in guerrilla warfare. Knowing Nancy wasn't up to so arduous a ride, he luckily managed to trade her for a likelier-looking mount, aptly named Pistol. Astride the new mount, over the next eight days he covered a distance of two hundred seventy-five miles, dodging the traffic of wagons and riders by taking back roads and isolated lanes. On the eighth day he was led to Colonel Jack Allen, CSA, the man delegated to come to Kentucky to recruit and organize what forces he could find and send them back to the regular army, in desperate need of more men. Though he knew Jack Allen only slightly, the colonel apparently knew something of him. To give Jarom some authority and credibility, given his youthful looks, Allen commissioned him a captain. Jarom didn't know what to make of becoming a captain at nineteen, had no time to muse on what becoming an officer meant to him.

Events crowded him. In Kentucky he came on more hard news. Adam Johnson had been shot blind at a place in Caldwell County called Grubbs Crossroads. A heavy pall of fog hung over the countryside when Johnson's small band encountered a troop of home guards. During the skirmish that followed, his own men—like Stonewall Jackson's at Chancellorsville—fired on him, a bullet striking his right eye and exiting through the left temple. He had been captured and sent north to a hospital or a prison, no one knew which.

That night as he lay in his blanket, Jarom had an image of John Patterson and Adam Johnson wearing dark glasses, their arms linked as they tapped their way down an unfamiliar street. They followed the clop of a horse on which Morgan was riding, backward. A rush of anger rose up within him, a lust to revenge himself against Patterson's enemies, against Johnson's. One equation formed in his mind: to deprive the deprivers. The army with its rules and orders, it lulls and sluggishness, would subject him always to the will of others. He wanted to fight on his own terms, not those of arbitrary commanders, good or bad. And not in Tennessee, not in Virginia, but in Kentucky, where he knew who and what he was fighting for.

Having returned to Kentucky after Morgan's death, he fell in with a small band of detached Confederates under a man whom he knew only as Captain Alexander. When Alexander was killed in a skirmish near a place called Big Springs, Jarom slipped into another funk. Patterson, Johnson, Morgan, every candle in his life snuffed to darkness. This last death prompted another change of heart. Now he wanted to leave the war behind him, to shed it like molt from a bird with new wing feathers. An inner voice spoke low and told him to stop fighting, to leave the army, to go back home. He'd seen enough of death and dying. Regretting his enlistment, he decided to do what a week earlier would have been unthinkable—to secede from the secession. Nothing would bring Patterson back to him whole, nothing would resurrect Morgan or return Johnson, shot by his own men, a symbol of how the war fed on itself. *That's all,* he told himself, *that's enough.*

He almost acted on this impulse to cut his losses and quit. Almost. He had to decide which direction to take—home, back to the army, or some middle ground between. He chose the ground between, trying to create for himself a zone of neutrality, a kind of voluntary purgatory where he could cleanse his soul and think things through.

He found a place to live in Nelson County with a sympathetic farmer whose name was Pruitt, a widower who needed a hand and asked few questions. For a few weeks he shed his uniform and put on citizens' clothes, some rough work pants and a jeans jacket. He turned to handing around the farm—milking, fencing, patching up a barn that had lost much of its siding in a storm. Pulling things out of the earth, he reasoned, was better than putting men under it. He worked, he ate, he slept. Pruitt lived alone, and Jarom welcomed the solitary life as a respite from the war.

Things went well enough until he visited a church in Bloomfield one day and overheard a woman describe him as a rebel soldier who had ridden with Morgan. The word would eventually reach the ears of federals who recognized no truce and would come for him, sooner or later, but most likely sooner. He knew he couldn't stay at Pruitt's any longer, that some night while he slept or some noon while he rested in the fields, they would take him into custody.

But he had no reliable horse. Pistol, the dappled gray he had ridden to Pruitt's, had come down with the heaves, an ailment Pruitt described as broken wind, a disease of the lungs. Nostrils flared, Pistol suffered coughing bouts and percussive breathing that produced a wheezing noise. He frequently passed noxious wind. Pruitt said the sickly horse needed to be pastured for a time, that chopped carrots and potatoes mixed with his oats would contribute to the cure, and that after a time he would probably recover. When Jarom said he had no time, Pruitt offered to take the horse in trade.

"In trade for what?" Jarom asked.

"Take that one over there," Pruitt said, pointing to a large mare grazing by a billowing oak in the lower pasture, downhill from the barn where they were standing. Her flanks, partially in sunlight, shimmered, the black mane nearly obscuring the face as the neck bent into the grass. When she rose and turned her long head toward them, Jarom saw the blaze along her muzzle; when she stirred, he saw white socks that rose above her fetlocks almost to the knees.

Even from a distance, Jarom could tell that this horse was better than the run of horses he and his companions had ridden, mostly hard-used cavalry mounts, many of them captured, with "US" emblazoned on their haunches.

"I don't have enough money to buy her," he said, "and she's worth at least three of Pistol."

Pruitt shrugged and turned out his palms in a gesture of generosity.

"Take her for your horse and your labor," he said.

"But I don't have enough to make up the difference."

"Take her," Pruitt said, as if trying to rid himself of something he didn't value.

"What do you call her?"

"Papaw."

Jarom liked the name. Pruitt explained that even as a colt she had what he called "the honey tooth." It was the fall of the year and near the house was a papaw, a small tree, almost a shrub. When the tree was in fruit, she would leave her dam each day at dusk and come to the fence, where she would, almost delicately, take the green, sweet, custardy-tasting fruit from his outstretched hand with her foreteeth, slowly working her jaws as if to savor the sweetness.

Before nightfall, Jarom made his goodbye to Pruitt, who forced him to take a few dollars and thanked him for his help and his company. Jarom packed his meager belongings, bundling most of his things in his rolled blanket, and saddled Papaw for the first time. She was docile, accepting his authority, his weight, almost immediately, as though she sensed that where she was going would be different from anywhere she had been. His two Colts he carried in a satchel made of carpet, whose handles he tied to the cantle of his saddle. Then he headed in the direction of Bardstown, the seat of Nelson County. Making some inquiries, he heard reports of a local band of partisan rangers near Bloomfield. Arranging a meeting wasn't difficult, and the next day he made the acquaintance of Henry C. "Billy" Magruder and Sam "One-Armed" Berry.

PART TWO

The term "guerrilla" is the diminutive of the word "guerra," war, and means petty war that is carried on by detached parties. Guerrillas properly may be defined as troops not belonging to a regular army consisting of volunteers, perhaps self-constructed, but generally by individuals authorized to do so by the authority they acknowledge as their government. They do not stand on the regular payroll of the army or are not paid at all, take up arms and lay them down at intervals, and carry on petty war chiefly by raids, extortion, destruction and massacre and who cannot encumber themselves with many prisoners and will therefore generally give no quarter. They are peculiarly dangerous because they easily evade pursuit, and by laying down their arms become insidious enemies because they cannot otherwise subsist than by rapine and almost always degenerate into simple robbers or brigands. Whatever may be our final definition, it is universally understood in this country at the present time that a guerrilla party means an irregular band of armed men, carrying on an irregular war, not being able, according to their character as a guerrilla party, to carry on what the law terms a regular war.

—Government Prosecutor, *U.S. vs. Magruder*

War imbrutes instead of refines.

—Eldress Nancy Elam Moore,
South Union Shaker Village

A POND OF WATER

Something unexpected happens when Jarom and Papaw enter the pond. Off to the left there is a splash, the wallop a bass makes against water, silence a moment, then another wallop. In rapid succession come more splashes, this time like gloved hands clapping. Jarom scans the surface for jumping fish but sees none. Whatever it is, he thinks, must be jumping from the banks. As he and Papaw move deeper in, something closer plops, his eye catching motion but no mover. Not a reptile, not a fish. A diving bird, a kingfish, say, would reemerge from the water.

Then something inside Jarom flashes, and he is at Aunt Mary's again, skipping stones that lie at the edge of the pond near the stock barn. It is early spring, sometime after supper. The grass is awash with dewfall, a first spray of gnats misting the air in feverish clusters. They are nearly absorbed by darkness when the pasture erupts with a dissonance that drowns out the low trill of insects his ear has become accustomed to. Now the air throbs with harsh, hammering noises that cancel other sounds, hushed fidgeting of the crickets subsiding. Patterson says the noisemakers are tree frogs. Aunt Mary calls them peepers, spring peepers.

"They're creatures of peculiar habit," she had said, "lying low during the day to come out at night. They're slow-pulsed, all leg and chest, the bellows of their chests pump little gulps of air that sound like wheezing. Nights, they deafen, filling the air with their ratchetings and love-sick complaints."

Jarom at first guesses that what he hears jumping in the pond aren't tree frogs because these creatures gather a cocoon of silence around themselves. When their zone of solitude is broken, they lob themselves into the water, withdrawing to a safer element. The first that jumps serves to raise the alarm. The others enter on cue as their zones are violated.

When Papaw and Jarom trip the alarm, the first jumps almost at their feet. The splashes take on a pattern, beginning almost underfoot and extending around both banks until the circuit is closed at the farthest end. Though Jarom tries to anticipate where the next one will jump, he cannot detect him, so perfect is their blending. Even the leaps are invisible. Where they land, the water spreads in wide, overlapping ribs. Each time the banks seem cleared, another detonates the silence like a flattened palm smacking a horse's rump. As the message passes, the pauses between slaps lengthen, as if the message has weakened in volume and urgency. Finally, one last straggler bellywhops in the shallows, raising mud clouds above the algae.

Papaw settles into the water, pond ooze up to her thighs, just short of Jarom's boot soles. Uneasy in this second element, her forelegs cut off at the water, she stiffens for a moment, then relaxes as belly and flanks accept the murky coolness. It is hot still, and the heat rises from her back in steamy vapors. As Jarom slackens the reins, she lowers her neck to water. When her muzzle touches, he feels himself slipping against the pommel. To keep from falling over her ears, he tilts his heels in the stirrups and pushes downward. Knees against her sides, he feels the rivulets passing through her gullet and swelling against his calves. As she drinks, air and water become one, perfectly still, the silence broken only by the rhythmic swishing of her tail and the ticking in her mane to worry the gnats.

The pond is not large, no larger than the acutest angle a farm wagon can turn, not half the size of the one in the Tibbs barn lot. Jarom imagines it as a flattened pear, the smaller oval belling into a larger, low for the season and banded with a collar of mud where the water evaporated or drained off. Stringy beards of algae show just beneath the surface, smoky thickets of phosphorescence that seem to him another world dominated by the sickly yellow of overgrown marshes or overripe corn. The water itself is a flat black with an unhealthy cast that carries no reflection.

As he sits locked to that moment, toward the center in the deepest part, a black knuckle protrudes from the surface, shedding almost indecipherable rings that widen across the water and melt into the banks. Like the rotating head of a hawk, this knuckle swivels until it comes to rest on a line with Papaw's chest. Several feet to the left by a clump of cattails, another knuckle appears. Then another off to the rear, to the right, others bobbing up until bullet-sized heads populate the water, a congress of eyes. At first Jarom takes them for snappers, a vat of them, but he knows them at last as peepers, bubble lungs drifting through a rim of light to spy him out.

Something about them troubles him—they make no sound, give

no sign, show no acknowledgment in their creaturely self-sufficiency. To him this signifies contempt. Only their eyes show above water, and Jarom senses that he and Papaw somehow have darkened their horizon, intruded against their light.

He has an impulse to draw his pistol for some practice—to detonate some heads. To do this not so much to humble them into recognition as to shake them from their study, jar them from their witness. Under their gaze he feels uneasy. He comes so close to firing he can imagine the beads of thrown water, the rise and slip-knotting of pond water as it escapes containment for a moment, stretches its sinews into rope, then drops back to it somnolent bulk. He can see featureless heads the size of marbles yanked suddenly beneath his sight or exploding into fragments with a lucky hit, the survivors popping up a few minutes later a few feet away, still taking him in, still waltzing in the slimy dark.

A DAY OF INDEPENDENCE

Jarom made no conscious choice to join the guerrillas. He knew such bands existed, that they had sprung up like crocuses, gaudy and short-lived, in one spot or another over the state. What options did he have? Though he still regarded himself as a soldier, he had no one to report to, no army within the borders of Kentucky to whose muster he could add his name. There was always the thought of Patterson living out his days in darkness, but there was no assignable moment when he made the choice. His allegiances known, his service easily traced, he could not elect to return home and pick up his interrupted life. Barely nineteen, he lacked the confidence and means to elope with Mollie Thomas somewhere west. Neither the Union army nor loyal Unionists bore him any love. Technically, he knew, his own army regarded him as a deserter.

So he entered the small war on the domestic scene almost by default, simply going along with the stronger personalities that carried him as a strong current pulls an oarless skiff. Chance and circumstances brought him to Magruder and Berry and to the stronger will of Bill Marion, who collected others about him in the way of bandits and princes throughout history, their followers attracted less by zeal for some great cause than by lures of adventure, profit, or lawlessness, the undecided submitting themselves to a dominating will. And so Jarom went along, not by choice, but by happenstance and casual momentum.

Counting Jarom, their number came to four, the others being Bill Marion, Sam Berry, and Billy Magruder. They spent the day in Louisville at several saloons celebrating their independence without any serious upset. None of them wore uniforms or other signs indicating they were anything but unaffiliated young men celebrating. Jarom, a little tipsy, felt relieved to be leaving the city where he knew they could be arrested at any turn. Every time he'd seen a bluecoat on the street he had an impulse to shoot the man and run. A mile or so out the Bardstown Road, south of the city, Bill Marion announced he was starving and meant to have some hospitality at one of the big houses that sat on the ridge along the pike.

"I could eat," said Billy Magruder, as if to cinch the matter.

All of them had been drinking since early morning but hadn't had a bite since breakfast. Despite misgivings, Jarom willingly followed the path of least resistance. If Marion had said they were off to congratulate General Burbridge at his headquarters and toast President Lincoln's health, Jarom knew the others would probably have gone along with him. Over the past few weeks with Magruder and the others, he had learned that relaxing was not inactivity but the art of not making any decisions.

Marion turned in at a likely-looking drive, unlatching the double iron gate and waving the others through, remounting and spurring his huge roan stallion. Mirroring the capacity of his owner to manufacture affront at every opportunity, his stallion hooves spewed gravel as he broke into a canter up the drive. Through the trees at the crest of the hill, Jarom could make out the shaft of a white column. Winding up the drive, they followed Marion to a large house behind shade trees that formed a buffer between house and road. It was sweltering hot, sultry and moist as only it can be during summer in the Ohio River Valley. Jarom felt as though every pore in his body was a spigot that purposed to drain him dry. Moisture sopped his shirt. The flanks of the horses steamed, their backs glossy as oiled metal.

Once he entered the shade of the ornamental elms that aproned the front of the house, the air cooled. The breeze stirred, and sweat beads under his broad hat began to tingle and pop. Marion's roan, anticipating a rest in the shade, began whisking his tail from side to side and nickering.

When Marion reached the porch, he slid off the roan's back and knotted the reins to a lilac bush as if he didn't plan to stay long. He clomped up the steps and rapped the butt of his pistol against the paneled door. No one came. He shrugged, eyed Jarom and the others with a silly grin, then rapped again, louder. This time the door opened, and a white-haired citizen in shirtsleeves asked Marion what he could do for him.

"We want some supper," he said, "and we want it soon as yesterday."

Their host, a polished-looking man in his sixties, surveyed the four of them, understandably worried from what Jarom could read of his expression. Jarom imagined what he and the others must look like from his perspective—hair unkempt, sweat stains in the block of his crumpled hat, scruffy shirt in need of laundering, a tear in his pants above the right knee, all of them dusty and rough around the edges. He tried to imagine his own reaction if, old and unarmed, he were confronted by a band of ruffians crowding his door and making demands to be fed, the sharp hooves of their slick-haunched horses poised at the edge of his wife's flowerbed. Jarom concluded that this homeowner, no fool from his appearance, would try to talk or bribe his way free of his predicament. He remembered the story about a fellow, a sheriff it happened, who was asked what he would do if faced by the whole of the band of rogues he was charged with bringing to justice. "I think," he said after due deliberation, "I shall bless them."

"My wife and I are here alone today," said their reluctant host, as if in apology. "The servants have gone to a picnic, and my wife is not in the habit of cooking. I hope you will excuse me."

He stepped back from the threshold and began to pull the door after him, but Marion interposed his boot, at the same time cocking his revolver in a menacing way.

"And we are not in the habit of waiting supper," he said. "We want vittles and want them now, damn you."

The householder quickly knew Marion as a man not to trifle with, for he did a turnaround and began to show his manners. He put on a face that exuded graciousness.

"Light and come in, gentlemen," he said. "We will do the best for you we can."

He seemed relaxed, almost confident now, though Jarom sensed beneath this facade a low, prickly hedge of formality and resentment. Despite his soft words, he stood as if supported along his spine by an invisible rod.

Then Magruder asked if he could feed his horse.

"Certainly," said their host, waving his hands expansively and gesturing toward the rear. "If you take your horses around to the stable, there you'll find plenty of corn and fodder. Use all you like."

Jarom saw the pale cornice of a large, whitewashed stable, visible from the edge of the porch.

"We're obliged," Magruder said with exaggerated politeness and began to lead his horse away.

Before he turned the corner of the house, Marion, considering the need to leave on short notice, called him back.

"Wait a minute, Billy," he said. "Better bring the corn and fodder around here. Let's take the bridles off and turn them out on the grass."

Magruder eyed the carpet of green and nodded. Leaving his horse to graze, Magruder set off to fetch some fodder.

Holding the door open, their host—Jarom never heard his name—summoned his wife, a petite nervous woman whom Jarom suspected of eavesdropping from a room off the hallway, cringing at every word. He led the way down the hall to a large kitchen at the rear of the house. They pulled up chairs around the table, and Sam Berry went on about bands of music and nothing in particular, asking questions in the manner of a schoolteacher, which he'd been for a time before the war. The wife, when she wasn't bustling about the stove and larder, kept stealing glances at the pinned-up sleeve where Berry's right arm had been. She soon had a meal laid out for them—cold chicken, parboiled potatoes, cabbage and onions, fresh-sliced tomatoes. The missus, at her husband's suggestion, fetched buttermilk from a cellar by the side of the house, putting a pitcherful at the center of the table.

"Is there anything to drink?" Marion asked, giving the clabbered liquid a look of scorn. With glasses of well water already before them, he clearly wasn't referring to soft beverages.

"We keep no strong spirits in the house," the missus said, still keeping her composure. She had a Presbyterian look about her, Jarom decided. Not a teetotaler but a person who seldom partook of anything that would alter her somber view of the world and those of Marion's stripe. Her husband rescued the moment.

"My wife does have a few bottles of native wine," he said with a wink. "But she is stingy of it."

"Well, then," said Marion. "Then bring a bottle for us to sample of it."

The old gentleman returned from the cellar with a dusty bottle, which he wiped with his sleeve.

Impatient of opening it and spoiling to make a show, Marion struck off the neck with the big bowie knife that he always carried on his belt. He poured his spring water onto the floor and proceeded to fill every glass with wine. Jarom took a sip of the pale mulberry liquid and found it too dry, but its cellar coolness made him feel refreshed.

After downing a second glass, Billy Magruder simpered and began to chortle. The missus, strained to her limits, started to cry, while her husband, his endurance stretched nearly beyond tolerance, stood stoically, helplessly by.

Marion sipped at first, then glugged down two more glassfuls, including the one poured Sam Berry, who said he'd had enough. Marion ordered the host to bring more wine, and the man returned with two more bottles, again wiping the dust off with his sleeve.

"Now, if I just had a segar," Marion said.

"Sir," the host said, "I have a few in a box. One moment and I'll fetch it." His voice now had a tinge of exasperation in it, a slight raspiness beginning to show beneath the civility.

He left the room, his face pinched in a martyr's smile.

Jarom had the impulse to apologize for Marion, though he felt no sympathy for the host who stood before them, superior, smoothed and polished to the point of glistening. He could picture him in his white sanctuary, sipping his wife's homemade wine from tulip-shaped glasses and bossing the servants about.

In a few moments he came back down the hall, presenting an opened box to Marion, who took one of the brown cylinders, pulled it under his nose to savor the aroma, then twirled it in his mouth to wet the makings. Their nameless host passed the box around, Jarom and the others each lighting up, the low-ceilinged kitchen quickly blueing with smoke. The host began to cough, asking politely if he and the lady of the house could be excused.

"Don't trouble yourself," Marion said, pushing back his chair. "We are just leaving."

Jarom knew that the longer they stayed the greater the risk of attracting notice and causing a ruckus that might result in their being killed or taken.

They rose from the table and trooped back through the hall, a pennant of blue smoke trailing behind. Magruder, having drunk too much, bumped along the wall in the passageway. They found their horses where they had left them. When they mounted, Jarom threw a mock salute to their host, who stood master of his porch again.

"Don't whisper a word of our being here," Marion warned. "If you do, we'll come back and burn this place to the ground."

It took little to convince the host, who said he wouldn't, relieved, Jarom thought, to see these scoundrels about to disappear through the same portal to hell from which they came.

Glancing back halfway down the drive, Jarom could just make him out, still standing in his shirtsleeves on the porch, small under the tall columns and the arc of trees, untouched by anything but the lengthening shade of his massive elm.

Weeks later, Jarom had to amend his impression when he came across an account in *The Louisville Journal* of the troubles their visit caused. For the poor man, a physician, he learned, had a second visit, this one from detectives dispatched from the commandant's office in downtown Louisville. The commandant, a man named Burbridge, was a war hero of Shiloh and, more recently, Cynthiana. For his services Lincoln appointed him military commandant of Kentucky. One of the neighbors reported to Burbridge that the doctor had been harboring bandits. Under questioning at headquarters, he confessed to having entertained a party of guerrillas under duress. The authorities seemed at first inclined to lock him up in the military prison as an example until the poor fellow explained in full the circumstances under which his hospitality had been offered.

And that wasn't their only expedition to Louisville. Late one sultry afternoon a month later, Jarom slipped into the city with Henry Medkiff, stopping for a drink at an uptown tavern on the Bardstown road. At the bar was the usual gathering of loafers and soaks: out-of-work mechanics, draft dodgers, a teamster or two, a drover, a professional panhandler. Most nuzzled schooners of beer against the heat and talked about the most recent doings off in Virginia. Then one of the teamsters mentioned that a person or persons unknown had shot a prominent Union man near Bloomfield. Guerrillas had been sighted in the vicinity but just whose band no one seemed to know. Mention of guerrillas roused a red-faced man at the end of the bar, a know-it-all wearing a faded hackman's cap.

"Mundy's your man," he said with conviction. "If it happened at Bloomfield, you can bet Sue Mundy's on one end of it, yessir."

Jarom tried to hold his anger by calmly continuing to sip whiskey from his tumbler. But the topic caught on, and others named crimes for which Sue Mundy was to blame: two pickets murdered in Middletown, a prize saddle mare stolen, a mail wagon looted near Muldraugh's Hill. In fact, Jarom, though not idle elsewhere, had no hand in any of these.

Taking up the theme, Red-Face proceeded to pour forth a tirade, badmouthing Mundy as a common highwayman, a poltroon, a cutpurse, a jackanapes of anonymous parentage, a polly foxer, an all of all that was base and mean against all that was pure and noble. A spoiler. Still Jarom kept his composure, nonchalantly bottoming his drink and ordering another. On impulse he stood a round for the whole company, including Red-Face. And this seemed to silence the insults temporarily. The topic was about to die a natural death when the hackman caught a second wind.

"I'll wager," he said, slapping a dollar down on the counter, "that any man at the bar is more than equal to Miz Mundy. More equal in all ways but one, and in that Miz Mundy is wanting."

He laughed, and the others joined in.

Jarom felt his fingers tighten around the tumbler until his knuckles blanched and he thought the glass would shatter. Only Medkiff noticed. The rest paid no special attention until he stepped back abruptly from the bar, the rowels of one spur making an ugly sound as they scraped across the foot rail. By turns he stared each of them in the eye, testing to see if anyone would challenge him. No one did, so he slumped back against the bar and took up his drink.

An uneasy minute passed as he gazed at the roomful of them in the mirror behind the bar, and they gazed back at him through the mirror behind the bar, his back to them as he leaned forward, resting his weight on his elbows. The pittings on the mirror's surface gave each object a grimy rash. Dust motes complicated the band of sunlight angling into the dim room through the tall window by the bar.

"Gentleman," Jarom said, speaking into the mirror, "you should be careful when you abuse anybody. I am Sue Mundy."

Having their attention now, he paused for effect. Then he turned, lifting his wide-brimmed hat, the mane of matted hair dropping to his shoulders.

His words hung in the air as the silence wove its invisible cocoon around them. No one wanted to be first to speak. But clearly what Jarom said couldn't be ignored. Everything became suspended, floating like the motes of dust in a closed room with sunlight sprawling across the rug. His revelation caught the barkeep contemplating the crumpled bloom of his towel in an upturned glass. The hackman had the look of doom. Several customers playing parcheesi at the back table began inching toward the rear door. Glaring directly into each face, as if for future reference, Jarom drained his glass and set it on the counter with a tiny clink. The kiss of glass on wood, light as it was, must have resonated in every ear, for the silence seemed reverent. No one moved as Jarom crossed to the doorway and turned to face them again.

"Now you can go down and invite your friends to call on me," he said. "I'll be glad to see any of them who choose to call out the Newburgh road this evening."

Motioning to Medkiff, he passed casually out the door, unhitched Papaw, and rode out the Newburgh road.

SAM BERRY

Like William C. Quantrill, his Missouri counterpart, Sam Berry, had been a schoolteacher before the war. Unlike Quantrill, he had also been a minister of the gospel, or so he told Jarom. For a time he had even lived with the Shakers at a large communal holding of interconnecting farms called Pleasant Hill, located in the highlands above the Kentucky River on the outer rim of the Bluegrass. It seemed an odd fit to Jarom, for he knew the Society of Believers, more formally the United Society of Believers in Christ's Second Appearing, did not countenance violence of any kind and practiced, with some slippage among the ever-erring few, celibacy. Given the pacific teachings of the sisters and brethren, Berry was the last person anyone would have expected to become a soldier, much less a guerrilla. He started his military career honorably enough, joining Company G of the Sixth Kentucky Cavalry, under John Hunt Morgan, at Lexington in October 1862.

Around the campfire Jarom learned that Sam's brother, Tom, a braggart much given to making exaggerated statements, claimed that he and his brother had killed as many men with their own hands as had any men in the Confederate army, excepting, possibly, a few sharpshooters. At any rate, at the time of Sumter, Sam Berry was teaching school in Mercer County at Harrodsburg, the oldest permanent settlement in Kentucky.

From the moment he met him, Jarom saw that Sam Berry was cut from finer cloth than either Marion or Magruder—his manner, his grammar, a certain bemused detachment in his interaction with his comrades. Slowly he began to piece together Berry's history. Watching him as he talked, Jarom could easily imagine him, a graduate of Lexington Normal School, lean and long-faced, not quite young enough now to pass for a student, not quite old enough or harried or haggard enough to pass for a teacher, still beardless, his right arm, which he lost to machinery working in a hemp factory, detached from his body long enough ago that he wasn't self-conscious about the loss. The loss, of course, had pushed him into a schoolhouse. Jarom could picture him standing before a roomful of young scholars, lining out the contents of a speller or going over tables in *Ray's Arithmetic,* one sleeve of his tunic folded and neatly pinned.

He could visualize the class, farmers' antsy sons and docile daughters, pacing themselves toward the moment when the hour told them they were free to quit the precincts of learning. Visualizing his short career as a preacher came harder. On Sundays, Berry told him, he had helped out at the church, occasionally giving a sermon, leading prayers for the sick or otherwise ministering to congregants in his neighborhood. As Jarom assayed him, he seemed too earnest, his face in unguarded moments betraying the slightest irritation, which would bloom later as disillusionment and spite.

War must have come as release for Berry, a prolonged recess, a reprieve from shirt starch and boredom. Berry gave the impression that if war hadn't come, a gold rush or the prospect of adventure in the West would have served as well. As it happened, Berry tried to remain neutral at a time when neutrality wasn't possible, given the deep fissures that divided his neighborhood, his region, into two armed camps. A few months before war broke out, a majority of Woodford County's citizens printed a notice of their allegiance to the Union, denouncing the secession movement. Very quickly the county split—those in the majority who had saved Woodford for the Union on one side, everyone else on the other. When the war started, the county's pro-Union sentiments made it a target of guerrilla raids. Berry thought the severed arm might exempt him from enlisting in either army, might win him status as a neutral noncombatant. After the war came to Kentucky, new acquaintances assumed he had lost it in some nameless skirmish. The death of his sister taught him a fuller meaning of enmity.

Just after Jarom met him, the two of them had their likeness made at a studio in Bloomfield, Kentucky. Berry, a little reluctant to depict for posterity his missing limb, contrived to pose in such a way that he seemed whole, placing the stump so that Jarom's upper body obscured it. For his part, Jarom raised his right hand and cradled it over the empty sleeve, his relaxed fingers acting as a partial shield, contributing to the illusion. Excessively proud of this likeness, Jarom carried it with him everywhere, showing it to whoever would look at it.

In his talks with Berry, Jarom learned Berry was descended from a family with long service in the military, harking back to peat bogs in Ireland for all he knew. For a hundred and fifty years every generation produced a crop of warriors, starting with his great-grandfather, who fought under John Churchill, first duke of Marlborough, in the war of the Spanish succession. His grandfather fought in the American Revolution. His father, Samuel O. Berry Sr., saddled his best riding horse one day and rode off as a volunteer to the Mexican War. After Sumter, he had enlisted as a private in Morgan's Raiders and claimed to be the oldest combatant on record in either army. Though Jarom had never met him, he did know several of the old man's former messmates, and questions after the senior Berry's health became a standard greeting among Morgan's riders.

"And how are you feeling today?"

"As fit as Sam Berry," the trooper would say.

In prison and out, the old man, as durable and lean as the walking stick he carried, stuck with Morgan until Morgan's death at Greeneville.

When asked the secret of his longevity, Sam Berry Sr. had a stock answer: "Pretty music, pretty flowers, pretty women."

Once when someone asked if he wasn't a hundred years old, he became thoughtful for a moment.

"I always thought that when I got to be a hundred I would turn into an old gray mule or go to Utah where I could marry me seven wives."

"What's keepin' you here?" another wag asked.

"The Southern cause," he said. "I can't strike out till we've licked these Yankees."

"And when's that gonta be?"

"Soon," he said, "soon. If the Lord has put up with Yankees all this time, I guess we can stand 'em a few more days."

Sam Jr.'s brother, Thomas F. Berry, had been among the first to join the Lexington rifles when it was re-formed to become the nucleus of Morgan's mounted infantry. A devil-may-care sort, he raised himself through the ranks from private to captain to colonel, claiming during his service to have been wounded sixty times, a claim that no one chose or dared to challenge. William, another brother, had enlisted as a private in Stonewall Jackson's old brigade, rising to the rank of major before dying at Malvern Hill.

The death of Sam's sister, Susan, marked the severest blow to the family's good fortune and drove an otherwise peaceable man to violence. Sam often cited it as the event that changed his life. After the Berry men rode off to war, she stayed behind to keep house and manage the family farm, situated out the Clifton Pike. Though both father and brothers worried about her well-being, she had a stubborn disposition, insisting she could go on living as though in normal times. She pointed out that she had hands on the place to work the fields, two servants to help around the house, and a few reliable neighbors who would look in on her from time to time. A spinster in her late twenties, she had earned a reputation for self-sufficiency. When she stated her intentions, the family relented and left her to her own devices.

"She's one woman who could saddle her own horse," Sam once told Jarom, a high compliment.

With four Berrys in the Confederate army, her family's politics were no secret in the county. In the Clifton neighborhood, sentiment was split pretty evenly down the middle. Life in that remote section of Woodford went on as usual until local papers brought news of the heavy losses at Shiloh and, closer to home, Perryville.

Then, families that had intermarried, shared labor and farm implements, and sat in adjoining pews for generations began to fall out over the death or injury of a husband or a favorite cousin or a brother. The world classified itself into a new taxonomy with two subparts—Lincolnite and Secesh. No luxury of a middle ground or free territory existed now, no individual neutrality for families connected with either side. And every family was connected, most of them closely. As casualties mounted and local rancor and local prejudices gained a purchase, fields full of cattle emptied overnight, tobacco curing in the barns went up in smoke, people sickened from drinking water from poisoned wells. Detachments of home guards formed to protect the property of loyal citizens from raids by bands of guerrillas detached from both armies. Answerable only to the county judge—a staunch Unionist—the home guard units quickly degenerated into bands whose primary motive was the pursuit of vendettas and accumulation of plunder.

So it was not wholly unexpected when, on some pretext or another, a party of local home guards rode out to the Berry farm one crisp fall afternoon. When they clattered into the farmyard, only Susan and a frightened house girl were at home, as the guardsmen probably knew. Knowing them to be up to no good, Susan locked the outer doors. The guardsmen forced their way in, pushed the women aside, and began ransacking the house for valuables. According to Sam, the family possessed an heirloom, a sword his grandfather had captured at Stony Point during the Indian campaigns while serving under "Mad" Anthony Wayne. Inevitably, one of the intruders took a fancy to it. As he pulled it from the wall above the mantel, Susan gamely tried to wrench it away. During the scuffle that followed, someone stabbed her from behind with a bayonet, the long triangular blade entering her right lower back—*her back, mind you,* Sam Berry had said, *her back!*—and lodging in the lower ribs. Realizing things had gone too far, the guardsmen quickly gathered their plunder, including the sword, and left.

When the hysterical house girl recovered her senses, she bolted out the back door and ran for the nearest neighbors. The neighbors in turn rode off for a doctor, who examined the wound and said Susan would die by nightfall. She didn't. Though the blade had penetrated the lower lobe of her liver, she hung on for nearly five days in the most extreme pain, long enough to plead with Sam, the first family member to arrive after the summons, not to take revenge on her murderers but to let things be.

Sam solemnly swore that he wouldn't, then set about sleuthing to discover the names of the culprits. With scholarly zeal, he meticulously compiled a list that eventually included every man who rode in the party, some forty or so.

"But why?" Jarom asked.

"For future reference and disposal," said Sam, not without some irony.

After burying his sister, Sam, who might have described himself as mild and gentle-minded, vowed that his life's business would be to wipe out the attackers for the injury perpetrated not only on his sister but on the wives and daughters of the entire state. What Jarom heard echoed chords in his own private war.

As a first step in carrying out his vendetta, Sam sent word to Tennessee where Tom was recovering from a knee wound received in Morgan's fight with Frank Wolford's cavalry at Cynthiana. Having no trust in the mails, Sam deputized a reliable friend to deliver the message to Tom personally. Tom, when the news reached him, needed little time to decide what he had to do. Though his wound hadn't healed completely and he walked with a pronounced limp, he got leave and mounted his horse, scouring the country for help. He spoke to anyone who would hear his story. He would describe the particulars of his sister's death, wait for the horror and outrage to sink in, then casually ask the listener if he had left a wife or sweetheart at home, a sister or mother. Within three days he recruited fifteen men, two of them veterans under Morgan, on leave while their own wounds mended.

Next, he sent one of them, Billy Magruder, to market at Georgetown to buy forty Colt revolvers and a thousand rounds of ammunition. When the arms arrived, Sam called for a muster, dividing his men into two parties, one of them under Magruder. Taking command of the second himself, he threaded along back roads to the most desolate place he knew, the rocky uplands and wooded bluffs above the deep gorge of the Kentucky, not far from Shakertown, where Sam had lived for a time, as he put it, "apart from the world." In the bluffs, screened by cedars—the primary tree other than scrub that would grow on such thin upland soil—Tom found a place apart from the world, a secluded retreat where he could rendezvous with Sam and the other recruits without worrying about intruders.

Cautious in the extreme, Sam set up camp in a nearly impenetrable woods just north of Dix River where it flows into the Kentucky, a place of spectacle where formations of limestone and fissured cliffs tower four hundred feet over a band of green water. A winding road, blasted and cut into the face of the rock, provided the access down to the river, the road ending at the base of the gorge where rock met water. Too rough, too steep for farming, the land on which his hermitage was situated touched no near neighbors, no village, no main roads. Not even a church existed in the whole section. The woods of the approach grew so dense that horses had to be led. To get to the camp, riders had to dismount, duck tree limbs, and follow a narrow game trail through thickets of sawbriers and coils of thorny smilax. All this was to Sam's liking. Magruder, acting as guide for the combined groups of riders, described these trails as rabbit paths. Even where the men were able to mount and ride, the shanks and undersides of their horses were raked by stickers until they bled. Nearing camp, they heard whistles from pickets and lookouts. Sam saw one posted above the trail in a makeshift deer stand lashed or nailed into the tree.

Sam told Jarom that the camp itself consisted of a single cabin snaggled with vines, a relic of the time when James Harrod and the country's first settlers abandoned their dugout canoes to hew and heave their way toward the broad skies of the uplands. Inside the cabin, located at one end of a failed pasture, Tom found his brother Sam dozing on a bunk of boards, his long legs propped on a splint-bottomed chair, the only other furniture in the cabin's one room. When Tom entered, Sam said his eyes popped open, alert for trouble. Recognizing his brother, he rose and threw his one arm about him in a bear hug. After commiserating over their sister, Tom introduced Sam to the men who'd followed him in, all having scores to settle with the local home guard, which they had come to see as an extended arm of federal tyranny that had reared its ugly head in Louisville.

With variations in detail, each of the wronged men had narratives differing in pattern only in incidental details from the account given by a farmer named George Enloe. A band of home guards burned his house and drove off his stock. They had traveled from a not-so-distant federal recruiting station called Camp Dick Robinson, a place in northern Garrard County named for an ardent Unionist who owned the farm. When Enloe complained to the nearest federal authority, Colonel Jacob at Camp Nelson, the guilty parties beat him and forced him into hiding. Among his friends he vowed that he always paid his debts with interest.

Next morning after breakfast, Sam Berry combined his men with Tom's in a fraternity of free men and bandits that went back to the Celts. Meeting in an informal ceremony of war, they elected leaders from their number and took oaths of loyalty to the Confederate cause. No one was surprised that Sam was elected captain, and Tom, who adopted the alias of Henderson, as first lieutenant, and Billy Magruder, as second. They selected George Enloe, whose mind was a map of every hill and hamlet for miles about, as guide and scout.

Magruder raised a question about how to travel the roads without attracting undue notice. He proposed the ingenious solution of having several men got up in blue overcoats and trousers to act as leads for the rest. They divided into three squads of sixteen to eighteen men, one for each of the main roads out of Camp Robinson.

They calculated everything to the finest degree. Most of the squad would hide in the woods while two parties of two would ride out on the road in either direction to act as decoys, keeping a sharp lookout for guardsmen or federal regulars, but especially guardsmen. Once they sighted prey, tactics would be devised to suit number and circumstances. Large units they would permit to pass like fish through a weir in reverse.

Smaller groups, up to four or five men, would be snared, tried, taken to the nearby ravines or thickets and shot if found guilty. Guilt translated to mean having accompanied the party that raided the Berry homeplace and stabbed Susan Berry. They decided to execute each of the condemned with a ball in the forehead, the band's agreed-upon signature. What they lacked in numbers they hoped to make up in armaments. Each member carried no fewer than four pistols and, where feasible, a sawed-off shotgun. Tom Berry himself carried nearly half his weight in a small arsenal of six pistols and two double-barreled shotguns, firepower that gave him forty shots before he needed to reload.

"Oh, he's a man of mettle," Sam joked. "His only fear is magnets."

The first day was a bust. The second, while patrolling a side road leading to the Harrodsburg pike, Sam's party netted six home guardsmen. After disarming and escorting them to a deserted place out of sight of the road, Sam pulled out his list, which he kept scrolled in his bedroll for safekeeping against the elements. Strangers might take it for a list of deacons or subscribers to some charitable cause. Consulting it, he asked each prisoner to give his name, and Enloe confirmed all were present at the Berry farm on the day when Susan received her fatal wound. They stood, most of them, with their eyes on the ground as if staring at a dropped object that they were afraid to pick up. Ranging from too young to shave to late middle age, they dressed motley; most of them, from the look of their clothes, were farmers dressed in jeans and scruffy jackets of homespun, men not in any visible way distinguishable from their captors. Without ceremony their captors told them to place their hands behind their backs. Billy Magruder came along behind them, binding them from a shank of rope he pulled and cut from his saddlebag. Most of the captives clung to the belief that, though at the mercy of strangers, these strangers would march them off to a camp somewhere or even parole them with a warning to shed themselves of the vocation of home-guarding. At least one had a chaw of tobacco in his mouth and respectfully turned his head when he felt the need to spit ambeer onto the ground. His teeth, Sam remembered, were the color of rainwater in a bucket of walnuts he'd picked and forgotten.

When all were bound, Sam faced them and introduced himself as the brother of the late Susan Lavinia Berry of Woodford County. This drew a sigh from one of the captives. Sam later remembered that another went into a blinking fit, his eyes aflutter in motions like the flexing wings of a butterfly, motions he could not control. Another man fell to his knees, looked to the heavens, a low hum emitting from the hollows of his chest.

"Lord, O Lord," muttered the man with tobacco balled in his cheek, 'Lord, O Lord."

Sam stood before them and looked each of them in the eye, his pistol lowered at half-cock and pointed toward the ground.

"I am Samuel O. Berry," he said, "and I intend to shoot you all to hell."

A visible tremor passed through the six, the kind of shudder a body might produce when thrust into cold air from warmer water, a muscular contraction neither bidden nor avoidable. Sam later told Jarom he recognized most of the men from before the war. They were farmers he might encounter at the hardware or feed store and speak to in passing, along with a layabout or two seen around the courthouse when court was in session and often when it wasn't. The man with the tobacco began pleading for his life, protesting that he shouldn't answer for what the others did.

"Robertson stabbed her," he said, pointing to a brawny, scowling fellow whose face was matted with whiskers that Sam described as resembling a curry brush, his person much in need of scouring with strong soap.

"It was a accident," he protested, "and not one of us saw it coming. We'd never do hurt to a lady. No sir, it's not right."

"Do you know this man?" Sam had asked Enloe.

"Only by reputation," Enloe said.

"Take Robertson and be done with him," said the man, whose eyes started fluttering. "Take him and let the rest of us git home. We never meant her, nor anyone, no harm."

Sam then asked Robertson if the others spoke the truth. Robertson denied stabbing Miz Berry, denied even being at the Berry farm.

"You going take the word of these goddamned liars?" he said. "Why, I haven't even set foot in Woodford County since tobacco setting last spring."

He went on in denial until he saw that Sam stood unfazed. Then he stopped, as though some voice in some recess of his mind had whispered for him to stop, because he wasn't gaining any ground and wasn't going to. He then started on another tack, admitting being at the farm but claiming he had not seen who stuck her.

Sam told Jarom that when the man's hands began to tremble he knew he was getting closer to the truth.

Sensing his advantage, Sam quizzed Robertson, pressing him to cite particulars. After more temporizing, more hemming and hawing, the man finally gave in.

"All right," he said, "I might of been there, but I never meant to harm her but only to give her a little scare."

He owned that, yes, he was standing behind her in the parlor, and that, yes, he might have kind of like pricked her with his bayonet, but he insisted he never meant her any real hurt. Cocking his head, the flutter finally stilling to an anxious squint, he asked Sam with a hint of bravado, for the benefit of the others, what he intended to do about it.

"I purpose," Sam said, "to shoot you like the dog you are and invite the buzzards of Mercer County to sup on your liver."

To his credit, Robertson accepted his sentence with a scowl and spoke no more.

Sam told Jarom that from the first something about the man—the cut of his lips across the grizzled terrain of the wide face, a certain cowering belligerence about him—told him that this man was capable of sticking his sister, amenable to any meanness.

"He reminded me," Sam said, "of a rat snake I cornered once in the stock barn one night after milking. By the light of my lantern I counted lumps of what must have been the cousins or in-laws of every rodent that ever burrowed in my corncrib. Caught as it was, it lacked the capacity to show any guilt because it was doing what nature had determined it to do. So I let it go."

"And Robertson," Jarom asked, "what did you do with him?"

Sam said he signaled Tom, who marched the unlucky six at gunpoint farther down the bluff into a deep ravine whose bottom was a dry creek bed. The rubble of rockfalls over the centuries sloped upward to ledges of rock layered in shadow, a place so craggy and narrow that sunlight shone directly on it only an hour or less each day. Part of the slope was a blow-down, an area where trees had been leveled by a high wind or tornado.

"It was late in the day," Sam told Jarom, "and what trees there were made a fretwork against the rocks. Over one end of the ravine I could just make out little bits of the river below."

They formed the six in two ranks, their backs against great chunks of limestone that spilled from the facings before any of them had been born. The rock faces looked mottled, scabbed with lichen and a yellowy moss.

One of the six, a gangly boy not out of his teens, started to cry. Several intoned prayers to their Maker. Then an executioner faced each of the six, Tom and Sam among them, each raising his pistol at Sam's order and leveling it at his partner. After a brief pause, Sam, his Colt dead on Robertson, gave the command to fire. An explosion convulsed that narrow space, and each of the guardsmen fell, each forehead bored by a single shot. Sam told Jarom he'd waited and watched the tendrils of blue smoke interweave before melting in the still air. Sure finally that none of them yet breathed, he ordered the guardsmen left where they lay. Then he holstered his pistol and started climbing back to the horses, one or two of them skittish from the unexpected reports.

Next day, they resumed their hunting along the roads and captured three more men, shot three more. On the fourth day the whole company assembled on a cliff overlooking the countryside for miles around. From the high point, the landscape, as Sam Berry described it, was a quilt, an imperfect geometry of stobby cornfields broken by little fringes of trees and brush along the boundaries, flatter land where only the ridges were wooded. He described a vista of pastureland with clusters of buildings and tiny wisps of smoke rising over the frozen ground. Here Sam felt the safest since his sister's death, able to take in half the county with his spy piece. He posted pickets and turned the horses out to graze on the sparse leavings of last season's fieldgrass.

Midday, when the pale sun reached its apex, Tom Berry made out sixteen riders inching along the valley road nearly two miles away. Eyeing them through his fieldglasses, Tom thought the cavalcade resembled a file of ants. It contained more men than any group seen since the hunting began. How to exploit the opportunity concerned Tom most. Instead of laying an ambush or attempting to capture a column so long with the usual decoys—a greater risk—he decided to gamble on something bolder and risk all. The whole company would meet the sixteen at some predetermined point. After conferring with Sam and Magruder, he decided on a chancy plan, bold to the point of rashness. Riding at the head of his own column, Tom would greet their captain and divide his men on either side of the oncoming column, springing the trap as he came abreast of their last rider. This sounded plausible enough and played well with the others.

Quickly resaddling their horses, Sam's party formed in two columns and trooped down the hill, picking up the lane that ran along the valley floor. Recognizing timing as crucial, Magruder galloped ahead as scout and gave arm signals to speed or slow the pace of the main party. About halfway to the advancing column Sam said he knew they had been spotted, for the oncoming riders stopped to parley among themselves. They bunched for a time, then came on again. Sam cautioned his men that each should proceed confidently and act the part of home guards with business at some distant destination.

As planned, the first riders met at a stream crossing. Sam hailed their captain, a husky, clean-shaven man astride a preening sorrel. Clopping through the shallows and spurring his horse up the embankment, Sam doffed his hat good-naturedly and went briskly on as though he had pressing business elsewhere. No one exchanged a word. They passed as though the men in both columns were mutes or members of tribes so distant in relations that they shared no word or gesture in common. Their captain, seeming at first a little perplexed, in turn worked his way down the bank and crossed the stream, the big sorrel's hooves poking through the membrane of ice along the edges. Without any obvious reluctance he proceeded purposefully past what he must have regarded as an itinerant troop of home guards. His fifteen men, tense and silent, followed and soon passed down the corridor formed by the two columns.

As their captain drew abreast of the last rider, Sam broke the silence with a shrill whistle. Instantly, the sixteen found themselves covered by revolvers. Some gaped in disbelief, some even laughed. Their leader, recognized by Sam as a combination haberdasher and outfitter in Nicholasville, quickly realized he had been duped. He slipped clumsily off the sorrel and spat in frustration. Even as Sam's men deprived them of their weapons and ordered them to gather under the bared canopy of an elm tree by the side of the road, most of the prisoners still resisted accepting these riders in blue as enemies. Sam, acting as keeper of accounts, efficiently took their names and checked them against his list, as a supplier might check off items on a bill of lading. Nine of the sixteen had been at the Berry farm. Thomas sorted the seven reprieved men from the condemned, not letting on that anything was amiss. Even after Sam explained why the nine were to be shot, several persisted in believing themselves victims of some monstrous joke. Enloe, wielding a long piece of cowhide, whipped the seven lucky ones and deprived them of their horses. Tom threatened to shoot them if they were taken again. Off they jogged down the road, the first shots sounding before they dropped out of sight. Susan Lavinia Berry. Thirty men in four days.

Sam's account of what happened to his sister inevitably put Jarom in mind of Patterson. He felt his own heart brimming cistern-full with hate. The sky ahead he imagined darkened by an expanse of thunderheads, a prospect of storm. Jarom told Sam what had happened to Patterson, the two of them linked in mutual suffering. To Jarom, Susan Berry might easily have been his Mollie or Mary Tibbs, or Patterson. Shooting Patterson had been equally senseless, part of a tragic consummation that impartially maimed and destroyed the innocent as well as those who knowingly undertook the risks.

At first, the annihilation of the thirty sickened Jarom. Though he understood the provocation as well as any and better than most, he felt the punishment was too harsh, knowing that it went against every parable of mercy he'd grown up hearing. Faced with shooting even so conspicuous a scoundrel as Robertson, whose heart was stained with the blood of his victim as surely as his shirtfront with tobacco stains, he knew he could not have pulled the trigger. Could he have shot the scoundrel who blinded Patterson? He knew that he would have squeezed the trigger without hesitation, having pulled it in his waking dreams time after time after time. Still, he knew he could not shoot unarmed men who had meant him personally no harm, not as long as he held some residue of faith in the human species, some notion of guilt that portioned into stations and degrees. He knew that earlier these moral distinctions graded like colors on a palette whose hues and variations covered the entire spectrum. He also knew that as the war progressed these patterns were losing their intricacy and subtlety, that even the primary colors from which all the others proceeded were distinctions dissolving in a wash of violence.

Sam knew he could no longer live in his home county. Having broken his neutrality, he went to Lexington, where he soon enlisted in the Confederate army. He joined Company G of the Sixth Kentucky Cavalry in a regiment serving under John Hunt Morgan. He mustered in as sergeant in October of 1862 when two Confederate armies invaded Kentucky, converging near a little town on the Salt River named Perryville, where a great battle would be fought and lost under the misdirection of Braxton Bragg.

He accompanied Morgan's mounted infantry on the raid through Indiana and Ohio in July of 1863, escaping across the ford into West Virginia with Adam Johnson and several hundred others, including Jarom, whom he had never met. Rejoining the remnants of Morgan's command, he had also been at Cynthiana, escaping again when Morgan's regiments were routed at the town's covered bridge, where Jarom had been wounded in the hand. Like Jarom, Berry came back to Kentucky with Colonel Jack Allen to recruit more troops but stayed home on the appointed day of rendezvous when they were to march back south. He sent word to Allen that he had taken sick but that he intended to rejoin the army when he recovered. Soon after, he met Magruder and took to guerrillering.

HARRODSBURG

Zay Coulter, Ben Froman, Sam Berry, Billy Magruder, and Jarom stopped the stagecoach on the Harrodsburg Pike about five miles outside town, not far from Pleasant Hill where the Shakers fashioned their flat-head brooms and worked their communal farm. The wagon was a Concord, drawn by four horses and controlled by a driver, or jehu, who sat in a box that rocked upon two through braces attached to a standard that ran between the axles. Its compartment, which rode in suspension to cushion the jars of the road, was built of white oak and strapped with iron. Each time he saw one, Jarom imagined its suspended state as a metaphor for humankind, caught between the hardpan of the roads and vagaries of sky, its occupants hoping to ride out the friction without too much injury.

Sam Berry knew the driver, an obliging sort named Billy Wilkinson. A teamster older than the combined ages of any two of the guerrillas, he'd become a "whip of the road" by dint of endurance rather than any crowning skill. To stop the coach, Coulter met him in the right-of-way with a drawn pistol and demanded that Wilkinson halt. While the horses stood in their harness pondering why they'd stopped at such a desolate and unaccustomed spot, Coulter demanded the mail. Wilkinson, hoping to hold back the Louisville mail, told him he could not throw it off the coach but that Coulter could take it off himself if he wanted it so much. He did not mean this as defiance so much as professional protocol, not to seem too compliant with a highwayman's wishes.

Jarom and the others sat their horses while Coulter dismounted and rummaged about the rack on top and the baggage hold on back, pitching down three bags with U.S. stenciled on their canvas. Coulter ordered a soldier inside to come out and help sort the mail, which with scant ceremony he dumped on the roadway. Coulter helped himself to what money he found, discarding bank drafts and other negotiable instruments of no use to them, since they were fearful of banks. When the soldier turned out his own pockets, Coulter found a total of sixty cents.

"Well, it's clear," he said, "that you didn't join for the pay."

More interested in horses, Jarom eyed the team and ordered Wilkinson to unhitch the left rear horse. With neither saddle nor lead, he hopped on its back, put spurs to its flanks, and took a brief trial up the road. Returning, he declared the gelding a poor horse for riding. About this time Sam Berry came up and greeted Wilkinson, asking about several citizens he knew Billy would know, both of them laughing at something Jarom couldn't hear. Then Berry went back to the coach, still containing two ladies, both middle-aged, with whom he struck up more small talk, mainly, Jarom guessed, to allay their fears.

Wilkinson, his own jitters beginning to show, asked Coulter if he could have the mail back when Coulter finished rifling through it. Coulter allowed that he could. Then Froman, who'd looked on in his amused way, told Billy Wilkinson that he would have to turn the stage around and go back to Nicholasville. When Wilkinson asked why, Froman explained that they wanted to use the road that night and that Wilkinson was not to pass until after three o'clock in the morning.

"Fine," said Billy Wilkinson. "That's just fine with me."

Coulter, before things became too convivial, warned the driver that in the future every coach would be burned if guards were put aboard them. Except for the obvious discomposure of the ladies, the robbery came off relatively free of rancor and observable tension. The coach went one way. They went the other.

In less than an hour the five of them rode into Harrodsburg, a place that eighty years before had been a stockade in the wilderness where survival had been precarious, as much from sickness and disease as from the Shawnee and other peoples determined to keep the vastness free of those they described as long knives. Sam Berry, who knew the town as well as he knew any place, directed them to the bank, which occupied a corner off the courthouse square. Though none of them wore Confederate uniforms, Jarom knew the plumes in their hats would immediately mark them as guerrillas.

Almost immediately, they captured two Union soldiers who had been lounging outside a local tavern called Morgan's. Not knowing what to do with them, Berry fetched their mounts and added them to what soon became a procession. In a moment of brilliance, he gave them back their rifles, unloaded, and told them he would shoot them if they discarded them. This increased the size of their party and gave belligerent townspeople additional targets. One of them had the name of Robinson. The other, never asked, never said.

Jarom, his pistol drawn, followed Sam Berry up to the Harrodsburg Savings Institute, an imposing two-story brick building whose doors were closed despite the courthouse clock indicating it was twelve ten, a time when, of a Wednesday, it would ordinarily be open for business. Sam Berry had got wind that the local home guard cached guns there to be dispensed among the loyal. Intent on making a show, Sam threw one foot over the saddle as he dismounted and started shooting pistol loads into the paneled doors. Jarom followed suit and fired two rounds, splintering more of the varnished oak. Not drawing any response, Sam Berry approached the door and gave it a kick. It did not give and clearly had been secured from the inside. Without hesitating, he strode to his horse and galloped up the street while Coulter unhitched his horse from some salt barrels near the porch of the express office.

At that moment Jarom spotted a young woman got up in full skirts and hat, carrying a basket of goods. Having stepped back into a doorway to wait out the storm, she looked like someone out of *Godey's*, proper and resplendent in her Sunday clothes. Something glittered from her mid-region. Lowering his pistol, Jarom went over and politely asked her to show him what had caught his eye. Frightened, unable to look at him, she managed to unclasp the fobbed watch and hand it over. Jarom, his need for bravado outweighing any guilt, thanked her, winked, and slipped both watch and fob into his pocket before she could protest. The watch would be a gift to Mollie Thomas, though he had no notion of when he might be able to give it her.

Sensing he had used up too much time, he quickly remounted Papaw and followed Berry up the street to protect his rear should there be firing from any of the buildings. Sam reined in at the front of a two-story building with "Bowman and Company" lettered across its front. Jarom could just hear him talking to the young woman whose fob and pocket timepiece he'd taken. Animated, she claimed the watch and its fob had been a gift from her deceased father and she must have it back.

"Miss, you shall have your watch," he assured her. "I'll go and get it for you. My name is Berry, and you shall have your watch."

Jarom looked on as Berry continued up the street toward Froman and Coulter. They raised their pistols as though expecting to be fired on at any instant. Turning to look back down the street, Jarom saw five or six men with guns outside a blacksmith's shop. Berry, still mounted, went back to the bank and waited outside. Following, Jarom saw a man come out of his way to speak to Berry, someone who seemed to know him.

"How are you, Tom?" Berry said. "Will you shake hands with a damned son of a bitch?"

"Certainly, I will," the man said, smiling and stepping over to where Berry's horse stood swishing flies with the black knot of his tail.

When Berry laid his pistol aside and reached out his left hand to the man, Jarom noticed that Berry had affixed a line to his stump and tied it round the pistol's grip to prevent its getting away from him.

"The last time you saw me," Berry said to the man, "I was a gentleman. Now I'm a damned thief, murderer, liar, and robber."

The man said nothing but continued to smile, stepping slowly toward the walkway.

Jarom glanced back toward the blacksmith's and counted five men in the open with guns at the ready. Across the street by the engine house he counted four more milling near a fence. As he watched, one of them crouched, rested his rifle barrel on the fence, took aim, and fired up the street toward Berry and him. Berry, now in front of the Baptist church, let out a whoop and fell over the side of his horse like an Indian. He may have been hit, but Jarom felt fairly certain he'd simply advantaged himself with the horse's flesh as a shield.

Jarom looked up the street again and saw a group of men forming a line about two squares up Main Street at the Military Asylum, where the state housed and cared for veterans of former wars, a large brick building that once had been a hotel and spa for those visiting the nearby springs. These against them now weren't regular soldiers but Saturday sportsmen, armed with antique muskets and shotguns as though equipped for a rabbit hunt. Jarom followed Berry, Froman, and Coulter up the street toward the men, who started firing as they approached. Jarom fired back twice and looked around him for cover, moving his horse to the corner where the road turned toward Perryville. About that time he saw Coulter boost himself onto his horse, his pistol leveled at two prisoners with their hands in the air.

The five of them reunited outside the asylum to make a dash up the street and out of town. A spatter of firing started now, but the only visible shooters gathered by the smith's shop, most of them filling the air with balls from shotguns gauged for bagging rabbits, not men. About fifty yards from the shooters, Berry's horse went down, pitching Berry into the dust of the street. Jarom saw him rise to his feet, shaken, dredging up the pistol still tied to the horse's reins. As it became clear he couldn't take both it and the horse with him, he turned it loose and drew another pistol from his belt.

Jarom, still firing at the jumble of men standing in the street, yelled to Berry that he would pick him up, at the same time jerking Papaw's head to the right to bring her around. At that moment Berry ran to one of the two captives, who was looking for a way to break clear but whose horse was whirling erratically in the street. The rider, a hatless man in a dusty federal uniform, still carried an unloaded Springfield rifle. He made an effort to turn his horse away from the firing. From the soldier's rear, Berry came up and poked the barrel against the man's lower ribs. Jarom interpreted this as a gesture to make the man dismount. Instead, Berry fired, so close the man's tunic caught fire, the impact knocking him senseless off the opposite side, his boot still ensconced in the stirrup, his weight in drag so heavy Jarom expected the saddle to wrench free. Coolly tucking the pistol in his belt, Berry went around the horse, whose eyes were bugged out with fright, loosed the dazed man's boot, then managed to grab the horse first by its mane and then by its bridle, lifting one leg deftly over his back. Swinging about, he fired several more shots at the men outside the smithy's before heading down the street that led south toward Danville. As a parting gesture of contempt, Jarom pulled off his plumed hat and waved it at the shooters, then ducked his head and spurred after Berry and the others as they rattled out of town.

A NAME IN THE PAPER

A week later, Sam Berry showed Jarom a tattered number of the *Louisville Journal,* its editor known as a strong Unionist.

"You have a new father," Berry said, amused at himself. "His name is George Prentice. Not only has he created a new name for you, he's created a new sex for you, to boot."

"Lookee here," he said, thrusting the paper at Jarom. "We've entered the papers. I'm a one-armed, notorious character, a desperado, and you're Lieutenant Flowers or Miss Sue Mundy, take your choice."

Flecked with mud and torn in one corner, the paper carried the date October 11, 1864. To Jarom it looked as if someone had wadded it up to start a fire and changed his mind before finding a match. Curious, his eyes ran down the columns looking for the black impression that would tie him to print for the first time in his life. He couldn't locate the item at first and thought Berry might be having a joke at his expense. Then, at the head of the first column, just under "Geo. D. Prentice, Public Printer for the Commonwealth," his eye fixed on an account of the whole affair, starting with the robbery of the stage:

Guerilla Desperadoes in Mercer County

A FEMALE GUERILLA—On Friday evening a band of guerillas, led by a notorious character, a man with but one arm, named Berry, formerly of Morgan's command, attacked the stage near Shawneetown, robbed the passengers and rifled the mail-bags. Mr. James Saffell, the stage conductor, was driving behind the lumbering vehicle in his buggy, and while attempting to make his escape from the guerillas, was thrown from his buggy over a stone fence and badly bruised by the fall. The horse and buggy were secured, but Mr. S. escaped discovery. The cutthroats then proceeded down the road and robbed the toll-gate keeper near Shawneetown of a small amount of funds. After this daring exploit, the band moved in the direction of Harrodsburg, relieving the toll-gate keeper near that place of cash and various articles, and then dashed into the town.

The Savings Bank was honored with the first call. The managers of the institution observed the movement, and hastily closed and barred the doors before the scoundrels could gain an entrance. The robbers fired several shots as the doors were being closed, but no injury was done by the same. Finding they could not force the doors, the guerillas proposed to fire the building but, before they could put the design into execution, the citizens, who had armed themselves and collected to defend their homes, commenced firing on the robber band. The outlaws were taken by surprise, and, greatly alarmed, fled from the town, retreating in the direction of Perryville. Capt. Berry had his horse shot from under him in the skirmish. He sprang to his feet, and deliberately fired at a Federal soldier on horseback, wounding him so badly that he fell from his steed, and, securing the riderless horse, the guerilla commander hastily mounted it, and escaped from the town with his band.

Up to this point, Prentice, as Jarom interpreted what he read, presented an evenhanded account of what had happened, though "desperado" carried a certain sting. He didn't think of himself as a desperado, a desperate fellow. Neither did he regard himself or even Magruder, the man among them who had shed the most blood, as a cutthroat. But it was what followed that captured his full attention:

> One of the peculiarities of this band of cutthroats is the officer second in command, recognized by the men as Lieutenant Flowers. The officer in question is a young woman, and her right name is Sue Mundy. She dresses in male attire, generally sporting a full Confederate uniform. Upon her head she wears a jaunty plumed hat, beneath which escapes a wealth of dark-brown hair, falling around and down her shoulders in luxuriant curls. She is possessed of a comely form, has a dark, piercing eye, is a bold rider, and a daring leader. Prior to connecting herself with Berry's gang of outlaws, she was associated with the band commanded by the notorious scoundrel Captain Alexander, who met his doom—a tragic death—a short time ago in Southern Kentucky.
>
> Lieutenant Flowers, or Sue Mundy, is a practiced robber, and many ladies, who have been so unfortunate as to meet her on the highway, can testify with what sangfroid she presents a pistol and commands "stand and deliver." Her name is becoming widely known, and, to the ladies, it is always associated with horror. On Friday evening she robbed a young lady of Harrodsburg of her watch and chain. If the citizens had not unceremoniously expelled the thieving band from the town, in all probability this she-devil in pantaloons would have paid her respects to the ladies of the place, and robbed them of their jewelry and valuables. She is a dangerous character, and for the sake of the fair ladies of Kentucky, we sincerely hope that she may soon be captured and placed in a position that will prevent her from repeating her unlady-like exploits.

Woman, she-devil in pantaloons, dangerous character, watch thiever—so inventive was Prentice's imagination that Jarom wasn't surprised when Berry informed him that the editor also wrote poetry in the style of sentimental versifying published in *Godey's* and other magazines, whose subscriptions were underwritten mainly by members of what he was too savvy to regard as the weaker sex. His verses regularly rounded out gaps in the gathered copy of his rag. Only a poet or a writer of romantic fiction like Sally Rochester Ford could rival the extravagance of Prentice's fanciful depictions. Was the article simply an extension of Prentice's facility in writing a ten-penny romance? True, Jarom wore his hair long and unkempt. He had no barber, he had lost his comb. His head, his hair, might have impressed someone as a woman's, but the frame it sat on, nearly six feet tall, made him distinctly masculine. Bold rider maybe he was, but only once had he ever got himself up in feminine garb, only once donned skirts as a kind of joke in camp when he became Queen of the May and paraded about on a pony in the spirit of playing a prank.

What puzzled him most was why Prentice seemed so intent on transforming him into a woman. As for Lieutenant Flowers, Magruder gave him the name in jest but also for a practical purpose. Each rider in the band agreed to take an alias to mask his actual identity, although Sam Berry, too well known in Mercer County, made little effort to conceal his. Even former friends he encountered on the street addressed him as Captain. But Prentice's christening Jarom as Sue Mundy was a horse of a different color. Though the alias might afford him some anonymity, he knew it must also have some unannounced purpose, one of more advantage to Prentice than to him. Who was this Prentice? What did he gain by gendering Jarom as a woman? Jarom suspected he would hear more of Miss Mundy if he followed the papers.

Some questions about Prentice produced some facts about his past and where he stood amid the political uncertainties that eddied around the military rule of Stephen Burbridge, the recently appointed military commandant of Kentucky. Jarom could not understand them fully, but he did know that Prentice was a New England Yankee moved south, an ardent supporter of the old Union, though his own house, like the nation's, was divided. Through questioning Sam Berry and others, he pieced together rough sketches of Prentice and Burbridge.

Born in rural Connecticut, Prentice could read the Bible or any text put before him by the age of four. He went on to graduate from an Eastern college. A Whig, he came to Kentucky to write a campaign biography of Henry Clay to support the senator's aspirations to become president. Though Clay did not go to Washington as the nation's chief executive, Prentice wrote so well he was invited to edit a newly founded paper, the

Daily Journal. His wife, a native of Louisville, became the mother of his four children. She entertained regularly and soon had a reputation as a socially prominent hostess. Two of their children, a boy and a girl, died young, probably of cholera or any one of a number of afflictions that plagued the river valley. Before her own death she made no secret of her allegiance to the South, nor did her remaining sons, both of whom joined the Confederate army. Clarence, the first to enlist, rose to the rank of colonel. The other, William, rode with Morgan's Partisan Rangers until he was killed in September of 1862 during one of Morgan's raids in fighting at Augusta, Kentucky, a small town on the banks of the Ohio. Tragically, a friend mistakenly fired the minie ball that killed him, confirming Jarom's experience that bullets play no favorites. Prentice, Magruder informed him, had little use for Confederates but neither did he cotton to the radical Republicanism of Burbridge, the most powerful name in the state.

Stephen Gano Burbridge was a native of Georgetown, one of the satellite courthouse towns in the Bluegrass that ringed Lexington. He graduated from Georgetown College and the Military Institute at nearby Frankfort, the state capital. At the time the war started, he owned a large plantation in Logan County, not so far from Mary Tibbs's Beech Grove. Though trained in the law, he farmed until the outbreak of war, when he organized the Twenty-sixth Kentucky Infantry for the Union, and was commissioned a colonel at the age of thirty. Having shown his valor at Shiloh, he became the commander of federal troops in Kentucky when Braxton Bragg invaded in 1862. He served in Mississippi during the siege of Vicksburg. For his bravery at Cynthiana he won the commendation of President Lincoln and the rank of major general of volunteers, a promotion that led to his appointment as military commander of the District of Kentucky in August of 1864.

Armed with power to subject the state to martial law and effectively write his own rules, Burbridge issued orders that eventually stirred the resentment of even the staunchest Unionists. As Berry explained it, President Lincoln had fueled dissension by suspending the writ of habeas corpus. Burbridge started his reign by ordering that any Confederate sympathizer within five miles of a guerrilla incident could be arrested and banished from the state. But his most infamous order was number

59, which provided that four guerrilla prisoners would be shot in reprisal for each Union man killed by guerrillas. In Louisville, Burbridge had executions carried out on the commons just west of the Nashville Depot, usually holding them on Sundays to draw the largest crowds. He had a problem because demand exceeded supply. Few actual guerrillas were at large, and those few were devilishly difficult to catch. His solution was to substitute regular Confederate prisoners of war. Of the more than fifty executions Burbridge approved, many were of duly enlisted Confederate prisoners of war, many of them Kentuckians. He was quickly condemned as a fanatical murderer and became the most dreaded and hated man in Kentucky. Going a step further, he decreed in October that all irregular bands of armed men disconnected from the rebel army were guerrillas and that no guerrillas would be received as prisoners.

"It doesn't take much guessing," Berry said, "to get a sense of what Burbridge means by no prisoners." His raised a phantom pistol in his hand and clucked off a shot.

As for the name Sue Mundy, Jarom supposed that someone at Harrodsburg had used that name to describe him. He'd never heard it before, either at Shaker Run or any of their stops outside the town. Prentice's statement about the name being well known was another fabrication. Never before, so far as he knew, had it appeared in print, at least in reference to him. Why would this stiff-necked old pen-pusher, Union down to his buttons, create a Sue Mundy? The only thing Jarom could imagine was that news of the more distant war had become so grim or so humdrum that Prentice wanted to season it a little and had come up with an ingenious idea. Why not put a brassy young woman in the saddle and sell more papers? Jarom also divined that the whole thing might be politics, something he had no head for. What he did know was that reading about himself in the paper sent an electrical current through him, both thrilled and scared him.

Over the next few days Berry the schoolteacher concocted an elaborate theory. Reduced to its essentials, the theory was that Prentice created Sue Mundy to embarrass the Union authorities, whose presence in the state had become intolerable to many loyal Kentuckians. Burbridge's murders swayed public opinion against the Union presence. Even if his tyranny won few converts to the Confederacy, it gained sympathy for victims whose only offense was loyalty to the Lost Cause. Shooting the innocent alienated Burbridge from both sides.

Scanning the papers when he could get them, Sam Berry began to record Burbridge's excesses and report them to Jarom. A firing squad executed two nonguerrilla inmates of the military prison for the murder of James E. Rank. On July 22, guerrillas killed a Union man named Robinson at Eagle Creek in Scott County. Burbridge responded five days later by sending a detail to shoot some so-called guerrillas in retaliation. On July 29, Burbridge sent two alleged guerrillas from prison in Louisville to be shot close to home at Russellville, where a certain Mr. Porter had been killed resisting some guerrillas. On August 12, four prisoners were shot at Eminence in Henry County. A firing squad executed three more in Grant County on August 15. And so on. The shootings of four men—Wilson Lilly, Sherwood Hatley, Lindsey Duke Buckner, and M. Blincoe—especially galled Jarom because they faced a firing squad near Jeffersontown in retaliation for the shooting of a Union soldier "by Sue Mundy's guerrillas." A damnable lie. Similarly, near Bloomfield, another party of executioners shot James Hopkins, J. W. Sipple, and Sam Stagdale for the killing of two Negroes by Sue Mundy's men. Also a lie. Neither Jarom nor anyone he knew had committed these murders. Prentice, not one to confirm or deny what lay in his interest, found it convenient to attribute any unexplained death to Sue Mundy.

The most shameful of the executions, in Berry's estimation, occurred at Frankfort, the state capital. In November, Burbridge's executioners singled out four Confederate prisoners in custody at nearby Lexington to be shot in retaliation for the shooting, presumably by guerrillas, of Robert Graham, a loyal Union man who lived in nearby Peaks Mill, a small community on Elkhorn Creek about nine miles from the capital. The unlucky prisoners, their names drawn by lot, were John Long and S. Thomas Hunt, both Kentuckians from Mason County, Elijah Horton of Carter County and Thomas Lafferty of Pendleton County. Hunt, a twenty-year-old lawyer from Maysville described as a "striking specimen of manhood," had been captured on his way to enlist in the Confederate army. Berry pointed out that technically he was a private citizen. Lafferty was in his seventies, emaciated and in poor health as a result of his confinement. The authorities held him for his unpopular political views, but he was never an active combatant. Berry knew nothing about Horton and Long except that they had been guilty only of opposing the federal intervention in the affairs of sovereign states south of Mason and Dixon's line.

Jarom later learned that the drawing had been made at nine o'clock of the evening preceding the executions. One officer drew slips of paper from a hat held by another man in blue. A third dutifully recorded the names as they were read out to give the procedure a greater semblance of legitimacy. Not one of the prisoners knew what the drawing meant, but a sanguine few believed it signified exchange or perhaps some special privilege. The prison blacksmith soon resolved the mystery. Jailers, as each prisoner's name was called, ordered him to place his right foot on an anvil so that shackles could be riveted to each ankle. The shackles were attached to a long chain, at the end of which was a forty-pound ball. Having one's name called, it became clear, was no privilege, but for good reason no one announced the penalty.

Early next morning, guards marched the four condemned men, who toted their balls on their shoulders, onto a railroad car and transported them by locomotive to Frankfort, about twenty-five miles away. Once in the capital city, wagons conveyed them through old Frankfort, crossing the covered bridge into South Frankfort, depositing them finally in a pasture belonging to a prominent farmer named Hunt. The guards gave them shovels and ordered them to dig their graves, four shallow trenches in a low corner of the field. Fifty soldiers stood by to prevent any irregularities, twelve of them designated as a firing squad. Reverend B. B. Sayre, a local schoolmaster and minister of God, offered up a prayer at the prisoners' request.

During the prayer Lafferty somehow managed to slip the weighted shackle over his thin ankle. With head still bowed, Reverend Sayre pronounced the amen, and the prisoners began rising to their feet. At that instant, Lafferty, amazingly agile for a man of his years, whirled and bolted across the pasture toward a stone fence that ran along the farm lane. A few seconds elapsed before the guards, taken by surprise, got off a shot. By that time Lafferty had reached the stone fence, nearly thirty yards away. Just as he mounted the top, poised to jump, several balls struck him, and he fell dead on the other side.

The rest of the execution, as reported to Jarom, went as planned, as though to compensate for the botched work of the executioners and the pluck of one old Confederate who should have been at home dandling his grandchildren. One of the prisoners asked for a sip of water, said to have been dipped from one of the graves. Without any more delay, guards blindfolded the survivors and lined them up before the shallow pits. Someone gave the "ready, aim, fire," and they dutifully fell a few feet from their graves. Even among the executioners few took pride in the work done that day.

Berry returned to Prentice's reasons for discrediting Burbridge. "Finally," he said, "the guerrilla scare is a means of discrediting Burbridge's standing as a soldier and his judgment as head of the military in Kentucky."

He explained that the war dividing the country had become as personal and as vicious in Kentucky as in Kansas and Missouri. Each day the papers contained reports of guerrillering, some shootings and robberies occurring in the very suburbs of Louisville.

"Whatever's in the pot," Berry said, "it finally boils down to politics."

Prentice, he explained, wanted to check the influence of Burbridge, his fanatical crony Reverend Robert Jefferson Breckinridge, and the rest of the radical abolitionists in Kentucky. Prentice also opposed Lincoln, and though he played up the crimes of guerrillas, he was careful not to be too critical of Burbridge, a powerful man who could censor the newspaper. Although he bridled at the order not to accept guerrillas as prisoners of war, he jabbed Burbridge with indirect hits that he could manipulate and defend. Many loyal Kentuckians also opposed freeing slaves, especially without remunerating their former owners. The Union initiative to recruit Negroes into the army stirred even more resentment. Berry told Jarom he'd heard that even Colonel Frank Wolford, Morgan's old nemesis, had been arrested for making a speech in Lexington opposing the induction of Negroes. "The people of Kentucky," Wolford declared, did not want to "keep step to the music of the Union alongside of Negro soldiers." Such a practice, Wolford said, was "an insult and a degradation" to Kentuckians "for which their free and manly spirits were not prepared."

So why create a Confederate guerrilla in the form of a woman? Because a mere woman fighting and ranging the state with no fear of capture proved that those commanding the army of occupation were incompetent and should be replaced. Berry, who had a touch of the poet himself, described Prentice's desire to undo Burbridge's harsh policies and remove Burbridge himself as "treading with a lighter step." Whether heavy step or light, Sue Mundy became the means by which Prentice portrayed Burbridge as a bungler and a fool.

Sue Mundy. On the one hand, Jarom had no objection to the name, especially since it kept his real name from the public eye. However, he resented deeply such characterizations as "practiced robber," "scoundrel," "cutthroat."

Jarom took Prentice's references to his being a woman less as a threat to his own manliness—his boyness?—than as an affront to his character. He liked to wear his hair long. Was it true that an individual's essence and vitality, like Samson's, resided in his hair? He didn't know. The feminine cast of his features, his whiskerless jaw, he could do nothing about. Did he feel an attraction to men? No, not in any sexual way. He had fantasies about having women constantly, though unlike Magruder and Sam Berry he did not resort to the company of whores. Often he tried to imagine Mollie Thomas, and other attractive women who crossed his path in country towns and farmsteads, nude. Yet Prentice kept playing up his identity as a woman, like a cat that toys with a captured mouse before killing it.

Beneath the playful surface he recognized Prentice's savvy and calculating nature. Prentice the teaser, he was sure, was Prentice the fox. He himself never encouraged the story that he'd impersonated a woman. Nor had he got up as a woman to pass through the lines and spy among the enemy. Perhaps there was truth to the rumor that the name originated with a young woman of easy reputation in Nelson County, an Amazon with unruly long hair who Jarom was said to resemble but had never seen. Who called him Sue Mundy first? He neither knew nor cared, but he suspected that it was Prentice, and that the name caught on with others, except his comrades, who continued to call him Jarom.

Nor did he appreciate Prentice's wit, though Sam Berry was of the opinion that the man had mastered the art of invective and innuendo.

Prentice once boasted that he filled his editorial quiver with quills of all sizes, from those of a hummingbird to those of an eagle. Jarom began to keep a little collection of Prentice's quips and puns, placing them between the leaves of an old account book he found discarded along the road near Bloomfield. Sometimes during a lull he would take them up. Most appeared during the fall in numbers of the *Louisville Daily Journal.*

Many think that it makes no difference on what day of the week a man dies, but we confess that we shouldn't like to die of a Mundy.

You have been an awful girl, Sue, we must say. You have killed so many persons, of all colors, that no doubt white, yellow, and black ghosts haunt you continually, the black ones coming by day because black doesn't show at night.

Our journal may bring you and your fellows to justice and thus be to you and them not only a newspaper but a noose-paper.

Sue Mundy, the she-guerrilla, who murders people for pastime, is said to be unmarried. There's a nice opening for some enterprising young rebel.

A Kentucky correspondent of a Richmond newspaper called Sue Mundy "a great woman." She is not very great now but she may be by and by.

Sue Mundy is reported to say that she won't marry any man. We guess she is reserving herself to marry Satan. The poor devil will have a hard time of it. She will broil him on his own gridiron, butter him with his own brimstone, and turn him on his own pitchfork.

We fear that we can't make a bargain with you, pretty and gentle Sue. Still if you will name time and place, and promise not to have any improper aims at us and not to look through other sights on getting a sight of us, in short not to be at all snappish toward us, and not to frighten us, as ghosts are said to be frightened by a cock, we may meet you and talk matters over with you confidentially. Abstemious as we are, we would rather accept the contents of one of your pilfered whiskey barrels than those of your pistol barrel. We would rather feel the wadding of your bosom than your pistol wad. We would prefer to see all the stock you have ever "lifted" rushing furiously toward us rather than behold your Colt's stock lifted at us. We should be almost as willing to see the nipples of your bosom as the nipples of your fire-arms. You may drill your troops as thoroughly as you please, but please don't go to drill a big hole through us.

And so on and so on. Prentice suffered fits of punning and created his own folklore about Jarom marrying the devil, endlessly inventing what he hoped were clever gibes to amuse and indoctrinate his readers. Prentice's jeering flights of fancy amused Jarom in one mood, irked him in another. He thought the old editor finally an author of dark fables. When he read one to Magruder, never seen reading anything, Magruder vowed that by God he could stop it by replacing the flow of ink with the flow of blood.

"Just how do you propose to accomplish that?" Jarom asked.

"Well," Magruder said, "I'll just ride to Louisville, find the damn newspaper, and shoot the son of a bitch. There will be as many to rejoice as will mourn. They may say the pen's mightier than the sword, but mighty few are willing to put it to the test."

———————————

A LEAKING ROOF

While in a crossroads store near Lebanon Junction the third week in October, Jarom found Sue Mundy in the news again:

> *Louisville Daily Journal*
> October 17, 1864
> SUE MUNDY AGAIN—HER ATROCITIES—A correspondent, writing from Jeffersontown, in this State, under date of October 14, furnishes some details of the operations of the outlaws under Captain Berry in that vicinity. We published last week an account of their depredations at Harrodsburg.

After passing Conley's toll-gate, the outlaws started from their camp in Spencer County, twelve miles from Jeffersontown. A number of citizens on the road were met, halted, and robbed of their valuables. Mr. Finley was knocked down and relieved of his watch and money. Abraham Fink was robbed of a fine horse and all the money on his person. Mr. and Mrs. Haller, Mr. Phillip and lady, Mrs. James Goose, and others, were treated in the same cavalierly manner—halted on the highway and robbed of their purses and valuables.

Up to this point, Jarom felt the account, though inaccurate in a few particulars, generally recreated the incident with as much fidelity as one could expect of someone who hadn't witnessed the events.

For Jarom and the others, robberies had become standard practice as they encountered strangers on the road or stopped at isolated farmhouses. He knew what he did was wrong, that no one who had brought him up would approve, that it was against everything he had heard for a lifetime of Sundays. But he also discovered that the turbulent world in which he lived lacked a compass, that it was a lost world, that the times in which he lived were such that the darker half of man's nature overbalanced the lighter. So he had no quarrel with what he read on paper, the words that gave voice to much of what had happened and only a little of what hadn't. And so he read on, knowing that the words evinced no badge of pride or act of generosity but only a world in which creatures struggled to annihilate other creatures whose only difference to sight was the tint of dye used in their clothing, blue or butternut:

About eight o-clock in the forenoon, the marauding gang, with Berry and Sue Mundy at its head, dashed into Jeffersontown, and took forcible possession of the place.

A negro boy, belonging to Mr. Vernon, was mounted on a horse, armed in the most complete fashion, and rode with the gang. He stood guard over the horses in Jeffersontown while the scoundrels were scattered about the town engaged in robbing the people. Sue Mundy dismounted at the Davis house and had her canteen filled with whiskey. The negro recruit had learned the duties of his vocation, and in the coolest manner imaginable, he relieved a number of his Ethiopian brothers of their pocket change. The outlaws had captured a Federal soldier along the road and retained him as their prisoner. After plundering the town, guerillas mounted their horses and departed from the place, moving on the Heady road.

They proceeded to a dark ravine in the woods of Mr. Joseph Latherman, where a halt was ordered, and subsequent developments proved that they murdered their prisoner in cold blood.

The discharge of firearms was heard by several parties residing in the vicinity, but they were ignorant of the cause. A short time after the reports were heard, Mr. James Simpson, on his way to Jeffersontown, was met in the road by the outlaws and robbed of twenty-seven dollars in money. He observed that Sue Mundy's pistol was empty, and the fresh stains showed that it had but very recently been discharged. While Mr. S. was being robbed, this she-devil was engaged in reloading her revolver. She pointed the muzzle at the breast of Mr. S., and smiled with fiendish satisfaction at his embarrassment, as she capped the tube of each barrel of the cylinder. After being released, Mr. Simpson rode directly to Jeffersontown and related his adventure. He was informed, that, with the prisoner in Federal uniform, the party numbered eight when in town. He met but seven on the road, and was positive that no prisoner accompanied the outlaws.

The Citizens at once surmised that the soldier had been murdered, and, following the trail of the guerillas, they approached the dark ravine, and found that their worst apprehensions were only too true. The day had passed, and the moon looked calmly down from a cloudless sky.

The dead body of the prisoner was discovered. He was stretched upon his back, and the rays of the moon fell softly upon his cold, white, upturned face, bathing it in a ghostly light, adding a strange, fearful power to the ashen hue of death. His body was marked by five pistol-shot wounds, and two deep stabs, as if made by the keen blade of a dagger. All the circumstances go to prove that the murder was committed by one hand, and that hand was Sue Mundy's, the outlaw woman, and the wild, daring leader of the band. By a record in a small memorandum-book found upon the dead body, it was learned that the name of the murdered man was Hugh Wilson. Upon his person was also found a letter, dated Mt. Vernon, Illinois, and presumed to be from his wife, as it commenced with "My dear husband." She wrote in an affectionate manner, and spoke with loving fondness of their pleasant home and the little darling ones who "sent love to pa." This letter, from the home of his love, and written with so much tenderness, was found in his bosom, pierced by balls and stained with the crimson blood that gushed in warm life-torrents from his heart. A new mound has been heaped in the little graveyard at Jeffersontown, and there the murdered soldier sleeps.

After the perpetration of this cold-blooded fiendish outrage, the outlaws rode directly for their camp. They were pursued a short distance by a party of mounted citizens from Jeffersontown, but without effect. Sue Mundy, the tigress, seems to be abandoned, lost to every kind, womanly feeling, and, exulting in scenes of blood, leads her desperate followers on to the perpetration of the most damnable outrages. Her many atrocities will be remembered, and we trust will be the means of bringing her to the gallows.

As he read Prentice's accounts, Jarom understood why others described him not only as a poet but as a talented prosecutor, a man who knew that words could turn events to advantage. Prentice knew how to milk the emotions of his readers, with both castles of sentiment and barbs of contempt, with quips and subtleties of tongue. In his description of the shooting he ignited his readers' prejudices, calling Jarom a tigress, a committer of outrages.

But Prentice couldn't know entirely what he hadn't witnessed, for reporters could only write about what others saw, more often about effects than causes. Jarom knew that no one conspired to kill the prisoner. Though killing him had been likely or even probable, the prisoner himself made his death a necessity. As they moved along a shady defile south of Bloomfield, the prisoner managed to pull Ben Froman's carbine from its scabbard and hightail it into the wooded slopes of a ravine, which, as the paper stated, probably belonged to Mr. Latherman. Catching everyone off guard, the prisoner succeeded in escaping before anyone had the presence of mind to shoot him. But he had misjudged the terrain, as it happened, fatally. Backed into a cul-de-sac, he had no choice but to fight. Dismounting where the ravine ended in shelves of rock that formed what had been a waterfall of a dried-up creek, he took refuge behind a large fallen rock as if daring Jarom and the others to come after him. Most of Jarom's party wanted to leave him be, but Coulter, his instincts aroused, insisted they root him out.

The seven of them, three newly joined, fanned out to come at the fugitive from different directions. By the time Ben Froman scaled the leaf-strewn bank and circled behind the lip of stone that formed the waterfall, it was over. Darting from tree to tree in the desperate man's line of sight, Sam Berry drew his fire, the bullet slapping the bark of the locust tree he stepped behind. As soon as the report sounded, the others rushed forward. Not having the makings with which to reload, the prisoner, a feisty little man in whose mouthings Jarom detected a trace of brogue, began to curse and swing his carbine about his head as though bereft of his senses. In an act of perverse chivalry, Zay Coulter put away his pistols and went after him with only a knife, working in close under the swiveling stock of the carbine to prick, then stab, the frenzied Hibernian.

When the stock of the rifle clipped Coulter's shoulder and rolled him defenseless on his back, Jarom and Berry intervened to slow the berserker with pistol loads. Rising, Coulter closed in for the kill, twice stabbing the thrashing prisoner, who managed to keep his feet but staggered as though drunk. Then, backing against a tree, he slumped against its trunk and slid to the ground lifeless. Admiring his pluck, no one touched him further or stooped to rifle his belongings.

Jarom remembered the story Mary Tibbs told him about the neighbor who noticed a leak in the ceiling of his porch. One day while this neighbor sat under the eaves during a spring shower, a drop of water filliped him on his forehead. He thought nothing about it until the next time it rained, and he discovered a small puddle on his porch floor. This time he said to himself that he ought to get out his ladder and climb up on his roof to tar the leak, but it might have been too dark or too cold or too pretty a day for house repairs. And before long it came winter, and snow accumulated around Christmastime. He noticed when it melted that the leak had spread and the whitewashed wood around the leak had turned the lime green of decay. That next spring, he finally put up the ladder and took some patching to plug the leak. When he stood on the spot, his leg slipped through the punky sheathing, and he scuffed up his shin. The point, Mary Tibbs drove home, was that by the time he got around to tending to what started as a drop of water, the underside of the roof had rotted, not to mention the floorboards that he also had to replace.

"So what do you think he did then?" Mary Tibbs asked.

"Did he build a new house?" Jarom asked, with a little archness.

"No, he had to hire a carpenter to lay down a new roof," Mary Tibbs replied, "spending more than he had to set it aright. Afterwards, he checked that porch each time it rained. A wet dog print was enough to send him off for the ladder."

Jarom considered the number and extent of his own leaks, his own moral failings. Especially killing. He took no special pleasure in it. Taking the lives of strangers was war's work. But he knew he'd moved from fighting for a cause in which he believed to fighting for the sake of fighting—robbing strangers, executing anonymous enemies, practicing acts of meanness under the guise of continuing a guerrilla war where armies had failed. He had a rare moment of self-reckoning, a sober weighing of the moral scales. He could find a few justifications, primarily the gratuitous shooting of Patterson, but that excuse was wearing thin. He could cite commendations as a soldier, acts of selfless bravery, but he also recognized that he had changed, that he no longer fought under any flag but that of self-gain and violent whim. Could he change directions? Could he mend his own roof? He felt that he had become who he was through slow stages; maybe he could work his way back. He hoped the porch was not too far gone to think of mending it.

PILGRIMAGE

Coming out of this reflective mood, on impulse Jarom paid his long-contemplated visit to Patterson in Hopkinsville. He awoke one morning with Patterson centered in his mind. Telling no one, and with almost no forethought, he threw a saddle onto Papaw's broad back, filled his canteen and packed a little food, and lit out toward the southwestern part of the state. He dressed in his best suit of clothes, hoping to pass as a factor if authorities stopped him. Traveling mostly at night, he slept or read during the light hours. In a vacated house he found a translation of Victor Hugo's *Les Misérables*. Transferring his attention to France in the early decades of his century, he absorbed himself in another life in times as troubled as his own. For the much-abused Jean Valjean he felt great affection and kinship, recognizing in that good man struggling to evade police inspector Javert a fugitive, unjustly persecuted, relentlessly pursued.

For two days he passed along unimproved country roads, possessed by the prospect of seeing Patterson again. Did Patterson still hold something of his old zest for life? What had he found to nourish his restless mind? Could he get around on his own? Had his injuries reduced him to a shadow man? In a kind of trance he dreamed of several versions of his reunion, meeting after so long the person who knew and brought out the best in him. In one half-waking dream doctors by some medicinal magic restored his sight, Patterson's eyes blinking under the glare of rediscovered sunlight. He imagined what the two of them would do together then, venturing somewhere far from the war, maybe sailing to Brazil where they would ranch and step the fandango with raven-haired senoritas. As he came closer to his destination, his visions sobered as he prepared himself to meet a broken Patterson, a man ruined and shattered beyond all salvaging.

Without encountering a single uniform, he arrived without mishap at the outskirts of Hopkinsville on Tuesday, almost two days to the hour after leaving Bloomfield. Laid out around a small but elegant courthouse, the town had an economy centered on marketing tobacco, though it had several mechanics' shops and a large tannery. Jarom counted the spires of six churches rising above the rooftops. It was a neat and flourishing place that did not seem much affected by the war.

Finding Patterson was his next task. He knew that Aunt Mary Tibbs had placed him at the home of a widow, a needy but caring woman of her acquaintance who took in boarders. He had only to ask the first storekeeper he met to learn where Patterson lived. How many blind men, after all, could be living in a town of sixteen hundred residents? Tying Papaw to the tine of a rusty iron fence, he walked up to a modest house a block off Hopkinsville's main street, where the storekeeper told him a blind man lived in a rented room.

A sallow woman, in her thirties he guessed, opened the door and introduced herself as Mrs. Kittridge. Yes, she said, there was a Mr. Patterson living under her roof. As if anticipating he might imagine her asking how he'd learned her address, she explained that all the neighbors knew Patterson, were accustomed to seeing him on the streets he'd evidently memorized, walking with a silver-knobbed cane given him by the woman who had brought him there over two years ago, a Mrs. Tibbs. Jarom told her he was kin to her and to Patterson and had come to pay his respects. She said she supposed that was fine and would take him to Mr. Patterson's room. On the way, she confided that her guest was a man of regular habits and that she was pleased to have him in her house.

Then she knocked on a closed door at the rear of the first floor and announced to Patterson that he had a visitor.

Jarom wasn't prepared for the Patterson who sat by an open window listening to the noises of the street. He'd sunk in on himself, his shoulders slouched, his long legs dwindled to sticks, a paunch in his middle. Dark glasses with lenses the size of dollars covered much of the area of his wounds. Tiny white scars nicked his cheeks and forehead, discolorations that would never fade. Some device that fleshed out, at least covered, the wrecked nose. He tried not to look at it.

"Here's an old friend come to see you," the widow said.

Patterson slowly straightened in his chair, turning to face his visitor.

"It's me," Jarom said, and reached for his hand to shake it.

Patterson slowly lifted himself to his feet. When his hand failed to rise, Jarom stepped closer.

"It's me," he said, "Jarom."

Patterson, as though struck dumb, slowly showed signs of reviving. At last he spread his arms and Jarom stepped into his embrace, the first time he had hugged any male in this manner. Patterson threw his arms about Jarom, choked by feelings Jarom had never witnessed in him, in any male.

Patterson asked him to draw up a chair and started asking questions. Where was he now? What was he doing? Was he still fighting with Morgan's old command?

Jarom summarized everything from the killing of Morgan to his taking up with Magruder and Berry. He described his life in Nelson County and the daily risks that had begun to form his routine, a life that added the randomness and violence of the soldier's life to spells of hibernation and hiding out. His lost personal identity, his lost citizenship, deprived him of ordinary rights and pleasures, of walking carefree down a street, not having to keep vigilant for anything around him out of the normal.

Widow Kittridge brought them tea on a tray, and Jarom self-consciously balanced the cup and saucer on the knee of pants he had worn in a dozen shooting scrapes in central and southwestern Kentucky.

After sipping his hot tea, the cup cradled in his palms, Patterson opened up a bit and described the half life he lived as a blind man, restricted to the barest necessities of warmth, food, and shelter—a life of privations. He said how lucky he had been to find lodging with Mina Kittridge. Her husband had been counted among the dead at Antietam fighting under another Kentuckian, General John Bell Hood, but she held out the hope that one day he would simply reenter her life, turning up when she least expected him. She gladly kept Patterson company, in the evening reading him the books that Aunt Mary sent. During the days Patterson hung around wherever he could listen, making friends with several veterans who no longer fought in the war and welcomed the obligation to look after him.

Afraid of the answer he would get, Jarom had no heart to ask the only question he wanted answered: was he happy?

After he described the directionlessness of his own life, he asked Patterson what he should do. Patterson sat in his chair and faced the window, musing, as though he could see into the future. He sat for a long minute before words came to him, his hands still steadying the drained cup.

"Quit," he said. "Put up your guns. Leave the service, leave off guerrillering and make a new life for yourself. Make a tame life in the wilds, where all you have to fear is Indians and grizzly bears."

"Just up and desert?" Jarom asked.

"You can only desert an army," said Patterson. "You're riding with men who are marked. For them there is no going back. Or for you if you stay with them. You're riding with wolves."

"But I can't just cut and run," Jarom said. "There's a price on my head, and the federals would never let me live in peace, not in Kentucky."

"Then go west," he said. "Pick up and go west. Go where there is new ground, new geography, new faces, where the war is just something talked about in the papers. Go where nature is still wild but you can limit your fighting to enemies you can recognize, to Pawnees and Fox and Sioux."

"Will you come with me?"

"Don't be foolish," he said. "I can hardly find my way to the privy out back."

"Will you come with me?"

Patterson sat sightless in his chair before the window, vague dronings and eruptions of the world outside drifting up.

"I am always with you," Patterson said.

And Jarom knew he had been dismissed, that wherever he went and whatever he did, it would not be with Patterson in any form other than that which he could conjure in his mind's eye.

After a lunch that Mrs. Kittridge served at her spare but adequate table, after hugging Patterson once more as though he might never again see this man who had fathered him into adulthood, Jarom said his good-byes and was off, traveling east, not west.

~~~~~~~~~~

NANTURA

On the night of November 1, 1864, Jarom accompanied Sam Berry and five or six others when they raided Nantura Farm in Woodford County. Located two miles from Midway and comprising about fifteen hundred acres of prime bluegrass, the farm bred race horses and contained some of the most celebrated racers in the state, including Longfellow and Ten Broeck, well known among those who followed the turf. The farm had been the property of Adam Harper, patriarch of a family long prominent in that section. From the papers Jarom later learned who occupied the house when he and the others came. Adam Sr. and his wife had died several years before hostilities commenced but were survived by four siblings—Betsy, Jake, Adam Jr., and John, all of them unmarried and living at the farm, all home at the time. Berry selected this particular farm to raid because he knew the Harpers as strong Unionists with prime horses. He also knew they had little use for any of the Berrys, especially since the war divided the county and put them on opposing sides.

Following Berry's instructions, Jarom and the others surrounded the house, a comfortable frame dwelling with porches on every side. After they found their positions, Zay Coulter clomped up the porch steps and rapped on the front door, demanding something to eat. By way of explanation, he said he and his men were soldiers on their way out of state to rejoin their units. Adam Harper hospitably opened the door. When he saw the men before him rigged out as guerrillas rather than uniformed soldiers, he let out a wail and started to retreat down the hall in search of a firearm to defend himself. Jarom still stood on the porch when someone, probably Coulter, shot the old man. A scream from upstairs told them that others occupied the house, and more shots followed, fired inside from the upstairs hall, some from an upstairs window. Jarom heard a crash and a tinkling of glass before the first shot from the upper floor, fired a minute or two after those from the hallway.

Zay Coulter, never a zealot in any contest of arms whose outcome was uncertain, thought it prudent to leave and hastened the others to their horses standing restive in the yard. Jarom hopped up on Papaw and drew his pistol to get off a shot should a target appear. As Sam Berry grasped the Texas-style horn of his saddle to pull himself up, Jarom saw a flash from one of the windows. Half in the saddle, Sam Berry gave a yelp and fell back onto the gravel drive, the breath knocked out of him.

"I've been shot!" he yelled, grabbing his hip just below his right buttock.

The reins ensnared one of his long legs, and he was trying, with little success, to kick himself free.

Seeing the danger, Jarom hopped off and dragged Berry out from under his spooked horse, picking up the reins, which had come loose. At first, Jarom thought the bullet had struck the horse too, which might have accounted for Berry being bucked and thrown to the ground. When Jarom saw the horse still standing, he knew it could still bear weight and likely transport Berry to safety. Acting by reflex, Zay Coulter raised his horse pistol and emptied it in the general direction of the window from which the shot was fired. The shooter must have been hit or scampered for cover, for the shooting stopped. Jarom and Ben Froman each put an arm under Berry's shoulder and lifted one foot to the stirrup and swung the other over the horse's back. They hoisted him on upright to center his weight in the swag of the horse's back. More screams came from the house, and Jarom half expected a troop of armed men to burst outdoors and loose a volley on them. Before remounting Papaw, he fit Berry's boots into the stirrups and had him clasp the horn of the saddle, telling him to hold on, that they were on their way to safety. Taking up the reins of Berry's horse, a trim roan more settled now, Jarom escorted Berry, hand still clamped to his buttock, down the drive and into the moonlit lane.

When they had ridden far enough from the Harper farm to feel safe, Coulter stopped at a house belonging to one of his drinking cronies, a part-time farmer and full-time bootlegger named Hayes. They half-carried, half-dragged Berry into the house and laid him out on the floor, removing his boots and pulling off his blood-soaked pants. Coulter, the most experienced with gunshot injuries, examined the wound while Jarom held a kerosene lamp over the bared skin. He saw a rash of birdshot that stippled the area just below the pelvic bone. Though he noted inflammation and a loss of blood, it appeared that nothing vital had been hit. Under the skin the birdshot festered like blackheads. Coulter told him that he required a doctor's hand to extract any shot that did not work its way out and that he should swab the wound with rubbing alcohol or, lacking that, whiskey, to prevent infection. The news relieved Berry. Zay Coulter kiddingly told him not to plan any running or trekking or dancing until the wound healed completely, that it would be tender for weeks, and that he would feel as though he'd aged decades overnight into an old man with a limp.

"Moving," he said, "will be slow as victory."

Not a week later, over the protests of the surviving Harpers, General Burbridge invoked order 59 and ordered a lot cast among Confederates imprisoned in Lexington. A detachment conveyed the losers to the Harper farm to be shot in retaliation for the death of Adam Harper. Three of the four who drew the fatal lots were young and healthy. The fourth, a pale youth in the final stages of consumption, was sickly and disabled. In an act of compassion—foolhardy to Coulter, noble beyond reckoning to

Jarom—the sickly man's brother, also a prisoner but unaware what lay ahead, took the lot of one of the other prisoners so he could look after his brother. They left Lexington and the guards escorted them along the Leestown Road to Midway. Not one of the four knew why he had been singled out until their executioners fetched them to the fatal spot.

On the way, the head of the party got word that the Harpers would not sanction shooting prisoners on their land, so he determined to shoot them in Midway. The guards drew the unfortunates up at a spot near the train depot and forced them to form a death line. The officer in charge, heeding his superiors, read the execution order then summoned what citizens he could gather by the depot as witnesses. According to the account Jarom later read in the *Midway Sun,* one of the victims emitted a hideous shriek at the instant the soldiers fired. One moment the innocents stood in sad communion, the next they lay sprawled and broken under the smoking rifles. A sorry spectacle, the paper called it.

The manner of their interment attracted notice too, for their executioners buried them where they fell in a hastily dug trench only eighteen inches deep. The guards arranged the bodies in a row side by side, then threw a blanket and shovelsful of dirt over them. When they finished their grim work, the executioners remounted and returned to Lexington. Local citizens sought and were given permission to remove the bodies, place them in decent coffins, and carry them to the burying ground, Jarom later heard. They even took up subscriptions to erect a stone over the graves. The stone they underwrote had an eagle with spread wings cut into it. Beneath the wings, they added an inscription:

RETALIATION
M. Jackson
J. Jackson
G. Rissinger
M. Adams
SHOT AT MIDWAY, KY., NOVEMBER 5, 1864
by order of Gen. Burbridge

Jarom recognized in these shootings the actions of brutes, a plumbing of new depths of depravity among those of his own species, among those who professed to walk in the ways of God and peace to preserve the Union. He felt his face clenching up, and he fought the impulse to cry when he finished reading the account. He also felt a strong inclination to smash something, smash anything—to break it into bits.

MAXWELL

Six days after the raid on Nantura, Jarom rode into the town of Maxwell in Washington County. This time twenty others accompanied him, all bent on a mission of mischief and profit. This time someone among the riders, probably Zay Coulter, fired his gun as a means of gaining people's attention. The first man who stepped into the street thought he'd come out to shush some drunken soldiers. On second look, he reconsidered. Undisciplined and dressed in motley, the horsemen could not be regular soldiers. He ran back into his house, rousing the inhabitants with a cry that could be heard up and down the street. "They are guerrillas!" he yelled. "Guerrillas!"

Tying Papaw to a rail, Jarom followed Coulter and two or three others through the front door of the apothecary, ordering those who had retreated to the back room to show themselves. Coulter stood with his back against the near wall, pistol raised.

"You God damn sons of bitches!" he yelled. "Come out of there, God damn you!"

No one came out.

"You God damn sons of bitches," Coulter yelled again, "come out of there! Do you two men intend to come out? Do you think you can resist twenty-five soldiers?"

Three men meekly emerged from the unlighted back room—one who identified himself as Perkins, a druggist; another who called himself Boseley; and a third named Walker, a store clerk. Coulter, in no mood to exchange pleasantries, quickly got down to cases.

"Give us your money," he demanded, approaching the nearest, pistol in hand. Jarom watched as Coulter felt about the man's pockets smartly, drawing out a roll of tickets of some kind and a pocketbook.

Without hesitation the other two pulled some greenbacks and change from their pockets and placed them on the counter. While Coulter kept his pistol leveled, Jarom helped himself to whatever he fancied, rooting through the drawers and behind the counter. Scattering some papers that lay on the desk, he lifted a blotter under which he found some treasury notes and what appeared to be a California gold piece. He took them, though money meant little to him so long as he had enough for dinner and incidentals such as horse feed. He didn't think about the long term. A saver he was not.

Then, for some unexplained reason, Coulter started cussing Walker, the clerk, a harmless-looking man who wore spectacles and for whom cringing seemed as natural as breathing. Coulter somehow got it into his head that this ineffectual man had written a pamphlet against guerrillas. The man denied it, saying he knew nothing of it, that he had never heard such a thing in his life.

For answer, Coulter scattered more of the papers around as if to find the offending pamphlet and confront him with it. Magruder went back to the room at the rear where the clerk slept and rummaged around his bed, finding a pistol under the covers. He cocked the pistol and came back to the front room where he pointed it at Boseley, who begged him not to shoot. When druggist Perkins intervened and started pleading for Boseley's life, Magruder turned the pistol on him, stuck it in his side, and pushed him across the room.

"God damn you son of a bitch!" he said, "I intend to kill you anyhow."

Perkins then appealed to Coulter, who was standing behind the counter taking it all in, and Coulter finally intervened.

"You God damn son of a bitch," he said to Magruder, "put that pistol down, God damn you, and let that man alone."

Magruder stiffened, and Jarom could feel his anger, but he lowered the pistol, easing the hammer until it rested harmless. He slipped it into his pocket and strode out of the room. Jarom climbed upstairs and helped prize open a wardrobe, taking some jewelry and silver secreted inside a trunk. Pulling the casing off one of the pillows, he stuffed the valuables into it. All of them, as Jarom saw it, took what they wanted, so why shouldn't he? Going back downstairs, he found Berry behind the counter on the medical side. For some reason the door of the counter would not open.

"God damn it," he said. "I can't get it open."

After trying again to strongarm it, he gave up, sticking his foot through the showcase with an awful crash, and everyone began to help himself to whatever struck his fancy. Berry, moving gingerly from the flesh wound he suffered at Nantura, took up a quantity of knives, most of the pocket variety, from what the clerk described as a fresh supply from Louisville. Someone had knocked Boseley in the head and blood runneled down his face.

Then Coulter demanded of Perkins some whiskey. By this time the druggist was visibly shaking.

"I've not got any," Perkins said.

"You God damned old liar," said Coulter. "I know you have, and I want some of that good whiskey you keep for medicinal purposes."

Perkins went out to find a bottle and glass. After a minute or two, he came back and poured Coulter a generous drink, probably praying that would be the end of it.

Before he could drink it, Magruder, who had returned from his prowl through the building, spoke up. "Make the God damn son of a bitch drink first himself," he said, as if Perkins might have tried to poison him. Jarom remembered reading about the Borgias in far-off Italy, who rid themselves of every obstacle to their advancement with poison. Perkins, certainly, was neither so clever nor so devious.

Several began passing the glass around, and Jarom took a drink, his first of rye whiskey. As it hit his throat, he felt as though someone had placed a hot poker on the back of his tongue. He nearly gagged from coughing.

Magruder and the others laughed, and he made a note to himself to take this firewater down in a more manly way, knowing now its power to burn. When Berry said it was time to leave, Jarom took up his pillow case. Coulter had Perkins refill the bottle and swaggered out grasping it by the neck.

But Maxwell, which was not unlike a dozen similar forays, wasn't what made an impression on him. Next day about dinnertime they stopped at a tall, unpainted farmhouse to muster something to eat. The house stood along a desolate stretch of road out from Hustonville. Maybe the owners had seen them coming, maybe they were off on errands—a barn raising or a corn shucking. Tobacco stood in full leaf, nearly ripe enough to cut, and might in some way account for their absence. Whatever the reason, no one seemed to be at home. In the larder Marion found a cache of homemade wine and helped himself, passing the unstoppered greenish-black bottle over to Jarom. There were only three of them now, and Berry had gone up to the second floor to see what he could discover. As Jarom stood swirling wine around his mouth, he heard a scream upstairs. Marion, taking everything in stride, told Jarom he'd better go up to see what devilment Berry had got himself into. Climbing the stairs, Jarom could hear commotion from a room at the end of the hall.

Gun in hand, he stepped in through the open door and saw Berry struggling with someone on a bolstered bed. Pants down to his ankles, he was hunched over a brown woman, a housekeeper probably left to watch after things, her bare legs thrashing as Berry, his one good hand still gripping his pistol, did his business with her. To Jarom, the pistol meant Berry had threatened to shoot her if she did not stop resisting. The wide unfocused eyes, the flaring nostrils in that tortured face, arrested him. His back to the doorway, Berry didn't hear him enter, but the woman, nearly hysterical, stopped screaming when she saw him standing there, expecting the worst. Jarom had never seen such terror in a human face, features twisted in such pain, the eyes dilated in fear. Her skin was the color of caramel.

Not until he'd finished and put his pistol aside to hike up his breeches did Berry become aware that Jarom had entered the room. Unrattled, speaking to him as though he had known all along that Jarom had been there, Berry asked if he wanted a turn, pitching a quarter on the bed as payment.

Caught off guard, Jarom felt a strong impulse to run, to bolt out of the house and take to his horse and ride until both were faint with exhaustion. Instead he told Berry that he would be outside with the horses. He turned on his heel and hurried down the hall, anxious for the whole hideous moment to be erased from memory, at the same time knowing he would carry the image for the rest of his days.

Jarom, who had never had congress with a woman but dreamed of it constantly, was revolted. The image of the wracked face would not leave him, though afterward the woman had pulled down her skirts and curled into a heaving ball on the bed, subdued now, whimpering with fright.

Where was the pleasure? he asked himself. What he had imagined as lovemaking now seemed an exercise in pain, an ordeal, a struggle of battling forms that tokened torture more than it did pleasure. Witnessing the gyrations of Sam Berry's white buttocks on the bed was the closest he had come to unraveling the mysteries of copulation, the act he'd heard bragged and whispered about since before the war. He'd never worked up nerve or desperation enough to visit one of the daughters of joy who followed both armies and sold themselves in tents. Like nearly every soldier he knew—even, he suspected, the religious Estin Polk—he'd stimulated himself when stirred by desire and found relief, but he'd never been on such terms of intimacy with anyone, had never seen a couple joined in such a knot.

Later, as they headed back toward Bloomfield, Berry asked Jarom if he was all right. Jarom said he was but spoke not another word as Marion and Berry chattered along the road until the three of them reached their billet for the night. And then all Jarom would say was that he would see them in the morning.

That night, lying in a stranger's bed, he couldn't sleep. Listening to a dog bark in the distance, he realized in a flash of intuition that he was a hunter, that all of them were hunters. Old Nether hunted for bees, Estin Polk for the face of God; Marion was fueled by the desire to reduce the world to lifelessness, Magruder by the greed of the dispossessed, Berry with lust that somehow compensated for his lost arm. Morgan, hunter of another ilk, strove for acclaim or honor or some basic fulfillment of a craving to be about in the world and thought a leader. Patterson he wasn't so certain about. Patterson's old wanderlust was a medium of conveyance, not a destination. What he searched for, impeded by blindness now, neither of them might ever know. His own quest? He didn't know, though he was beginning to believe it might be for survival. He did know that now he was a hunter hunted.

CALDWELL

Magruder found a tailor and tavern keeper in Bloomfield named Tinsley who agreed to make gaudy suits for the group. Berry politely but firmly declined the offer, saying he reckoned the clothes he had on suited him well enough. From the same bolt Magruder and Tom Henry selected black velvet. Jarom picked his from a quantity of red wool, giving instructions to trim it out with a tinsel fringe on the sleeves and breeches. Tinsley tailored jackets in the roundabout fashion with gold lace and staff officer buttons or brass buttons stamped with the Kentucky state seal—two men shaking hands, one in a coonskin cap, the other, obviously more citified, in a cutaway coat. *United we stand, divided we fall.*

The suits were ready in early November. Tinsley charged them double the regular price because other guerrillas had left him high and dry. Everyone willingly paid, not wishing to jinx themselves with stolen clothes.

Marion tricked himself out in a gray sack coat with yellow stripes and a low black hat from which protruded the speckled feather of a pheasant, the hat set off with a tassel of yellow and black. Around his neck he wound a red and white comfort, giving him more color than the others. Around his Magruder was wound a victorine, a long ladies' fur piece that Berry said was properly called a tippet and was named after the queen of England, who wore them in winter and set the style. On the first night wearing the new outfits, they began painting their faces in Indian style and added long horsehair wigs that gave them the look of troglodytes.

Though Magruder insisted the outfits cowed and intimidated their enemies, Jarom interpreted his as a combination playsuit and declaration of exuberance and devil-may-care. To Marion, their outfits signified that no quarter would be given, no prisoners taken.

One overcast morning, not long before noon, a band of twelve of Berry's group were returning on the Bardstown road from a scout near Pitt's Point, a village situated at the junction of the Rolling Fork and the main Salt River, nine miles from Shepherdsville in Bullitt County. In the village, they took what they wanted from the stores. At one of the two merchandising establishments Magruder picked up an item of gossip: Edward Caldwell, whom both he and Marion had known since childhood, had come home to visit his dying father. The store owner shared this intelligence, Magruder suspected, to get them off his premises and out of Pitt's Point. Magruder saw this news as an invitation to proceed on a second adventure and serve up some revenge. Since no one knew the way exactly, they pressed into service a guide, a farmer named Pastle, who said he could take them.

Caldwell had come home on furlough from the Fifteenth Kentucky volunteers, and Magruder especially hated Kentuckians of his acquaintance who had enlisted in the Union cause. Four of them—Marion, Magruder, Tom Henry, and Jarom—along with their guide formed a squad and broke off from the others at the appropriate side road to make their way to the Caldwell farm, arranging beforehand to catch with up the rest of the party at the abandoned iron furnaces near Belmont; whoever arrived first was to set up camp. The five of them rode in a mizzling rain that worked into their new suits, only Tom Henry having thought to bring his poncho. Jarom worried that dampness saturating the material would cause the colors to run and give off a stink of mustiness.

The party reached the Caldwells' near suppertime. Located about two and half miles below Shepherdsville, the house stood at the end of a wooded lane on top of a rise that sloped down to the Salt River. The house in sight, they dismissed Pastle with a warning not to tell anyone what he had seen or done. The guide lost little time in getting shed of them. Then they debated whether to tether their horses so as not to announce their coming. Jarom thought it a good idea, but Magruder overrode him, saying those inside the house would never hear them for the rain.

As they approached, lighted windows in the house indicated the family was at home. With no preamble, Magruder walked up the porch steps, pistols drawn. He pushed open the front door and found the family seated solemnly in the darkening parlor, a man about twenty, a boy in his middle teens, another still younger—all obviously brothers, differing only in size and small details of physiognomy. The boys' mother sat at one end of the table.

The first to realize their peril, Mrs. Caldwell screamed. Then her three sons, George, Edward, and the youngest one, whose name Jarom never heard—none of them with weapons at hand—realized they had been caught helpless.

"Where's your husband?" Magruder demanded.

"He died not an hour ago," said Mrs. Caldwell, "of his sickness."

"Just keep your seats," Magruder said, "or he'll have company soon."

Jarom knew she was upset, noting the red around her eyes, a quavering in her voice.

Only Edward and the pinch-faced Mrs. Caldwell had risen from the table on which the dishes held the remains of their supper—plain food, plainly served. The two seated glowered. Mrs. Caldwell, still glaring, took her seat again, but Edward, looking from face to face of his captors, remained standing.

While Magruder kept everyone at bay with his pistols, Marion and Tom Henry explored the house, ransacking the bureau for money, searching the cupboard for silver, ripping and tearing sheets off the beds in sheer joy of destroying what belonged to their enemies. Tom Henry came into the room sporting a nearly new military overcoat. Jarom, curious but not feeling much acquisitive, went along to see what plunder they might find. He heard Tom Henry open a door off the main hallway. "Hey," he shouted to no one in particular. "Come lookee here."

Jarom went over and peered through the open door. Inside on a makeshift trestle table lay a dead man dressed in a suit of Sunday clothes, a white cravat under a beard that half covered his face. He lay on his back, hands at his sides, his skin pale and waxen. His eyes had been shut as if in repose, his hair slicked and combed over his broad forehead.

Tom Henry came back through the door and spoke to Mrs. Caldwell. "Ma'am, what was your husband's name?" he asked.

"Benjamin Franklin Caldwell," she said. "He was known to his friends as Frank."

"And what was it that took him?" said Tom Henry.

"He came down with a fever," she said. "Caught a cold chopping wood in a chill rain a few weeks back. Said he'd chilled himself and got into bed and heaped on the covers. The cold moved to his lungs, and things went from bad to worse. Was the pneumonia that took him, the doctor said. And there was nothing to be done but make him comfortable as we could."

Marion then thought to demand any weapons in the house.

"We're plain people, farmers," said Mrs. Caldwell, wiping the tears from her eyes with a handkerchief she pulled from her sleeve, blowing her nose. "We don't keep guns here except for the squirrel rifle my husband used to bring in game when his chores let up on him, which wasn't often. And that's broke."

"And how about you?" Marion said, turning his attention to the eldest son. "Where do you keep your gun?"

With some reluctance Edward, a boy on the verge of manhood wearing a soldier's blouse and some military pantaloons, gave up his pistol, the only weapon found in the house. Magruder then ordered the three youths to turn out their pockets, relieving them of some change and a wad of greenbacks that Edward said was to pay for his father's coffin. In addition, he confiscated Edward's penknife, his pipe, and some smoking tobacco. Mrs. Caldwell—a slight woman, her body taxed and depleted from birthing—wore boots and a plain frock covered with an apron on which Jarom saw a spate of cooking stains. Though she'd heard no threat or warning, through some inscrutable resource of maternity she somehow divined their purpose.

"Mr. Magruder," she pleaded, "please don't shoot my boy." She knew him from the times when he and Edward played as children.

"Shut your trap," Magruder said curtly, "or I'll blow him to blazes right here."

Edward, obviously fearing for his life, knew to be silent and accommodating. Not so Mrs. Caldwell. She had just lost her husband, and she wasn't going to lose a son if she could help it.

"Let him be," she said, "he's just come home to bury his father."

"Then bring us his horse," Magruder demanded.

Those around the table exchanged glances, and none but the mother offered any resistance

"George," Mrs. Caldwell said finally, "go fetch them the horse. If that's all these men want, they can have it." Though sobbing, she spoke in a tone that left no margin for debate.

"But she's not mine," Edward protested. "I had to borrow her to get here, and there'll be the devil to pay if I don't bring her back."

"There be the devil to pay," Magruder growled, "if you don't give it over." He patted the blue barrel of his Colt.

"I'll get her," said George, the second son, pulling his chair back from the table with a screech as it grated across the uncarpeted floor.

"You know where the key is kept," said his mother, sinking low in her seat, a study in dread.

"You must come too," Magruder said, turning to fix his eyes on Edward, whose shoulders were shuddering, the perplexed expression still imprinted on his face, the eyes still flitting from one to the other as if he knew this might be the last he'd see any of them.

When this demand registered, Mrs. Caldwell began screaming. Her knuckles whitened as she sat up again and gripped the edge of the table for support. Jarom himself felt uneasy and wanted to leave the room, leave the house, maybe leave the country. But curiosity to see how things played out held him. Remembering Patterson, he felt a slow surge of wrath, premeditated and undeniable. Though he knew what was about to happen, he had no energy or will to resist it, no reason if Patterson entered the consideration. He looked on as if fascinated, following Marion and the son named George out to the locked stable, Edward stopping to look back at her when he reached the front door.

"Don't go," Mrs. Caldwell ordered, finding some new source of determination. "Don't go outside with these men. They'll kill you."

Edward tried to reassure her, reassure himself, putting on a brave front.

"They won't kill anybody, mother. They just want to be sure they get the right horse."

"Mr. Marion . . . Billy," she said, rising up to grasp Marion by the arm. She knew him also as one of Edward's playmates and hoped she could prevail on him to prevent whatever was about to happen.

"Do something to stop this," she pleaded. "Please, please, do something."

Marion stared at her indulgently but said nothing.

"Are you just going to stand by and see him shot? He's never done wrong by you. He's never done a spiteful thing to anybody."

Marion shook loose from her and grunted something unintelligible and strode out of the house to join the others at the stable.

Jarom made his way across the muddy yard to the barn where he found Magruder, Marion, and the boy-man Edward leading a large bay mare out of one of the stables. When Tom Henry stepped out on the porch, off which a curtain of water was dropping, Magruder shouted for him to go unhitch and bring up the horses. Jarom ordered Edward to make the horse ready to ride. Edward, just cinching the saddle, offered the reins to Marion when he'd finished.

"No, no, it's for you," Magruder said. "Git on and go for a ride with us."

His drawn pistol left little room for negotiation.

Jarom was surprised that Edward went along with them so complacently. He tried to put himself in Edward's place. He guessed Edward could not imagine they would actually shoot him. He had cooperated. Though he fought on the other side, he had no quarrel with Marion, with any of them. He'd known both Marion and Magruder since they were children skinny-dipping in the creek. So why would they want to take his life?

As he entered the barn, Jarom saw George leading a bay mare from one of the stalls. Saddled, the snaffle bit and head strap fit over her ears, she stood outside, wagging her head and snorting at the humans who had taken her from the manger and warm stall. Tom Henry shut his played-out stallion, an iron gray, into the emptied stall as a replacement. Outside, George held the reins just under the reddish brown of the bony nose, waiting for his brother to mount. Jarom rose to the back of his own horse, as did the others, including Marion, who'd come out of the house. Mrs. Caldwell stood on the porch wailing, framed in the light of the open door of the house in which her husband lay on the cooling board, her arm around her youngest son.

Though he had come this far obediently, Edward chose this moment to balk. Jarom guessed that finally it dawned on him that the intruders wanted something more than an exchange of horses.

"Git up on that horse," Magruder repeated, his patience thinning.

Again Edward refused, his brother holding the stirrup for him now. Without uttering another word, Magruder raised his pistol and fired a single shot. Edward went down with a bullet wound just above his left eye, dead or dying. Then, in some unrehearsed ritual, each of the others, all on horseback, shot down on Edward where he lay, as though to ratify the deed. Jarom fired first, riding over to where Edward lay in the mud and putting a load into his chest. As the bullet struck, Jarom thought he saw the torso twitch, whether reflex of the dead or coup de grace he didn't know. Henry went next, followed by Marion, the shots dying out in the steady fall of rain.

George stood helplessly by, afraid he was next. Instead, Magruder threatened and warned him not to cross his path again. George stood wordless, his face clenching up, his chest heaving. Jarom saw the boy's hands knot into fists and recognized his anguish but would not have undone what had been done even if he were able to. He had no doubt that Edward would have been shot if he had gone off with them. What surprised him was how long Edward chose to believe that death could not touch him, that all he had to do to preserve his life was what he was told to do. Good faith would not shield him from the world. Denial had been his mode when he exited this life, refusing until the last to believe that those whom he'd known not so many years ago could do him harm.

Magruder showed them a bundle of greenbacks he found in the barn as well as a book with the pictures of three comely young women in it. Jarom noticed a pinewood coffin leaning upright against one of the stalls. It must have been bought in anticipation of the father's death. Now someone would have to order another. As Magruder spurred his horse to leave, Mrs. Caldwell rushed out to meet her living son and mourn her dead one. Jarom followed the others, feeling little satisfaction as the rush of blood coursing through his body began to ebb. Once on the road again, Magruder commented, not in any way as justification so much as statement of fact, that they'd left as good a horse as the one they took.

Over the next few weeks Jarom participated in a series of raids that became a killing spree. In Scott County the band raided the home of a farmer named Medley Powell, who, with his twenty-two-year-old son, had successfully resisted an earlier attack and driven the guerrillas away. After robbing him of his money and all the valuables they could find,

Magruder kidnapped the son, Fielding, whose mother, like Mrs. Caldwell, begged them to leave him be. Marion bluntly told Mrs. Powell she was on the wrong side and could not save her son. Fielding's sister attempted to follow on horseback, but Marion told her that if she did they would shoot her, too. Instead, Magruder and Marion forced Fielding—his flaxen hair stuck in Jarom's memory—to mount a horse, which carried him about a half mile to some woods near a dip in the road. There Jarom and the others emptied their revolvers into him, riddling the body with shot. The shooting took place close enough that Fielding's parents could hear the reports of their pistols.

After they shot a federal soldier captured near Jeffersontown, the military commandant in Louisville ordered Captain Hackett of the Twenty-sixth Kentucky to take four captive Confederates to the spot and shoot them in retaliation. Their names, Jarom later read, were W. Lilly, S. Hattey, M. Briscoe, and Captain L. D. Buckner. He wondered if Buckner was kin to his old commander, General Simon Bolivar Buckner. To be so broad, Kentucky seemed a very small place. Sickened by the reprisal, Jarom began to see the war not as battles but a series of small but vicious exchanges of tit for tat.

The shootings of Surgeon Shirk and Lieutenant McCormack he remembered for the unusual circumstances and the fact that Magruder joked about the episode. Riding by a farm belonging to a man named Grigsby, Magruder, ahead of Jarom and the others, discovered two finely caparisoned horses tied to a fence paling in front of the house. After surrounding the rather large dwelling, Jarom and seven or eight others bolted in and found the family room filled with young men and women preparing to have a party. Surgeon Shirk, a major, and McCormack, a captain, had rushed out of the room and hidden themselves under a bed in a room off the end of the hall, hoping they would be overlooked. Magruder entered first and began firing at the bed. By the time Jarom entered, he found bedclothes strewn on the floor, the room a mess. Surgeon Shirk lay with a half-eaten apple in his hand. McCormack sprawled close by, his cape thrown over his head. Rifling through his pockets, Magruder found a handsome pocket watch. Outside, Magruder also claimed Shirk's finely tooled saddle, pulling his own off the back of his big bay, aptly named Grit. And he would remember his part in shooting another soldier at Hustonville after raiding the town on a Sunday morning. They had searched every stable for horses, stopping at the town's main hostelry, the Weatherford Hotel. He, Magruder, and some untried new men, one or two dressed in federal uniforms, posed as soldiers belonging to the Fourth Missouri Cavalry in need of fresh horses. Using this ruse, they bamboozled eight prime saddle horses from the skeptical keepers of the livery stable adjoining the hotel. One of the mounts, a fine gray mare, belonged to a Lieutenant C. F. Cunningham, just mustered out of the Thirteenth Kentucky Cavalry. Learning his horse had been taken, Cunningham rushed to the stables and demanded its return. He stated his name, said he'd served two years and that the horse in question was his favorite. While Magruder ordered him to disarm himself, Jarom and one of the Missourians shot him in the face, killing him instantly. Others started shooting at the two men who had accompanied him—one of them the Weatherford who owned the hotel—but they escaped through the door and down the street with only a bullet hole in Weatherford's hat. Someone went through Cunningham's pockets, finding his pistol and two hundred greenbacks. Magruder slipped a ring off the dead man's finger.

In the newspaper account of the murder, Jarom later read that Cunningham, an orphan like himself, had been raised by his uncle and entered the service at seventeen, fighting first with the Eighth Kentucky Cavalry and then with Colonel Weatherford's regiment of the Thirteenth Kentucky. According to the writer, he was not only the youngest officer but the youngest man in the regiment. The article, probably sent over the wires from someone who knew him, referred to the men who shot him as fiends. What stayed with Jarom was the gist of lamentation in the article. Cunningham had been taken from the circle of his associates just in the bloom of life with hopes and bright anticipations of success in the new business he was commencing. "None knew him but to love him," the article stated, " none lisped his name but to praise." The article went on to say that gloom still lingered in the midst of those who knew him and that the tear of sympathy had been freely shed over his bier. One seemingly innocuous sentence toward the end of the article especially got to Jarom. The writer, describing the reactions of those who witnessed the raid, quoted one of the town's citizens. "They are," he said, "a vicious set of men, very." It was the "very" that troubled him more than the "vicious"—the afterthought that "very" was needed to describe the intensity of the viciousness visited on Hustonville.

Reading the piece, Jarom, remembering his loss, felt a pang of conscience. They had no reason, no provocation, to gun Cunningham down. He had surrendered. He was giving up his pistol. Why had they shot him? Was it instinct, an ingrained reflex of some kind? That the men he shot had lives and hopes similar to his own he well understood. But until that moment he had not considered himself a fiend who snuffed out the life of someone his own age, a person with characteristics that made him more than another abstraction in blue. Until then he had not felt the anguish of those who knew Cunningham.

So far as Jarom knew, George Prentice wrote about each of the killings, and occasionally Jarom happened on a back issue at a grocer's or hardware. One he came across in mid-December typified the notices:

> *Louisville Daily Journal*
> December 8, 1864
> Sue Mundy's Gang—A Chapter of Robberies and Murders.—On Saturday last, a gang of twelve guerillas, led by Sue Mundy and a scoundrel named Dick Mitchell, started on a tour of robbery and murder, and the outlaws were quite successful. They first visited Springfield, robbed the stores and private parties of about two thousand dollars in money and property, and, without provocation, shot two citizens down in cold blood. T. W. Lee, a wagon maker, was one of the murdered men, and Wetherton, a shoemaker, was the other. The marauders then started from the town, paid a visit to the villages of Texas and Pottsville, and robbed each of them of small amounts. Just after dark, on Friday night, the town of Perryville was thrown into a commotion by a report being brought in that a band of guerillas, said to be one hundred strong, was approaching the place by way of Mackville. The citizens were terribly excited, and a number of them were up keeping watch over the town all night. They were without arms, and came to the conclusion, that, if the force was as large as represented, it would be useless to attempt to offer any resistance. About two o-clock P.M., the next day, Sue Mundy dashed into the town at the head

of her gang of twelve men, which, it appears, report had magnified into one hundred. An unusual number of men and women were in the streets at the time, and, in less than fifteen minutes, under the effects of a pistol argument, everyone was relieved of their purses. The scoundrels did not dismount from their horses, but rode up to store-doors, and made the merchants bring to them the contents of their money-drawers. Money appeared to be the sole object of their raid as they carried away with them but little, if any, goods. They "confiscated" several horses and saddles.

A young man named Lawson, a Federal soldier, was shot and mortally wounded while in the act of handing over his purse. The miscreant guilty of the cowardly outrage claimed that the shooting was an accident. The gang did not remain in the town more than twenty minutes.

From Perryville the outlaws moved to Nevada, then to Cornishville. When last heard from, they were at Bloomfield. About an hour after they had departed from Perryville, Captains Fiddler and Wharton, from Lebanon, in command of a detachment of soldiers and armed citizens, arrived and pushed forward in hot pursuit. We did not learn with what success the pursuers met. It is fair to assume that they did not overtake the outlaws.

As a general thing, a scout manages to keep about one mile behind the force that it is sent in pursuit of. Surely, if a proper effort was made, some means could be devised for the capture of Sue Mundy and her horse-thieving, murdering gang. If the citizens would exhibit a spirit of bravery worthy of Kentuckians, the handful of marauders might be picked up and turned over to the military authorities as prisoners without anybody getting very badly hurt.

Jarom had to admit that, aside from name-calling, Prentice reported things as they had happened. Dick Mitchell, another adopted Nelson Countian, had been with him, as had Dick's brother Tom. But Jarom only partially agreed that an exhibition of bravery would bring him and the others to their knees. He emphatically disagreed that they could be taken without, as Prentice might put it, great effusion of blood. He fingered one of the metal buttons on his jacket: *United we stand, divided we fall.*

REDEMPTION

Jarom could think of no special reason for any of them, on a bitter cold Monday morning, to be in Taylorsville, a town of no special importance except as a watering place on the way to Bloomfield and other destinations in Nelson County. Not one of them—neither Magruder, Berry, Bill Marion, nor Jarom himself—had any business there until Marion manufactured some in the form of abducting four persons of color from the local jail.

Like much that begins as mischief and ends in calamity, it opened by chance and played out in the old molds of predictability. Knocking about the town, Marion stopped a man named Dunstan, a carpenter, and asked him what the news was. Froman told him that four Negroes had been jailed on Sunday, two of them women. Marion asked what they'd done, and Dunstan told him that they had been charged with burning and looting a house a mile or so north of town. He explained that at the time of the fire someone saw the woman near the site and that when questioned, none too gently, she'd named three others. So the constable enlisted some good men and true, men who happened at the time to be idle, and they scoured the country gathering them up, fetching them from the farms of their owners. At each place, after the circumstances had been explained, the owners reluctantly gave them up, all except the Widow Hume, who had to be restrained while the men bound her young domestic to a spare horse and led her away. The others went willingly enough to the jail in Taylorsville, where they sat behind bars until an inquiry could be made.

"Inquiry be damned," Marion said. "They ought to be shot, and we're just the boys to do it."

Without any other prompting, he went over, as he put it, to reason with the jailer, a man named Samuel Snyder, a part-time turnkey, who made most of his living as a blacksmith. Snyder had gone across the street to fetch cigars requested by one of the prisoners, a man possessed theretofore of a good reputation. When Snyder returned with a handful, Marion and Magruder confronted him outside on horseback with pistols presented. Pistolless himself, still clasping the cigars, Snyder was in no position to resist even if he had been inclined to. Marion demanded the prisoners, ordering Snyder to unlock the door and to do it quick.

Marion and Magruder then dismounted and bullied Snyder into the jail, pushing him up the stairs and down an ill-lighted corridor to the cell where they were kept. Snyder, afraid that giving up the prisoners too easily might make him appear lax, lamely protested that he held the prisoners in his custody and that all good citizens should let justice do its work. He and the growing number of onlookers knew that he protested mainly for show, as he had not the faintest hope of dissuading a man as determined as Marion, a man well known to all of them.

He went on to promise Marion that justice might take some time but that it would be done and done proper. Taking the undelivered cigars from Snyder's hand and stuffing them in his jacket, Marion responded with curses, forcing Snyder at gunpoint to unlock the cell door. Leaving him with a key in his hand and an empty cell, Marion and Magruder escorted the four prisoners downstairs and onto the porch. Which was when Berry rode up, meeting Dunstan and some other citizens who had assembled outside the jail, more out of curiosity than outrage.

Dunstan and a man named Kirk appealed to him to prevent the Negroes from being killed and to let the civil law run its course. Berry told them he would do what he could to save the Negroes' lives. He slid off his horse and joined Snyder, who was still pleading with Marion and Magruder on the porch of the jail. They talked a few minutes, then Berry came back and said there was nothing he could do, that his friends were determined to kill the Negroes. He said that he feared for his own life and that he'd been threatened for arguing on behalf of the Negroes.

"The long and short of it," he said, "is that I won't risk my life for any Negroes."

Dunstan then appealed to him not to have the Negroes killed in town.

"What difference does it make," said Berry, "if the Negroes are killed here or killed out of town?"

"Because," Dunstan said, "the town already has a bad enough name. If you're determined to kill them, have the courtesy to take them out of town."

A body of twenty or so citizens had now collected outside the jail.

They did not appear in any way threatening, but Marion willingly granted them this small concession. "In town or out of town don't matter to me," he said. "I estimate I can shoot them out of town just as well as in."

Hearing the hubbub, Jarom, who had been up the street at a stable having a loose shoe on Papaw's right forehoof checked, rode down to the jailhouse where Marion and Magruder were prodding the Negroes into the street. Berry stood by with a hangdog look on his face. Marion and Magruder, who said not a word, mounted their horses and marched the Negroes ahead of them toward the Salt River bridge. Berry held back a minute or two, explaining for Jarom's benefit what he knew of what happened before he'd come to the jail. What Berry himself had not witnessed he pieced together from Froman and Snyder as well as from what he could gather from Marion and Magruder. Then Berry, resigned, hoisted himself onto his horse in his one-armed way and went after the others.

When the three riders with their four charges were halfway to the bridge, Jarom, disgusted by the whole episode, went after them. He caught up just as the party vanished into the dark mouth of the covered bridge, a structure that had been the town's pride for over thirty years and that Marion threatened to burn each time he crossed it, just as he threatened to burn the courthouse, a threat he later made good on. When they came out at the other end, Marion ordered each of the Negroes to hop on the back of a horse, each of the four behind a rider. And Jarom went along with Marion's instructions, as the older of the two captive men, with some effort, climbed up behind him. Sensing that the crowd at the jail might gather pluck enough to set up a pursuit, Marion put spurs to his big gelding, and the eight of them took off upriver as hard as they could go on double-weighted horses. Still worried about the shoe, as Papaw strained under the double weight, Jarom slowed while the others steadily widened their lead.

Jarom learned that his passenger, a burly man with a wreath of white stubble around his mouth and jowls, was named John Russell. His breath smelled of rancid bacon. Jarom, lagging behind the others, ordered John Russell to clasp him about the middle and hold on. In response to Jarom's questioning, John Russell said his master was Cal Grigsby, a farmer from up around a section called Little Union. Russell said Grigsby treated him "pretty tolerable."

Jarom explained to John Russell what the man already knew, that he'd got himself into serious trouble and asked him to tell straight out what had happened. The Negro, speaking over Jarom's shoulder into his right ear, said the first he knew of the house burning was from a cook in the neighborhood named Sallie Bell, a plumpish yellow woman in her forties who belonged to a not-too-prosperous farmer named Eli Cooper. She told him that there had been a fire in a vacant house and that he could take what he wanted that wasn't burned. He'd gone to the place and found most of the upper floor a blackened ruin, the downstairs damaged by smoke but mostly intact. Where the fire had burned, the roofline was broken and filled with unfamiliar light, the sticks of charred sheathing poking up to suggest the ghost angle of the structure when it had been whole. From among the clothes and belongings strewn on the floor he had taken a few things, nothing valuable, and carried them back to Cooper's. No, he hadn't set the fire, and, no, he didn't have any notion who did.

"And that's all I know about the fire," he said, "until the gang of them come for me and put me in the prison house. I've never messed with any real trouble in my life. I do my work, I mind my business. I don't do thataway."

Jarom was inclined to believe him and said so, unable without turning completely around to read his expression. Though he didn't know what involvement John Russell had with taking items from the house, he didn't think the man had struck the fire. If he had scavenged some clothing from the abandoned house, no one, to Jarom's way of thinking, would be the less for it. Snatching up useful things struck him as closer to practicing good husbandry than "looting," an ugly word better described as "salvage" here.

On this side of the river the going was less sure because they followed no road. The pike to Bloomfield ran on the town side of the bridge, but Jarom knew there was a passable ford a mile or two upriver where they could double back. Marion chose this side for its relative remoteness and to discourage followers. It was easy to lay an ambush along such an unformed route. But for an occasional clearing the landscape was hilly and densely wooded with great rough-barked hickories and flanks of dusky oaks whose limbs formed fingerlike canopies over their heads. They passed up and down steep, bridgeless declivities that dipped to ravines and dry creek beds that fed into the river whenever rain fell.

"What kind of man did you say Cal Grigsby is?" Jarom asked.

John Russell, the warmth of his bulk behind almost an extension of Jarom now—physically closer to him than anyone, even than Mollie Thomas, had ever been—did not answer at first. Jarom reckoned the man pondered how honest he could afford to be, white people sticking up for white people, black for black. Finally, he broke the silence with the answer of someone who had survived servitude a long time, a hybrid of truth and fiction. "Oh, Cap'n," he said, "he's better'n most and worse than some. He's fine when he's not been drinking."

"And how often is he drinking?" Jarom asked.

"Most the time," John Russell said, "most the time."

"Do you have a wife?"

"I do, and three children, but they live up in Shelby County at Dickson's and I am with them only a little. A son and two daughters."

"And what did you have to do with this house burning?" Jarom asked. "Are you sure it wasn't you who set the fire?"

"On my soul," John Russell said, "it wasn't. I swear to you. I only came to the house when Sallie Bell told me things were out for the taking, that they would be ruint if someone didn't take them. So I says to myself, says I, 'If they're here for someone, I might as well be that someone cause ain't I someone too?'"

They were passing under a large sweet gum, and one of the lower limbs brushed the hat off Jarom's head.

"Woops," he said, "I've lost my hat," sweeping his arm back in a vain effort to catch it.

John Russell, wonderfully limber, slid off the Papaw's rump and fetched it up, handing it up to Jarom, who pulled it over his snaggled head and thanked him. Jarom was surprised to hear himself thanking this stranger who had done him a kindness at a time when he was designing to take the man's life—which did not accord with whatever conventions of kindness governed even so wild a place.

As they entered an overgrown pasture of sedge that grew in sallow spikes, an eroded slope choked with scrub and cedars, they heard a spatter of shots some distance ahead. Sound carried in the river bottom, and it was hard to determine how far away they were. As the tattoo of firing fainted away, more shots sounded, and Jarom knew he'd better catch up to see for himself.

They made their way down through a copse of thick timber into a wide field that spread and scalloped up the steep slope of another ridge. At the far end of the field, maybe two hundred yards away, Jarom could make out two riders straining through the stubble toward the trees. The first was charging up the hill toward the trees. Just at the treeline, he saw the form of a woman, her skirts hiked to her waist, sprinting faster than he had imagined anyone in skirts could move. The second rider, mounted on Marion's big gray gelding, not far behind, was chasing up the hill, his passenger, a male from the looks of him, still hugging the man in the saddle.

As he and John Russell rode down into a swale, Jarom lost sight of the riders and the running woman, but more shots placed them somewhere off to the right. As they rose again to higher ground, he saw that Marion had turned and was heading back toward the river. He couldn't see Magruder but guessed he was somewhere in the woods still after his own rider. Where Berry and the other woman were, he didn't know. The shooting stopped, and he angled back toward the river following the direction in which he'd seen Marion moving. Marion and his burden disappeared again, a tongue of trees separating them, but he knew Marion would close the gap and likely would pop into view, sooner and closer than he might expect. Out of the blue came John Russell's question. "Cap'n, are you going to shoot me?"

Jarom had no ready answer, not expecting so blunt a question from someone whose death he debated even then. His every instinct told him not to tell the truth, whatever he intended to do. He knew that the easiest way to placate him would be to tell John Russell, that, no, he, John Russell, was a good man, that Jarom had no intention of shooting him, would not think of it. He could then make up his mind before joining Marion and Magruder. He did know that if he closed with them again with John Russell still alive, he wouldn't be after meeting them.

"I don't know," he said, and he felt John Russell stiffen and sigh, sigh again, and then go silent. The breath he felt on his neck from his fellow being who reminded him of Uncle Nether, the patient man who had shown him how to run a beeline half his life ago. It was best to come square with John Russell.

"Uncle," Jarom said, "I believe they are going to kill the last damn one of you."

"Then, Cap'n, why don't you jest let me go?"

"Because if I do they might kill *me*," Jarom heard himself saying, knowing this to be unlikely and amounting to a lie.

Then he saw Marion pop out of some trees in the uplands, cutting a diagonal across the pasture where he and Marion and John Russell would likely converge. Marion held a pistol at the ready, pointed toward heaven, with no rider at his back, no woman. And Jarom knew that she lay in some upland thicket, that Marion had come back without her because he had caught and done violence to her, for Marion was not a man who would have returned until he had snared whatever he was after.

Then he felt John Russell slide off Papaw's rump and hit the ground. John Russell was up and running before Jarom could turn Papaw back to face the figure whose feet were beginning to get their purchase up the hill. John Russell vaulted over a clump of buckberries and tore off toward cover. The woods were maybe fifty yards away, though large single trees with spraddled limbs broke the skyline in the old field, one just ahead of him with its top knocked out by lightning. As Jarom passed it, he had to dodge the remnant limbs where they had fallen. Instinctively, he drew his pistol and raised it to align on the center of John Russell's back.

Not once did the fleeing man look back, though he must have expected the shot at any instant. Nor did he zig and zag but beelined for the fringe of trees that rose to the ridge. Crossing it seemed the goal toward which his whole body and mind were striving. Jarom could see Marion coming in his direction now, his gelding bounding across the open ground in a steady lope.

Jarom raised the pistol, cocked back the hammer to steady his shot, and followed John Russell's back as he made for the trees, gaining some distance now.

"John Russell!" he yelled. "You, John Russell, stop!"

But Jarom knew John Russell wouldn't stop, just as he knew that he himself would not exert the pressure necessary through his crooked finger to trip the trigger. He glanced back and saw Marion getting closer. By now surely Marion, whose hatred of blacks was endemic, could see the upraised gun and the fugitive as he flew. Marion must have been wondering why Jarom didn't fire, or why he didn't at least spur Papaw into what would still be an easy pursuit.

Then what had been swelling inside him without shape or substance rose like the head of an infant crowning at birth.

I can't do it, Jarom said to the part of him that was poised to fire. Finger, hand, hold back. *I can't shoot this man, just can't do it. Won't.*

In plain sight of Marion, closing within eighty yards now, he raised the pistol and fired well over John Russell's head. John Russell showed no sign of slowing but kept on clambering uphill, his run slowing to a dogged trot as he reached the thickets and undergrowth near the crest of the ridge. Jarom fired again, again for show, the pistol kicking up in the familiar way but the ball cutting air well wide of John Russell, who had nearly reached the ridgetop. The limbs and shelves of rock under Papaw's hooves checked her progress until she stopped, as if frustrated by impediments she could not overstep. A third time Jarom fired, and then John Russell was over the crest and out of view.

Marion, pistol still raised, reined in next to him.

"Did you hit him?" he asked. "Myself, I couldn't get a clear shot at the son of a bitch."

"I might have have pinked him a little," Jarom said, taking comfort in his lie. "It'll take more than either Papaw or me to find him now."

The two of them made their way to the summit and looked out over an expanse of gray timber, a great cone of wilderness that formed a mesh of limbs thicker than any man could negotiate on horseback. A blush of lavender showed in the buds of some of the near trees, a smear of it in those distant, filmy and blue. After checking his remaining loads, Jarom holstered his pistol, which seemed now to hold some new heaviness. But in his chest he felt that some great stone pinching his lungs had been lifted so that he could breathe again.

He knew he was all right when Marion holstered his gun, still scanning the woods for some sign of the fugitive.

"Did the others get away?" Jarom asked.

"Not hardly," Marion said. "They're down the river, the three of them."

"Dead?" Jarom asked.

"Dead."

First they came to one of the women, Berry's charge, off to herself in a little clearing on a bluff near the water. Her feet with her laced-up shoes stuck pathetically from under her sprawled and twisted skirts. She lay on one cheek, one eye fixed in startlement, her arm outthrust, the caramel brown of her forearm contrasting with the pinkish cup of the exposed palm, her fingers clenched in death like the claws of a stricken hen. One arm was tucked under, and her billowing skirts formed a kind of fan. Around her neck hung a spotless yellow bandanna.

Marion led him to Magruder and Berry, who still sat their horses on a little sandbar that extended into the river. The horses showed fatigue now, especially Magruder's, whose flanks heaved from exertion. The neck of Marion's arched toward a ragged hole in the ice through which Jarom could make out gelid water. The men themselves were smoking and talking quietly in somber mood. Jarom studied the hole as he would something dark and ominous. Beneath the water with its collar of jagged ice Jarom could make out two forms, one male, one female. Whether they had been drowned or shot was not easy to tell, but the woman named Sallie Bell had a hole in the side of her cheek. Her woolen dress was sopping and heavy, her head clearly visible. Under the cold water her skin had blenched white, her frizzed hair turned the blackest black, the greenish black of a grackle's wing. Jarom could see more of the man but could detect no visible wounds, no bloodstained jacket or shattered face, the eyes squinched closed as if contracted against the cold.

On the other side of the river stood a mill and some outbuildings, half visible through the trees. Smoke from the chimney told him someone lived there, decent folk, he hoped, who would investigate and see to the burials, people who would fetch the owners to claim their property, someone in the end who would say that in some crude way propriety and custom, if not justice, had been served. Marion, puffing on one of John Russell's cigars, was obviously pleased with himself. Magruder seemed more furtive, blowing little rings of blue smoke that unraveled in the invisible turbulences of that place. The breath snorted from the horses' nostrils condensed as it met the frigid air of morning, making it seem for an instant that in some peculiar equine way they were smoking too.

When Berry and Jarom had a moment to themselves, Berry told him that Magruder, after ridding himself of his rider, had come along and ordered the woman off Berry's horse. Protesting at first, Berry finally helped place her foot in the stirrup of Magruder's mount, and the two cantered off. When Berry heard several shots a few minutes later, he did not have to be told what had happened. Hearing this, Jarom congratulated himself that he would never have surrendered John Russell. Savoring a satisfaction new to him, he tried to imagine John Russell, shivering but alive, hunkered in some hollow tree or doubling back to whatever friend or family he had in that place until he found someone who would work to restore warmth to his body—to spoon him some broth, chuck another stick of kindling on the fire.

MAGRUDER

From the first time he met Billy Magruder, Jarom felt the man had a fatal streak in him and was superstitious to the point of madness. Magruder seemed a creature made up of contraries. He never hesitated to take an enemy's life, but he would suffer discomfort and sleeplessness rather than flick a mosquito from his forearm. He harbored the same fellow feeling for crickets, hoptoads, and ladybugs. One fall when the ladybugs were thick, somehow he bit into one as he ate some bread, spitting out the remains, which he swore he recognized by the bitter taste. For weeks afterward, he carefully inspected everything he ate for fear of consuming an insect, a creature to which he believed he was related, if distantly, in the great family of living things. "You don't eat family," he said.

Born a bastard in Bullitt County, he regarded his illegitimacy as a stain on his character that justified almost any behavior. His condition, as he saw it and believed others saw it, disgraced him. He felt himself an outcast with no need to answer to the rules by which others lived. "My life was darkened in its morning," he once told Jarom, "and it has known no sunshine since." For this, he asked no pity from anyone, no mercy, no sympathy. But he did not take kindly to anyone, even his friends, making reference to his origins.

Joking around one day at Bloomfield, Bill Marion called him a bastard.

"Woods colt," Magruder corrected him, "woods colt."

Marion allowed he'd never heard of such a thing and asked what he meant.

"It means this," Magruder said, slapping one of his thighs on which he wore a holstered pistol. "And this Colt has a kick!" he added, tapping the pistol butt emphatically.

Henry C. Magruder joined the Confederate army in Nelson County in 1862, recruited by Colonel Jack Allen at a place called Camp Charity. He had been part of Albert Sidney Johnson's bodyguard at Shiloh and saw the blood poured from the general's boot before he died. Ordered to deliver dispatches across the battlefield after the first day, he rifled the pockets of the dead and dying, Union and Confederate alike. He told Jarom and anyone else who would listen that he courted death and had a heart for any fate. He joined Morgan's cavalry and served until Morgan was killed, whereupon he returned to Kentucky and took to guerrillering as naturally, he used to say, as a baby suckles his mother's milk.

Magruder's knowledge and practice of moral character were at best exploratory. To him, the natural world was a living organism consisting of worlds within worlds, some being too great for the mind to encompass, some too small scarcely to reckon. To him, every creature, every action, was a sign writ in Nature's hand. Once, Jarom saw him pull pegs from his tent rather than disturb a brown spider that had spun its filaments over the opening.

Though lacking moral substance, he was the kind of philosopher that might be found at any crossroads store, full of earthy wisdom. Jarom remembered Magruder's little lecture on the leg as a means of escaping one's enemies. He called it the philosophy of running. "Any man," he said, "who imagines that his leg is simply an ornament to his person has failed to discover the purpose for which it is fastened on him. A man's legs are to bear him out of danger. And the man who uses his arms and legs, the faster the better, is wiser than the man who rests his legs and stands."

He loathed religion in general and Christians in particular. Though born a Catholic, he often seemed to be competing with himself to see how many of the Ten Commandments he could break and how often, and while he acknowledged no fear of the hereafter, he would not take up arms on Sunday. If circumstances dictated that he defend himself on that day, he would do his best to disappear until the contest was over or Monday came. He kept his nail parings in a mason jar as though they were jewels, and he refused to sit on tables. He upbraided Sam Berry for counting the wagons in a funeral procession that passed through Bardstown one day. Even if he were famished, at table he would not take the last biscuit or crust of hot bread from the plate. Believing his image could be spirited away, he would not look into mirrors and consequently often appeared unkempt and barked around the edges. He told Jarom that he once spent all the money he had, a fairly considerable sum, laying out his palms for an old black woman to read his fortune. He would not knowingly fire bullets from a dead man's gun nor wield weapons or utensils captured from a corpse. This did not, however, prevent him from removing an item of apparel or a horse before the owner became a corpse.

Unschooled beyond the rudiments, Magruder's philosophical strain was a mix of fatalism and pessimism with only a tiny dose of ethical sensitivity. Despite his off-centered self-centeredness, he at times could be insightful, even clever. As he and Jarom were riding back to Bloomfield one day, Jarom mentioned reading of troops routed at the Second Manasas. Magruder impressed Jarom by quoting some Latin, some bit of knowledge he'd picked up God knows where.

"I tell you," he said, "I have long ago discovered this fact: that when a fellow is spoiling for a fight, when he's hungry for blood, it answers the purpose just as well to let a little drop of his own as it does to take a great deal from his enemies, but it takes confoundedly little of his own.

"I have seen," he went on, "a fellow go yelping out of a fight at the loss of a finger, when nothing less than the heads of a dozen Yanks would have satisfied him. That is to say, there is a difference between *meum* and *tuum*."

Magruder had convinced himself of his own invincibility on odd days of the month, except for the thirteenth. Placing great faith in talismans, around his neck he wore a locket his mother had given him. It held a likeness of his grandmother, dried up and toothless, who looked, he confessed, like everyone's grandmother. The knots and tangles in a horse's mane he referred to as witches' stirrups. The horse with the snarled mane must have belonged to someone else, for his own he kept immaculately combed and curried. His life was an endless inventory of prohibitions and mandates, not a few of them lacking any rational explanation. Magruder shot one poor man, an itinerant tinker who lived in a covered wagon, when he became convinced the fellow put the stink-eye on him.

One clear night in November Jarom found Magruder outside staring into the heavens. The sky was stippled with stars in their constellations, and the dippers were in their customary relations. The air carried a chill, and Margruder had pulled a blanket about his shoulders. Not seeing Jarom approach, he continued to sway this way and that as though searching for something high and distant. Suddenly, he clapped his hands and shouted, "Moneymoneymoney!"

Stepping over to hand him the blanket that fell from his shoulders, Jarom asked what the outburst meant. Magruder explained with the absolute conviction of a child or true believer that if a person who saw a shooting star should shout the magic word three times before the star dimmed, he would be in for a budget of luck. When Jarom said that for luck he himself relied on the silver crescent pinned to his hat, Magruder shook his head and told Jarom that such a device held no power, that Jarom was superstitious.

SIMPSONVILLE

About this time, Captain Edwin Terrell, a turncoat who had deserted the Confederate army and sold out to the Union, began a series of raids on farms whose owners he knew to be Southern in their sympathies. Killing and arresting a number of individuals in Spencer, Washington, and Shelby counties, he confiscated cattle and horses conveniently described as contraband, part of what others later described as an enormous swindle. Hearing of the herd, Berry gathered men whose families had been mistreated, including some of Morgan's veterans who had been left behind, a few wounded men not mended enough to fight, and four or five boys from Louisville, no older than Jarom, off on a tear. Sam Berry's brother

Tom had returned after escaping from Camp Morton. Altogether Jarom counted forty-two men bent on satisfaction, but some didn't show up when it came to belling the cat.

The place agreed on for a rendezvous was an abandoned farm near Finchville in Shelby County. On the night of January 24 Jarom and a dozen or so veterans of the guerrilla war—"survivors," Jarom called them—met in a tumbledown, abandoned farmhouse sitting a respectable distance off the road. The weather turned cold enough to freeze five or six inches of water in the trough to a platter of stone. After feeding the horses some spoiled hay found in the barn, Jarom helped drag in some fence rails to kindle a fire in the wide hearth of the dry-laid stone chimney. When the room had warmed as much as it was going to, Berry asked those gathered what they proposed to do. The company included Zay Coulter, Henry Medkiff, Magruder, the two Berry brothers, Enloe, Jim Quince, and Bill Marion. Several of the Louisville boys arrived late, but Sam Berry welcomed them, less because he trusted them or greatly valued their martial skills than because in a scrap he felt more secure with more targets for his enemies to shoot at.

Marion and Zay Coulter wanted to rob the savings bank in Shelbyville, but Sam Berry made it clear he thought such an enterprise was folly. He opposed it under any conditions. Word came that a force of Yankees with a drove of cattle had left Mercer County on their way to Louisville, where the livestock could be corralled and butchered at the stockyards near the city market. Marion backed off the bank, allowing that though apples were sweet, too large a bite would choke the eater. All of them acknowledged the greater risk in raiding the county seat and saw the benefits of recovering stolen cattle.

"Stumble into a fire," Zay Coulter said, "you just liable to get burned."

And that settled it.

They devised a plan to strike the cattle train at or near Simpsonville, a small town eight miles west of Shelbyville that once had been a stagecoach stop on the Louisville-Frankfort pike. Fairly close to Louisville, the town lacked military value; no troops were garrisoned there. As Jarom remembered it, the village comprised little more than a cluster of modest houses along the right-of-way and one or two general merchandise stores. Add the inevitable Baptist and Methodist churches, a smith's shop, a steam sawmill, and a stone tavern dating from pioneer days that served as a stopping place for drovers and teamsters on the road to Louisville. Jarom estimated a population of no more than a hundred within a mile of town.

From Finchville to Shelbyville was no more than eight or nine miles, but the weather the next morning turned raw and even colder. The thermometer dropped below zero before they reached Simpsonville, which but for some chimney smoke seemed to be depopulated. Overnight the temperature had slid nearly thirty degrees, and Jarom heard himself complaining to Sam Berry.

"My blood just hasn't adjusted," he said. "My bones feel as cold as blue metal."

"You'll survive it," Sam Berry said. "You'll survive."

Snow had accumulated since early December; the cold so severe that all traffic had disappeared from the road. Farmers along the pike left the comfort of their stoves only to feed livestock and bring in more firewood.

Jarom longed to join them, feet propped before the fire, reading Charles Dickens, his eyes following a caravan of ink into spring. His hands had stiffened with cold, his feet going numb through his boots and thin wool socks. Once during the morning he spied an old farmer feebly trying to smash a hole in his pond so his stock could drink. So far away was Jarom that the sound didn't reach his ears until the ax was halfway raised for the next stroke. Winter locked each house they passed in its grip, smoke threads rising out of the chimneys whiter than the sky they rose into, everything else gritty and as gray as Zay Coulter's gelding. The trees about the houses stood rigid and leafless, the ponds covered with glaze in fields that bristled with spikes of frost above the snowfall.

Jarom looked about him and saw that few of his companions were equipped to stave off cold, bundled as they were in whatever came to hand. Tom Berry and Marion wore captured overcoats, but the unexpected cold forced Jarom to improvise, cutting a head-hole in his blanket and winding scarves around his head and neck like an Arab. Under his blanket Jarom wore a mangy surtout with a fancy silk collar that he'd found in a vacant house. Long ago, Jarom had lost his rabbit-skin gloves.

Since none of them had any, they wrapped their hands in linen or bandage gauze, anything that would sheathe their bare skin from the cold. Every couple of miles Jarom felt the need to dismount to beat the blood back into his hands and feet. The juice from Magruder's tobacco froze to his whiskers in icy shards and the hooves of the horses clacked like wooden blocks on the brittle road.

Entering town from the east, the men passed some houses and a neatly clapboarded church. Marion put up his horse and went inside the grocery, a smartly fitted-out article run by a notorious skinflint named Prince whose ties with the Union were close and profitable. Known locally as a sharp dealer, he had two prices for everything on his shelves—one for Lincolnites, another for followers of Jeff Davis. Zay Coulter didn't dicker with him but simply insisted on unlimited credit, coming out with several pink hams of meat and a quantity of other foodstuffs, including some buttermilk and a wheel of German cheese. Marion doled out cotton work gloves, two pairs to a man. Jillson, one of the Louisville boys, devoured several tins of canned meat and made a silly joke about dying of lead poisoning. Jarom wondered if he himself ever appeared to his comrades such a fool and decided he probably did.

Zay Coulter went back in for a second armload and stumbled onto the porch hugging a jar of pickles the size of the dinner bell Aunt Mary Tibbs used to call hands from the field. With the jackknife stolen from Perkins's store he speared the contents and served them around like a prince dispensing favors, yellow brine still dripping from the knobby lobes. Jarom reflected on how ridiculous they must have appeared to anyone who dared to watch—the fifteen of them in the dead of winter picnicking on horseback in the center of a windswept road in Simpsonville, Kentucky.

When the pickles had nearly made it around, Coulter spied a weathercock on the livery across the way. Drawing his navy pistol, he took aim and emptied it at chanticleer's profile, the last shot chipping off one of its tin hackles. This brought huzzahs from the Louisvillians, who had been passing a flask of cognac around and were feeling no pain.

Almost before the chips hit the ground, several bluecoats darted out of the tavern about a hundred yards down the road. They disappeared around the corner and reemerged a few moments later on horseback.

Jarom and the others looked on as they crossed the pasture behind the stone building at a pretty brisk rate, dissolving in a screen of cedars at the base of the ridge.

Zay Coulter took up the challenge first. Dropping the pickle jar, whose fragments splashed on Papaw's hocks, he heaved himself into the saddle and spurred off in pursuit. Jarom, going more for sport than with any hope of catching the fugitives, joined the others, romping down to the tavern where they met the proprietor standing in the road. A rickety man in his sixties, obviously a noncombatant, he needlessly identified the runaways as federal officers.

Just as they were about to take up the hunt, Jim Davis came loping up with news that the company of Yankees, who had left Camp Nelson with a large herd of cattle, had been sighted west of town on their way to Louisville. The tavern keeper, understandably anxious to get them out of Simpsonville, volunteered that the herd had passed through town less than a hour earlier and that the three they had flushed had been stragglers from the very party that Davis described. Davis added that Louis Berry, Sam and Tom's uncle, had lost nearly a hundred head of prime cattle and John McGraw, another kinsman, forty. Louis Berry estimated the number of guards escorting the cattle at a hundred or more, mostly Negro recruits from Fort Nelson, commanded by a few white officers.

Jarom wasn't surprised to learn that the army was stealing cattle, for rumor had it that profiteers regularly shipped cattle, hogs, horses, shoats, jewelry, even furniture, out of the state in carloads. Without anyone needing to say it, they formed an unspoken pact to prevent this particular contraband from reaching Louisville. The issue became how to rustle them with maximum of success and minimum hurt—at least to themselves. Marion calculated that the guards outnumbered the sixteen of them at least eight to one, if Louis Berry's estimates were accurate. This meant they couldn't count on winning in an open fight without losing men. To set an ambush, they had to know the exact number and disposition of the drovers. With this knowledge they could choose a place that worked to their advantage and even the odds.

Tom Berry, recovering from one of his perennial gunshot wounds, stepped in. Behind him trailed his servant Toby, a willowy stripling of fifteen, fiercely loyal to all the Berrys. He had been a favorite of Susan

Berry, who gave him privileged employment in the house rather than back-breaking labor in the fields. Toby readily agreed to ride ahead as a spy. To prevent his attracting much notice, Jarom suggested that they get him up a disguise. Removing his warm clothes, he changed into a shabby work outfit such as any farmhand would wear. Wrapping himself in a blanket shawl, he looked in every particular an ordinary fieldhand but for his fine bay horse. To remedy this defect, he exchanged it for an old mule that Jarom liberated from a nearby field. To make it appear that Toby had been snaking logs, the mule wore a blind bridle, a collar, old harness, and trace chains that someone fetched from a nearby stable.

Jarom worried that the simplicity of the plan made it too transparent. Toby would ride ahead and fall in with the cattle train. He was to gather all the intelligence he could without seeming to meddle—how many soldiers, their condition and morale, how many cattle, their destination, and any other particulars that might be useful. When satisfied with what he'd learned, he would slip out again and make his report.

Looking confident, Toby said he would be back before you could say "Versailles, Kentucky," bade the Berrys goodbye, and jounced off on his mule toward Falls City. Admiring his loyalty but wondering if he himself, in a condition of slavery, would serve his masters so, Jarom watched until he dropped below the horizon, a boy in tatters bobbing almost comically on the mule. Just before he topped the rise, Toby turned and waved his hat.

Aware of how critical timing was to the success of his plan, Coulter called on Enloe to a find a route that would put them ahead of the column. He also wanted Enloe to suggest a likely place to set an ambuscade. To know precisely when the column would reach the spot to be designated, Coulter sent Marion, Magruder, and all but one or two of the others to form an invisible corridor down which the caravan would pass. Five riders were to be posted out of sight at intervals along the road. Each was provided with a tin horn that Zay went back inside the store to fetch, bringing out a basket of them that he found by the counter. Jarom speculated that they were stocked to amuse children or to call in cattle at feeding or milking time. At ten-minute intervals the heralders were to blow their horns as the caravan passed so those waiting in ambush could mark the progress of march. Spaced an eighth-mile apart and keeping out of sight, the heralders, placed on either side of the road, were to sound their horns until the column reached within a quarter mile of the chosen site. As each rider was passed, he was to hurry forward, keeping invisible if possible, to where the others waited. Marion was not averse to using the horns to spook the cattle guards.

Keeping out of sight of the road, Jarom, Marion, and two others broke the crusted snow and made their way cross-country, through farm gates and across icy creeks, to arrive at the designated spot, where they waited forty minutes before hearing the first blare of a horn. It sounded thin and shrill, passing like tremors in the still air over the frozen landscape. Jarom tried to find a word to describe what the horns sounded like. Not a blaring so much as the bellowings of a calf being smothered. After a few minutes, they heard still other blasts, this time nasal and more distinct, a "brer-rare, brer-rare" of dual horns almost in concert—menacing, metallic. One sounded slightly sooner than the other as though exchanging salutes or dialogues through some coded language peculiar to horn blowers, the buglings hanging in the air for an ominous instant before kiting off in the wind.

As the minutes passed, the trumpeting came progressively closer.

Jarom was tightening the cinch on Papaw's saddle as Toby rode in astride the mule. He reported that the escort consisted of parts of two companies numbering upward of a hundred men. He had counted nearly a thousand cattle divided into bunches of twenty or thirty, a man or two assigned to each bunch, the rest forming advance and rear guards. According to Toby, who possessed a flair for the dramatic, the column was so disorganized, its progress so slow, that it stretched a mile along the road. Most of the white officers had stopped at a farmhouse outside Simpsonville to warm themselves, leaving the enlistees to drive the cattle as best they could. The sound of the first horns mystified the guards. They became wary, then afraid, especially when no blowers came into view.

"What do those horns mean?" Toby was asked.

"They're calls to dinner," he said.

"At three in the afternoon?"

"Maybe folks in these parts have they suppers early," he said, "or they dinners late."

Waiting for Sam Berry's signal to attack became, as Zay Coulter would say, tetchous. Enloe contracted a case of the fidgets and could hardly hold his horse's reins, his hands were shaking so. To bolster his own confidence, Coulter cracked his knuckles and chattered incessantly.

"Christmas ain't over yet," he said, "you bet your candle. No sir, it ain't over yet."

It fell to Sam Berry to worry about particulars. He directed each of them to check and recheck their weapons, a process that took some doing since most of them carried from four to six revolvers plus one or more sawed-off, double-barreled shotguns.

When Tom kidded his younger brother about the arsenal he carried, Sam smiled and came back at him, patting his holster with the hand of his good arm.

"If anyone tries to pick on *this* Berry," he said, "they'll find he has briars."

With a hunter's eye, Coulter and Sam carefully chose the spot for a classic ambuscade. About two miles west of Simpsonville the road narrowed to pass between two hillocks, one side lined with a rail fence, the other densely grown over with post oaks and chinquapins. Off to one side was a fine spring, a wide pool sheeted with ice laid down with a blueish sheen to it. The trees provided ample cover to screen a body of horsemen from those passing.

Weather conditions suited their design perfectly. They found themselves in a pelting snowstorm in which the air filled with white platelets that cut across their vision diagonally. So Jarom smelled the caravan minutes before he saw or heard it, a rich odor of barn-lot manure and fermenting fodder that carried downwind so pungently Coulter swore he could touch it. Once Coulter sensed the nearness of their prey, his confidence swelled to cockiness. He stood up in the stirrups to make out what he could along the road, thumped his sidearm against his thigh, his knuckles cracking like castanets. Cold as it was, he seemed to Jarom to be sweating, beads of moisture forming about his nose and neck.

At last the vanguard came into view, not as individual steers but as a shaggy mass of ambulant meat, steak on hooves. Jarom imagined a single great beast, a lumbering behemoth coated with grizzled, bark-colored fur, stamping out of the wildness into the chock-full lane. Here and there on its back and sides specks of blue clung to the hump like some strange species of parasite. The mass moved toward them as mindlessly as flowing water, the order of march being simply to fill the space in front and shoulder into the trees. When those foremost in the herd reached the spring, the single beast broke into pieces, the bits forming into discrete steers that, smelling water, lumbered about stomping holes in the ice so they could extend their long necks to drink.

The men behind trees all watched as the firstcomers lowered their heads and took their fill, those behind moping and nudging their way forward, a few beginning to graze on tufts of scrawny grass along the road. Jarom could see the herd contained mostly shorthorns, husky brown steers fattened by unhusked corn and hay stored in the feed barns of Louis Berry, John McGraw, and who knows how many others whose farms lay along the route. At least some of these beef, Jarom felt persuaded, had been illegally confiscated from Southern sympathizers. They *had* to have been. Some others may have been legally bought with greenbacks from brokers and profiteers, men who did not let conscience or principle get in the way of making money. Others must have been simply stolen or appropriated as strays.

As they crowded about the spring, not one of their protectors took precautions or attempted to keep the cattle moving. No one prodded. No one goaded them on or went ahead to scout the road. No one sent pickets out. Most of the guards simply cleared off to one side and squatted along the roadbanks, slapping themselves and stamping to keep their blood circulating. They laid their rifles by and rummaged in their haversacks for crackers or meat, anything to restore precious heat to their bodies, to replenish the energy expended as they trudged the road. Despite the cold, the period of rest seemed welcome to keepers as well as kept. As still more of the cattle shouldered their way toward water, those first served wandered off toward the oaks and spilled onto the unfenced strip along the road.

Though it was frozen, they stamped and hashed the ground to bits, steam rising from mounds of fresh dung. The spring, its edges still glazed with ice, acted as a natural lure. Under the first poking hooves, the crusted surface popped, then minced into icy shards. Two or three of the guards tried to prod the steers back onto the road, using the butts of their rifles as goads. This failing, they stepped back to escape the press and the chance of being crushed underfoot. Those on the banks, the predicament slowly beginning to dawn on them, stood by bewildered. Not an officer in sight.

As the movement took on a life of its own, what started as a problem became a crisis. The roadway became a funnel clogged with tons of beef, the moans and bellows of the crimped cattle adding to the confusion. The foremost cows stalled and bumped themselves into tight wedges like cogs and ratchets in some outlandish rig of machinery. Smelling water, those to the rear pressed forward until their bodies wedged into prisons of flesh. Soon the forepart of the herd fixed itself in place as though soldered, making movement in any direction almost impossible. It was, Jarom felt, as though the forces governing nature conspired to bring about this impasse, as surely as the gods of the Greeks exacted retribution for the offenses, real and imagined, of erring humans.

Even the weather conspired to undo those attempting to unravel the snarl of cattle, for snow had started to fall, at first in sporadic floating tufts that stippled the air. Then the wind picked up from the east and blew in a blizzard, a blinding snowfall that shifted to the diagonal and pelted the faces of oncoming men and cattle alike. Jarom's world reverted to the half-tone of a daguerrotype, a blurred and colorless landscape of tree limbs and slope that lacked all depth, anchored only by a few objects that stood solid before the eye. Things more than ten yards away were hard to make out. What seemed a tree was a fence post. Articulated forms melted into more elemental shapes under a sky that obscured the known world while bringing it closer, reducing all to subtle inflections of grayness. Jarom lifted his hat and wrapped the scarf about his head, leaving only a band of skin where he could peer out blinking. He regretted he hadn't thought to cut eyeholes in the woolen cloth. In spite of discomfort, he knew snow for an ally. He wished each flake as it fell could be transformed to a bullet speeding toward those who blundered toward him.

As snow continued to fall, Coulter signaled for Jarom and the others to blow their own storm and smash what lay before them. Glancing to either side, one finger to his lips, he motioned for the sixteen—including Toby—to form the attack. Sam Berry, his pistol connected to its lanyard, took a position on the extreme left to nerve the city boys. Bill Marion and the main body, masked by the chinquapins, spread out along the right. The line they formed ran cheek by jowl to the road, maybe forty yards beyond the spring. The center Coulter reserved for himself. Next to him and slightly ahead was Jim Quince, a black man known as the Duke for his elegant manners and the fancy spotted vest and stovepipe Lincoln hat he sported. Other than Toby, who had done no actual fighting, he was one of only a few men of color to ride with them as trusted ally.

Jarom knew enough of the Duke to characterize him as an odd fish, an opportunist unduly fastidious about his person. The Duke was so conscious of his dress that he would not mount a white or dark-colored horse for fear the hairs would shed and show up on his clothes. As a compromise, he straddled a fat-haunched mare whose sandy shade nearly matched his own. Now, as the snow capped him in white, he hunched like a racer over the neck of his mare, a pistol in each hand, one garish gold tooth glittering in his whiskers like a promise.

Coulter, whose personal motto was "Hold your head up and die hard," gave the cue for the attack by discharging one of his pistols. "Hooraw for hell," he shouted, "and who's afraid of fire!"

In that instant heels and spurs kicked the flanks of all sixteen horses, driving them pell-mell through the fringe of oaks and onto the road. The Duke broke into the open first, still hunched over jockey style and bobbing as his big horse found its stride, Jarom, Marion, and the others tagging several lengths behind. As they cleared the trees, the horses found surer footing and worked into a gallop, fanning out across the lane until they formed a phalanx of horseflesh, four or five riders abreast, each rank shaping into a ragged V. Looking over through the pelting snow, Jarom made out Coulter shouting something at him. His mouth opened and closed, but from it came no sound, the clatter of hooves deepening to a deafening rumble as horses and men fashioned themselves into a single implement of thrust. Gripping his pistol in one hand, the reins in the other, Jarom lost the first rank of riders in the snowfall, forcing himself not to fire until he could distinguish friends from the cattle guards.

Twenty yards from the mass of shaggy cattle, those ahead raised the local version of a rebel yell, a piercing caterwaul that started deep in the lungs and burst out as a shriek. To the guards, yanked from their daydreams by they knew not what, the attack must have been terrifying. In those first seconds, Jarom was conscious of the horses' snorts and the creaking of leather as their cinches chaffed against the flanks in time with a gallop, at first only tentative and faltering. The weather that benefited them was now a leash, and things slowed almost to the slackened rate of dream.

From among the gray humps men began to appear, buckles glinting against the dark wool of their overcoats. Stunned, some gaping in horror, they turned to face the riders, each encumbered with a canvas knapsack, a plump white turtle in the center of his back. The riders' first shots stampeded the cattle and scattered the remainder of the rear guard. Hundreds of cattle, packed chock-a-block in the roadway, collided with those pushing from behind. Bellowing hoarsely, steers on the outside tore through sections of fence, sweeping rails and posts before them. To escape being trampled, several panicked guards shot into the herd, but the firing only stirred the steers to greater frenzy. When one or two went down, they tripped those that tried to scrabble over them, causing still others to stumble and pile in the roadway.

As Jarom closed in on them, most of the advance guards broke and ran, each preferring to go his own hook than face the pummeling hooves and pistols of the riders. Jarom saw a dozen or so take cover behind some downed steers and fire a few shots before the horsemen milled among them, before Marion and the Duke and the Berrys began squeezing off rounds at the plump white turtles on their backs. One minute the vanguard had been comfortably lolling along the road, the next each man was fighting or running to keep breath in his body.

As he leveled and fired at two of the runners, Jarom saw Bill Marion, still yelling, storm his big mare up the embankment where several guards scrambled toward the fence. He fired until he'd emptied the pistol in his hand, then hurled it at one of the runners before pulling out another. Enloe's blaze-faced mare, blood streaming from her hindquarters, furiously tried to throw him, rearing and turning pinwheels in the middle of the lane. Gripping his pommel with one hand, Enloe calmly poked and fired his revolver as she spun, men collapsing around him. Without officers to direct them, those behind the steers made a poor showing. Most got off a wild shot or two before dropping their rifles in capitulation. Those who did resist were shot out of hand. All told, it took less than four minutes from the first shot to the last.

After the shooting stopped, sixteen soldiers still stood, all sons of Africa. Jarom scanned the full gray faces, the upraised palms pink and somehow childlike against the government coats, gawking unfamiliarly at so many Indians on horseback, especially at one black Indian. With great dignity several stared back in defiance, but a few already lowered themselves to their knees. The snow had stopped falling, and their gyrating world was settling again to one more familiar, more fixed, more sobering.

No one ordered what happened next. It came naturally as reflex and as predetermined as the follow-through stroke of a thrower's arm completing an arc. Marion, Magruder, Coulter, and several others dismounted and pushed the survivors to one side of the road, the fenced side. No houses or buildings stood along this stretch, which formed a natural trough between the two embankments. Dry tangles of honeysuckle choked the ditch next to the road and the uneven slope above with its pockets and drifts of snow. Downcast, humiliated, the condemned filed before their executioners in ill-fitting overcoats with buttons too shiny, their government brogans lost under ballooning trouser cuffs. Marion and the Duke were already trying on overcoats from two of the prisoners as the group dressed ranks in a ragged line before turning to face their captors, all of them knowing what would come next.

Someone started a death moan, which was joined farther down the line. Beginning as a low-hummed monotone, barely audible, it expanded into a crooning that wavered and rose to a feminine pitch. Jarom shuddered not from the cold but from the apprehension and fear that racked his body. To him, the sound took on a life of its own, a heft in the quieted air after the guns. The chorale of pain and frustration was the saddest sound he had ever heard, an acknowledgment of the long, somber history of human suffering, the fronting of captor and captive that had sounded through the ages as men had confronted each other, first over clubs and bows, then with sabers, flintlocks, and mortars.

Who fired the first shot Jarom didn't know, but he stood with the others and leveled his pistol at one of the prisoners, a defiant one who seemed intent on staring him down as if to stay the finger poised against the trigger. Jarom had a vision of Patterson lying in the pasture belonging to the Locke sisters, then sitting his horse helplessly as Windrup and the home guardsmen silently debated what to do with him. Then he felt the kick of his own pistol as his wrist involuntarily lifted, and he saw the standing man pitch backward into the ditch, thrown sprawling against the bank. The body snapped tensely, then loosened, the eyes fixed now in a terrified concentration that Jarom had come to recognize as the emphatic wonder of death. As the reverberation faded, a heavy silence returned, and he felt something pass over him, pass over the whole company. Something deep in his being told him that all of them, executioners and victims alike, had paused to consider their mortality, the frail slip-knot that bound them to this earth. The hesitation was grudgingly reverent, if one could imagine reverence in Marion or Magruder or the Duke. Then a pistol beside him cracked, and others began cracking, the claps smacking through his scarf to fill his head with ringing as everything around him went floating and unreal.

Off to his right he saw the Duke, already wearing a captured coat, pot one of the kneelers with his Colt. After his own first shot, Jarom felt a stab of remorse at shooting an unarmed man. He stepped back from the slaughter. Despite his need to settle accounts, his longing to vindicate Patterson's blinding, something held him back. Fighting was one thing, execution of the helpless another. He looked over at the Duke, who seemed sublimely unconcerned, casually sighting as if unaware that the discharges came from his own pistol until one of the bluecoats he faced winced and reeled into the ditch.

But Jarom found no force of will to withdraw. He looked on as the Duke aimed at one of the stoics, a large, almond-faced man gazing indifferently at the octagonal barrel of the gun until the percussion jarred the man from his vision. At that moment Jarom froze. He would not call it conscience, but some voice inside restrained him. He knew as certainly as he knew anything that he would not fire another shot that day unless forced to. He could watch, but he couldn't, at least today, take another life that no longer threatened his. Though his hand still gripped the familiar handle, he couldn't complete the procedure he'd learned so well: raise, aim, let out a little breath, slowly squeeze the trigger. Then he was distracted, as even those horses not shy of guns began wheeling and skitting, the yellowed squares of their teeth showing as they tried to bite through their bits.

In the confusion several prisoners broke for the rail fence above the road. To reach it, they had to leap the ditch, wade through snarls of honeysuckle, and scale the embankment before climbing the fence that enclosed a large pasture bordering what had been a field of corn. One was shot halfway up and slid reluctantly back to the ditch. The second, poised to jump from the uppermost rail, was boosted by a shot that tumbled him into the pasture beyond. The third successfully cleared the fence, miraculously unhit, as bullets swarmed about him like so many impotent wasps. When his long limbs touched the hardened ground, he sprinted across the stubble and disappeared among some stalks of withering corn, his footfalls making dark blotches on the frosted grass. Though the tracks could be followed, no one seemed inclined to cross the fence and follow.

When the ringing stopped, Jarom, still having fired only one shot after the surrender, forced himself to look down in the ditch. Sprawled or hunched up along the road and mixed with the stiffening cattle, the victims lay topsy-turvy in every attitude of death. The guilty knowledge of what had been done did not shake him so much as the spectacle, the familiar disarranged, slovenly, prone, emphatically still. He remembered how he'd felt when he saw new light filling the space in the Tibbs's side yard where a familiar landmark, a great sugar tree, had toppled during a storm. Or in this instance, a whole grove of trees. Some of the dead lay composed as if sleeping off a knockabout. Others lay twisted rigidly in contortions no gymnast could duplicate, the limber cocoa faces hardened into porcelain, glazed with startlement, alarm. The skin of those slain was brittle and ridged like hulled walnuts, each cheek stiffening in its husk of death.

The corpses remained undisturbed just long enough for the whole ugly composition to fix itself in Jarom's memory. Then the Duke, Bill Marion, and Magruder began rifling pockets and packs, littering the road with goods and trifles: papers, trinkets, mess kits, canteens, a shaving kit, a few books, and spare clothing strewn everywhere. From the scattered belongings, they removed valuables—watches, rings, greenbacks, and coins. In less than five minutes all the dead had been thoroughly picked over, their pockets turned out, knapsacks emptied, linings ripped out for hidden bills. Magruder collected a small arsenal, mostly Springfields, efficiently breaking each walnut stock over a fence rail.

Zay Coulter stepped his mare off the road and pretended to scan the hills. Unusually morose, he sat his horse like stone. Offering no excuses, the Berrys rode off to round up steers, driving them into the woods where they would be safe until their owners came. When he had smashed the last rifle, Magruder piled all the usable ammunition onto a blanket, then poured it into a tow sack. Around his neck was a necklace of pistols that made him look like some monster of mayhem, a mechanical apotheosis of Samuel Colt. He carefully unloaded each piece and strung it through the trigger guard. Being superstitious, he kept not even one for his own use but parceled them out like Christmas gifts among the band to whoever would take them.

Then Jarom caught sight of a discarded daguerreotype, the image hinged between cardboard backings and cased in oval glass. Picking it up from beside the ditch, he gazed on the likeness of a broad-faced young man standing unnaturally erect in his uniform, the chevrons on his sleeve signifying a sergeant. From the tinny surface the earnest eyes stared on some invisible superior behind the camera as if awaiting the next command, one of the white officers by the stove in the stone inn perhaps, whose acknowledging salute he was waiting to receive. The stiff bill of his kepi cut across the ball of his forehead like a wedge, everything sliced off three buttons below the collar. Examining the case, Jarom found nothing to identify the man: no name, no date, only the stamp of an artist's studio in Louisville. Though the face signified nothing to him, he could not toss it away, so he stuffed it in the bottom of his saddlebag.

Poking among the bodies, Henry Medkiff, whom some called Metcalfe—a name Jarom recognized as belonging to a Kentucky governor—announced to anyone who cared to listen that he'd counted thirty-five dead, no wounded, no prisoners. As for their own hurts, a bullet had pinked the shin of one of the Louisville boys, a flush-faced cherub named Adkins. The saddest loss among the attackers was Enloe's sable mare. Downed by a wild bullet and bleeding to death, she had to be shot.

By then the remnants of the guard had gained some distance, on its way back to Camp Nelson or Louisville where Jarom knew another fuss would come in the papers, another piece by Prentice criticizing the

Union conduct of the war, probably something disparaging, too, about the employment of colored troops.

The attack scattered cattle in pastures and country lanes all over Shelby County. Some, he heard later, even strayed into Shelbyville, where some Odd Fellows quickly butchered them and served them up, holding an impromptu barbecue. Coulter sent several of the men, including at least one of the Berrys, to spread word among the claimants where their cattle could be found. Everyone also knew the news would soon reach the small garrison at Shelbyville where a pursuit would form.

As they readied themselves to leave, Jarom noticed Medkiff again. He sat hunkered on the bank, occupied with loading one of his revolvers. Next to him lay a dead private, a forearm crooked casually across his brow as though shading his eyes from a strong light. Someone, maybe Medkiff himself, had removed the shoes, and the naked toes in the raw air had a blueish cast. Ignoring the body as he might ignore a passerby on a crowded street, Medkiff concentrated on the task at hand, expertly spinning and testing the cylinder with his palm. When the spindle clicked, he prepared a load in the chamber and spun it again, repeating the process five times. Finally, he lifted the cylinder next his ear and gave it a last gratuitous flick. The tiny, well-oiled rachetings seemed to satisfy him, for he placed the pistol in one of the giant holsters that hung from his belt. He didn't seem to notice Jarom, though he stood only a few feet away.

"What day of the month is this?" Jarom asked.

Without looking up, Medkiff raised his eyes over the barren fields, blinking into the weak light of the westering sun. Jarom ticked off the seconds as the coldness cut through his coat again, chilling him to the bone as he looked down at the carnage along the road.

"The twenty-fifth of January," Medkiff said finally.

Two days later, January 27, George Prentice gave an account of the killings, as Jarom predicted, needling the Union authorities whose laxness had made the massacre possible:

> Sue Mundy, at the head of a small band of guerillas, has been going to and fro through a few counties of the State

for several months, committing outrages and atrocities of the worst [kind]. The theatre of her operations has not been a wide one; she has confined herself within a rather narrow circle. How very strange that she isn't caught. She has no reputation, and probably deserves none, for military sagacity or tact or any other kind of sagacity or tact. Nevertheless she goes where she pleases, and does what she pleases, and none of our military leaders seem to have the ability, if they have the disposition, to lay their hands upon her. We can't imagine what the matter is; surely they are not afraid of her. To permit this she-devil to pursue her horrid work successfully much longer, will be, even if the past is not, a military scandal and shame.

Jarom almost felt at times that Prentice, embittered and cranky, worked to undermine the Union through print just as he himself did through bullets. How little the old editor knew how cleverly the attack at Simpsonville had been planned and executed. Though Jarom had witnessed the feats and blunders of Morgan and Grant, had read accounts of battles reported and analyzed, he could boast no training as a military strategist. But he felt he'd learned well the tactics of survival and attack of a small band, the method of horseflies that stung a horse's rump and buzzed off into the airways.

By the end of 1864 Prentice stepped up the stories, in one instance stating that he had received a letter from Sue Mundy herself:

> We have received from near West Point, at the mouth of Salt river, a communication signed with the names of Sue Mundy and three of her chief officers, together with a note in Sue's name alone. Sue, in her individual note, asks us to publish the communication of herself and her officers, and proposed, when she and we meet, to pay us in whatever currency we prefer.

A lie, Jarom said to himself, probably one to confirm the female gender and to give Prentice license to take off on one of his flights of fancy. Here, Jarom concluded, is a man who loves his own jokes, revels in them. And Prentice proceeded to follow one bad pun with another:

Well, let us think what we will take pay in. We don't want it in Confederate notes, for our pockets wouldn't hold enough to pay for a "nip" apiece for Sue and ourselves. We don't desire it in lead, for we have mettle enough in us already. We don't want it in steel, for we have quite as much point now as we need. We prefer not to place it in hemp, for we are a temperance man and have objections to getting high. We won't accept it in kisses, for we would rather be kissed by the Devil's daughter with her brimstone breath than by a tomboy. We'll not submit to have it in hugs, for those who have seen Sue in her guerilla costume say that she is a little bare. So we'll not sue to Sue for favors of any sort. She has done a great deal of stealing, but she can't steal our heart, and we don't care to have her steel her own against us. She has committed great waste, but she can't commit her own little one to our arms.

The terrible puns he could tolerate. They would be funny had they not hit so close to home. What bothered Jarom most about Prentice was his imputation of female gender, Prentice's persistence in playing up the idea of his femininity to embarrass the Union military, to make him a pawn. Typically, when the news ended in Prentice's stories, the taunting began. He would twist the knife with gratuitous speculations, complaining first that after months of atrocities Miss Sue hadn't been caught, then flaunting gender before his readers:

Some say Mundy is a man and some say she is a woman. We don't suppose the sexes will quarrel for the distinction of owning her. If she were captured and it became important to ascertain to what sex she belonged, would the committee consist of women or men? We have this moment received a communication that Sue is a compromise between a man and a woman—a hermaphrodite. Sue, whether of the masculine, feminine or neutral gender—whether he, she, or it—is certainly a grammatical puzzle. Which of our grammar schools can parse Sue Mundy?

Reading such libels, Jarom almost wished he could confront Prentice in the nude and put an end to the game. Maybe he should have a portrait made and sent to a rival paper. Though the paper wouldn't, couldn't, print it, the editor could report Jarom's rightful gender and spoil Prentice's game. But then everyone would know that Jarom Clarke was Sue Mundy—his family, Mollie Thomas, his enemies. He wished he'd fathered a child and could prove it. He came back to the fantasy of disguising himself and sneaking into the editor's office with a kit from which he could don his plumed hat with the silver crescent, his most garish outfit, his boots, and his Colts. When he had Prentice alone, he would identify himself and drop his pants, saying, "Miss Sue Mundy, at your service." He would threaten to shoot the editor the next time he read the name Sue Mundy in the news. Would this stop him? Probably not.

MCCLOSKEY'S

Apart from home, the country where Jarom felt most himself after nearly four years of war, was a cluster of counties on an invisible line between Lexington and Louisville and mostly to the south. They included Bullitt, Marion, Spencer, Shelby, and, to the north, "Sweet Owen," which claimed to have produced proportionately more Confederate soldiers than any other county in the state. With few exceptions, people in these places treated Jarom and the others not as bandits and felons but as soldiers and kinsmen. Much of the country formed a no-man's-land of farmsteads and villages whose citizens fundamentally wanted to be left alone. Though few of the landowners held slaves, the military presence they increasingly felt riled them. They bore no love for Stephen Burbridge and by extension the federal army, which they regarded as an occupying force in a free state.

So Jarom, the Berrys, Magruder, and company came to rely on a few friends and many strangers, on local farmers and keepers of crossroads stores. Without the aid of this anonymous association, Jarom knew he and the others would not last more than a week or two before being rooted out and shot. Resented and lacking this help themselves, the federals barked but could not tree Magruder or the Berrys, who came and went in these counties at will.

To counteract this advantage, Burbridge hired what others called federal guerrillas, many of them desperate men and professional killers, to track and hunt down guerrillas. Edwin Terrell and Captain Bridgewater's bands had orders no more specific than to follow where Sue Mundy led and whittle as they went. Burbridge tried to wipe out the guerrilla menace by executing the innocent.

In February 1865, President Lincoln—who had narrowly won reelection the previous fall, and who had failed to carry Kentucky—replaced the despised Burbridge with General John Palmer, naming him commandant of the new Military Department of Kentucky. The posting was something of a homecoming for Palmer, who, although he had made his name as a politician in Illinois, where he was influential in organizing the Republican party, was a native of Kentucky. The appointment prompted editor George Prentice to write, "It is said that General Palmer came to Kentucky to relieve General Burbridge. Perhaps it might be more proper to say that he came to relieve Kentucky," a sentiment with which Jarom agreed, even though he knew Palmer would be no friend to guerrillas.

In fact, Palmer, following the adage that it takes a thief to catch a thief, hired Terrell and commissioned Bridgewater to go after the guerrillas, following wherever they led. A turncoat and scoundrel as bad as, or worse than, those he hunted, Terrell had been a bareback rider in a circus before the war. Reputed to have murdered a bartender in Baltimore, he relished the role of hunter hunting the hunted. Enlisting in the First Kentucky (Confederate) in 1861, it was rumored that he deserted after he killed an officer. In 1863 he joined the Thirty-seventh Kentucky (Union), a unit of mounted cavalry. By the end of 1864, he managed to secure a discharge and returned to Shelby, his home county, where he became a captain of the home guard. Palmer, distrustful of his hired killer, kept a loaded revolver by his side when Terrell delivered his reports.

Though he had never met Terrell, Jarom felt an immediate affinity for him. True, they fought, now at least, on different sides, but they were about the same age, had a taste of war, and found themselves fighting in small bands outside the regular service. Terrell changed sides for convenience and profit; Jarom, whatever the changes in style and order of command, kept his. Jarom painfully felt one other inescapable difference. Terrell had chosen the winning side. Whatever wrongs he committed, at least for the present, would be forgiven, even rewarded.

What could Jarom expect?

When Terrell and his handpicked thugs took up the pursuit of guerrillas, Jarom and the others, accustomed to their role as predators, knew they had become prey. If pursuit became too hot, Jarom and his saddlemates faded into the hills, the knobby backlands of Nelson and Spencer counties. The most favored hideaway belonged to Dr. Isaac McCloskey and was on his farm near Bloomfield in Nelson County, though everyone felt equally welcome with the Thomases, the Russells, and the Pences, who would open their homes, their larders, and their purses to anyone in gray. The McCloskey farm lay in the northern part of the county near the heart of the Salt River watershed, west of the Bluegrass. Though a few parts were level and arable, irregular rolling hills broke up the country, low ridges dissected by V-shaped valleys. These valleys, many of them picturesque, rose sharply to narrow ridgetops largely inaccessible to men on horseback, especially those unfamiliar with the skeins of cattle paths and game trails too narrow for wagons. Higher on the hillside farms, the fields and pasturelands dissolved in briars and dense cedar thickets, a desolate place consisting of outcroppings of rock whose dominant texture was the jagged bark of trees, a monochromatic country that would rasp a man to pieces.

Viewed from high ground, these uplands looked to Jarom like a succession of rooster combs. People inhabited only the base and lower slopes so that each wide space between the twisting spines had its hardscrabble farm, consisting of small plots of scraggly corn, a leaning barn or two, and a patch of dark-fired tobacco. Not much suitable for cultivation. Men and horses were doubly handicapped with natural barriers, which made it difficult to get about. Travel to market towns followed circuitous routes. Sometimes, even getting from one side of a farm to the other required a day's ride. This worked to the advantage of Jarom and company, who counted inaccessibility and remoteness a virtue, affording them a perfect natural sanctuary.

"God, I've come to love this place," Sam Berry said, "like the knife loves its sheath."

Dr. Isaac McCloskey and his brothers confirmed the biblical text that adversity always turns up a Samaritan, the doctor becoming one of Sam Berry's angels. Though the hopes of the McCloskeys rode with the

South, the doctor never queried a patient about his politics before bandaging his wounds. True to his oath, he offered his services to anyone who needed them. For this reason, and this reason only, given his politics, the Union authorities, who controlled the area under martial law, left him unmolested. The McCloskeys held considerable property, about three thousand acres of woodland near the west boundary of Nelson County and the east line of Bullitt. On the periphery of cave country, the property had several large caverns, one reportedly large enough to shelter two hundred fifty men. Secure from outsiders and shielded by and from the weather, McCloskey's became a combination of refuge and aid station, a place of respite.

His skills as a physician and surgeon gave Ike McCloskey a reputation as one of the finest doctors in the state. His specialty, by dint of long apprenticeship, was gunshot wounds. Visitors never worried about food because the family kept an abundant garden, butchered its own beef, and took great pride in the table they set. Though the farm possessed every comfort, Jarom never felt entirely comfortable there, constantly measuring it against Beech Grove. He missed the familiar lay of land in Logan County, a flatness that bespoke ampleness and generosity, a wider sky under fields more fertile and less hindered. He missed in particular a contrast of light set by the relation of house to ridge to treeline. In this stark and alien place, he felt the lack of the feminine, the absence of Mollie Thomas. Whenever Jarom heard the McCloskey name, he remembered a story the Berrys told about touching heels with Captain Terrell one fall afternoon. During one of the brief lulls between scouts, Sam and Tom Berry rambled over to nearby Fairfield to freshen their store of ammunition, riding back along a narrow road up one of the hogbacks. It was dusk, Sam Berry related, the sun lowering behind the ragged edge of a timbered ridge, the valley below them already steeped in shadow.

Just as they reached the summit, they heard a horse nicker a little distance away. Not thirty yards off, they spotted their implacable enemy Captain Terrell at the head of about forty riders, approaching along the trail that rose from the other side. As Sam told it, the Berrys immediately drew their pistols and veered to one side of the wagon road so as to better maneuver and fire. Also caught off his guard, Terrell and his men drew their arms and pulled off to the left of the byway, not really a road, not much more than a set of twin stripes cut by wagons and implements across the countryside.

The Berrys quickly calculated they were outnumbered about twenty to one, a not very favorable ratio. Knowing they would be summarily shot if they surrendered or turned to make a break back downhill, they considered several choices. They could attack and take down six or eight of their assailants before going down themselves, not a very promising tradeoff. Going back would put them at greater disadvantage since, unlike their pursuers, they would be firing over their shoulders. Their other option, even bolder, was to ride out a bluff, hoping to pass by their enemies with dignity and surviving to fight until the odds of survival improved. Without exchanging a word or slowing their pace, they came to a tacit accord that Jarom attributed to some mystical link between siblings.

At this point Tom Berry took over, displaying great flair when he came to the crux of the story.

"Then we closed the final few feet between us and Terrell's dark bay. Holding our pistols cocked but aimed skyward so as not to provoke him unduly, we met the hostile looks of each rider. As we passed, I remember seeing a black tuft of hair curling from Terrell's near nostril. We were so close I saw a shaving nick on one rider's cheek. Near the end, one of the horses, a strawberry roan, swished its tail against my calf, the only actual contact we had with Terrell's men. Everyone maintained his finest Sunday manners, and nobody fired. According to Tom, who took up the story again, not one word was uttered as all forty riders passed, close enough to clink spurs by raising a leg in the stirrup.

"As we met," Tom Berry said, "the silence wasn't human—no cough, no whistling of underbreath, not a syllable uttered." He described an animal presence, a steady chaffing of leather against the flanks of the horses and a chuffing of labored breath above the cloppity-clop of the hooves.

Terrell, though caught off guard, performed his role to perfection, cleverly marshaling his wits for this test of survival. He wasn't, after all, too startled to realize he would be among the first to fall if shooting started.

"What he could not resist," Tom Berry said, "he wisely chose to ignore."

Tom estimated that it took less than a minute for the whole column to pass, and the *tut*-ta, *tut*-ta, *tut*-ta of the horses as they moved became a kind of music that guaranteed their safety so long as it lasted. Sam Berry found the pressure almost unbearable. He told Jarom that by the time he cleared the last horse his body shuddered uncontrollably and a spasm of relief ran up his spine. A minute or two clear of them, he reported that Thomas relaxed the tension by snapping his cockerel head from side to side, both still rattled. Sam confirmed this when he confessed having to pry open Tom's hands so his brother's pistols could be reholstered.

Jarom had no doubts that singly or together Tom and Sam would have fought on open ground until breath left their bodies, but neither had been prepared for what he encountered on that lonely hillside—the Berrys too cunning to fire the first shot, Terrell too surprised to. Instead, they enacted a truce by default, what Tom Berry described as a mutual suspension of mayhem. By not acknowledging the original condition, they could mutually pretend that the meeting never happened. With no threat to their manly view of themselves, they could conveniently erase it from their minds. Unlike their other encounters, they bore no painful souvenirs of the meeting. No one lay dead or wounded, moaning along the roadside in pain. Tom confessed, however, that after he'd passed the last horseman, all parties widened the distance between them at a brisker gait.

QUANTRILL

By the last week of the first month of 1865, word reached Bloomfield that William Clarke Quantrill, "Bloody Quantrill," had crossed the Mississippi and entered Kentucky with several dozen of his followers. He crossed the Mississippi above Memphis near a place called Devil's Elbow on the first day of the year. With him came forty-eight seasoned guerrillas, men who preferred not to stay in Missouri. Though Quantrill held a commission as a colonel in the Confederate army, the federal authorities regarded him as an outlaw, especially after his 1863 raid on Lawrence, Kansas, where he and four hundred fifty of his men looted the town and massacred at least a hundred fifty civilians. As a result, west of the Mississippi Quantrill and his border band held low status as fugitives whose names and faces made survival a relentless and unending chore.

Like the Shawnee Indians whom Jarom had heard tales about, Quantrill seemed to regard Kentucky as a happy hunting ground, a place where he could continue fighting his private war with more profit, fewer rules, and less fear of an accounting. Jarom, like everyone, knew Quantrill's reputation long before he met him. Masquerading as federal cavalry hunting guerrillas, he and his men murdered and robbed their way across the state, Quantrill vowing that his destination was Washington City, where he would kill President Lincoln, the granddaddy of all the greenbacks. Dressed in stolen federal uniforms, his band moved east across Kentucky until they reached Nelson and Spencer counties. Quantrill adopted the alias of Captain William Clarke of the Fourth Missouri Cavalry. When asked what his mission was, he claimed to be hunting guerrillas, specifically Sue Mundy and his band. Which was true, though he wanted not to capture but to join them.

Jarom was later to learn a great deal about Quantrill, some of it from the man himself. When they eventually met, Quantrill recounted to Jarom his activities when he first arrived in Kentucky. At Hartford in Ohio County, in the guise of Clarke, whose papers he had stolen, he had persuaded the Union commander to furnish him with a guide to hunt Sue Mundy and Billy Magruder along the Ohio River. A captain named Barnette volunteered to accompany him, as did two others, a discharged veteran homeward bound and another soldier on furlough looking for a little excitement.

Three miles from Hartford out the Greenville pike toward a place called Paradise, Quantrill hanged the veteran in some tall timber along the road. Nine miles farther along, he had the furloughed soldier, a prisoner by then, unceremoniously shot. Fourteen miles out of Hartford, Barnette himself was called, quite literally, to the other shore. At sunset, while crossing a creek, Quantrill gave the signal, and Frank James, whose younger brother Jesse was beginning to make a name for himself, calmly rode up from behind and shot the captain. The body tumbled into the creek waters, and Quantrill's party rode on a little farther before settling down for the night. Quantrill told Jarom that the next morning they passed Barnette's corpse lying face up, head and neck wreathed in ice, the forehead with its bullet hole covered by a light mantle of frost. "His eyes were set," Quantrill remarked, "as if making an appeal."

Quantrill next stopped for a duty call to the federal garrison at Greenville. Accepting his word that he belonged to the Fourth Missouri, the post commander agreed to put up Quantrill's men for a couple of days. The first morning, while several of his men joked and roughhoused in the barracks, another came in and chided them without thinking. "You fellows had better stop," he warned. "Quantrill will be here directly and give you hell."

His messmates kept playing as though nothing had been said, and apparently the remark did not register with any of the Union soldiers with whom they shared quarters. Only after they left Greenville did Quantrill, hearing about the incident, ride casually up to the careless man and coolly shoot his brains out. The story shocked Jarom, who realized that someone in his own band with Quantrill's compulsions about secrecy and discipline would not last long. Jarom would have shot Quantrill himself at the first sign of turning on his own.

Farther east, at Houstonville, Quantrill stole some horses, one of his men accommodating a federal major who said that the particular horse Quantrill's man had saddled would leave the stable only over his dead body. That would have been the end of it had the major been alone. But he had entered the stable with a squad of escorts, who instantly raised their rifles to even the score. As might be expected, Quantrill's men drew their own pistols. At this point, Quantrill stepped forward as mediator, threatening to shoot the first man on either side who broke the peace. And here he applied what Jarom could only guess was his silver tongue, defusing the face-off by ordering his men to leave the barn. Once outside, they lost little time in mounting and leaving town, taking a string of thirty fresh saddle horses as they went.

After this incident, remaining in the Bloomfield area as Captain Clarke of the Fourth Missouri was impossible, so Quantrill gave up the pose. Bloody Quantrill, as Jarom saw it, simply became Bloody Quantrill. Jarom decided that the man was purely—if that was the word—a creature of expedience, a beast whose inclinations fell below the lowest rung of human decency. Quantrill wouldn't hesitate to turn Jarom in, even shoot him, to save himself. And he remembered what Patterson told him about the Titan Cronos, one of the Greek gods, a beast-god really, who devoured his progeny as they were born. "Only the cruelest father," he had said, "eats his son."

A week later at nearby Danville, Quantrill once again impersonating a federal officer, quietly stood at the bar in a local saloon when a young lieutenant got the drop on him, leveling a heavy muzzle loader at his chest. Quantrill calmly put down his glass of whiskey and turned to face the man. As he told it, he knew he couldn't fight because he had buttoned his pistols inside his overcoat. Instead, he laughed and denied being Quantrill, insisting he could prove it.

"I have special orders," he said, "from none other than Secretary of War Stanton to bear me out."

This comeback surprised the lieutenant, and Quantrill, as if to verify his claim, stepped to the door and yelled across the street for his crony Sergeant Barker, one of a group of men loitering in front of the hotel. Barker came in, saw the muzzle loader, and immediately drew his revolver.

"There's no need for that," Quantrill said, and Barker put his weapon away.

Quantrill then explained the situation and asked Barker to show his papers to the lieutenant. For a moment the lieutenant relaxed his guard, and Barker instantly pulled a smaller pistol out of his jacket and deftly disarmed the challenger.

"Colonel," Barker asked, "should I put the mark between his eyes?"

Greatly relieved, Quantrill confessed to Jarom, he charitably let the matter go. He finished his drink and made ready to leave Danville. But before he left, he turned his Missourians loose on the town. In need of footwear, they ransacked a boot store. The also tore up the telegraph office and stripped some citizens of their watches and other valuables.

Stopping in a remote area a few miles north near Harrodsburg, he split his men into three groups so they could, as he put it, better take advantage of local hospitality. Generally, this meant stopping at an isolated farmhouse and demanding a hot supper and lodgings for the night. The party under Sergeant Barker went to the home of a widow named Vanarsdoll, asking for a meal. Their mouths were full of fried chicken when they were interrupted by a company of Captain Bridgewater's militia.

The captain, a man not easily put off, had tracked them through five inches of snow.

Bridgewater surrounded the house and shouted for Quantrill's men to surrender. In reply, Barker's men fired a volley from the windows and door of the farmhouse. As they broke for their horses, Barker and several others fell dead, and the rest were captured. All this had been witnessed by one of Quantrill's men who had been sent from the next farmhouse to investigate and himself fired upon. His force cut by a full third, Quantrill confessed that he became all the more anxious to combine his forces with Sue Mundy's, mouthing the adage about safety in numbers.

Jarom sensed vividly that Quantrill had been stamped with the mark of death. What gave him this impression he could not define, but this did not stop him from speculating. First, Quantrill seemed "wore out," the first stage of sinking into fatalism. His vocation of extinction had no specific end other than to be the last man standing. His life reflected the habits of nomads who drifted from place to place and from one livelihood to another; he had been college student, prospector, schoolteacher, husband, teamster, gambler, soldier, and now outlaw. Jarom also detected a nervous disorder of some kind that compelled Quantrill to keep on the move, to flit from place to place, a trait that may in the short run have contributed to his longevity but had obviously done little to improve his character. He seemed, like Morgan, constitutionally unable to stay still. When Jarom asked him where he called home, Quantrill answered that he called home wherever he happened to be.

Was it something in Quantrill's appearance that foretold an early death? Not really, Jarom decided. Quantrill had no special physical quality that set him apart from others. Above medium height, he carried himself with a military bearing that made him seem much taller. He had wavy brown hair and affected fancy manners and dress. His face, as Jarom interpreted it, had a feminine cast, deceptively gentle, and his thick, drooping eyelids gave him a drowsy or inattentive look. But his eyes shone steady and hard, his irises the color of blooming chicory. They seemed most naturally employed sighting down a gun barrel. Like some hunters a dead shot, unlike most he had the look of a person who delighted in extinguishing life.

Bud Pence, one of the Missourians who had been with him longest, told Jarom that as a boy Quantrill delighted in nailing snakes to trees, torturing dogs and cats, and one time stabbing a fractious cow. Whether this was true Jarom couldn't verify, but the eyes made a persuasive case. Quantrill himself told Jarom that in the late fifties he had divined that war would break out within the next five years. He welcomed that prospect as some men would welcome an opportunity in some lucrative career or enterprise. As Jarom read his comments and what he knew of his performance in the West, he believed Quantrill dangerous in the extreme, a man with a natural aptitude for cruelty and mayhem.

Pence also mentioned that Quantrill prided himself on his power to strike fear into those weaker, and he told a story to illustrate the point. Once, on a jaunt with his sweetheart, he acted surprised when her affections cooled after he pointed to a certain tree and said it would be ideal for hanging a man. By the time he reached Kentucky late in his twenties, he was a man wholly without illusion.

Quantrill told Jarom that since entering the state he had been down on his luck, a resource he relied on daily. He had come to Kentucky on the supposition that he would enjoy a certain anonymity, and that things would cool down for him and his men. He was wrong on both counts. As for bad luck, Old Charley, the horse he'd captured from a Union officer and rode for most of the war, cut a tendon outside Canton, Kentucky, and had to be shot. Charley, on whom he lavished affection, was the closest thing he had to a bosom friend and had delivered him from death a number of times. Quantrill interpreted his horse's death as an ill omen.

Events bore out his predictions. Two days later, he lost his second-closest friend, Jim Little, in a skirmish with Union cavalry. Jarom learned that Little's death was the motivation for the murder of Barnette and two other soldiers outside Hartford, a balancing of accounts. The loss of followers at Harrodsburg, killed or captured, brought the full weight of despondence on him. The captors took some of his key associates to the prison in Lexington, including Jim Younger, Bill Gaugh, and several others whose names Jarom couldn't remember. When Bridgewater attacked the dozen of them outside Harrodsburg, Quantrill had been in earshot of their guns. He knew that only by some fluke had he been spared. What if Bridgewater had come to his farmhouse first? He learned the painful lesson that to survive in such an alien place, he must secrete his men among those intimate with the country and its people.

William Clarke Quantrill. Jarom wondered about the Clarke. Were they related at some remove through generations that broke off from their Virginia cousins and emigrated to Ohio? Was there something in the blood that linked them? He hoped not. If Patterson and Morgan were substitute fathers, Quantrill was a false one—devious, autocratic, devoid of all fellow-feeling, a man who had seceded not only from the federal Union but from all humanity. Jarom took some consolation from the fact that William Clarke Quantrill was wifeless, childless, a line that likely would end soon and violently.

When Bill Marion first met Quantrill, at a farm near Taylorsville, he suspected the man was just what he had been saying he was—a federal officer leading a party whose mission was to hunt guerrillas. Quantrill originally asked to meet Sue Mundy, and Marion told him that Sue Mundy wasn't in the county. True enough. Quantrill had then said he wanted to join forces with Marion. But Marion was suspicious. Before he could seriously consider the offer, he insisted that the newcomers prove they were who they claimed to be. He would put them to a test. After consulting Magruder and Sam Berry, Marion agreed that a party of Quantrill's men would accompany him to Georgetown, a smart little county seat north of Lexington, to do some mischief to the Yankees garrisoned there. Quantrill readily agreed, especially when it became clear that he was to remain behind.

"A hostage, you mean," said Quantrill.

"A token of good faith," Magruder said.

So in early February most of the Missourians and a few Kentuckians set off for Georgetown to test the mettle of the Missourians. Jarom, at large in Owen County north of Georgetown at the time, didn't join them until later, but Marion grudgingly reported what happened. The night before, the whole band, posing yet again as federal cavalry, lodged at the house of a Union man who lived within a two-hour ride of Georgetown. Their host, a middle-aged farmer who served as a deacon in the Baptist church, seemed to accept their story. At the supper table, however, someone let slip a remark about hoodwinking Union troops the next day in Georgetown, and the deacon's daughter heard it. After everyone turned in, she saddled a mare and rode to town, where she alerted the military. Then she rode back, returning before dawn with no one, at the time, any the wiser.

Next morning the party, still costumed in federal uniforms, rode into the sleepy town with its college and Baptist seminary, unaware that an ambush had been set. None of them knew that the plucky daughter, fearing for the life of her fiancé, who was stationed there, had sounded the alarm. Frank James, whose father had attended the college as a ministerial student, noticed something amiss when he saw the main street deserted. While he was telling Marion things weren't as they should be, they spotted four men a block away, stooped and running across the street, rifles in hand. Marion was swinging his horse around when the street erupted with gunfire, shots coming from almost every shop front and second-story window in the business district. Frank James had his horse shot from under him, and several of Quantrill's men took wounds. Ducking his head, Marion ordered a withdrawal, though in fact most everyone had already skedaddled. From one of the pickets they captured on the way out of town they learned that the deacon's daughter had alerted the town.

Marion later told Jarom that he had headed northwest into Owen County, where sentiment strongly favored the South. When he was certain no one had followed, he veered south, where he met Jarom, Magruder, and five others on the Owenton Pike near Monterey, a little steamboat town on the Kentucky River. At a crossroads Jarom beheld Marion's riders, bedraggled and saddle sore, a little unnerved. Even the horses seemed used up, listlessly grinding the shelled corn purchased from one of the hill farms they'd passed. Several of Quantrill's men nursed minor wounds. Two of the other Missourians, one of them Frank James, had to double up because they'd lost their horses in the fusillade that greeted them at Georgetown.

In need of fresh mounts and hoping to scrape past any large units of cavalry, they continued south through country dingy and gray, the weather having turned bitter cold. Midway became their destination, where they hoped to press more horses from a region that Marion described as producing the best horseflesh in the world. Situated eight miles or so from Versailles on the railroad between Lexington and Frankfort,

Midway had a display of handsome houses and a few storefronts, a village of some pretension. Marion, never one to forget an affront, reminded Jarom and the others that Burbridge had murdered four Confederate prisoners there in retaliation for the death of Adam Harper, an incident whose particulars he didn't dwell on.

Marion stated his intention to burn the train depot on the main street, and neither the Missourians nor Jarom raised any objections. An eye for an eye was an exchange that even the dimmest lights among the federals could understand, a just response to Burbridge's policy of reprisal—a policy that Palmer seemed to have embraced as well.

Jarom doubted that Palmer would change his ways, no matter how many lessons were delivered.

HORSE COUNTRY

After riding into Midway about suppertime one February day, Jarom witnessed Quantrill's men, masters of the craft, quickly gather the makings of a fire and ignite the railway depot. It was vacant but for the agent, whom they ushered out to mild protestations but little real resistance. They disconnected the telegraph and robbed the depot's safe, then helped themselves to provisions at several stores and chopped down two dozen telegraph poles, hoping to retard the inevitable pursuit. They also robbed several citizens of their pocket watches and greenbacks. Helping stack and upend the poles into an enormous teepee, Jarom stood by as two of the Missourians poured lamp oil on the wood and ignited it, fueling a fire that soon rivaled the one at the depot. He watched the spitting flames in that semihypnotic state that is fire's fourth power behind consumption, heat, and light. The Missourians lost little time in bagging a sizable amount of cash and loose silver from the agent and a nearby storekeeper, both of whom stood helplessly by. Though citizens came out of their houses to watch, no one spoke or dared offer any objection.

The fire provided some welcome warmth against the weather, which again turned bitter cold. Bud Pence, his forearm bandaged, passed Jarom a flask of something that distracted him from the cold more than it relieved the numbness. Watching the flames as they stabbed through the shingled roof of the depot, Jarom felt the raw alcohol burn a course down his throat, a parallel conflagration that fired his vitals. On the Good Book he would have sworn he could feel it in his feet. As the flames rose higher, he and the others pressed closer until the roof groaned on the brink of collapsing. They all stepped back as it caved in on itself, shooting cascades of sparks into the heavens. When the fire at the depot dwindled, Jarom and the other onlookers backed up to the burning telegraph poles until Marion summoned them to their saddles. Even as he mounted Papaw, Jarom couldn't keep his eyes from the fire. It formed a bright parabola against the darkened houses, throwing wavery shadows against the water tower on its wooden stilts, the blue flames and billows of sulfurous smoke illumining the darkness with a yellowish tinge. He hadn't seen such a blaze since the destruction of the trestles at Muldraugh's Hill.

Leaving town without having fired a shot, they rode briskly out the Midway-Versailles road into the heart of horse country. At dusk the large farms they passed seemed remote and deserted, only a dim light or two showing in the odd window as they passed. Along the way they saw everything from tenant and slave cabins to well-fenced stockfarms whose manicured lawns lay under a bed of snow, the twin wheel tracks on one driveway silvered under the high winter moon. Well back from the road stood columned houses where Jarom pictured owners sleeping and dreaming their lives away, pampered and safe. When they awoke, someone would make their beds, cook their breakfasts, and empty their slop jars. Everything was done for them except sire their children—and that wasn't always certain. Whoever won or lost the war, he sensed that those behind the columns would prosper. These were not his people, at least not any longer. Stopping in the road, he could still see over his shoulder the fire's faint glow above Midway, a fading rose of pinkish light.

At a crossroads Frank James pointed out the stagecoach inn where his mother had been born, a combination of log and stone. Rather than pass through the intersection, they turned west on the Lexington-Frankfort Pike, an unusually beautiful stretch of macadamized road that ran between stone fences and remnants of the old forest, whose unleafed limbs formed a woven basketry over the right-of-way. In the darkness the mesh of dark limbs seemed to crowd down on them, and Jarom braced himself for the flash of carbines he expected at any moment from behind the fences. Their shield of stones he recognized as perfect for ambush.

In the gathering dark Jarom looked for remembered landmarks, for he'd been to the farm briefly once before, toward the end of October when he and six others one beautiful fall afternoon simply trotted up the drive and past the house to the stables. No one anticipated that they would maraud a horse farm in daylight, since such raids in the past had occurred only after dark. Intimidating those at the stables, they seized six valuable horses—the unbeaten colt Asteroid, the promising Bay Dick, and three choice two-year-olds sired by the great stallion Lexington, and one trotting mare. Before anyone resisted, they fastened leads to their halters and led them away, the seven of them, including Berry and Magruder, making off with six horses that would not seem out of place in the stables of princes.

Knowing a chase would come next, they rode hard about ten miles to the Kentucky River, where the owner Alexander and his men caught up with them, charging before they could cross. When the others scattered, leaving the horses to Alexander, Jarom, riding Asteroid, managed to swim safely across, though not without being fired on while still in the water. From memory he could not still the pang of the bullets striking around him. He also remembered that afterward Alexander put up a reward of a thousand dollars for the return of Asteroid and five thousand dollars for Jarom's capture.

Not one to give up easily, Alexander deputized his neighbor and friend Willa Viley to negotiate Asteroid's return. Viley later claimed that during their caper Berry had been wounded in the heel by a gunshot, a claim Berry denied. Viley and two other men had dogged the progress of Jarom and the others for forty miles to Bloomfield. With great luck they happened on Magruder and Jarom, still on Asteroid, riding along a rural lane. The minute he saw Viley, Jarom knew what he'd come for, and the negotiations began. When Viley offered him three hundred dollars for the horse, Jarom finally agreed to the return, conditioning the deal on Viley replacing Asteroid with his equal, though at least one of them knew that Asteroid had no equal. As a gesture of trust, Jarom accepted his check along with the promise that another horse would be provided soon.

So Jarom revisited, as Alexander might put it, the scene of his misdeeds. Five rode in the first time, over twenty now. When they arrived at the entrance of the farm, Jarom confirmed the location, and the whole troop passed the twin gateposts and up the slight incline to Woodburn. They had entered the domain of R. A. Alexander, celebrated for producing the best purebred racing stock in America. Just after they left the pike, Marion announced his need—his yen really, since his mount was in fine fettle—for a new mount.

"And I know just where to get me one," he said, "and not a nag neither but a prize."

Anyone who read the papers or listened to talk about horses knew that Alexander's thoroughbred foals performed as equine aristocrats of the racing and trotting meets. Chief among them was Lexington, for years acknowledged as the most important sire on the continent. In some mysterious way he represented a convergence of traits whose pedigree spawned winners and fortunes—bloodline, stamina, speed, conformation, and, in some mysterious way, a zeal to win. Through Jarom and Sam Berry, both with an inexhaustible passion for horses, Lexington's reputation obviously had reached the ears of Bill Marion. A heaven for horses, the farm provided a home for over two hundred.

Looping up the long drive that was as yet printless under new-fallen snow, Jarom made out the silver roofline of an enormous house topped by a cupola. To his left, next to the main elevation, stood an extensive wing flanked by hedges and walkways. He remembered the formal garden they passed as the largest he had ever seen in which nothing was produced to eat—except, perhaps, some sprigs of mint for juleps. He kept his eyes open for the Union Jack Alexander reputedly flew to proclaim his British citizenship, which made him neutral and exempt, he hoped, from any national squabbles in America. More pointedly, Alexander raised and displayed the flag in hopes of preserving Woodburn from guerrillas. Marion, following Jarom's directions in every particular, bypassed the darkened mass of unpainted brick, passed through the kitchen yard, and started for the stables. As they came abreast of the house, a light appeared in one of the upper windows and several dogs began to bark.

"Halt!" a voice shouted from the kitchen doorway as they filed past.

Onto the porch stepped a frail-looking, florid man in his mid-forties, a pistol in his hand, another in his belt. Slight, with a high forehead and thinning brown hair, he looked to Jarom every ounce the child of privilege who might own such a place.

"Halt!" the man shouted again as the file kept moving until all but Marion, in the front rank, stopped and turned back, the other mounts forced to stand as one came upon the other. A minute passed before the entire company had reined in. Looking down on the small, neatly dressed man in his sober clothes and trimmed whiskers, Jarom at first thought him a lost Quaker who had wandered or been carried south of the Ohio.

"What will you have, gentlemen?" the man asked curtly, placing the slightest edge on "gentlemen."

"We only want some provender," said Marion.

"How much?" said the man on the porch, apparently wishing to waste no time on amenities but to get down to cases.

"Oh, I would expect enough to feed two hundred horses," Marion said.

"That's a pretty large order," said the man on the porch. "I have provender enough but no place to feed to so many."

At this juncture Marion took another tack, explaining that his detachment had been sent to press horses into the service.

The man on the porch identified himself as R. A. Alexander and asked to see his orders.

At this point Marion and the others drew their pistols.

"This is our order," Marion said, holding his pistol up as though to admire its mechanism.

Alexander said he had a body of armed men in the house prepared to fight to protect his property. In fact, Jarom had learned that after the first raid Alexander thought it in his interest to hire armed watchmen to protect his stables. Alexander added that he held British citizenship, that as a foreign national the law of nations protected his property.

"I suppose," he said, a bit imperiously, "if you are bound to have the horses there is no necessity for a fight about it, but if you are disposed to have a fight, I have some men here and we will give you the best fight we can."

Marion announced that he had a hostage with him, Alexander's neighbor and friend Willa Viley. Jarom recognized him as the man who had negotiated the release of Asteroid at Bloomfield. Viley had been captured when several of Quantrill's men stopped at a neighbor's and liberated a buggy horse from the stable. Outraged, Viley, a man in his late seventies out paying his neighbor a visit, became so worked up he mounted a horse in his bedclothes and pursued the marauders riding bareback. Brought along in custody, Viley urged his friend to give up his horses without causing bloodshed.

"Alexander," he pleaded, "for God's sake let them have the horses. The captain says he'll be satisfied if you let him have two horses without a fight or any trouble."

Alexander apparently reconsidered, for he gave in and told Marion that, all right, he would surrender two of his horses. He even agreed to seal the bargain with a handshake, walking over to where Marion was sitting astride his horse and extending his hand. Marion surprised Jarom by taking it.

"But," said Marion, "you and your men must also surrender your arms."

Alexander paused as if weighing his alternatives. "I am to give you two horses," he said finally. "You shall have the horses, but I will neither march out my men nor give up my arms."

After some consideration, Marion grudgingly agreed to let Alexander and his hirelings keep their arms. ""But," he said, "if you fire a shot at us, I will torch the place."

"If a shot is fired," Alexander retorted, "it will be you that fired first."

"Where're the horses?" Marion demanded. "We're in a hurry and have no time to dance with shadows."

As Jarom read the other raiders, they began to grow weary of so much talk and so little do. Alexander pointed to the nearest stable and told him that inside they'd find the horses they wanted.

Alexander went along with them to the stable, wading through the snow in what appeared to be slippers. Stopping in front of a long, dark stable, he told Marion that he would bring out the first of the two horses he'd promised.

"Is he a good 'un?" Marion asked.

"Yes, as good as you will find anywhere."

"Bring me the bald horse," Marion said.

Jarom deduced that Marion had very specific knowledge about Alexander's holdings and this confirmed it. By bald horse he meant the one with the white blaze in his face, the one known as Bay Chief, the prince of Alexander's entire stable of horses.

Alexander agreed that the bald horse was a good trotter but protested such a horse had more value for him than for Marion, that he had twenty horses better suited to his use.

But Marion insisted on having the trotter.

"If he's valuable to you," he reasoned, "he's valuable to me."

Alexander went off and consulted a man named Hull, his stable master, apparently to arrange to give up some horse of lesser value. Alexander returned to say that there was some confusion about who had the key to the stable. Jarom sensed that this was another stall, another ploy to eat up time. Finally, Alexander said he would fetch his own key and strode off toward the house.

What happened next, Jarom later pieced together from Tom Henry, one of Quantrill's men who'd gone into the Alexander house. Seeing two horses without riders in the kitchen yard, Alexander surmised that two of the raiders had gone inside. He rushed in, going down the long passageway from the kitchen room to the dining room where he found three females: Mrs. Daniel Swigert with a babe in arms; a nurse with child in her arms; and Mrs. Swigert's teenaged daughter Mary. An armed raider stood by the fireplace with a cocked pistol in his hand. The other guerrilla—most likely Bud Pence—stood at the other end of the room loaded down with pistols and a rifle or two he had collected from around the house. Though neither of the women seemed frightened to the point of hysteria, Alexander, seeing them considerably upset, stepped in. Determined to get the guerrillas out of his house, he told them that their captain said that if he gave up two horses without a fight or any trouble, he could keep his arms. And that he meant to do just that.

Highly displeased with this challenge to his authority, Tom Henry, the guerrilla with the cocked pistol, approached Alexander and raised it menacingly.

"Damn you," he said, "deliver up the rest of those arms or I'll shoot you dead!"

According to Henry, Alexander knocked his pistol away and started to grapple with him, pushing him out of the dining room and into the hall, in an effort to bolt the door. But when Alexander tried to trip Henry, Henry pulled him down on top of him. Before he knew it Alexander had pinned him to the floor. Henry shouted for Bud Pence to shoot Alexander, but Pence refused, saying that Alexander wasn't armed and couldn't really do much harm. Thinking he could end the fracas, Pence ordered Alexander to let Henry up, but Alexander again refused, saying that Henry would shoot him. They grappled again and Henry's gun went off when it struck an iron safe that was in the hall. Henry thought that he'd broken his arm, and while he fought the pain, Pence pushed him into the kitchen, prompting Alexander to close and bolt the door.

As the light grew fainter, Marion ordered a fire of straw built in front of the stables so they could inspect the horses as the groomsmen led them out. Frank James took Mr. Hull aside and explained that that if anyone resisted their taking the horses, that person would be shot. So Hull and some of the stable hands stood helplessly by as Marion, James, and other guerrillas selected the horses they would take with them, including such highly valued ones later identified as Abdullah and Bay Chief. Jarom felt some sympathy for Hull and others of Alexander's men, who offered large sums to the guerrillas if they would forfeit Bay Chief and Abdullah, two of the most exceptional horses in America. The amount offered not to take Bay Chief reached ten thousand dollars, but Marion refused it. Jarom was fairly certain that Alexander's help had switched some of the named horses, including Asteroid. They had no time to determine which was which.

When Jarom asked specifically for Asteroid, the stableman told him that Alexander kept Asteroid in another barn, along with his sire Lexington, blind and too old to ride now. Jarom had a hankering to see the famous sire, having heard that he still stood stud, housed in special quarters of equine splendor. But Jarom didn't want to push the point because he knew that to the Missourians Lexington was only a place, not a prince of sires. Skittish and unfamiliar with this alien setting, they had no wish to stay a minute longer than necessary. These men, Jarom considered, had been hunted not for weeks or months but years. Whatever else they were, they weren't sightseers but desperate men primarily bent on survival.

Jarom suspected one of the trainers, a trim little man whose pointed ears gave him an elfish look, of working the switches, but he didn't betray him. Though he didn't like being trifled with, he knew that without knowing each of the horses individually he had in the end to accept what they brought forth, hoping for serviceable mounts and not jades. He also suspected that Alexander had no jades, no spavined, foundered, or inferior stock—not a man who owned the garden so carefully cultivated by the side of the house.

Alexander, surrounded by a growing circle of groomsmen, trainers, and hired watchmen, turned up at the second stable. Here he reintroduced an old theme, though even he must have known it would bear no fruit except possibly to stall the inevitable.

"Before you do anything you'll regret," he said, "I must inform you again that I am a British citizen, and that Britain is yet neutral in this war. My property as a British citizen is exempt from appropriation by either army."

"British or skittish," said Marion, to take him down a peg or two. "I don't give a damn! War's war, and I need some horses. In particular, I want your man to bring me Bay Chief."

"Bay Chief is mine!" the little man shouted, "No one is going to steal him from me, no one!"

Losing all composure, he began to move toward Marion in a menacing way, elbows outthrust, arms swinging as though he might knot his hands into fists to thrash him.

"Don't get in my way," Marion shouted, drawing his Remington and motioning him back.

He turned to one of the trainers who had been standing by, trying now to dissolve into the shadow of the stable.

"Fetch me Bay Chief," Marion ordered, and "bring him to me now!"

The trainer looked to Alexander for approval. Alexander, more subdued and apparently resigned, nodded for the man to do as he was told.

In a few minutes the trainer returned with a fine trotter, slender-legged and high-rumped, his coat rich and burnished as a buckeye worked free of its hull. Alexander stood helplessly by as Marion inspected Woodburn's greatest prize, patting him with a possessive hand and lifting the head to examine his teeth. Jarom considered that Marion's touching his stable's pick must have been as offensive to Alexander as another man fondling his wife. For a time, Jarom believed that the man would break down and cry.

"If you leave me my horse," Alexander offered in one last attempt, "I'll see that you're paid five thousand American dollars."

"I'll not be bought off," Marion said. "Not at that price anyway."

Speaking with a Scottish burr, which he must have reverted to when his dander was up, Alexander upped the offer to seven thousand five hundred. Still Marion refused, saying he wanted to try a horse whose owner prized him so highly. Again Alexander protested, finally raising the offer to ten thousand greenbacks, but Marion would hear nothing of it.

Jarom dreamt of what he would do with so much money, how he would spend it, where on the face of the green earth he would go. Would it be somewhere like Argentina, where he could buy a ranch and not worry about Burbridge or Palm and such scoundrels catching up with him? Maybe California. Maybe even Ireland, where some of his forebears had burned peat and stacked stone along the treeless hummocks.

The trainer, sent off for more horses, emerged from the stable leading three more likely ones, including at Marion's insistence the trotter Abdullah, the one that Jarom valued as the handsomest of the lot.

The next stable housed racehorses, and Marion claimed four more, including a bay mare, a filly, a gelding named Norwich, and a colt that the groom identified as Asteroid, though Jarom had his doubts. This last attracted Magruder, who'd heard the name, but as it happened someone had slipped in another counterfeit, and Magruder learned later he'd come away with only the name.

As Marion had some of the horses saddled and others provided with halters or leads, Alexander made his final appeal. Haggard-looking, distraught, once again he offered to buy back his own horse. Once again Marion turned a deaf ear.

"Take the others," Alexander said pitifully, "only leave me Bay Chief."

All the defiance had gone out of him. His voice quavered, pleading now. He wondered how Alexander treated his children, if he had children. Would a man who valued his animals as though they were his children value his children as though they were animals?

Marion turned to his business, attaching the bridle over Bay Chief's neck and fixing a bit in his unwilling jaw. He threw a blanket onto his back and cinched his saddle over it. Then his men tethered the other horses with leads, no more than one to a rider, and the whole troop clattered down the drive and into the darkness, leaving R. A. Alexander and his awakened help—Jarom counted at least twenty-five—shivering in their clothes and keenly aware that misery came in all sizes.

The last Jarom saw of Alexander he stood in the drive, the hulk of his house rising among the trees and hedges, a surtout draped over his narrow shoulders, the chiseled face still florid with outrage and disbelief. His feet, he thought, must be freezing.

And Jarom felt a wave of sympathy pass over him. He had no personal quarrel with Alexander, who seemed decent enough if too much wedded to his possessions, especially those of the equine stamp.

He knew what it meant to love a horse. Papaw, almost instinctively sensitive to his intentions without prodding or whip, was more than enough horse for any one man to claim. He felt fidelity to her and wondered if this was some perverse variation on what it meant to be faithful to someone—Patterson, Aunt Mary Tibbs, Sarah Lashbrook, Mollie Thomas. The world that he knew he knew over Papaw's neck. The world would not seem intact to him without her upright ears to frame it. She knew his weight, his ways, the messages of his heels. He convinced himself she could read his mood through something so subtle as the pinch of his calves against her flanks or the pull she felt through his stirrups, his tone of voice. He wondered if she felt resigned to him as the burden she was fated to carry. These dainty trotters and thoroughbreds had speed and carriage, class, looks, even nobility. What he valued in Papaw were reliability, stamina, and fearlessness, and less definable qualities he described as heart. She was, he realized, what he possessed instead of home, instead of spouse, instead of bonded friendship. For him to take another would be betrayal, a kind of equestrian adultery. He imagined acquiring a new mount as something as strange and discomfiting as slipping on a dead man's boot.

A TIGHT SPOT

After they trotted out between the gated pillars of Woodburn, Marion led them back to the Kentucky where they found the river nearly at flood stage. The men, leading the stolen horses, managed to get across by ferry, breakfasting at a farmhouse near Lawrenceburg. While Jarom sat at the table finishing his ham and scrambled eggs, Frank James, sitting next to him and gazing casually out the window, raised the alarm.

"Yonder they come!" he shouted, knocking over his chair as he leapt to his feet. "To the stable, boys, for your horses and your lives!"

Hearing the first shots, Jarom peered out to see a stream of bluecoats pouring into the farmlot through the open gate. Frank James and several of the Missourians, accustomed to such drills, recognized the danger first, sprinting out the back door toward the barn to bring up their horses. Helter-skelter, they scrambled forty yards or so across open ground, dodging bullets, flitting first one way and then another. From the back window, Jarom saw at least one of the Missourians fall. Telling those who remained behind to follow him, Marion bolted out the door and jumped behind a stone wall. Jarom and some of the others ducked behind one of the outbuildings.

From the barn Jarom heard more firing and knew Frank James and the three other Missourians were struggling to get their horses saddled. Jarom steadied himself and popped off four of his loads at several bluecoats who hopped from their horses and poked their pistols through the chinks in the barn. Magruder was firing too, and two of the attackers dropped to the ground with the first shots. Of the eight horses put up in the barn, only four made it out. Among the first to fall was Bay Chief, best of the horses taken at Woodburn, hit as he exposed himself for a few moments at the barn door.

Some voice of caution told Jarom to make his break for Papaw while he could. Fortunately, Papaw and the other Kentuckians' horses were hobbled at the rear of the lot where they couldn't be seen from the road. Jarom told Magruder he felt now was the moment to go. The others agreed, and together they broke cover, getting halfway to the trees before those at the barn turned their attention to them and started firing. As he ran, Jarom saw a big man on horseback waving his gun. Bridgewater, he felt certain. Though the big man's mount pranced some distance off, Jarom paused to draw a bead on him, popping off two shots that had no visible effect on the hulking figure still waving his pistol.

Then he untied Papaw and hiked himself up on the stirrup, the others following him out onto the road, the firing behind them diminishing into little pops no louder than a puckering kiss. Not until they felt safe from pursuit did Jarom call a stop to rest and recover themselves. Marion and several stragglers soon caught up, all of them en route to a farm near Bloomfield where they'd agreed to rendezvous. Eight of Jarom's bunch had been wounded in the fight—five Missourians and three Kentuckians. Except for one, they'd been able to take everyone with them. Tom Henry fell early with a shot in the breast that appeared to have killed him. After Jarom mounted Papaw before making his break, he saw one of Bridgewater's men trot over to where Henry lay on the ground, poke his pistol at his prostrate form, and shoot him twice more from the saddle. Jarom assumed that Henry was killed then if he hadn't been earlier, especially when he saw the man hop off his mount and crouch to go through Henry's pockets. Jarom felt the impulse to charge over and shoot the man. But his prudent self cautioned against it, and he put spurs to Papaw, scurrying off with the others.

Assured they had shaken off pursuers, Jarom, the four stolen horses, and the other survivors took refuge at Wakefield's in Spencer County, a place where they felt safe enough to collect themselves and doctor their wounds. To Jarom, all seemed pretty well used up, especially Alexander's blooded horses, lot-tamed and unaccustomed to rough use. Two in addition to Bay Chief had been wounded and left to die in Anderson County. One they had to desert. As Alexander had warned, Abdullah wasn't conditioned for hard riding. Forced to swim the freezing waters of the Kentucky, he'd emerged, dispirited and limping, a pale nominee for death. In Lawrenceburg they had to abandon him, ridden until literally he could not take another step. Word soon got back to Alexander, who sent some men to care for him, but the newspapers reported he died four days later. The papers quoted Alexander as saying that Abdullah had been the most promising sire of broodmares in Kentucky.

When news of the raid came to Quantrill and he saw the abused horses, he reacted with outrage. Despite the fact that he desperately needed more mounts, his men had broken these horses, used them up without forethought or pity. Answering to some residual impulse of rightness, he insisted they be returned to Alexander. Having lost his own prized Charley, Quantrill must have pitied Alexander, feeling for once another's loss. Jarom recognized Quantrill's gesture as the only sign he'd seen in Quantrill of a softer heart. Marion had no such feelings. Though a little intimidated, he didn't want to give up what he regarded as plunder rightfully his, relenting only when someone warned him of Quantrill's mercurial temper. So Marion, cowed for once, had the four surviving horses collected and delivered through third parties to Woodburn. Alexander was so grateful he presented Quantrill with a magnificent stallion named after a popular stage player whom Jarom had never heard of—Edwin Booth. The morning after their return, Quantrill and his bedraggled survivors, many visibly sagging in the saddle, parted company with the Kentuckians and went into seclusion to the extent they could find it, needing a few days to mend and to mull over what misfortune to perpetrate next

And that wasn't all. There came a windfall. Two of Quantrill's men, riding ahead of the main body, fell in with a strong Union man who, seeing their federal uniforms, mistook them for federal cavalry. He praised them for their sacrifices and proudly declared his own dedication to the Union, his willingness to give up all of his property if that would further the cause. One of the two Quantrill men, Bud Pence, decided to take him up on his pledge. He asked the patriot if a man of his sentiments might be willing to exchange his fat and fresh mount for the jaded one that he, Bud Pence, was riding. Though the patriot hesitated longer than seemly, he realized that to save face he must make good on his boast. He allowed that his horse could be a temporary loan and that for his part he would fatten Pence's horse so they could work an exchange when he returned. Pence pronounced that a capital proposal and set about putting his saddle on the stranger's horse, all the while congratulating the man for his loyalty. Not until several days later did the patriot learn that he'd awarded his fine horse to one of the hated rebels. This was the only levity Jarom remembered during the ordeal, and he knew he would tell and retell the story long after he'd forgotten more sanguinary details of the horse-stealing venture.

Jarom thought no more about the supposed death of Tom Henry until a week later when word came that Henry still breathed and was expected to recover from all three of his wounds. The second shot, fired inches from his face, entered his mouth and exited through the left side of his neck. The third burrowed into the right cheek an inch below the eye, passing near the base of his right ear. When fired, the muzzle, all but resting against his upper cheek, blew powder into him, burning off his eyebrows and lashes, making an imprint that Magruder described as a gunpowder tattoo.

His unconscious state probably saved him. When he came to, dark had fallen and the place was deserted. He had presence of mind enough to know he would die of exposure without a warm berth and caring hands to see to his wounds. Unable to walk, he dragged himself across the frozen ground for three miles until he reached a log house in which he saw no light. He managed to crawl up the steps onto the porch, where he used a piece of firewood to thump against the door until someone came. The Samaritan who took him in, suspecting what had happened, sent for Marion, who at great risk to himself sneaked to the place and guarded Henry until a doctor could be found—the first, the only, noble deed Jarom ever knew of Marion performing for one of his men.

A few days later Jarom put his hands on George Prentice's account of the raid. As usual, the editor managed to get some of the facts wrong. He accused Marion of stealing thirteen instead of fifteen horses. The piece contained other errors as well as the usual provocations. Reading Prentice's character through the man's writings, Jarom came to believe that the editor picked his phrases as an amateur orchardist would plums, more for their color and eye appeal than for their sweetness of taste. No one who regularly read his columns would accuse him of being fair-minded when he crafted such phrases as "punish the rascals as they deserve." Prentice's account also raised questions of degree. What Prentice characterized as a "hot pursuit" Jarom described as tepid at best. But what he most resented was Prentice's habit of augmenting facts with judgments, shaping what he should have been describing. As a merchant of words sitting at his editor's desk, Prentice, he decided, had little sense of who deserved punishment and who didn't. Though Jarom conceded to himself that he didn't know much better, he at least observed from the field where he could quickly learn to sort friend from foe. He'd also learned that a rival newspaper had questioned the guerrilla articles Prentice's journal published, charging that some of them were the coinings of a fertile imagination.

~~~~~~~~~~~~~~~~~~

MARION

For weeks Jarom pondered what made Marion in so many ways so despicable. Jarom didn't like him, didn't trust him, and felt it necessary to understand why. Size wasn't a factor. Marion could never intimidate others by his size. He was thickset but modest of stature, standing about five-four in his stocking feet. To compensate, he wore Western boots with elevated heels that gave him another inch or so. These boots, tooled by some nameless artisan of the old Southwest, were his only concession to stylishness. Usually he wore a scruffy jeans jacket over a checked shirt much in need of washing, much in need of darning. Hard use had worn the denim of the jacket threadbare, the blue of an ideal summer sky long ago bleached out by wind and weather.

Marion's personal habits gave little cause for boasting. He never shaved and seldom bathed. His face formed a thicket from which the eyes stared out with a blend of wonder and malice, a look Jarom imagined a bear might give waking at the mouth of a cave or culvert from a winter sleep. A blunt mustache bristled above his thin upper lip. Hair thinning on his crown, he wore the scraggly remnants long and unkempt. It billowed from under his hat in dark snarls through which a comb seemed never to have passed. He adopted Remington pistols as his weapon of choice because they had drop cylinders that permitted quick reloading. Marion never ventured out without a half-dozen or so replacement cylinders, each holding six loads. He had Tailor Tinsley sew large pockets onto his vest with which to carry them, creating a fad that others called "guerrilla pockets." Berry once commented to Jarom that the bulges on Marion gave him a lumpy look. Marion's most characteristic expression was a look of intense concentration, a fixity of mien that masked his emotions. Jarom seldom, if ever, saw him put down his guard and wondered how he could sleep—if he *did* sleep. Jarom wasn't long around him before discovering that Marion had an ungovernable temper, a whiplash tongue, and a weakness for peach brandy—not a combination that made for lasting friendships.

In fact, the man answered to every descriptor of villainy that Jarom could summon: ruffian, miscreant, wretch, monster, reptile, imp, demon, cutthroat, incendiary, knave, rascal, rogue, scoundrel, scapegrace, blackguard. Berry referred to him as the Devil's spawn. Being human remained a continent that Marion had little interest in discovering or exploring. Thinking of him, Jarom remembered an expression Aunt Mary used to describe everything from odd behavior to lunacy: "Not all of his birds roosting in one tree." Berry, who likewise had little affection for Marion, once told Jarom he regarded Marion as a shark with teeth at the top and spurs at the bottom and not much in between but a paunch and a saddle.

Marion lavished his greatest affection and care on his weapons. While others loafed or breezed around the cookfire, he would be cleaning one of his eight Remington pistols or ramming a rod down the barrel of his shotgun, meticulously swabbing out the bore with a wad of cotton or a cleaning patch. Piece by piece, Jarom noted, he would take his pistols apart like a lapidary working his jewels, spreading them on his spare shirt. With a surgeon's deft touch he would adjust this spring or test that mechanism, oil every working part to a blue sheen. Pistols he used for individual targets, small game. Shotguns he preferred for close work because in a fracas targets could be multiple and expansive, the wide swath of the balls making allowance for his weak vision, his eyes so close-set they seemed at some angles to be crossed. Notoriously nearsighted, he could not distinguish a wagon from a windmill over thirty yards away. Early in the war he was rumored to have shot one of his only friends, mistaking him for an enemy. Despite his handicap, he counted more hits than any three of his cohorts.

As far as Jarom could tell, Marion had no mottoes or teachings by which to direct his life, no articles of faith, other than his welcoming of perdition in, "Hooraw for hell! Who's afraid of fire?" His major motivator was hate, indiscriminate but focused on the nearest object at hand. He burned down the Spencer County courthouse to make good a threat. The papers, especially George Prentice, could not get his name straight, sometimes spelling it Merriman or Meriman. Bereft of letters, Marion probably could not offer a correction; he boasted he'd never been to school a day in his life.

Jarom learned that Marion had joined Berry, Magruder, and the rest when he realized that guerrillas were a more efficient instrument of hurt than massed troops or solo malevolence. His past was vague, but he once told Jarom that local Regulators—the home guard—had ruined his family. Picking a time when his father was away, they had stripped and beaten his mother and two sisters with hickory withes until blood ran to their toes. The punishers left them unconscious, their hands still bound, until the neighbors found them. Though his mother didn't survive, the sisters recovered in a few months, at least physically, in time to bury the father, shot by never-identified bushwhackers. After that, his sisters had not been right in the head. Where or when this happened, Marion would not say, but Jarom believed every word of it, for he almost never saw Marion show a glimmer of feeling for anyone.

"I haven't a friend in the world but my pistols," he told Jarom one night as they sat by the campfire, Jarom sipping coffee, Marion guzzling brandy from a flask. Jarom sensed that Marion made this statement not for sympathy, not as boast, but simply as a declaration of fact.

This statement partially explained what happened to Tom Berry's Toby after Simpsonville. Before the attack Tom Berry, for reasons he didn't explain but which everyone understood, instructed Toby to stay behind in the woods. When the shooting stopped, he rejoined the Berrys as they and the rest of the party made their way south to Spencer and thence to Nelson County. As a reward for his part in scouting the cattle train, Tom Berry exchanged Toby's mule for a handsome sorrel saddle horse found after the ambush. Near Bloomfield, Toby, proudly astride his prize, happened to find himself riding next to Bill Marion. In an unoffending way, he tapped Marion lightly on the leg.

"The fight was a hot one, wasn't it, Marse Bill?"

For some reason Marion reacted as though bitten by a water mocassin. As Jarom heard later, Marion cursed poor Toby and told him that he was going to kill him but would first order his coffin. Mortified but not wanting to believe anyone capable of spewing such venom, Toby apologized profusely and begged him not to do it, that he had never meant any offense.

For answer, Marion spurred away after giving Toby a menacing look, refusing to speak or hear another word. When the party reached Bloom-field, Jarom thought Marion had forgotten his threat, for he seemed to act normally, or at least to act like himself. But true to his promise, Marion ordered a coffin, the cheapest, though custom-made to accommodate Toby's long legs.

The next morning, before Jarom and the others rose from their beds, Marion roused Toby and told him to say his prayers. He announced to him that his coffin had been fitted and already paid for. With an expression of dread and disbelief, Toby dropped to his knees and began to pray. Without any more ceremony Marion raised his pistol and shot him in the forehead, then galloped casually out of camp.

Jarom never learned his reasons, for the same day, about four o'clock in the afternoon, news came that Bill Marion himself had been killed by Captain Terrell's men in a fracas near Chaplintown. No one offered any regret or sentiment of grief. Fresh from laying Toby in the cold ground, the Berrys already were planning retribution when the news came. Later, Jarom learned that when the news reached Terrell, he grabbed up the body, lashed it to Marion's compliant warhorse, and rushed off to General Palmer in Louisville to claim the reward.

For Jarom, Marion's death served as a lesson in incivility. He and Sam Berry, musing by the fire one night, tried to put a name to all the things they didn't like about Bill Marion and why the world would not be a lesser place without him.

"What it comes down to," Jarom had said, "is that he was more brute than human."

"What that means," Berry the schoolteacher said, "is that he was by nature undomesticated, feral. Take animals. They are of two types, tamed and wild. A pullet or a house-raised spaniel can't make it in the wilderness. Nor will a raccoon or a ferret or a water moccasin make a house pet. Marion lacked any ties to human sympathy, a wild thing who lived during a time of civil breakdown."

"Does that excuse him from shooting poor Toby?"

"No," Berry said. "But it's incorrect to understand Marion by measures of right and wrong, for he was a man who lacked any moral compass to guide him. He lived by brute promptings. As for moral sense, he was hollow as a gourd."

"And that's what led to his killing Toby?" Jarom asked.

"In a way," said Berry, "I believe it did. You and I are superstitious enough to believe in some moral balance, the play of providence to ensure a balance necessary to keep the world turning on its axis, the work of angels and devils to keep things in balance."

"And Bill Marion?" asked Jarom.

"Bill Marion," he said, "upset the balance. When he stepped beyond the bounds, he destroyed the balance necessary to all things and must be prepared to accept what's fitting to set it right—a run of bad luck, mishaps befalling someone he loved, though that's unlikely—some hurt to his person."

"So Marion died to set the balance right?"

Looking into the darkness beyond its nimbus of fire, Jarom felt himself on the threshold of some new understanding.

"Something like that," said Berry, cupping his stump in his good hand and rubbing it, a gesture Jarom had never noticed before.

"So when crimes are committed against us," said Jarom, "are we warranted in helping the angels to set that balance right?" Patterson came to mind. He expected Berry to remember his sister Susan.

"Angels or devils," Berry said as he stirred the fire, the log that he turned spewing up a funnel of sparks.

Jarom, rolling into his blankets later that night, could not stop thinking of Toby and ultimately the wrong of putting one person, one race, under the direction of another. The limb that broke under Marion, he thought, broke under his own weight. The bullet that had brought him low hadn't been fired by Terrell or his men in Chaplintown but by Marion himself in Nelson County nearly forty miles away where poor Toby was lying in his coffin, custom built, custom fitted.

EXODUS

Early in January word came that General Breckinridge had ordered all remaining Confederate troops in Kentucky to withdraw to Tennessee by March 1. By order of the War Department in Richmond those who did not comply would be remanded to the Union military as deserters. The message left little leeway for misunderstanding, and Jarom felt as many of the others did that time was a peach whose ripeness required they leave Kentucky or risk being executed with the connivance of what from time to time, for convenience mostly, they still recognized as their own government.

As a farewell, their friends in Spencer, Nelson, and Bullitt organized a mammoth barbecue and fandango for all the Confederates in the area. The appointed day, February 27, was cold and clear, with not a cloud in the sky. At Newel and Isaac McCloskey's farm the guests arrived by dribs and drabs before noon and in droves during the afternoon, some coming from as far away as thirty or forty miles, from Shelbyville and Elizabethtown and Hodgensville but mostly from hamlets and road crossings too remote or too small even to have a name. They came by wagon and carriage, on horseback, some even on foot, walking the humps in the road between the crust of snow and ice that had been minced to mud.

From noon on, they congregated before a large fire in the parlor and fed on gossip and stories that distorted the truth less often in the service of modesty than of grandeur. By suppertime over two hundred people had congregated, more than any house in the county could hold. A fair number wore skirts, more than Jarom had seen in any one place since before the war—mothers and sisters and maiden aunts and sweethearts, wives and brides-to-be as well as hopeful spinsters and ladies of the church who felt the thrill of patriotic zeal. A good many of the younger ones wore miniature flags pinned to their dresses. Too many of them, old and young, Jarom thought, wore black. He fantasized that Mollie might miraculously appear. Several of the girls reminded Jarom of Mollie in one department or another, a dark head of hair, a pitch of the neck, a slope of shoulder or conformation of the nose. Facets of Mollie appeared in a dozen of the girls, but no feat of sorcery could make the parts materialize into Mollie herself. The more he ogled them, the more he thought of her, holding out hope until last light that she might bob in astride her piebald mare or inside one of the wagons that pulled up by the house under the grove of bare-limbed locusts. She moved closest in his mind when war stayed most remote. He missed her to the point of pain. From fighting to being listless and bored, he came to fluctuate between manic states of excitability and longing.

In addition to an array of familiar faces, many strangers showed up, including some recuperating from wounds and anxious to travel south in company. Though no one talked of leaving, all seemed full of what they would do when they came home and what their world would be like when the war ended. They speculated about conditions for failed rebels when the Yankees won. Sherman had recently completed his march through the Southland and swung back to the Carolinas, deftly cutting the country in two, demoralizing the population.

Quantrill showed up, making a grand entrance on one of the blooded horses that Alexander bestowed on him, the one that came to replace Old Charley in his affections. Its proud carriage and Quantrill's own stiff bearing made him look taller, more imposing. Jarom sensed that whatever the occasion, Quantrill, like the engraving of a puff adder he'd seen in a book of curiosities, had the knack of seeming larger and more important than he was. And it seemed to him that this exaggerated self accounted for his holding sway for so long over lesser lights around him. What surprised him was how in several weeks Quantrill had managed to age so much. His always serious expression had grown more somber, hard and angular as flint, relieved only by the tufts of sparse reddish hair sticking out from under his wide-brimmed Western hat. Around him clustered the familiar survivors of four years' fighting: Bud Pence, John Ross, Frank James, Payne Jones, Clark Hockensmith, Dick Glasscock, and twenty others he imported with him from Missouri, plus the few he'd managed to recruit in Kentucky. The riskier and more fatal his maneuvers became, the more he attracted a certain breed of blades around him to die. Even in this company, he introduced himself as Captain Clarke of the Fourth Missouri Cavalry, leaving the persons who met him to assume that he meant Confederate cavalry. The ruse fooled no one. Only a blind man or an anchorite could fail to identify the strutting madman.

When Quantrill entered the parlor, everyone seemed to take a respectful step backward as though royalty or lord high executioner had appeared—or some dreadful but perversely alluring combination. As Jarom looked on, he considered that maybe a collective intake of breath had created this sense of the crowd recoiling or shrinking into an attitude of subservience. Nowhere, not even with Morgan, had he seen a man who so successfully created an aura of power and invincibility. As Quantrill entered, Jarom realized as a corrective that some of the onlookers did not actually move. They retracted, drew in on themselves the way a threatened animal, the possum he once` cornered in the henhouse, drew in on itself in the custom of defense. Many did not appear conscious of their fear of him.

But Quantrill, in the way of egomaniacs, tried to take the edge off by cracking jokes and affecting an easy manner. No matter how many light words, his face, Jarom noticed, never softened. His nature, tensed like an archer's bow, seemed to have no give. Haggard now, his deepset eyes, rimmed with redness, reminded Jarom of concentric rings on a drillmaster's target. Magruder, who made no secret of despising Quantrill, would not refer to him as Colonel or even by his surname but always as Hair-Trigger. Thinking of rabbit blood, Jarom wondered if he meant Hare-Trigger.

When the rooms inside overflowed, McCloskey had large fires built outdoors by the sheltered side of the house. After the fiddlers came out, most of the revelers followed, and after they struck up "Soldier's Joy," the less inhibited guests bundled up and came outside to dance, looking to Jarom like a congress of dancing bears escaped from some gaudy and exuberant circus caravan. Inside on the trestle tables Jarom saw more food than he had seen and eaten for months—meats, apple fritters, sweet potatoes, hominy bread, shortbread, almond cakes, pones of baked Indian meal, pastries that tasted bland for lack of sugar, pies, and rabbit soup. Along the tables set up in the drafty hall, he served himself from every dish he could reach, going off to a corner of the room with a mound of food he wasn't sure he could finish. One of a multitude of cooks smiled and ladled him a cup of hot punch from a large silver tureen. When he'd emptied his cup, he sampled some blackberry wine but passed on the brandies and colorless, popskull whiskey.

Outside, he heard the deep thrumming of the guitars as the fiddles scratched and wheedled their melodies from resonant cavities of wood, instruments that replicated every human feeling: longing, carefreeness, lament, and, most insistently, melancholy. He remembered Patterson commenting on the Celtic origins of such music, attributing its magic to giving its listeners memories of experiences they'd never had. As he listened, he closed his eyes and imagined border clashes and clan rallies where cymbals and pipes and drums echoed in the highlands. But he also remembered Aunt Mary Tibbs's fundamental distrust of any music not performed on an organ. She said that the guitar and the fiddle were a summons from Satan and that such music, accompanied by dancing and who knows what other shenanigans, represented a dinner bell to perdition sounded by the unsaved for the tottering. She had a special injunction against the banjo, which she loathed and would refer to only as "that low instrument." Jarom himself thought of these familiar harmonies and rhythms as manufactured joy, spun melodies that relieved worries of the day and held up a prospect of better things, better times. He couldn't keep his feet from tapping, the music filling him with a sense of well-being, temporary as he knew it would be.

He stepped outdoors just as girls, young and not so young, paired off with partners for dancing, those finding none pairing off among themselves. The shuffling and awkward steppings lasted till after midnight, when most of the guests not staying the night saddled or harnessed up for home. Too self-conscious himself to dance, Jarom watched with envy the couples as they reeled and waltzed and scooted, never summoning nerve enough to ask one of those who stood on the fringes for a turn on the tramped ground that constituted the dance floor. As for drinking, remembering how much he'd retched the last time he tasted John Barleycorn, he restricted himself to cider. He consoled himself with small success with the notion that he had been faithful to Mollie.

Though he longed to see her and though she lived less than two hours away, he was glad he'd decided not to invite her. First, he doubted that her mother would have permitted her to come. He also feared the questions she would ask, knowing he couldn't lie to her about the questionable company he kept, his service in the army, his career as a guerrilla. If she knew of his link to Sue Mundy, she would have read of him in the papers. For him to discount it all as stuff and lies would probably feed rather than remove her doubts. He could not simply dismiss accusations by saying Prentice bandied the name Sue Mundy about for political purposes having no connection with him.

Finally, the risk of conducting her would have been too great for them both. Prentice from his pulpit of print seldom missed an opportunity now to trumpet the name Sue Mundy until Jarom felt himself quarry in a hunt that would end only with his capture. If the number of his reported crimes was any measure of the number he'd actually committed, he would be a kind of wonder boy (or woman)—deadly, ubiquitous, uncatchable. If guerrillas anywhere shot someone, burned a public building, stopped a train of cars, or stole a pony from a cart, the victims attributed the crime to Sue Mundy and his band, no matter how sketchy or slender the evidence. Through news accounts and editorials, George Prentice had elevated "Miss Sue" in the public eye to the first order of rogues, the most sought after man, or woman, in Kentucky. He could not tell Mollie that if he were caught he might be charged with guerrillering and sent to prison after the war. Or worse.

Painfully aware of this newfound notoriety, Jarom found himself taking more precautions—skirting towns, using back roads, riding mostly at night or early morning across fields stiffened with frost. He slept less, and then more fitfully, feeling a new languor that wore him down like the workings of a rasp on punky wood. Now he always rode with the flap that covered his holster unsnapped.

Toward the end of the party someone started to sing "Dixie," and everyone took up the words with a rush of feeling and wistfulness. The evening ended with some sentimental songs about home and campfires, enough to tell him to get on. Mounting Papaw, who stood well-fed in the stable, he rode under the clear sky to Bedford Russell's farm several miles away. There he and some dozen other party guests curled up in the barn loft with their blankets. They all planned to rise at dawn, eat breakfast, and depart for Paris, Tennessee. There they hoped to rendezvous with other elements of the army being evacuated from western and west central parts of the state. Jarom sensed new possibilities, and he rolled into his blanket with a feeling of hopefulness and expectation.

Next morning he woke to the sounds of low voices in the barnyard as some of the early birds saddled their horses. He emerged from a dream in which he had been home, Aunt Mary Tibbs stirring in the kitchen, smells of fried bacon wafting up to his bedroom, a cock crowing, a cowbell, sun lifting over the sill of his open window on a summer morning. Stiff from sleeping in the hayloft, he studied the light that passed between the pieces of vertical siding and splayed itself in intricate stripes and patterns across the hay-strewn floor. In the hay he found the faintest residue of summer, that sweet cloying freshness that settles over a field just cut, the windrows giving up their ghosts of greenness.

After a glorious breakfast of hot biscuits and ham served up by Mrs. Russell and her daughters, they finally broke camp and followed the Lebanon Road toward Campbellsville on the first leg of their long journey. At the last minute Quantrill joined them, the rump of his frisky purebred pumping rhythmically as a shaft on a steam-powered engine.

Magruder, William Hulse, Bud Pence, and Frank James rode forward, Jarom hanging back with the main body of riders where Quantrill, in a funk, jogged sullenly along, keeping counsel with himself. As a precaution, those in the front ranks had donned Union garb. Before they'd gone five miles, Hulse galloped back with news that he and James, riding ahead, had sighted a wagon train on the road from Lebanon, a winding caterpillar of white canvas. Keeping out of sight, they sneaked close enough to see wagons being escorted by a convoy of soldiers, four of them riding well in advance as scouts.

Knowing that any hesitation would spoil the semblance of friend meeting friend, Magruder gamely cantered ahead to meet the front riders. When they approached within a few yards, Magruder and his four companions drew their pistols and ordered the four opposing scouts to surrender. The officer, a stocky man whose full mustache had bristles stiff as a curry brush, sat on a gray charger, the most powerful saddle horse, Magruder told Jarom, that he had ever seen. Foolishly, the lieutenant tried to draw his revolver. Magruder and his men fired, killing him and two of the others instantly. The fourth managed to swing his mount around and make off toward the wagons, pressed hard by Frank James. When it became clear that the rider had gained too great a lead, James took aim and essayed a long shot as the rider pulled steadily away. It caught him at the base of his skull, tumbling him from his horse just yards from the first wagon, whose startled driver looked on in horror. Made at full gallop at a moving target, James's shot certified marksmanship that impressed even Magruder.

Jarom gave the dead man not another thought but spurred Papaw to the head of the attack that Magruder formed. He caught up with Magruder and thirty-odd others as they loaded and primed their arms in preparation for the charge. Magruder struck off in the lead, zigzagging his bay among the skittish mules and working his pistols in every direction. As they made their first contact with the teamsters, Jarom imagined a dam breaking, restrained force suddenly spilling into a channel, sweeping aside and crashing into whatever less resistant objects stood in its path.

Though they heard the first shots, the cavalry escort responded slowly, and Quantrill's veterans dropped many before they could fire a round. The fighting lasted no longer than five minutes. Of the thirty-eight horsemen and wagoners, twenty-seven were killed and ten wounded. Only a sutler who took refuge under his wagon surrendered alive and unhurt. Jarom counted twenty wagons captured, and Quantrill ordered them burned after removing what could be used. Out came a variety of foodstuffs, most of it crated metal cans in which government contractors found a way to package profit. Magruder, at heart a looter, rummaged about and found some fresh hams bagged and packed in straw, the cold providing a kind of natural icebox to prevent the scarlet pork from spoiling. Everyone helped himself to as much ammunition as he could carry. Feeling generous or perhaps fearing consequences, Quantrill turned the survivors loose on foot, knowing that wounded men would not go either far or fast and that some would not go at all.

The pursuit that Jarom knew would be coming, as soon as the telegraph could alert the nearest garrison town, did not catch up with them until they reached the tollgate two miles west of a little town named Bradsfordville. Jarom first noticed a spatter of fire at the rear of the column. They were passing along a narrow wagon road with dense cedar woods to either side, and at first the shots sounded far off, muffled by the wall of boughs and needles. He imagined the sound like shots fired from under a pillow. As Jarom reined in Papaw, her ears pricked in warning. He turned to see the roadway full of blue riders pressing down on them at full gallop, rapidly closing the hundred yards that separated them. Before Quantrill or any of them could react, the riders bore down on them. Relying solely on instinct, Jarom, along with Magruder, a man named Barnwell, Quantrill, and a dozen others, instinctively swung their horses around and charged back down the road to meet them.

By that time the riders had come so close that Jarom could see the determined faces of the oncomers as they hunched over their horses' necks, sidearms drawn for business. Turning to face them in the constricted road was like corking a bottle. With no room to maneuver, only those in the forefront could work their weapons without risk of shooting their own. Jarom popped a man in blue who had jumped or fallen from his horse and was firing from behind a thickish cedar. The man spotted him as he aimed and dodged behind the trunk, which lacked width to shield all of him. Jarom saw him snuggle against it as protection from the shot he anticipated, hugging the bark as though to merge with it. When Jarom fired, he saw the man drop his carbine and grab his thigh.

Those to the rear of the point of friction reeled under the tide as front riders, those surviving the first fire, fell back against the mass of men and horses clogging the road. Jarom felt a flash of anxiety as he closed among them, working two Colts as fast as they would fire. When he would empty one, he would pull out another from his belt and then his two pommel holsters. He shot three riders in as many seconds before Papaw reared and fell sidelong in the road with a shot to her chest. Before he could clear his leg, she'd pinned him under, her full weight falling against him as she hit the ground.

Now is my time, he said to himself, struggling to work his way free, expecting the fatal shot at any instant. An image flashed before him of Mollie Thomas and Patterson, still sighted, standing wordlessly over his grave.

He looked up to see six or eight bluejackets, having scented a kill, closing in to finish him.

Now is my time, he said to himself again, *now is my time,* as he struggled to work himself out from Papaw's writhing bulk. She neighed in pain and fright, a hoarse bellow he interpreted as a death song.

Two of the riders carried sabers, the first he'd ever seen outside a parade ground. One waved the gleaming metal above his head, and the other shifted his weight, leaning over his horse and jabbing it downward at him like a lance. The eyes of the man seemed strangely calm, oblivious to what went on around him, like someone intent on performing a difficult and intricate task. His face flushed crimson, his eyes shone cold and hard and blue as gunmetal.

Jarom realized that the burden of Papaw was his only protection. Papaw's exposed rear and front leg pummeled as though to gain purchase on what was only air, in vain hope that the motion would give her momentum enough to rise. But her bulk formed a barrier between him and the jabber. This cool-headed patriot, jaw and chin spiked with an untrimmed growth of reddish whiskers and wearing a faded uniform, made several more swipes at him before his own horse, a dappled gray, stumbled and fell motionless in the road. Whiskers must have been hit at the same time, for he pitched over to one side and did not rise.

From that moment Jarom felt unmoored from events, which happened too fast for him to translate into sequence. From his low perspective the fighting went on not so much around him as above him. The horses seemed to be dancing, throwing their heads, their legs thrashing and stomping about as though stuck in mire or immersed in water. Then horses and men meshed together in a shambling waltz, their bodies locked on a teetering toy carousel that reeled and staggered about under a weight no single one of them could shoulder. The movement slowed, the path of each arc or thrust joining the swirls of motion around it. Jarom imagined himself floating down a flooded river choked with driftwood. The current carried logs and pieces of debris in its flow, bobbing and sinking. Some caught in black eddies that formed swirling cones. Others shifted and freed themselves from the current to beach and pile in the backwaters. Jarom could see no joinder between action and consequence, only the broad, roiling sweep of movement and color whose dominant shade was that of mud. That no pattern emerged both terrified and fascinated him. He felt more helpless than ever before, as though adrift in a watery world in which predictable motion had been suspended, all laws by which the universe ran, all assurances, had gone.

The bullets whumping into Papaw's flank confirmed this feeling. He expected at any instant the projectiles to penetrate his own vulnerable skin. He saw around him a wheel of riders, passing and spinning, spinning and prancing, poking and prodding at him with pistols. Though he could see fire spit from the barrels, he couldn't hear the individual reports, drowned out in the uproar. For an instant he held an image of himself dead under the trampling hooves. Again he strained, again to no avail, to push the dead weight off. Papaw, no longer flailing, wouldn't budge. He no longer felt the comforting heave of her lungs as she pressed against him. He felt himself under a weight from which he could never arise.

Into this maelstrom Billy Magruder and little William Hulse prodded their horses as though dragging heavy loads up a steep incline. They emptied their pistols in the faces of their enemies as those enemies passed on the carousel. Then Jarom could register only fragments of sense: the square, yellow cusps of a wounded horse forming a death smile under its curled muzzle, a glint of burnished metal against some coarse blue wool, a riderless horse standing calmly by the road rubbing its rump under a cedar bough. He worked one of his hands free to grip the pommel, but still he couldn't pull out from under. The faces of his murderers ballooned up in pitiful mime, their antics performed against the whinnying of injured horses and a deafening thunder louder than any storm.

How long the fight lasted he did not know, but after a time he felt the surge pass over and beyond him, the crush of muscle easing and ebbing back down the road, where he glimpsed the survivors limping through the splintered cedars in the direction of what he guessed was Bradfordsville. As his senses readjusted to what lay before him, up rode Billy Magruder, a red scarf wound about his head like a turban. He jumped from his horse and shouted for several of the others to help him drag Papaw off. Magruder, together with Bud Pence and Sam Berry, doing his best with one arm, commenced to push and prize, sliding the carcass off inch by inch until Jarom could roll free.

Jarom didn't know how long it took for the message that the weight had been removed to penetrate his numbness. Though he knew he would mourn Papaw, in that moment he felt a powerful elation. Seconds earlier, death, with all certainty, had snared him in its grip. Snatched back to life by Billy Magruder, he felt renewed, emphatically alive at the center of a field radiant with intense light, where every grass blade, every leaf and shimmering stem, had life and breath of its own, the smallest motion quivering to permeate the whole. A power not physical so much as psychic swept through him. For the first time he felt preternaturally aware of everything about him: the fissures in a fencepost, a shattered canteen, the minutest twig, crow caw, the ruined bodies pulsing among the stones. He felt great release, a freeing not from death's hold but from all that held him from the fullness of things.

Then he became aware that Billy Magruder, his deliverer, stood next to him, grinning innocently above the carnage. Picking up Jarom's hat,

Magruder wet his finger and applied it to the lucky crescent, rubbing the silver against his sleeve until it shined. Finishing, he plopped the hat on Jarom's head.

"You better stop napping," he said, "before someone comes and buries you and the horse both."

THE BARN

The wound in Billy Magruder's chest had finally stopped bleeding. The pea-sized hole with its carnation of dried blood was stuffed with cotton and bound over with several lengths of gauze. Magruder slept on his back in a nest of sour hay Medkiff had raked up from the barn floor, as comfortable as he and Jarom could make him. While he slept, Jarom and Medkiff speculated on his chances of survival—on their own chances. The wound seemed clean enough but in a nasty place. Entering just below the collar bone, the bullet punctured Magruder's left lung before exiting through the upper back a half inch from the spine. Jarom guessed it a pistol ball from its size, too small for a rifle or carbine, too uncomplicated for a shotgun. The wound had suppurated, the lung collapsed, and Magruder's breathing took the form of labored wheezing. Even in sleep his chest heaved in shaky spasms, the breath sucked in deep and passed out weak with a sound like air being blown through a torn paper sack. It rose and fell in sputters, reminding Jarom somehow of pulsating butterfly wings.

If Magruder was bad off, he fared better than Sam Jones, the man who had brought the order for Jarom and the others to report to Paris, Tennessee. He'd tumbled off his horse in the first volley of fire, the life gone out of him before he hit the ground. Not one of them would have picked the spot their enemies chose for a bushwhacking, a stretch of open ground in country veined with narrow trails through dense timber. The fact that it was a bad choice made it a good one for those who lay in wait for them. In the open the four of them had put their guard down, not reckoning on amateurs. He, Medkiff, Magruder, and Jones trekked the back roads toward Paris, Tennessee, where they hoped to rejoin the remainder of the Confederate army in the West. Though they anticipated some trouble on the way, especially after the fight when Jarom was nearly killed, they didn't expect to meet it at this place or to meet it so soon.

Without hint or warning, the first volley came from a patch of stobby tobacco about thirty yards to the east of the road, the second from a rise about an equal distance to the west. As Jarom ducked, he glimpsed two figures stooped behind a pile of fencerails, another in a gully to one side of the tobacco. Eight he counted in all, eight against three. Struck by more than one bullet, Jones had pitched from the saddle. Sprawled motionless in the roadway, he was clearly dead. The road ahead appeared unobstructed, so the three goosed their horses, Jarom riding a chestnut filly that had already proven her spirit and staying power. Stolen two days earlier from a pasture not far from where Jarom had been born, she was beginning to respond when he called her Memphis. The three of them had ducked their heads and put spurs to the horses. They had nearly ridden out the storm when Billy Magruder dropped his reins, freeing his chestnut gelding to veer off the road and nearly unseat him. Magruder now seemed to be seated upright in the saddle more by habit than any obedience to gravity's law. Before he could slip off, Medkiff wheeled about and steadied him, snatching the loose reins to bring the chestnut around.

As soon as they had outrun the bullets, Jarom swapped horses, mounting behind Magruder and passing the reins of Memphis over to Medkiff. Placing Magruder's hands at his side, he formed a cage with his own to keep him from falling. Neither he nor Medkiff had to debate whether Billy Magruder needed a doctor, but neither had an idea where one could be found. Jarom did know that they rode in Hancock County and that they would need a place to lie low until Magruder's wounds healed—or he died. He knew Magruder wasn't in any condition to ride and that plainly his wounds would kill him it they didn't find a doctor soon.

They passed through a desolate and meager country, a land with few people and farms that did not guarantee even subsistence. One grim little farmstead after another had the look of land in a primal stage of settlement, as though the first generation of settlers had arrived and started to carve cornfields and homesteads out of the landscape but somehow had its energies sapped until progress slowed and finally stopped. With their remaining energy, the survivors held against the vagaries of weather and conditions of privation. Despite an occasional church or intact farmhouse, the landscape showed little sociability or change. The unpainted houses and ill-repaired dependencies stood lamely in their path, neglected and wasting. Jarom called it the Land of Missing Boards after counting dozens of outbuildings that needed siding or roof sheathing replaced.

Because Magruder might incur further injury if they moved faster than a walk, the progress on horseback slowed. Riding double, Jarom and Magruder would go six or eight miles and then change horses. Medkiff often rode ahead to scout the way. From time to time Billy Magruder would raise his head to ask their whereabouts and then nod off again. When conscious, he moaned from the jolting as the horses plodded under a double load. Jarom tried to imagine Magruder's thoughts. He knew him for a fatalist, grimly making casual and oblique references to the mark being on him. Once he asked Jarom to deposit him at the next farmhouse. Jarom replied that his wound would be seen to once they found a place of refuge. Neither Jarom nor Medkiff, so far as Jarom could tell, considered abandoning Magruder, especially since they knew Magruder would never desert them in the same condition.

Whenever Jarom tired of ministering, the image of Magruder rolling Papaw off him on the road to Lebanon came back to him. Then, Magruder had become a frenzied wasp, stinging whatever threatened and stinging hard. His impetuousness saved Jarom's life. Though no one said as much, Jarom knew he had a debt to repay. Hope for relief lay in finding sanctuary within a day's ride, the closer the better, a place where they could get a doctor and sit things out.

"If you won't leave me," Billy said, woozy but finally coming to, "carry me to Meade County. There I can claim kin to some who'll look after me."

When questioned further, he named a Dr. Lewis, a physician who lived somewhere between Webster and Brandenburg. He guessed the doctor's house lay about thirty or thirty-five miles to the east.

And that decided it. Making their way along more back roads the rest of that day and night, next morning they reached the section where Dr. Lewis lived. An old farmer they stopped along the way gave them directions. Billy's shirt was sopped with blood, and the protrusion of the makeshift bandages under it gave the appearance of misshapen breasts.

When they neared the place, Billy recognized the road. He directed them to a vacant barn out of sight of passersby where they could wait while someone, either Jarom or Medkiff, fetched the doctor.

They found the empty barn located in the boondocks not far from Webster, a stopping place ten miles south of the county seat along the market road. Webster itself they passed through, a village sequestered among a profusion of knobs that seemed an aberration of nature, a series of bumps on the landscape as if God had stamped them on with a muffin pan. The barn belonged to James S. Cox, a distant cousin of Billy's mother's people. Billy relied on Mr. Cox's good will to let them stay for a time if they would go along with the fiction that he didn't know it. By edict, harboring guerrillas was a criminal offense punishable by fine and imprisonment, possibly death. If someone could prove Cox in cahoots with guerrillas, he could be shot as a traitor to his country. On the other hand, informing would earn the betrayer both commendation and a hefty reward. So Jarom and Medkiff agreed that one of them would stay to care for Billy, the other would fetch the doctor. Already edgy in the confines of the barn, Medkiff volunteered to go.

Sometime before midnight, Jarom, drowsy against one of the stanchions, heard the clickity-clack of horses on the frozen ground outside the barn. Medkiff whistled and led in a dapper little man lugging a leather satchel. Without any comment he knelt by Magruder and reached into his bag for a pair of scissors, carefully snipping open the shirt to examine the wound. To Jarom, it looked like a ruptured plum, a purple mass of shredded flesh on which blood stood too long, giving it the consistency and color of congealed gravy. The doctor deftly swabbed it with a clear liquid poured onto a cloth, dabbing and wiping with a delicate touch. When he'd cleansed the wound, he dressed it from a spool of gauze, saying there was nothing more he could do in that place to prevent infection.

Jarom looked on, impressed with his obvious skill, especially since many of the country doctors he'd seen knew more of delivering calves than treating humans. The doctor seemed more attuned to treating his own.

"Where did you learn to tend such wounds?" Jarom asked.

"Before the war," he said, "I'd hardly seen any but innocent blood, the cut of a misapplied scythe, a gash from a fall. Since it started, I've seen barrels of blood, more than I thought to see in a lifetime."

Trimly built and formal in his bearing despite the crude conditions, the doctor wore a gray swallowtail coat at least two generations removed from what Jarom recognized as current fashion, something as antique as billowing pantaloons or knee-length stockings. To his credit, Jarom thought, the doctor acted as though in his practice he commonly visited patients in tobacco barns. If troubled, he withheld showing it, either too polite or too canny to let his concern show through. Though below average height, he bore a strange resemblance to the latest tintypes of Lincoln, a long haggard face cut deep as the gullied terrain about them. He appeared irremediably sad, his eyes unnaturally alert and probing. The wound, he told them finally, was open, and there had been a good deal of discharge. The bullet had entered the left side of his torso, halfway between the nipple and the sternum. Though the ball punctured his left lung as it passed through his body, the right lung seemed sound and functioned properly. Then he told them what they already knew, that healing, if it took, would be slow and that the patient must be given adequate rest. None of them, including the patient himself, reasonably expected Billy to last over a day or so, two days at best.

"It's only a matter of time," Medkiff said. "Old Death is a' stalking and won't be put off the scent."

Before leaving, Dr. Lewis laid down the law.

"For at least two weeks," he said, "he must—I say, must—not be moved, as he has already lost more blood than he can spare. Move him and he will die."

He didn't tell them, and didn't need to, that staying in one place for that duration substantially increased the risk of their being discovered. As the doctor packed to go, Jarom emptied his pockets and tried to put money in his hand.

Dr. Lewis refused it. Instead he suggested they offer some to Mr. Cox, who had already compromised himself and his family in giving shelter and agreeing to provide their meals. At the entryway he promised to come back the next evening at a time when he was less likely to be missed, less likely to meet anyone on the road. Prior to going, he knelt to readjust

Billy's bandage, then picked up his instruments, carefully placed them in the satchel, and slipped into the darkness.

Jarom came to know the barn as intimately as he had known any other place he had been since the war began. It was old, a barn within a barn, a survival from the days of earliest settlement. At its heart stood a log crib sixteen by sixteen feet, with a crude door cut into one wall, but no windows, the mud chinking long since fallen out. Light coming between the logs gave the interior a latticing that would have been more pronounced had the light been more direct. Its hand-hewn timbers bore clefts where an ax had scored the barked log for the adze to follow and square into planes. Though none of the wood had finish applied to it, it had worn smooth, as oiled and splinter-free as the old furniture in Mary Tibbs's sitting room.

Around and above the crib rose a three-bent barn built of generously wide oak boards nailed vertically to a scantling of cedar posts and beams, whole trees shorn and trussed together by mortise and tendon. The intricacies of its construction fascinated Jarom. The boxlike interior was trellised with poles lashed together or pegged to the six main posts in such a way that heavy sheaves of tobacco could be hung and smoked on their skewered sticks in tiers, four high over the alley, two on the shed sides. The undersides of the poles and roof sheathing showed soot-black from seasons of smoke used to cure the hanging tobacco. Ash pits spotted the hard-packed earthen floor. A stale smell of burnt hickory hung in the air that gathered cool and still like the interior of a cave. Randomly spaced along two walls were long slits on hinged members that could be opened or closed, so the hanging tobacco, as Medkiff described it, could breathe.

With little to do but tend to Magruder as best he could, Jarom studied the barn in its particulars and fancied crews of phantom tobacco workers ribbing one another, exchanging stories as they hoisted sheaves from the lowest tiers to the highest. The floor around him was strewn with leavings from previous crops that seemed as old as the barn itself, split stalks with leaves as fragile as parchment or the tissue-thin pages in the Tibbs family Bible. The dry leaves, shaped like a lolling tongue, had the tinge of the auburn or dusky bronze of leatherbound books, and Jarom thought it not unlike a library in ruins, a site of interest to antiquarians.

When it rained with the doors and slits shut, his eyes teared from the burning acidity of tobacco, as intrinsic to the barn as its trusswork. After a few days, he noticed that the structure must have doubled as shelter for stock, at least during winter, for old road apples lay in piles. The faint smell of dried manure blended with moldering hay in the improvised log crib where Magruder lay and where he and Medkiff slept. These combined with the tobacco smell to densen the air with a too-sweet odor of decay. He felt in some tie of kinship with the wider world of mammals that he and Medkiff and Magruder had found a burrow, a den to withstand harsh weather.

After a week of lagging days, Jarom felt a niggling sense of unease that he couldn't discount as restlessness. The days took on a routine. In the morning and late afternoon Mr. Cox's son Drury brought leftovers from the Cox kitchen, a chicken breast or joint of tough beef and always some biscuits, though often as cold as the ground on which they sat. Drury, a lank, slow-witted boy whom Jarom judged to be ten or eleven, always brought a small pail of chicken broth, which they ate of themselves and spoon-fed to Billy. After a week of such thin eating, Billy complained to Dr. Lewis during one of his evening rounds.

"Mend or break, Billy," was all he said, "you can either mend or break."

Water was not a worry, for a spring fed the pond above the barn, its pooled mouth fenced off from the stock. The horses slaked their thirst from the branch that ran past the barn. For provender the three horses fed on spoiled hay during the light hours. At night either Jarom or Medkiff hobbled them near the beds of tender grass beginning to green the hillside. Jarom took the precaution of confining them by day and turning them out at night. Watering them one night, Medkiff pulled some greens that neither of them could identify. Using a small skillet that Drury brought from the kitchen, he fried them in bacon drippings, and Jarom praised them as delicious. For the first few days, they supplemented house meals with the small cache of trail food in their saddlebags—some crumbled cornbread, a few tins of federal meat, even some brandy Magruder had packed along, he said, for snakebites. After the first few days, they made do with whatever Drury brought. When Medkiff complained, Jarom reminded him that they lived in a barn by sufferance, not in a hotel.

Every other evening Dr. Lewis tethered his horse in the grove of trees near the spring and slowly made a path that his feet seemed to know without lantern or moonlight. Sometimes he changed the dressing, but usually he examined the wound for the discoloring of infection and spoke little of Magruder's condition. Though Billy breathed and slept with less strain, Jarom could see he hadn't really improved much. Dr. Lewis, who practiced his science in monastic speechlessness, volunteered nothing, but his silence on the subject confirmed Jarom's worries. Day and night Billy slept, often eight or ten hours at a spell. Like a banked fire, his slack body seemed to smolder, lacking some condition that would either cause it to reignite or extinguish itself. He had withdrawn himself from the world, reminding Jarom of John Patterson's pet collie after being kicked by a mule. It lay on a pallet for a week or ten days, eating and drinking little while the body restored itself, regenerated its ravaged cells, rebuilt its broken ribs. Pacified, still, Magruder lost all reckoning of time and place, all interest in the world. Sometimes he became delirious, once or twice talking in his sleep. Whatever happened, Jarom repeated the oath he'd made to himself not to desert him.

As the waiting began to fret on him, Medkiff grew less certain. He moped and shambled about, kicking up dust until his edginess got to both of them. Much of the day he spent in the small loft above the two plank doors, his eye to a knot-hole in the siding, keeping a vigil on the fringe of trees within his angle of vision. Brooding on him, Jarom remembered a type Aunt Mary described as "having few eggs in his basket." Unlike the English essayist whom Jarom had thumbed to in a student reader, Medkiff lacked means to amuse himself. The essayist claimed that he was never less alone than when alone.

Jarom, sometimes restive too, put himself to fulfilling that test with only modest success. He yearned for a book or newspaper and asked Drury to bring him something to read, but nothing in the farmhouse had print on it, and it wasn't clear that James Cox could read it if there had been. So activity became his antidote to boredom. When he wasn't squinting through his own peephole, he counted bullets or arranged his loads in geometrical patterns. Once he used their entire stock of ammunition to build a castle, complete with towers and moat. He imagined it as citadel of the Black Prince, himself as the forest bandit Robin Hood. He spent most of one afternoon watching the antics of a red squirrel in a nearby oak. He counted the number of crow caws in an hour and determined the time of day they were most garrulous, concluding that they, like a certain lazy planter he'd known in Logan County, seemed most active in the hour before noon. He imagined himself with Mollie Thomas and the outings they would take when the war ended, the great Mammoth Cave at the top of his list. His ambrotype was worn around the edges, the emulsion softening with wear. He unfolded "Lillibulero" again and tried to hum the notes, mostly on the basis of whether they were high or low on the fence of parallel lines. The tune he improvised sounded like no tune he'd ever heard. He confirmed to himself that he would never be a serenader or valued member of a choir.

Or he was with the horses, nature's true stoics, who accepted the world in which they found themselves with no discernible resistance or reflection. He spent hours rubbing them down, glossing their tack with gun oil, soothing them endlessly in whispered monotones. Nights he would lead them out for an hour to graze, to water, to exercise, to void themselves. Jarom knew that adopting this brotherhood with horses benefited himself more than it did them. Memphis, accepting the privation as though such treatment was naturally her lot in life, kept him from going low and sullen, helped him strike a truce between the ever-warring domains of mind and heart. For hours on end neither Jarom nor Medkiff spoke, each wrapped in his mantle of gloom, separate worlds within the world of the barn.

Jarom felt after a time that he'd gained a kind of honorary citizenship in the Nation of Barns. He acclimated himself to the discomfort, the dankness, the subtle scents of decay and death. The heady fumes of manure no longer bothered him, nor the stink of horse piss from the corner of the barn where the horses were hobbled during the day. His senses stood persuaded that at some juncture the odor had been naturalized and no longer merited notice, that it had become a part of him, or he of it, so familiar it could no longer be detected. If the smells had dissipated and the air perfumed with the crushed heads of a million roses, Jarom felt certain he would still be uneasy, not really knowing why.

One night when the stars seemed particularly cold and remote, he dreamt the barn transformed into an enormous coffin, a sealed box in which the three of them slowly smothered, cut off from air and food, from light and motion, from the reassuring sounds of ordinary human speech that reminded them they partook of this world not as exiles but speech-gifted witnesses. Earlier, he and Medkiff had played at cards, mostly rummy, with a tattered deck that Drury smuggled to them one noontime with dinner. But Medkiff had grown bored after an hour or two, especially after he discovered that he could win only when Jarom allowed him to. Next morning Jarom marked the progress of silver light striping the strewn floor. As the earth completed its diurnal rounds, he mentally charted their cubicle as it registered change, shifted into new angles and planes, new patterns of alternating glare and shadow. After his early supper he found himself sitting rapt for hours in the thousands of taps a drizzle made on the leaky roof, the tremors it sent along the grains as water seeped into the rotting shingles. He understood that beneath the boredom he and Medkiff were lonely and scared, knowing sooner or later word would reach the wrong ears that the barn had become a hospital.

A SOUND OF COCKS CROWING

Jarom awoke to the usual sound of cockcrows far off and the barking of the Coxes' house dog, something unusual, for it barked only in the presence of strangers. Medkiff lay curled up in his blankets next to Magruder, both, as Jarom remembered in Patterson's phrase, still in the embrace of Morpheus. Bootless, pistol in hand, Jarom stood up and put the mechanism on cock, dreading the metallic racheting that announced his presence, though he realized the sound could not be heard beyond the interior of the barn. Moving to the double doors, he put his eye to one of the cracks in the siding and studied the treeline. Light was washing the tops of a butternut tree maybe forty yards away, the brush and scrubby undergrowth beneath it visible only in halftones. Using this butternut tree as a point of reference, he stared at the trunk, acutely aware of any motion that his peripheral vision might detect.

He saw nothing unfamiliar but soon heard a rustling he associated with insects in their millions on still nights in late summer, a persistent fidgeting felt almost as mild tremor. He waited as the intensifying light slowly applied color to the objects, the duns and earth colors whose assembly into morning he had become accustomed to. Though he could detect nothing amiss, part of him sensed another presence behind, within, the screen of trees.

Then one, two, a half dozen crouching figures crept out of the brush and moved toward the barn, rifles in hand. They moved with the stealth of men hunting, one even tiptoeing down the hillside. Jarom readily saw from the blue of their tunics they meant him no good. As he watched them approach, birds began to pipe along the woodline, though the dog continued to bark in its monitory way. Medkiff, also aware of something amiss, had taken his pistol and carbine to the other side of the double doors and observed the bent figures as they approached, so close now Jarom could read the features on their faces. He felt a wave of anxiety as one of the figures, ahead of the rest, marched up to the door. Jarom could see the black belt that girded him with the "US" emblazoned in brass, could see the man's ankle boots standing just outside the door, close enough for him to touch from under the planking. The man boldly rapped on the stout oak with the aplomb of a neighbor coming to borrow some flour or a dollop of lard. Jarom could see only two of the others, but they stood by with rifles at the ready, suspecting but not knowing for certain what occupied the precincts of the barn, as gray and undisturbed as the entrance of a cave or a sealed mausoleum.

Jarom could hear the breath of the man outside the door, could even see the dark, unshaved follicles on his chin. *My only strategy,* he told himself, *is muteness, to wait for those outside to push ahead or retreat to the treeline with a report that the barn is deserted.* This latter, he realized, was a wish with no fulfillment, neither likely nor even possible. Then the man at the door stepped back, whispering something inaudible to one of the others, and the two of them moved back to a patch of horseweed to heft a large pear-shaped stone. First putting their rifles down, they lifted it to their waists and came forward under the heavy load. Six or so feet away, they heaved it against the door with great force, knocking off a rusted hinge and splintering some planks. The blow came with such effect that the upper portion of the door collapsed into the barn, bent from the still secure lower hinge. The impact exposed the dark interior of the barn, and light splashed across the earthen floor.

Jarom and Medkiff, realizing their stratagem had failed, both fired at the same instant, placing the muzzle of their pistols between the slats and awkwardly directing the barrels toward wherever they could see or imagine a human form. In the confusion, Jarom saw two of the six bluecoats fall and not get up and two more wounded, though remaining on their feet. Shots from the treeline thunked in the oak planking around him, and one or two penetrated the interior, but no one was hit. One of the two remaining members of the assault party sprinted back to the cover of the trees while the other held his comrade, who was dragging one leg and hopping. Jarom heard a shout in the direction of the trees, and the firing stopped as abruptly as it had started. *This is to give all of us some time to weigh our choices,* Jarom thought, *and reload.*

Putting his eye to the crack again, Jarom saw Dr. Lewis making his way down the hill, waving a tobacco stick with a handkerchief affixed. It occurred to him that Dr. Lewis had led them there, probably because he was forced to. When he came within earshot, two troopers stepped out of the woods and cautiously descended the hill part way, taking up another wounded man, who hobbled, half-crawling, up the slope. They dragged him into the woods.

When the doctor approached within a few feet of the door, Jarom shouted for him to stop right there. Jarom put his mouth to the slit and asked what regiment the troops were from, who commanded it, and, most importantly, how many men he was facing.

"Major Cyrus Wilson of the Thirtieth Wisconsin is in command," Dr. Lewis said, "and he would like to speak for himself if you'll let him come down under a flag of truce."

Knowing he had little choice, Jarom said that he would. But he also knew that whatever this Wilson had to say, he and Medkiff and Magruder were done, that they would leave the barn either as prisoners or corpses.

Neither escape nor negotiating their freedom seemed possible. The doctor trudged back up the hill to fetch the major, the sunlight off his bald dome bright as a breakfast dish.

Jarom made certain that the first object Major Cyrus Wilson saw as he stepped into the interior of the barn was the business end of his navy Colt. As the other door swung open, light flooded the interior and forced Jarom to blink, shaking his concentration. Medkiff stayed in the loft where Jarom had posted him. Magruder, helpless but awake, was still rolled up in his blankets.

Jarom suppressed the urge to scream and turned his mind to business. He hunkered onto his bare heels, resting his back against one of the stanchions. He motioned for Wilson to do the same as one might offer a seat to a visitor in one's office or parlor. Wilson, a decent-looking man of fifty or so, lowered himself and folded his feet under him Indian style. Jarom looked him in the eye to read what he might find there.

"Would you like a smoke?" Wilson asked.

"Yes, I would," Jarom said, after considering a few moments.

So Wilson rolled one for himself and passed the fixings over to him. Jarom carefully laid his pistol aside, discreetly placing it beyond the major's reach, shaking some of the red makings onto a paper, sealing the edge with spittle on his tongue and passing it across his underlip. Then he drew the strings and with exaggerated politeness passed the bag back. From his breast pocket he drew a packet of lucifer matches, whisking one into flame against the post.

When the cigarette was lighted, he took a drag and spit out an invisible particle of loose tobacco. Jarom sucked on the cigarette, the first in many weeks, and spewed forth a stream of silver smoke that hovered like a miniature cloud in the chill air.

"You've got yourself in a pickle, Sue Mundy," Wilson said. "You're surrounded and cut off from any help. This barn may keep you dry but it won't keep you whole. It's indefensible."

Jarom nodded to affirm the essential truth of what he said.

"Under the circumstances," Wilson asked, "wouldn't it be wise for you to surrender?"

"You will kill me if I do."

"That isn't true," said Wilson matter of factly.

"Then your men will," said Jarom, gesturing toward the open door.

"That isn't so. My men won't shoot you unless I order them to, and I have just promised that I won't do that."

"How many of you are there?"

"One hundred cavalry and fifty infantrymen," Wilson said, not averting his eyes or blinking. Jarom assumed that Wilson overstated his number to bolster his position so Jarom and Medkiff would surrender without a fight, knowing they couldn't hope to escape unscathed.

He felt Wilson's stare as an auger boring into his forehead. A stinging sensation in his index finger told him the ash of his cigarette was burnt to the nub. As he snubbed it into the dust, a lazy ribbon of smoke still wafted toward Medkiff in the loft. He fixed his gaze on Wilson, weighing their chances. Their possibilities were fading, their predicament setting like wet plaster into something solid and permanent as anything could be in the flux of things. Despite his pretense of steadiness, he felt himself growing desperate as he moved on to the next phase.

"If we decide to surrender," he asked, "where will you take us?"

"To Louisville," Wilson said. Just as Jarom reckoned.

"Then you will kill me there," he said, his mind stepping to the next phase as if each was a slippery stone in a stream he was trying to cross without wetting his feet.

"Probably so," Wilson said, since there was no denying the forces that demanded his blood. "But," he added, "consider the alternatives. If you surrender today, you'll be alive tonight. If you don't, you'll have one chance in a thousand, in ten thousand, of seeing noon tomorrow."

Jarom glanced over to Magruder on his pallet ten feet away. He was propped up on one elbow, clearly taking everything in.

"Don't fight on my account," Magruder said. "I don't expect to live. I've been a bad boy and I expect to die. But you," he said, "shot now or shot later is a poor choice, but a choice still. And who knows?"

"Don't push me, Billy," Jarom said, feeling more than a little pushed. Despite his efforts to control it, he could feel his face drawing into a pout. He felt the muscles in his jaw setting up their own authority. "When I'm ready, I'll let you know, but please don't hurry me, please."

He was irked, though he knew Billy was trying to do the generous thing, freeing Jarom to do what seemed best for himself rather than feeling constrained by what was best for Billy Magruder. He sensed himself wavering, and he knew that Wilson sensed it too. Which, he thought, is probably why Wilson turned his attention to Medkiff, who'd been listening from the loft.

"What do *you* think ought be done?" said Wilson, looking up now at Medkiff, even more jumpy now and obviously confused.

For answer, Medkiff, not much on words, simply shrugged, turning his attention to a crevice in the planking.

Jarom, running his possibles, knew he had no choice where he'd imagined one, that all he might salvage was a little dignity and some precious time. Escaping fifteen or twenty was possible though unlikely. But a hundred and fifty? Even if he and Medkiff left Magruder, the odds were too steep. One shot could bring down a horse. Even if he had inflated the numbers, Wilson clearly had a sizable force to their two. He considered his chances in taking Wilson hostage but knew he couldn't break his word under a flag of truce. That would only confirm what his enemies believed, that he was rogue to the bone. Only one question remained to ask.

"Will we be treated as prisoners of war?" he asked. This was a discreet way of asking whether they would be treated as soldiers within the usages of war or as guerrillas, another word for outlaws.

"You will be treated as Confederate prisoners of war," Wilson said, though Jarom knew that he couldn't make such a guarantee. Sensing the full weight of his predicament, Jarom believed for a moment he would cry.

And then Jarom surprised himself, moving as if controlled by some force beyond him, by putting his hands on the buckle of the belt that held his pistols. From what seemed like a great distance away, he watched himself unbuckle, putting down the three and putting aside the fourth, still where he'd placed it by his side.

He then motioned for Medkiff, wide-eyed in the loft, to do the same. After hesitating some moments, Medkiff put his pistols aside and sighed an expansive sigh that seemed a distillation of all the winds.

Wilson still stared as Jarom felt his own concentration break. Releasing himself from Wilson's stare, he tried to focus on the abstract patterns of leaf and litter on the barn floor. He could hear some movement outside, the Coxes' dog still barking, birds twittering in the trees.

"Where did I leave my boots?" was the last thing he could remember saying, addressed to no one in particular.

PRISONER

Even after they put leg irons on him and shackled his wrists, Jarom did not learn who played them false. When he asked why irons were necessary, Wilson told him that the papers had described him as a very dangerous fellow. Jarom did his best to persuade him that he and Medkiff posed no great threat, surrounded by guards and played out as both were. He told him that half the stuff printed about him in the newspapers was untrue, the rest exaggerated. To make his point, he told Wilson that there was even a story about his dressing up as a woman to fool General Morgan and to act as a female spy. All damn stuff, Jarom assured him, the stuff of campfires, wanting to set the record straight.

Magruder had been carried to a wagon for the trip back to Brandenburg, a ride that must have banged him up considerably along roads rough as a creek bed. Captain Marshall, Wilson's second in command, had heard that at least three other guerrilla bands were in the area. As a precaution he ordered his men to bolster themselves for an attack, since all of them seemed to believe that once the capture became known, no effort would be spared to spring the captives loose. The citizen who imparted this information warned Marshall that the guerrillas would "hit them like wildfire." Jarom also learned that Marshall questioned Wilson's judgment in permitting Dr. Lewis, a civilian of doubtful loyalty, to visit the barn under a flag of truce. Marshall's own preference had been to incinerate the whole building if its inmates didn't surrender. Along the way Jarom remembered a scriptural text—was it a psalm?—wherein he looked to the hills from whence cometh his help. He scanned the ridgeline, but help didn't come.

Though gawkers gathered along the way, especially in the river town of Brandenburg where the sternwheeler put in, no one raised a hand in protest or anger. No one, in fact, said anything, staring in silence. A large crowd of Sunday afternoon loafers congregated to see them board. Magruder's litter was placed on the floor of the captain's quarters beside the four wounded federals, resting places memorialized by stains of blood on the floorboards. When they boarded the *Morning Star*, a steamer similar to the one on which Company B of the Thirtieth Wisconsin had come down the Ohio from Louisville, Jarom pieced together the events leading to his capture, mostly from what he picked up talking to Wilson. He also noticed that not once did Wilson let him out of his sight. The last time he saw Memphis, one of Wilson's men was leading her away, her long tail switching, the muscles of her tan rump working indifferently, distracted by the strange company after three weeks of solitude and inactivity.

He learned that Cyrus Wilson, a miller in Larue County retired from service in the Twenty-sixth Kentucky Cavalry, had been promoted to major and called back to special duty to capture the guerrilla Sue Mundy. On Saturday Wilson and his Wisconsin troops had left the wharf at Louisville on a river steamer named *Grey Eagle*. They had cleared the falls and passed Shippingport, heading west downriver to Brandenburg. From there they had marched southeast ten miles at night to the hamlet of Webster, where they pressed Dr. Lewis into service to lead them to the Cox farm. Who had informed the federals Jarom didn't know.

The trip back to Louisville took longer since the *Morning Star* now pushed upstream against the current, and they didn't arrive until Monday morning. The wires carried the message of his capture to Louisville, where a large crowd assembled by the wharf at the foot of Fourth Street to see him debark. Under heavy guard they proceeded to the military prison at Ninth and Broadway. Guards raised Jarom and Medkiff, still chained, to government horses, their hands and legs secured by chains that girded the horses' underbellies. The soldiers formed a hollow square around them and marched them up the street from the dock, Magruder bringing up the rear in an army ambulance. All the way to the prison their captors paraded them through crowds that stopped to ogle the unfortunate duo trussed in chains. Many received word that the prisoners were expected and had waited to get a view of the banditti princess they had been reading about for months. Jarom noticed that many women came out to see a member of their sex who had given herself over to violent excess and vile impersonation. Jarom felt relieved to escape the prying eyes when the little caravan reached the prison's walled enclosure. The last time he saw Medkiff they nodded before guards led them to different cells. Medkiff shrugged his shoulders, then winked at him.

The guards conducted Jarom to a cell at the far end of a long corridor of cells in a brick building that resembled a factory, one that produced nothing more useful than suffering and wretchedness. Cold, sterile, depressing—Jarom discovered a place of unforgiving metal and unscaleable walls where misery seemed the currency, and hope, as poet Prentice might put it, had not one friend. He fought to keep his "lamp from burning low."

The next day, one of his jailers, thinking Jarom might like to read about himself, brought him the papers, and he read an account of his own capture in the *Daily Democrat*:

> *Louisville Daily Democrat*
> March 14, 1865
> CAPTURE OF THREE NOTORIOUS OUTLAWS—SUE MUNDY, CAPTAIN MAGRUDER, AND CAPTAIN MEDKIFF IN LIMBO—The notorious outlaws, Sue Mundy, Jerome Clark, Captain Billy Magruder, and Henry Medkiff have been captured and are now securely lodged in the Military Prison of this City. It will be recollected that Magruder was severely wounded about twenty days ago in an encounter with Federal troops. Colonel D. Dill, the Post Commandant, a few days ago received information that the outlaw was lying in a tobacco barn on the place of Mr. Cox, near a little village known as Webster, about ten miles south of Brandenburg, being nursed by Sue Mundy and Captain Medkiff. On Saturday evening he despatched a detachment of fifty men of the 30th Wisconsin volunteers down the river, on the steamer Grey Eagle, to make an effort to capture the illustrious trio. About sunrise on Sunday morning the soldiers arrived at the place, and quietly surrounded the barn.
>
> The door was broken open, and Sue Mundy, as they approached, with a pistol in each hand, fired two shots in quick succession at the boys in blue.
>
> The aim was true, and four of them fell wounded, one

mortally. She remained bold and defiant after this desperate exhibition of her prowess with firearms, and refused to surrender only as a prisoner of war. The terms were agreed to, and the three notorious guerillas were taken prisoners. The scout returned to the city yesterday morning, with the prisoners securely guarded. Magruder is in a weak condition and suffering greatly from the effects of his wound. It is thought he will yield up the ghost before morning dawns.

Sue Mundy, or Jerome Clark, is a rosy-cheeked boy, with dark eyes and scowling brow. Medkiff is a fine, stalwart specimen of humanity. He was confined in the Military Prison here about one year ago, but escaped from the guard while on his way, with other prisoners, to Camp Douglas. He has led a wild life, and we trust that he will expiate his many crimes upon the gallows before many days. Clark and Medkiff are now ironed, and closely confined in cells in the Military Prison. Magruder is receiving medical attention in the Military Prison Hospital.

The *Daily Democrat,* a rival of Prentice's *Louisville Journal,* had provided its readers a fairly straightforward account of the capture, but again the writer hadn't bothered to get the facts straight. Someone who didn't know the facts might conclude, for example, that he and Medkiff managed to wound four Union soldiers with two shots. Twelve or more would have been a more accurate count. The most remarkable error, however, was the transformation of gender that Sue Mundy underwent between the beginning and the end of the article. "*She* remained bold and defiant" became "rosy-cheeked boy" in the space of two paragraphs. Jarom thought a rival editor had called Prentice's bluff, that in fact George Prentice could call Sue Mundy a woman only when she, or he, was not before the public eye. With Jarom in custody, Prentice would be forced to concede the game he'd been playing and put the best face on it without acknowledging his persistent lie.

From the March 14 number of the *Daily Journal* he found two notices relating to his capture:

☞ The four soldiers of the 30th Wisconsin who were wounded by Sue Mundy, were sent to the Barracks Hospital yesterday. Their names are John A. Robbins, company H, gunshot wound in the bowels, which passed through; John G. White, company F, wounded upper part of the right lung, ball still in his body; W. A. Wadsworth, company A. wounded in left ankle; another of the 30th Wisconsin was slightly wounded.

Jarom studied the names as curiosities. Seldom had he known the names of the men he'd shot, nor had he read a description of their wounds. Did this intimate knowledge loose arrows of compunction and guilt? Not one. Set in the printer's font were names of men out to kill him. Had it been otherwise, they would have been raising congratulatory toasts in a Louisville saloon by now. In the same number he found a notice that arrested his attention to a greater degree:

> ☞ All persons having any evidence against the captured outlaws, Sue Mundy, Captain Magruder, and Captain Medkiff, are requested to call at the Provost Marshal's office today or to-morrow, and file their affidavits. The authorities will give the scoundrels a speedy trial, and we trust that they will receive their just deserts—hanging.

Prentice's story of the capture didn't come until the following day when the august editor had sufficient time to study the other papers and put his own rhetorical spin on events. Unlike the account of the day before, it was, as Jarom saw it, part news account, part editorial, with little indication where one ended and the other began:

> THE CAPTURE OF SUE MUNDY, &c.—Some individuals have waxed exceedingly wrothy over a statement published in the Journal in relation to the capture of Sue Mundy and her or his confederates. We said that the outlaws refused to surrender only as prisoners of war, which terms were agreed to. Our amiable friends assure us that we are greatly mistaken. They say that the guerillas surrendered to be held as prisoners of war until they should be delivered up to the authorities at Louisville.
>
> We omitted the proviso, and we are extremely sorry for the omission. When we look at the question fairly the

mistake is not such a monstrous one after all. The outlaws did surrender as prisoners of war, and on board the steamer, from Brandenburg to Louisville, they were treated as such. We trust that we offend nobody by asking why this was so. Who ever heard of Sue Mundy, Magruder, or Medkiff extending a privilege of the kind to a Federal soldier? Who ever knew of three desperate cutthroats treating a prisoner in a kind and humane manner? Sue and Medkiff made a desperate fight, yet, certainly, they were not invincible. Magruder was lying upon a bed of pain in a weak, tottering condition, therefore unable to offer any defence. Fifty Federal soldiers, fully armed, surrounded the house, yet the two outlaws kept them at bay, and were permitted to dictate terms for surrender. They were guerillas, deeply steeped in blood and crime—they were recognized as outlaws—a price was upon their heads, yet they were allowed to surrender as prisoners of war.

We are at a loss to understand how a Federal officer, knowing all of these facts, could accept such terms. Military usage and military law do not sanction such a proceeding. An outlaw cannot be permitted to surrender as a prisoner of war, even with stipulated conditions. To accede to such a proposition is to acknowledge the individual as being engaged in waging a legitimate warfare.

We rejoice at the capture of the cut-throats, and freely say that the planning of the expedition reflects great credit upon the officers connected with it.

THE TRIAL

After breakfast on Tuesday morning, to the sounds of drays and wagons on the cobbles outside, guards transported Jarom from his cell in the military prison at Ninth and Broadway. His legs chained, he scooted, with the assistance of two guards, to a hackney and was conveyed to the headquarters of Colonel William C. Coyl, judge advocate, the man designated to officiate at his court-martial. The building was a handsome, two-story residence built of salmon-colored brick with a small but immaculate graveled yard, rake marks clearly inscribing its surface. Before the army acquired it, Jarom heard one of the guards say, the house belonged to a prosperous tanner. It stood on Chestnut above Third Street, a block or two north of Broadway.

As the guards lifted Jarom from the hackney, he faced twenty or so onlookers collected in the yard and along the street. To the extent that he could read their faces, they seemed curious, having somehow heard or divined when and where the court would convene. The irons on his arms and legs made it awkward for him to get down from the closed carriage, and two neatly uniformed privates stepped over to help. They escorted him past a few old men and a menace of brats, up the walk, and through the front door into what had been a large drawing room, now set up for the trial.

From the moment he climbed to the stoop he felt a sinking in his stomach. The eyes of the curious didn't sicken him but rather the sense that he was living the most important day of his life, that the outcome of this trial would determine whether he lived or died, survived the war or entered the list of its casualties. He looked at the impassive figures around the room and knew he couldn't count one friend among them. At one end he saw a long table with six seats drawn up to it and a furled United States flag standing to one side in a metal sconce. Along the outer wall sat several officers and four or five common soldiers standing.

As soon as they motioned for him to take his seat, one of the officers, a stocky, serious-looking man old enough to be his father, stepped over and introduced himself as Major Wharton, counsel for the defense. Jarom tried to read his face. He was thick-necked and ruddy, much of his face burrowed between the heavy sideburns that General Ambrose Burnside had made so popular among faddish officers in the Union army. A limp mustache obscured his upper lip. What skin showed through seemed to be in bloom, flushed as if he had overheated himself or had some condition physicians talked about in hushed voices. Something about his manner told Jarom he could handle himself competently before such a tribunal—the question was whether he felt inclined or free to.

Speaking in a lowered tone that reminded Jarom of Dr. Lewis, he told Jarom he'd been assigned to defend him that morning and that he'd just been given the charges and a list of government witnesses. He added, almost as an afterthought, that he would do what he could to defend him. Jarom thought Wharton probably realized, as he did, that this case flowed like water in a streambed—it would run its course no matter what obstacles either could throw up to stop it. Jarom mentioned that he'd prepared a written statement to present in his defense. Wharton said that was fine and at the proper time he would present it to the court. Jarom handed it over, and Wharton stuck the papers in his file, not bothering to read them. At that moment Jarom realized he couldn't count on Wharton for much; like the gingerbread trim he noticed along the building's eaves, Wharton served no function beyond giving things a good appearance. Wharton must have read his doubts, for he explained that he had only a few minutes to prepare the defense and that Jarom should listen closely.

First, Wharton informed him that the proceedings would be conducted by a military commission and that as defendant he would be asked to plead guilty or not guilty to each charge as it was read.

"Can I call witnesses?" he asked.

"I don't think your witnesses will be allowed," he said, "especially if they can't be instantly summoned."

Jarom asked what the charges were, and Wharton said the commission was about to convene and that he could hear them for himself.

Jarom noticed the swatch of saffron light that shone through one of the windows and laid itself on the bare floor. *I wish I was here as bright and as untouchable as that light,* he said to himself, *and that my fleshly self lay as distant.* Over the murmuring of the three men seated along the wall he heard a wasp. It thumped against the window, lighting a few moments on one of the mullions before bumping against another pane. The band of wavy light slanted across the room, cutting above the cap of one knee and splaying across his upper thigh. The air in the room seemed depleted, used up, and he knew it would be worse in a few minutes if no one opened a window.

When he asked how much longer they had to wait, Wharton removed his watch from his pocket and tapped the casing, which showed a couple of minutes to ten. At precisely ten Jarom heard a little commotion in the hallway. A clerk or a bailiff of some kind, who'd been standing to one side of the door, told everyone to rise for a military commission of the United States of America, Brigadier General Walter C. Whitaker presiding.

The door opened and six men paraded into the room, seating themselves at the table. All six wore dress uniforms, all were middle-aged or older. Their insignias, as Jarom read them, indicated two generals, three colonels, and a major. They reminded him of an assembly of aldermen or church deacons, grave and businesslike, practical men with little time either to generate or endure nonsense. They appeared vaguely uncomfortable, unbendingly stern. He hoped that, unlike most elders in the church, they dedicated themselves to virtue rather than the semblance of virtue. The one nearest the center, one of the generals, drew a sheaf of papers from his bag and leafed through them for a minute before glancing at his watch, which he pulled out ostentatiously on its fob from a pocket in his vest. Before starting, he looked soberly to either side, and the room went quiet.

From the deference everyone paid the paper-puller, Jarom surmised that he would officiate—a grandfather in his sixties. The general had suaveness, the look of a man at home in cities. Jarom noted that what hair he still had was princely silver and he brushed it back over his ears like folded wings. His eyes flitted about intense and humorless, constantly in motion but intent on business. Patches of gray streaked his beard, the head glossy and efficiently designed as an egg. Jarom was struck by the fact that, aside from the watch, which arguably was a necessity, this man showed not a hint of ornament or excess. Jarom interpreted him as disposed toward fair-mindedness but preoccupied, a little impatient. In the darkest view of things, Jarom concluded that he'd probably been picked because of his devotion to procedure and flexibility when it came to justice.

When he had everyone's attention, Whitaker needlessly cleared his throat before introducing himself as president of the military commission appointed to hear the case. Continuing to study him, Jarom for some reason thought of overripe fruit. Whitaker had the shape of a pear. He puffed out his chest as though pumped up by some inflation device that stretched him, wrinkleless like a balloon. Everything about him seemed taut and distended. Whitaker, White Acre. He also intuited that this fellow intended to do him in, no matter what the evidence showed.

Starting at the far end of the table, Whitaker introduced the members of the commission, identifying their ranks and units. Not one nodded or otherwise acknowledged the introduction. Finally, Whitaker announced that Colonel William H. Coyl of the Ninth Iowa infantry would prosecute the case. Jarom immediately associated the name with snake and cautioned himself to be on his guard, attentive to every word this man spoke at every instant. Low-built, stoop-shouldered, Coyl must have been in his middle fifties. Despite his bureaucratic pallor, he looked canny and self-aware, not likely to sleep at his desk. He carried a mole on his lower jaw, another to one side of his Adam's apple that jogged and jerked as he spoke.

Whitaker turned the proceedings over to Coyl, and Coyl nodded to the court clerk, the same man who stood at the door. Now he wrote furiously what must be the official record of the proceedings. He stopped taking notes long enough to read the order of Major General John Palmer, military commander and so on and so on, authorizing the commission to convene and decide the case of United States versus Jerome Clarke, alias Sue Mundy. Jarom knew Palmer as the man who had replaced Stephen Burbridge in February, the man more than any other he would like to have lined in the sights of a serviceable firearm.

After this preamble, Jarom for the first time felt Whitaker's attention turn to him.

"Have you objections to any members of the commission?" he asked politely.

"No," Jarom answered, wanting to avoid a fight at this early stage.

"Speak more loudly, please," Whitaker said.

"No," said Jarom, "I have no objection," louder this time. None of the names registered but the states did. *What business,* he asked himself, *did Iowa, Indiana, and Wisconsin have in Kentucky? Was there no one in Kentucky qualified to hear the case of a Kentuckian?*

Whitaker then asked everyone to take his seat and further informed them that the commission had been assigned by such and such an order and authorized by General Palmer, commander of the Military Department of Kentucky. Needless repetition. Then he directed the clerk to read the charges and specifications.

Once Jarom sifted through the thickets of legal-sounding words and elaborate locutions, the meaning came surprisingly clear. Charge the first was being a guerrilla. The specification recited that though he was a citizen of Kentucky and the United States, "owing allegiance thereunto," he "did unlawfully take up arms as a guerrilla, not acting with or belonging to any lawfully authorized military force at war with the United States" and that he had acted as a guerrilla and cooperated with guerrillas in the counties of Nelson, Marion, Henry, and Woodford during the months of September, October, November, and December 1864.

Translated and distilled, the second specification meant that he had taken up arms as a guerrilla in Meade County and fired on a detachment of the Thirtieth Wisconsin Volunteer Infantry and "by reason of said shooting did wound Privates White and Wadsworth on the 11th day of March." Jarom guessed that White and Wadsworth were two of the six rightly served when they heaved the stone against the barn door.

When the clerk finished, Whitaker asked Jarom how he pleaded to the first specification.

"Not guilty," he said.

To the second specification?

"Not guilty."

And to the charge?

"Not guilty." Jarom decided that though he was compelled to ride the railroad, he would not grease the tracks for them. He didn't detect even the faintest scent of clemency in the room.

After the charges were read, he knew what the foundation of his defense would be. First, he had to prove that he held standing as an officer in the Confederate army during the last months of 1864. To do that, he needed his commanding officers, Adam Johnson and Colonel Jack Allen. Allen, he knew, served on the staff of General John C. Breckinridge and would be found wherever his commander was. Though he could hardly expect them to appear, he knew that even summoning them would take a minimum of eight or nine days, assuming they were still alive, could be found, and would come. So far as he knew, both were actively fighting somewhere in Tennessee or Virginia. Even if they could be located quickly, which was doubtful, he wondered if they would be permitted safe conduct to travel several hundred miles to testify in an effort simply to save his neck. Probably not, he decided. Defending the second specification, as he understood it, seemed less problematic. His argument would be that in the shooting at the barn he was defending his life from persons seemingly bent on taking it.

There followed a succession of six witnesses, all but one of them Union soldiers. First came Major Cyrus Wilson, duly sworn in and asked what he knew about the taking of Sue Mundy on the twelfth day of March in the year 1865. Wilson described Mundy's capture at the tobacco barn, including his version of the negotiations for surrender. Fundamentally true, his testimony impressed Jarom as convincing and honestly presented, as honestly as his perspective allowed.

"As I stepped out of the sunlight," he said, "I met a drawn pistol leveled at my heart. The hand holding it belonged to a frightened, gangly, wild-eyed boy. He was blinking at the flood of light behind me as though just awakened. As he most likely had, for his rumpled hair had hay straws in it, and he was barefooted. Beyond him I could make out two other human shapes, a man's form crouching in the loft and one lying on the barn floor, propped on one elbow in the crib, his body wrapped in a horse blanket. Beneath the pistol's nose I could see the defendant's index finger curled around the trigger, ready. Though concerned, one look at the owner told me the finger would not crook unless I compelled it to. I was less certain about the nervous one fiddling with his pistols in the loft."

Wilson paused and straightened himself in the witness chair before going on. As he spoke, Jarom noticed that once or twice he looked over to him, as if for confirmation. He then reported substantially what happened as they parleyed in the barn, including Jarom's willingness to surrender if treated as a prisoner of war. He reported that he sensed behind the steady eyes Jarom's awareness of the predicament, that Jarom was desperate and willing to bargain for his life.

When he finished this part of his testimony, Jarom wished that Wharton would question Wilson a little about his impressions and the certainty with which he referred to Jarom's feelings. Who could know his feelings when he himself was so uncertain? But Wharton never objected or interrupted. The judges sat enchanted as Wilson recounted the episode in the barn.

Jarom found himself caught up in Wilson's testimony as much as the others. It was strange to hear someone else give an account of what he had experienced and said, to see the complexion that person put on things. Though Wilson wasn't correct in every particular, Jarom had the eerie sense that Wilson had peered deeply into him. He felt for the second time that Wilson exerted some mysterious power over him. He'd felt uneasy, yes, but for the first time genuinely afraid, not so much by what Wilson said as by the absolute control over events that the major seemed to possess. Jarom saw himself as a guilty child must feel when confronted by his parents about some unthinkable wrong.

When Wilson finished, Coyl asked whether Jarom had made a statement about their being evidence enough to hang him.

"Hang" was not the word, said Wilson. "I believe he said there being evidence enough to kill him."

Coyl asked whether Jarom fired first.

"I believe he did," Wilson said. "I certainly had given no order."

Jarom acknowledged to himself that Wilson was right, that he had fired first, but only after the stone crashed against the door and demonstrated that those outside intended violence against him. He fought the urge to stand up and shout something about throwing the first stone.

Wharton, the statement still in his vest, came back on cross-examination and asked an innocuous question or two about what Jarom had said, and then Wilson came off the witness chair looking relieved, the look of an honest man who had acted an honest part in a dishonest game, and knew it.

Next came a Captain Lewis Marshall, a muddleheaded man in his mid-thirties, willing to take his cue from any leading question that Coyl asked. He confirmed most of what Wilson said about the exchange, though he didn't hear most of it and couldn't be characterized as a disinterested interpreter. When he referred to Jarom as Sue Mundy, Whitaker asked if by Mundy he meant "the man sitting there." The witness affirmed that he did, pointing to Jarom. Jarom reckoned that one Wilson was worth a dozen Marshalls, no matter whose ox was being gored, whose hen being broiled for Sunday supper.

"Captain Marshall," Coyl asked, "can you tell this commission where the name Sue Mundy came from?"

Marshall answered that a girl named Sue Mundy had stolen a horse and started the report that it was Jerome Clarke.

Jarom leaned over and whispered to Wharton that George D. Prentice had bestowed the name on him in the papers.

To his credit, Wharton asked Marshall if the defendant had not actually said that the name had been given him by George Prentice, editor of the *Louisville Daily Journal*. Jarom saw a shudder pass through Marshall, who shifted his weight in his hard-bottomed seat. He hadn't expected Wharton to challenge him.

Marshall replied that he didn't think the defendant had said any such of a thing. This was a lie, and everyone in the room, Jarom believed, knew it.

Again at Jarom's suggestion, Wharton asked if the defendant hadn't also said that at least three men went by the name of Sue Mundy.

"I disremember," Marshall said. "If the defendant made that statement, I hadn't paid it any mind."

Jarom nodded to Wharton to indicate Marshall was lying again.

Sensing that this line of questioning would prove harmful to his case, Coyl interposed an irrelevant question of his own that got Marshall off the hook. As Jarom saw it, George Prentice for his own purposes had written that Sue Mundy was the author of almost any anonymous offense committed against the Union. At least three others—Magruder, Quantrill, and Marion—had used the name in connection with their own misdeeds, whether to shield their own identities or to fuel the threat of guerrillas, he didn't know.

Questions followed about whether Jarom had surrendered as a prisoner of war. Jarom recognized this point as central to his standing before the court. The court accorded certain courtesies to bona fide prisoners of war not owed to guerrillas. Coyl recalled Cyrus Wilson. Still under oath, he denied that Jarom had surrendered on condition he be treated as a prisoner of war. This was a blow. So Wilson was a liar too. That ended the testimony of Wilson and Marshall, and at that point Jarom would have consigned them both to a tenement in the fiery pit reserved for those who have orphaned scruple.

The next four witnesses Coyl must have picked up on the street or as a result of the notice placed in the paper calling for witnesses. Not just any witnesses, Jarom reminded himself, but those who could offer evidence against him. The first answered to the name of William Brady. He testified that he was one of four Union soldiers shot near New Castle on February 2. Military dispatches corroborated this information, attributing the shootings to a gang headed by Quantrill and Sue Mundy.

Coyl asked Brady who shot him. He didn't know. Coyl then asked if the accused was among the party, and Brady answered he couldn't say for sure. Pressed harder, Brady allowed that he supposed that the "defendant there" was the chief and that he assumed the shooting was performed on orders of the chief. Coyl asked what kind of horse Jarom had been riding, and Brady said a dark bay. When asked about Jarom's dress, Brady said the chief was "got up neat in pretty tolerable light pants and a neat something on the shoulders all fringed off." There was then a dispute about whether Jarom wore his hair short or long, all very critical facts in Jarom's opinion. Coyl had to drag the answers from the dimwitted Brady, who had only the vaguest recollections of the incident, if any at all.

Wharton's trying to establish Quantrill as leader of the party pleased Jarom. He purposed to distinguish Jarom's hair, which was long and dark, from Quantrill's, which was curly and reddish. The man Brady saw had a mustache—Jarom obviously didn't. The man he saw or thought he saw, Quantrill, was two to three inches shorter than Jarom.

Brady hemmed and hawed, finally admitting that the man just might have been shorter than the defendant. To Jarom's way of thinking, Brady lied consistently, and he fought the impulse to stand up and scream it to the world.

Next came an extraordinary liar by the name of Hiram Meadows, who said he was attached to Company C, First Wisconsin Infantry. While out "foraging on his own" during Christmas of 1864, he claimed to have been taken prisoner by Sue Mundy, whom he identified as "that man sitting there." He testified that Mundy force-marched him and his brother for a night and a day and into the next night. When his brother "gave out," the prisoner ordered someone to shoot him. This, according to Meadows, was done "right then." Curiously to Jarom, at no time was the slain brother named or identified. Nor did Meadows state where the alleged murder occurred. Jarom had no recollection of any such event and acknowledged to himself that if for some reason he had wanted a prisoner shot, he would have done it himself rather than ask someone else. He was pretty well convinced that Hiram Meadows had no brother, at least not one who accompanied him foraging at Christmas. This death, he knew, was not his doing, if in fact there had been a death at all.

The commission absorbed this fiction without comment, and Coyl brought on the next witness. He introduced himself as Private Alfred Hill, stating that he'd seen the defendant while riding on a train. A citizen, he said, pointed Sue Mundy out to him as the defendant rode along outside, shooting into the train windows. Hill said this incident had occurred "a little this side of St. Mary's" and that he would have shot Mundy if the scoundrel had not ridden off before he could load his gun.

At no time was Hill asked to fix the event to a time certain. It irked Jarom that his counsel let things ride without objection as if worried about taxing the judges with too much detail. As best Jarom could determine, Hill referred to the train Magruder robbed early in September. Fair enough, but he wasn't with Magruder. Given the chance, he knew he could prove he was at the time with Morgan in Tennessee.

A final witness, whose name Jarom missed, did not add anything material to what had been alleged. When he left the chair, Coyl rested his case, and the hearing was all but over. Through his attorney Jarom protested that he hadn't been able to produce any witnesses. General Whitaker, ingenuous as Cinderella, said that none had been summoned. After Jarom requested Adam Johnson and Jack Allen, Coyl said these men's testimony would be tainted because they fought with the rebel army and couldn't readily be brought before the commission because they fought far away in an opposing army. At this moment Jarom knew he'd lost, knew that he'd probably lost before the trial began, and that he was playing a bit part in a larger charade in which he would be expected to pay with his life.

After the last witness left the room, members of the commission conferred a little. Whitaker cleared his throat and spoke on their behalf, saying that the urgency of the proceedings required a timely disposition of the case. To this Jarom wanted to shout, "Bull!" Instead, Wharton took the opportunity to submit Jarom's statement for the commission's review, and Whitaker reluctantly agreed to append it to the record as exhibit A.

Though Jarom didn't expect anything to come of it, Wharton asked Coyl to send to Camp Chase and other places so that the defendant could prove he was indeed a Confederate soldier. Whitaker regretted that there was not sufficient time to call witnesses from all over the country, especially since there was, after all, a war going on.

Even if there were time, he added, proof that Jarom was a Confederate soldier would be immaterial because the crimes he stood accused of were sufficient to convict him even if he was. The only charge, he reminded the commission, was that as a guerrilla Jarom had fired on the Thirtieth Wisconsin.

Jarom, staring at a spot on the wall behind them, knew further debate was useless. They would do what they would do.

After a brief pause in which Jarom listened to the ticking of the clock on the mantle, a twin of the Seth Thomas in the Tibbs parlor, Whitaker announced that the case had been heard and it was time for the members to confer and reach a decision based on evidence and law. With this, Whitaker rose, and the other members of the commission trooped out of the room after him, to give the matter, as Whitaker put it, "mature deliberation."

Momentarily confused, Jarom began to understand what "mature deliberation" meant. The hopeful could regard it as possible clemency. The cynical could interpret it as a way of saying that in fact the case had been decided and the tribunal did not wish to state its prejudices in the presence of the defendant. Jarom felt suspended above a chasm such as several he'd seen near Pound Gap in the Kentucky mountains. The rope that held him was in the grip of strangers who bore him no love. One of those standing by, less indifferent than hostile, was George Prentice, the editor holding his pen poised to see what more mischief he could do.

So that was all there was to it, he thought. *No decision announced, no resolution.* He felt a constriction in his lungs that threatened to cut off his breath. He felt himself run through a gamut of emotions: frustration, betrayal, outrage at injustice, foreboding, a tinge of self-pity. He couldn't imagine what Patterson would do, what advice he would give, what possible solace he could offer. He was perplexed and finally downcast, left with words to the effect that the commission would render its decision concerning his guilt or innocence, his life, his death, after "mature deliberation."

After the commission left, the same guards escorted him to the hack and drove him back to prison. This time people on the street seemed to go about their business ignorant of or indifferent to the doings of their government. Women carrying grocery sacks gabbled on a corner outside a sundries shop. A servant in a red vest and rakish hat cut a little caper as he passed a stooped workman pushing a wheelbarrow full of bricks.

Only the guards in the spare brick prison showed him deference, most of them having tasted the inequities of war, the homicidal whims of officers, knowing what it meant to be vulnerable. They stood back as he passed, holding their tongues, their stares. Jarom remembered a piece of wisdom his father recited when he spanked Jarom—then about ten—after he'd caught him teasing a neighbor's dog that had strayed to their kitchen door.

"Be kind," he said, "for everyone you meet is fighting a great battle."

"Even dogs?" Jarom asked.

"Even dogs," his father said.

When his cell door clanged to and he was alone, the feelings he had stifled all morning knotted in his chest. Though he fought it, his body began to shudder. Along his arms he felt goose bumps. Crying for the first time since he'd discovered John Patterson bleeding in the hayfield, he buried his face in the rough blanket that covered his pallet.

After he'd calmed himself, he mined his memory for each piece of testimony and imagined the impression it would make on impartial judges. And then on partial judges. He hashed everything over and over again, searching for any scrap of evidence or gesture on which he could fix his hopes. Even after he'd eaten his bread and beans and was staring at the plaster of the cell's ceiling in the dark, he sifted through what he now thought of as a script, staying awake most of the night. He wondered where Medkiff was and whether Magruder had been given a bed in the infirmary. He wondered if Berry knew of his capture, if he was organizing to spring him from prison. He reflected on the trajectory of the trial. The turning point had come when Whitaker refused him witnesses. From that moment on, he knew he was doomed. The only thing he needed to know was how much time he had before they shot him.

CHURCHED

Early the next morning the Reverend J. J. Talbot, rector of St. John's Episcopal Church, came to visit Jarom in his cell. Even if he had not worn dark clerical clothes and collar, Jarom would have identified him as an official of the church on some dark mission, not a bearer of good news. Though the minister approached him kindly, Jarom detected the same patronizing air he had experienced with others of his tribe, who, because of their special relationship with God, monopolized all the answers. Whether Talbot was sincere in sharing his special knowledge he couldn't say. When Jarom first heard the name, he immediately thought of the Talbot in the song, who by the singer's "shoul" would "cut all the English throat," the Talbot who would be made a lord, Talbot the dog. One part of him recognized his flirtation with coincidence. Another plumbed the implications of the name—was his the "English throat"? Talbot. Lord. Was Talbot the perverse God who held Jarom's fate in His divine hands?

But the Talbot before him only asked how he'd slept and how he felt. Jarom said he was feeling as well as he could, sitting in a cell certain about his future but uncertain about how soon.

There came a silence that did not seem awkward to him, to either of them. And then Talbot changed the subject.

"You are called Sue Mundy," Talbot said. "I'm curious. What is your real name?"

"Clarke," Jarom said, "Marcellus Jerome Clarke. Marcellus was the name my father gave me, expecting I would be a soldier, a follower of Mars."

"And Jerome?"

"It was the name my mother gave me," he said, "though she shortened it to Jarom. A kind of pet name."

"And do you know who Jerome was?"

"No, not really. I guess he was a minister of the church."

"A saint," Talbot said. "A great student of the Word."

"Don't the saints die terrible deaths?" Jarom asked. "How did he die?"

"In his sleep," Talbot said, "peacefully in his sleep."

Then Talbot pulled him back to his troubles with all the force of gravity, asking if he had heard the result of the court-martial. Jarom instinctively knew that if he had only intuited the outcome before, he would have it now as fixed and readable as letters chiseled into stone.

"They will shoot me, I suppose," he found himself saying.

"When do you suppose that will be?" Talbot asked, Jarom hearing in his voice the tone he knew Talbot must use to console the bereaved or the dying, a voice unctuous with concern and kindliness.

"In a few weeks, I guess," Jarom said, having heard that authorities customarily gave the condemned time to settle their quarrels with God and prepare their souls for eternity. He stared at the lump of Talbot's Adam's apple as if he could discern the words before they were spoken. His own throat tightened, and he knew the worst was coming.

"Who knows?" Talbot said gently in the way an adult might speak to a child. "Who knows that it may not be in a few days? Can I come around and be of some service to you?"

"Yes," Jarom heard himself saying, "come around," as though the words were novel to him, wholly unexpected. "Yes, sir," hearing himself use the word for the first time since leaving Morgan's command in Tennessee. "I'd be glad to have you come and see me."

Talbot seemed willing to listen, a decent man he was sure, if nothing else company who could keep his mind from sinking. Talbot had kept an emotional distance, a clerical dispassion. Though he seemed sympathetic, he remained strangely placid, affected but detached. Jarom felt like a displaced boulder poised on the edge of a precipice above a lake. He already felt a terrible turbulence, the displacement of stone, obeying the only laws it knew, striking the placid water. And Talbot, as Jarom conceived him, was that water. This might have ended it, but he sensed Talbot had something more to say, that he had a boulder of his own to drop.

"My young friend," he said, "if in a few days, why not a few hours? You'd better train your thoughts to preparation now."

The reality behind Talbot's words struck Jarom and hit with the force not of a dropped stone but of a tidal sweep, a force that broke over him and shattered what self-control he had been able to muster. When the words penetrated, he felt a constriction in his gut that preceded heaving, a realization that his execution—a word that cut him—was not a far-off event in an indeterminate future but something that would happen today—in the small breadth of hours and minutes. And he was powerless to prevent it. His breath shortened, he found himself gasping. The heaves moved up to his chest, and for a few seconds he felt he would throw up.

"Parson," he said, "are you telling me I am to be shot today?"

"Father," Talbot said.

"Father," Jarom said, "am I to be shot today?"

Talbot lowered his eyes in answer.

Then Jarom met Talbot's eyes as they rose kindly to meet his own.

"You are to be executed this afternoon at four o'clock." He hesitated, "And there is one other thing. You are not to be shot."

"Hung then?" Jarom asked.

Talbot nodded and looked down at some object invisible on the floor of the cell. How could he be surprised? Since he had surrendered in the barn, the dark prospect of execution loomed over him like a span of invisible wings, a presence like the shadow of a cloud moving across the landscape. Or the scissoring silhouette of a hawk skimming across a stricken pullet caught in an open field. Now he was the chicken that sensed something dark pass over him. Time after time he had imagined himself standing blindfolded against a wall, neat balls of lead punching through his open shirt, his ears concentrating on a band of music or hymnody. A clean shot to the chest and that was that. But hanging. He wasn't prepared for such a leave-taking, hadn't acknowledged the possibility.

"They have no right!" he shouted in Talbot's compassionate face. "I was commissioned in the regular service by Jack Allen, and I can prove Marion killed the men I'm charged with killing."

"Well, that may be," said Talbot, "but this is not the time to say, nor am I the one to hear you say it. What I can do for you is pray."

As the reality began to take root in him, Jarom realized that at one level he was guilty. The evidence was not right, the judges not impartial, but at root he knew he was guilty. It occurred to him now that it was possible to be innocent and guilty at the same time, that both were summations of degrees and millimeters balanced here and tipped there, and that a final accounting could not be made until that person had performed his last act, leaving nothing more to measure. At some level Jarom realized he was being called to account not only for charges that had come before the commission but for everything—every shot he'd ever fired, every spark of anger he'd felt toward those who hurt the people he loved, every time he'd gone along when Marion or Magruder had overstepped the bounds. The charges brought against him were weak, but the moral weight of his other crimes bore down on him.

Hate, like the generations of ancestors of whom he was composed, had a complex genealogy. The particular wrong that unnameable others had done him had aggregated into a hatred that was general—a hatred fueled not only by Patterson's blinding but also by the bayonet that pierced Susan Berry's side, the shot that downed John Hunt Morgan, the spent bullet that thumped Estin Polk, the blinding of Stovepipe Johnson by his own troops, and, yes, the shooting of good-natured Toby by Bill Marion. And finally, he was guilty in the sense, he thought, that everyone is guilty—guilty of believing in a cause more indefinite than himself, guilty of being his parents' child, guilty of being taught to act according to what he believed without considering consequences. The guilt he was willing to accept he did not own—it was shared. Under this reckoning, his judges were as guilty as he the moment they let expedience and bias dictate the outcome of the trial. Tainted, they too were no more than their parents' children.

So Talbot knelt and Jarom joined him on the slabbed stone of the cell floor, the coldness working up through the knobs of his knees into the marrow of his bones. Without a book Talbot prayed for more than an hour. At first he spoke of the sickened heart and the perfect harvest of death that the war had visited on the world.

"Let us rejoice," he said, "in the hope of glory that will bring a surcease of human suffering on this sphere of rock in this shattered country where men take the lives of their neighbors and put stock to the sword and pillage their neighbors' crops and incinerate what their neighbors have built so that it chars and blackens to ruin. So that not one stone stands on another."

He prayed for the vision to forsake mortal blindness and find a fuller vision encompassing Kingdom Come, that blithe and beautiful day that, like human hopes, shines but to hasten away. He acknowledged the frost and snows and storms that will hide the blue sky and lock up the riffling rill while man and beast go shivering. He affirmed that the only blue sky that persists is the Lord's firmament in whose domain there is no storm, no strife, but only a pureness of spirit and warmth and splendor that is joy eternal. He invoked the years of deep sorrow on the land and the deep gloom that still enshrouds it and the coming years that might witness an increase in our sorrows, except that we accept the Lord in his mercy and enter his Kingdom where sorrow shall cease and the broken and dead shall be uplifted and made whole.

Jarom felt the consolation of Talbot's words, the comfort that only words can give, though in the end they were not comforting or soothing enough to erase his guilt or the vision of what lay ahead: the gallows, the trap, the noose that would strangle and wrench the breath from his lungs, his feet withdrawn from the solid earth he loved, dangling, suspended, dancing in the void.

But then he came back to the more familiar world he loved: the crow of the cock, the exquisite motion of a running horse, sunlight translated across the yard through a grove of sugar trees late on a fall afternoon, the voices and features that defined poor Billy Magruder and the peace he found in Mollie Thomas's earnest face. And the force of goodness that made these and others like nothing else that lived or had lived or would live for all he knew—these things and all things until every object and creature and influence that filled this life and made it both tolerable and wonderful could be touched and savored until there was no more to touch and savor.

To be severed from all this was more than he could withstand, a loss no words or sentiment could describe. Expressions like "numbing void" or "utter emptiness" meant nothing to him because they could not finally delineate his feelings. For him—for the majority of us, too, he thought—the transition into nothing was everything. Letting it come was not enough—that is, blanking out or dimming the senses and mechanically accepting what followed in the annihilation of consciousness. He had to be at peace somehow, and gentle words and Jesus, he knew, would carry him only so far.

He realized he wanted to send, had to send, some messages to those he loved. A vague Mollie appeared to him, and he pulled out the ambrotype to coax her features into resolving themselves.

Talbot had been looking at him in that indulgent way of ministers who sometimes lead by being led.

"Will you get me a pen and some paper?" Jarom asked.

"Of course," he said, "though there is a prohibition against my carrying messages beyond these walls."

"Will you carry them for me?" Jarom asked.

"Of course I will," he said. "I would be happy to."

Talbot went to the cell door and through the bars asked the guard for some pen and paper and a bottle of ink. When the guard returned with the things he had requested, Jarom, unsure of the steadiness of his hand, asked Talbot if he would act as scribe. Talbot dutifully wrote down what he was told to, letters to Aunt Mary Tibbs, Nancy Bradshaw, John Patterson, and Mollie Thomas. Jarom saved Mollie's for last because he knew it would be the hardest to compose, the most wrenching. What could he say to her, knowing that by the time she received it he would be dead? For a time the words wouldn't come. Talbot used up several sheets of foolscap with false starts and falterings before Jarom could find the words he wanted her to read, something simple, something from the heart:

> My dear Mollie,
> I have to inform you of the sad fate which awaits your true friend. I am to suffer death this afternoon at four o'clock. I send you from my chains a message of true love; and as I stand on the brink of the grave I tell you, I do fondly and forever love you.
>
> >   I am ever truly yours

He read what Talbot had written, then bent to sign the letter, debating for a few seconds whether to give his name as Jarom or Jerome. Unable to forgo this last gesture of correctness, of extravagance, he signed, "M. Jerome Clarke.". Then he thought of sending something of himself with each letter, a token. At his request Talbot asked the guard for a pair of scissors, assuring him that they wouldn't be used for any act of violence. The guard must have trusted him, for he came back with a small pair of snips. Having Jarom hold his head still, Talbot clipped some locks of his uncombed hair to be enclosed in each letter. With Mary Tibbs's he included the brass button from his father's uniform. He asked Talbot not to say anything about any of this, and Talbot gave his word that he wouldn't. Then he took from his pocket the folded-up music sheet in which he had wrapped the ambrotype of Mollie and him, he on the settee with his arm about her, she sitting on its edge, her hand in his. He wrapped "Lillibulero," the song he had never heard—and never would hear, he realized—inserting the letter to Mollie in its folds. When he'd given the letters to Talbot, he felt relieved. He thanked Talbot, who clasped his hand and said he would pray for him and would stay with him until the last. As Talbot stepped from the cell and the door swung to, Jarom vowed to himself that he would make his own exit from this world as neatly as he could, picking up after himself each step of the way until there were no more steps for him to take.

Around midday, the guard brought him dinner on a tin plate, lean beef and boiled potatoes. Bite by bite he ate what he knew would be his last meal. Afterward, he lay down on his cot and closed his eyes to the world. In the half-light of the cell, he found himself reviewing the budget of what he loved and things to which he owed allegiance, an inventory that grew as he combed his nearly twenty years on the planet: Logan County, blind Patterson, the loyalties of his messmates—especially One-Armed Berry and the wounded Magruder—Mollie Thomas, Aunt Mary Tibbs, farmscapes, whatever configuration of land lay before him in Kentucky, Samuel Colt, Papaw and Memphis, John Hunt Morgan, breast of chicken and collard greens, the regenerative power of rain, the sanctity of shape and texture in trees, the essential holiness of every animal in creaturedom, the interminable interplay of light and shadow.

Chief among the things he had learned through the tutelage of blood, his apprenticeship in suffering, was that this so-called civil war was at root uncivil, a distemper of wolves.

He composed a mental list of what he would never do or know: reach the age of twenty, marry, lead a stable life, grow a beard, dwindle into old age, see an ocean, lie with a woman, lie with Mollie Thomas, earn his own livelihood, go to California, voyage to the land and seat of his Clarke forebears, collect his own library of books, own a boundary of land, know the pleasure and satisfactions of constructing things, outlive Memphis, chronicle whatever peace followed the war, take pleasure in the roll of seasons as things grew and prospered under his hand, savor foods as yet untasted, feel the respect that accrues to elders like deepening mulch in a forest, attain maturity of mind, read the complete works of Mr. Charles Dickens. Nor would he ever get his hands on Windrup, even know the man's first name. He would never become a father.

Jarom would never meet or even see George D. Prentice, his failed father, the author in part of his son's destruction. Would he come visit? No. Had he been at the wharf or somewhere along the route to prison? Would he be among the throng that gathered for his execution, armed with sharpened quill to get the last word?

Looking fresh, Talbot came back after the noon hour and began going over the catechism, reading from the *Book of Common Prayer* and the King James Bible. Jarom accompanied him in prayer, and Talbot conferred with him about the nature of his beliefs.

He asked if Jarom accepted Jesus Christ as his Lord and Savior and if he believed in life everlasting. Jarom answered that he did, wanting to believe and be believed though he knew nothing would alter what he had to go through and in the end make things any easier. How to get through the execution, the ritual of murder, gave him more concern than what lay in the Hereafter. For some reason he also wanted to please Talbot, the good shepherd who did not seem to doubt or question the words. About three o'clock Talbot conducted the sacrament of baptism, and Jarom for a brief moment felt he had been wrapped in the white garment of Christ's infinite mercy. As the words had said. In his heart he was still terrified, still not one with himself and others, still unsure of what had to be done. There may have been a verdict in his military trial, but he knew his trials were not done. They had just begun. His hope was that his remains would be gathered to the dust of Kentucky, though he had no notion where. He had asked Talbot to contact Mary Tibbs, who would see that his remains reached a resting place in his home county.

One face among the shadow army of faces that rose before him came unsummoned, a furloughed soldier—was Caldwell the name?—rousted in his shirtsleeves from his supper table at a farmstead in Bullitt County, a man Magruder had known before the war and had been watching as a hunter might observe the habits of a buck that raided the truck in his garden. Prodded out to his barnyard, the man was shot by Jarom, Magruder, Marion, and a fourth man whose identity Jarom couldn't remember, though it may have been Sam Berry. He remembered pulling the man's mother loose from him, remembered her trying to shoo her other children back into the house so they would not see. But most he remembered the terror in the man's face as silently he drew his last few breaths there in his own yard, the four of them cocking and preparing to fire, the man unsure from which pistol to expect the first load. Later, as they rode away, he'd wondered what the name, pronounced "kah-well," meant, speculating that the dead man's Scottish forebears lived at the place of the Cold Well. Caldwell.

His father also rose up, the late Brigadier-General Hector M. Clarke decked out in his braided militia uniform and plumed hat. Sitting at his large desk in the parlor, he asked Jarom to explain himself. Envisioning him, Jarom thought of his own gaudy duds, the red suit he'd worn with the fringe and tinsel along the sleeve and pants legs. How could he explain the past months, the shame he had brought on his family—the pitiless thefts, the low company he kept, the blood he'd shed? No better than his not-so-distant cousin Branch Clarke, the murderer. No better than Branch's son Tandy, sitting in his Frankfort penitentiary cell, idle and handless. What would the old man think of him now—not a soldier but a fugitive from soldiers, a guerrilla at best, no longer fighting under a banner that would claim him, no longer associated with a cause beyond his own survival?

"Short of the glory," his father would say, "short of the glory," shaking his head, erect even while sitting, his back not touching the chair.

Jarom took consolation in his father not having lived long enough to know, for the knowledge would have killed him.

How did I come to find myself here in this place? he asked finally, eyeing the neat but monotonous courses of brick on the cell wall, a striped trapezoid of light against it from the small barred window.

He had no answer, nothing he could say by way of justification or excuse.

"What clemency do you hope for?" asked the voice inside.

"All," he said.

"What clemency can you expect?"

"None."

He no longer kindled even the faintest hope of Berry or Quantrill or Tom Henry or any of the others cheating the hangman by a dramatic rescue. The risks were too great, the rewards too small. Magruder, were he able, would not have hesitated. He felt a constriction in his chest and the beating of his heart, imagining the valves as fists beating frantically against a closed door. In his hopelessness he cried as the sequence of his last moments came to him. He remembered feelings like these only one other time, descending a steep ridge along a very narrow path, uncertain of Papaw's steadiness. One misstep and the two of them would pitch to their deaths in the craggy bottom. Then, as now, he could only center his weight and try to concentrate on the way ahead. When he'd looked down, he saw the sleek muscles in Papaw's upper right leg, the knobs and bony competence of her step, a few dark bristles protruding, knowing not to lean over, not to look down, until the path widened into a wagon road.

All the while, Talbot sat patiently in a corner of the cell, seemingly communing with the higher powers—there if needed. Jarom kept staring at the tiers of bricks with their stripes of lime, saying nothing. About three-thirty Talbot tactfully excused himself so Jarom could collect himself and think his final thoughts.

RECESSIONAL

March 15, 1865

As the reality of his execution bore down on him, Jarom tried to forestall his fear by registering every detail, as though by amassing everything, he could preserve all that was his life. He counted three others in the hack, a roomy leather nest perched on great spring bows with facing seats and a collapsible top. The two whose names he knew were Captain George Swope and the Reverend J. J. Talbot. The third was a hayseed with a blotchy complexion whose task, Jarom realized with grim amusement, was to shoot him if he jumped in his chains and attempted to run.

Between Swope and Talbot he saw a bond—the man of war and the man of God making the best of their temporary association, one pretending the next world primary, the other agreeing to the extent that he would lend a hand to transporting Jarom there. He noticed that neither seemed comfortable speaking directly to the other, so they talked through or to him so the other could hear.

To Jarom, they were players in an elaborate performance, a pair of mismatched horses carting precious baggage—himself—through each stage of an awkward and bumpy journey from one kingdom to the next.

The Power and the Glory. One was Power, the other Glory. Where did he stand in this hierarchy? At best he thought of himself as Aunt Mary's last-minute Christian, a reluctant Christian, a Christian by necessity. He remembered the story his aunt told him about the New Madrid earthquake of 1811, when the earth ruptured so strongly the Ohio River flowed backward for a time. So powerfully came the tremors that great numbers of wastrels and felons and scamps suddenly converted to the ways of Christ. In droves the churches reported converts, those who'd finally come to recognize God's message to infidels. So long as there remained a possibility of more tremors, attendance remained high. After a few weeks, the tremors ceased and attendance dropped back to prequake levels. And Jarom recognized that though the church had its hold on him, he fell into the category of earthquake Christian, gallows Christian.

Forward on the driver's seat were another guard and the hackman, an ancient whose hands, grasping the reins, were smudged with age spots, a brown archipelago mapping his skin from knuckles to wrist. Jarom was drawn to these hands as to a map on which the sum of all the man's winters had been imprinted. With a pang he realized that though he'd weathered his share of storms in his three years of war, his skin would not feel another rain, would not feel the warm palm of another sun.

Across and to his right sat Talbot, riding backward, the light on his blind side. He didn't seem to mind, his eyes half-shut under his steel spectacles. He had the look of one of the mystics of the early church, a desert dweller who had removed himself from one world in contemplation of the next. For a time Jarom raised his handkerchief to his eyes to lessen the glare, leaning his head against the side of the cab as if to hide his agony from those who looked on. The intensity of these last minutes engulfed him.

As they passed down Broadway, the widest street in the Falls City, Jarom noticed that Talbot ignored the crowd, the commotion in the street, the music of murder. He looked beyond as if he knew everything by some higher intuition accessible only to priests. His lips were moving, reciting a prayer or maybe an appropriate psalm, a litany of whispered hisses and exploding consonants, sounds that hovered, like the church itself, feasibly on the edge of sense. What he said, Jarom concluded, wasn't meant for his ears but instead was audible only to angels, the membership of the Heavenly Host. He tucked his right forefinger into his black book, marking what was probably the prayer for the dead in the Book of Common Prayer of the Episcopal Church: "I am the resurrection and the life, saith the Lord," a text that he had heard as a child and had heard in his own mind since Talbot came to his cell at nine o'clock that morning.

Fighting off tremors of anxiety, Jarom looked at the guard on a leather seat directly across from him and next to Talbot. He had the fidgets, could not keep still. Swope addressed him as Ruckles or Rockles, Jarom couldn't tell which. To Jarom he was Jack-in-the-Box. Never completely at rest, he shifted his weight, cocked his head from one side to the other, drummed and clenched his fingers, flicked his eyes about him nervously. Pimples formed a red constellation on his chin; across his nose was a generous pepper-spill of freckles that reminded Jarom of the Indiana farmlands he had seen after the escape from Camp Morton. He couldn't have been much older, if any, than Jarom. His holstered pistol—a Colt issued for the occasion and with which, he would bet, he was not overly familiar—was placed butt forward, the flap unfastened for easy drawing. Jarom wanted to assure him that he had nothing to fear from his hands, itching in their metal bracelets. The two steel rings yoking his wrists rubbed and chafed with the slightest movement. Freckle-Face knew and Jarom knew there would be nothing to worry about so long as the metal didn't slip or melt from his wrists. What worried the guard lay beyond, ahead, behind. As he squirmed, he scanned the streets for desperadoes, invisible armies of gray rescuers. Even Jarom had heard rumors that guerrilla cronies would snatch him from the jaws of Death. Jarom wanted desperately to believe it but couldn't—Magruder wounded, Marion dead, Berry God knows where. But to Rockles—or Ruckles—every alley or side street was a point of attack for which he braced himself.

Captain Swope sat supremely untroubled to Jarom's right, every pound of his considerable self cushioned and confident. Jarom thought of the vast muttonchops forming a double hedge across Swope's upper jowls. They rose out of his collar and up his cheeks like tails of pet squirrels, twins, their furry sleekness buried in the expansive folds of his uniform. The hairs of his coat were coarse as steel filings, gray-tipped and slightly coiled. He had the rooted, ponderous look of a small-town banker or alderman, the shape of a possum with eyes pink and feral. Or a rain barrel. He wore the uniform as masquerade, a blue safe-conduct from one snug burrow to the next. Short of breath, he huffed at reliable intervals and looked on everything he saw with an appraiser's eye. To Jarom, the now familiar warmth and bulk of the overfed body against him felt oddly comforting, almost paternal, though this father was composed of betrayal. He knew that when the wheels stopped their rotations Swope would escort him to destruction as casually as he would bid the regimental cook twist the neck of his Sunday chicken.

"Where will it happen?" Jarom asked.

"At the fairgrounds," Swope said, "Eighteenth and Broadway, a few more blocks."

As he spoke, Jarom could feel the steady expansion and contraction of the man's chest like a bloated concertina, his voice offensively nasal.

"How much is the admission?" Jarom asked, trying to rankle him a little.

"Not a cent for you," he said. "Free, in fact, for all comers." He could have said, Jarom thought, that you will be admitted at the cost of your neck.

Jarom wished his hands were free so he could wipe the smirk from Swope's face, his sidelong glare of outrage when he realized that Jarom baited him and remained defiant yet. Swope's chest rose and fell undisturbed though the breath came deeper and his face flamed red. Jarom took some small pleasure in bringing Swope's water to a boil in the way he took pleasure generally from pretense being exposed and any balloon of self-importance punctured.

Finally, the wheels came to a stop. The well-fed horses stood in their harness, tails switching at the flies. Jarom imagined himself outside on the curb with the onlookers, watching the radial blur as the iron-rimmed wheels slowed into focus, the spokes arranging themselves around the hub, locking into sight. Jarom watched the others as they sunk lower into the hot leather of the seats. In turn, each stepped off, the balance shifting as the tensed springs beneath them shrugged free of their burden. When it came his turn, Swope and the guard supported his underarms and lifted him down, his feet momentarily suspended. He felt their support as he hobbled, half-hopped, onto the yellow crust of the fairground. To either side of him stood soldiers of the Thirtieth Wisconsin, forming a corridor of blue that led to a high wooden scaffolding well off the street. From somewhere nearby, a band began playing the Dead March.

The gallows consisted of a raised platform supported by a trusswork of crossbeams and uprights. He'd overheard guards at the prison mention it had been rebuilt with materials used to hang Nathaniel Marks, "the outlaw of the mountains," executed out of public view in January. The planking appeared almost new, blond and clean-smelling, as though fresh from the mill yard. Jarom detected a faint scent of pine resin. *What a waste of good lumber,* he thought. *Better a bullet.*

The guards turned their backs on him now, as if what they had to fear was not from Jarom but from the crowd around them. They formed a barrier of blue and held their rifles at port arms, taking every precaution to see the hangman wasn't cheated. The guard from the hack and a new guard undid Jarom's ankle chains so he could mount the stairs of the scaffold to the platform. A turn of the key and he felt the manacles snap off his ankles.

Instantly, he had a feeling of lightness, of boundless possibility. He felt his legs extending beyond the restriction of the chains and knew they would lift him up the steps. He felt a surge in his limbs and imagined escape, a picture in which he was running, running, the crowd parting in amazement, the stiff line of guards crumbling into motion, tentative and confused, a few of them dropping their rifles to take up the chase and pursuing until he'd outdistanced them all and lost himself in the maze of alleyways and backyards, blocks away. He saw Mollie Thomas wearing a pressed gingham dress standing on her porch and opening her arms to him as he came up the steps of her father's house unfettered and buoyed with possibility and hope.

The chains clanking in a brittle pile as they slipped off his ankles brought him back. There was small relief in this small freedom as he felt a nervous tic in his legs, a tingling in his ankles. For the first time in three days, he could move without hindrance. He imagined coffles of slaves as they plodded across the landscape, droves of them yearning not for anything so abstract as freedom but simply for the fetters to be removed and movement restored to their ankles and wrists. The illusion of freedom, he realized, was enough for most of us. Freedom itself was a burden most seemed unwilling or unable to carry.

They moved toward the platform then, guards in front, guards behind. For the first time Jarom became aware of the din about him, the gabble of thousands speaking in words from which he could not extract any sense. He thought of the honeybees fretting in an opened hive, an incessant and indecipherable music whose song carried only the drone of busyness. Those standing toward the crowd formed a buffer of flesh, but Jarom knew the going would not be easy as pushers elbowed their way to the front and into his path to paw at his jacket for souvenirs. He felt their eyes scan his face for signs of fear or whatever they looked for there. He'd almost made it to the steps when someone jostled him off balance. His weight shifted out from him until Freckle-Face dipped under his shoulder and lifted him back again, steadied his step. Jarom heard himself thanking him kindly.

The stair treads that Jarom felt under his boots were reddish blond— pine, he guessed, from the knots. They looked so new he could imagine them still powdered with yellow leavings from the saw. They sounded hollow as step by step the five of them clopped up to the platform, square nail heads shining four to a step like eyes. Halfway up, he looked out over the crowd. A blinding light splayed off the brass of the band instruments in golden spangles. Tilted parasols capped many of the heads, popping out of the multitude like mushrooms. A great swell of flesh spilled across the fairgrounds and lapped against the buildings, a gumbo of simmering faces. Rising from it were mixed odors of cigars, sweat, and a cloying sweetness he couldn't name but had smelled among masses of men on marches early in the war. In it hung a pervasive staleness like the must of some long-unopened trunk in the attic.

As he stepped onto the platform, he felt what Patterson had described to him as buck fever, a nervous anticipation that would cause the hunter to shiver before hammer struck cap and sent the load home into the flank of a browsing deer. Jarom felt it the first time he drew a bead on a man on the second day at Donelson and afterward each time he knew himself about to visit ruin on someone's body. He felt it now as he stepped onto the platform into a crow's nest, a point from which he could see as well as be seen. *Courage keep me,* he said to himself, *give me strength to go through,* as he turned to look over the sea of faces. The exertion, the anxiety, quickened his breath. Looking out, he discovered that the ten feet of elevation did not permit him to see more so much as it altered his perspective.

At a glance he could see almost every available swatch of ground occupied. He remembered Aunt Mary Tibbs's account of her father saying that during Kentucky's first settlement the wilderness was so dense that except for some waterways it was possible for a squirrel to traverse the state from limb to limb, tree to tree, without touching ground. The mass of humanity before him was the largest he'd seen under one sky except for the surrender at Donelson, if one counted those prostrate on the ground. Five thousand, eight thousand, ten thousand, he could hardly estimate the number. Packed with people, the open ground extended south for two blocks before ending at another wall of storefronts and row houses. Shade trees here and there broke the flatness of the fairgrounds, upright funnels of bared limbs with nipples of half-opened buds.

As he looked out, faces began to emerge from the mass: a gristle-jawed farmer wearing a tattered hat, a middle-aged trollop blued about the eyes, a jumpy bootblack, a bonneted heroine from an engraving in Mr. Dickens's *Pickwick Papers,* a whole ladder team from the firehouse got up in ridiculous helmets. He could see tribes of ragamuffins burrowing through the crowd like moles. Less obvious were the pickpockets and snatch-purses. From the courthouse he made out politicians and clerks, barely distinguishable from their retinues of hangers-on. *What was it,* he asked himself, *that brought them?* Passersby, sometimes whole families, seemed drawn to spectacle like ants to spilled sugar.

Across Broadway each window above the storefronts and offices had its display of faces. Even the rooftops attracted watchers. A few game souls, mostly teenage boys, perched precariously in the trees, hanging like some out-of-season fruit. Looking back toward Broadway, he could see the crowd backed up the steps of a Catholic church nearly two blocks away. The number of flags surprised him. Competing with the band, a group off to his left started up a patriotic hymn, but the breeze wafted it up so it didn't catch on. Vendors selling sausages and souvenirs worked their way along the fringes of the crowd. One enterprising citizen, at some risk, appeared to be hawking miniature Confederate flags. Another adjusted a tripod to support an enormous box camera while his assistant wrote down orders from a line of enthusiasts. For the first time Jarom felt that he'd stepped forward naked, exposed.

Having seen enough, he now familiarized himself with what occupied the platform. Perched on top, the gallows was wobbly, the work of jacklegs, a word that Patterson defined as someone who takes a long time getting to where he's going to go and doesn't do much when he gets there. The only part adequately built was a six-by-six with one arm rising above the platform, well-braced and sturdy. Looking at it, he was sure it would support twice his one hundred fifty-three pounds. Crude but effective, it extended horizontally over a trapdoor in the center of the platform. This trap was hinged, supported from under by a prop to which a rope was attached. Remove the prop and the trap would fall. Centered above it and secured to the arm was the rope itself, two yards of braided hemp, obviously new. Looking at it, Jarom felt a quavering in his lower back just above the rectum, a lightness, a queasiness that shot along his spine, tingling. He felt his body in rebellion. Snapping his shoulders didn't rid him of shudders. He felt the ligatures in the joints of his arms begin to jerk sympathetically, and it took all of his concentration to compose them again. Nervously, he shot a glance at the crowd.

From the platform everything seemed more pronounced, more finely etched in space, even lighter, as though he'd walked into a familiar room one morning after a snowfall and found walls and objects, the air itself, brushed with bright intensity. Again he centered his attention on the rope, knotted in a hangman's noose. Irresistibly, it drew him like filings to a magnet. Though he tried to look away, he found himself counting the coils—one, two, three . . . thirteen, as he knew there would be. He imagined the rope as a caterpillar with thousands of tiny hairs. In the sunlight they glowed fine and honeyed as wisps of a woman's hair, the hair on Mollie Thomas's head.

Jarom felt unnerved, the feeling he'd had in his previous life when he sensed but could not remember some task he'd not completed, something important left undone. Mollie, Aunt Mary, Billy Magruder, Sam Jones, Patterson standing sightlessly—all rose in his mind. They huddled before him, an improbable grouping, strangers randomly assembled to pose for a tintype, held for a minute before the lens as the shadow-catcher counted the exposure, the light recorded, released.

Then George Swope, watching Jarom, fumbled with the handcuffs, his stubby fingers unable to fit the key. Finally the lock tripped, and Jarom felt the heavy rings slide from his wrists. Relief. Rubbing, he felt the blood return to his fingers, felt the itchy-tingling sensation as it irrigated his palms, his fingertips. He felt the corners of his mouth twitching and ran his tongue along his lips.

"I am the resurrection and the life," he said to himself.

On all sides of him was the platform, an almost perfect square. Nailed to the corner posts ran a single rail, waist high. Jarom saw himself as part of a composition: Swope, Talbot, Freckle-Face, and a black-hooded hangman. The center had been reserved for him. He took no pleasure in recognizing that the executioner, true to folklore, didn't speak but communicated only with nods. Jarom felt his stare through the eye holes in his hood. Significantly, he thought, the hood had a nose slit for breathing but no opening for the mouth. Nothing about him seemed human—no name, no identifiable features, no age. Even the sex wasn't certain. Who was he? Jarom suspected a regular soldier chosen or volunteering because he fit a soldierly ideal—impersonal, efficient, unquestioningly obedient, possessed of an undersized conscience impervious to guilt. *A machine,* Jarom thought, *to perform a machine's work.*

"Lord have mercy on my soul," Jarom whispered to himself, conscious that his lips were moving now.

The hood that covered the hangman's upper half hung in droopy pleats, much like a judge's gown. Beneath, he wore shapeless pants of ragged gray twill, holding too much heat for this weather. Jarom noticed his high-topped shoes, cheap and spotless.

Then down his neck Jarom felt the hangman's breath, familiar and tropical with a faint reek of garlic. He felt his wrists being bound with rope, this time from behind. The hooded figure stooped to bind his legs with a second length just above the calves, and he expected the noose itself to follow. From the corner of his eye he saw Swope ceremoniously put his hand to his hat, and the band stopped playing the Dead March, one stray horn blaring on for a few bars before dwindling into silence. There came a pause, and after a few moments the silence seemed to make everyone uneasy. Jarom could almost feel the respiration of ten thousand lungs as someone feels rather than hears the wing beats of low-flying geese, the air rippling as they pummel past. From the crowd came an incessant murmur of expectation that reminded Jarom of gravel being poured slowly from a cart.

Then Talbot stepped from his corner and knelt next to him, his bony knees on the hard decking.

"Will you kneel with me?" he asked, and Jarom knelt.

"Do you still take the Lord Jesus Christ as your Savior?" Talbot asked, not daring to look at him.

Remembering their sessions over the better part of two days, Jarom didn't answer. He remembered his baptism in the body and blood of Christ.

"Jarom," he said, "do you still take Jesus as your Lord and Savior?"

"I do," Jarom said.

"Have you confessed your sins and made your peace with God?"

"I have," Jarom said. He hadn't, wasn't able to enumerate them all, but thought to himself, *This is important to Talbot and it costs me nothing to say it.*

"Will you join me in the Lord's Prayer?"

Jarom looked over at him. His eyes, not yet ready to look at Jarom's, held to the plank floor on which Jarom's complaining knees were throbbing.

Not waiting for Jarom's answer, Talbot started the recitation.

Hearing Talbot's voice begin, deep in his throat Jarom felt his own breath shaping the familiar syllables and his lips trying to sound out the words. But no words came. Instead, his best voice produced a croaking whisper.

When Talbot reached the forgive-us-our-trespasses, Jarom couldn't find the words though he had them by heart, had recited them a thousand times. He glanced over to see if anyone noticed. Freckle-Face had lowered his head and closed his eyes, a perfect altar boy. Swope gazed off at some imaginary battlefield, dreaming of promotions and glory. Only the hangman looked at him, appraising him through his black mask like a wood-splitter sizing a stump. His eyes formed twin islands isolated from all the seasons and the world's ocean of feeling. Jarom considered that the eyes, marooned as they were from the other features of his face, knew everything, knew nothing.

Stumbling over the forgiveness part, Jarom picked up again with "for thine is the kingdom, and the power, and the glory."

Talbot's protracted "ahhh-min" consumed his own. Despite his show of piety, Jarom couldn't help wondering if this good man did not love more than a little the resonance of his own rich baritone.

Then Swope gathered his bulk to take the stage. He stepped forward and stiffened straight, tugging the ends of his tunic tight over his swelling chest, the slackness temporarily secured by the thick leather belt that girded his middle. He unfastened the front and produced an official-looking packet bound in blue ribbon. He untied it, unrolling an elaborate government document. Clearing his throat, he read the charges, the same Jarom had heard at the trial. Jarom did not listen to the sense but concentrated instead on the sounds, hoping Swope would falter or trip over a phrase, a tricky word that would grant him this small victory. In this he was disappointed. Swope's voice droned on faultlessly, mechanical and precise. As Jarom picked up the gist of it again, he noticed that the sounds had no life or spirit to them. They fell on the ear flat and gray, pennies on tin. Gray was Swope's color, a dull, dolt, possum gray.

As Swope droned out the specifications, Jarom gazed from his crow's nest over the fairgrounds. He saw a multitude of upturned, egg-shaped faces, the features painted on, as fixed and interchangeable as profiles on dimes. The mindless gawkers and bloodlusters he'd expected appeared somber, respectfully curious. In some of the faces he read a kind of reverence, that mix of cherub and undertaker he'd recognized at church funerals in Logan County among the faces of his neighbors. In the lifted chins and squinting eyes of others he detected expectancy and the mildest terror, an aura of disbelief that must pass among witnesses of miracles and climatic disasters.

Nearby, under a gray locust, stood an army express wagon, four broad-assed government mules plastered with flies twitching in the heat, their glistening rumps striped with harness. In its bed he saw a long plain pinewood box, wedge-shaped and shoulder-wide at one end, tapered where the limbs narrowed at the feet.

"Lord, have mercy on my soul," he heard himself saying. "Lord, have mercy."

Though he knew the army contracted for coffins by the tens of thousands, he couldn't remember seeing one before. The wagon driver, a pudgy man with pants cuffs stuffed into his boots in the way of teamsters, was palavering with some rough-looking customers gathered about one wheel. The driver must have made a joke, for they grinned and smirked before raising their heads to look up at him. No one else on the platform seemed to notice. They appeared to be listening intently as Swope read Jarom's full name, adding "alias Sue Mundy" in his lusterless monotone.

Jarom picked up snatches as Swope continued to read. Jarom had been duly tried and convicted of taking up arms as a guerrilla and outlaw in the counties of Nelson, Henry, Marion, Woodford, and so on, during the months of September, October, November, and so on. Jarom twitched involuntarily as Swope added that the prisoner had been sentenced to hang by the neck until dead. And then, almost as an afterthought, Swope asked if he had anything to say before sentence was carried out.

Jarom felt the impulse to repeat his request to be buried in full Confederate uniform or that, as a Confederate soldier, he be executed by firing squad rather than hanged as a common outlaw. But he knew it wasn't any use. He'd given the letters to Talbot who'd promised to see them delivered. He could see Mollie and Aunt Mary Tibbs opening theirs, ripping or cutting the mucilage where he had run his tongue across it. John Patterson stood glumly between them, his sightless eyes fixed on a horizon only the blind can see.

Jarom combed his memory for any last thing else he needed to say that would disburden him. He felt a tiny waver of relief as he considered that for the first time in his life his slate was empty—not clean but empty—his conscience as clear as ever it would be, as white as the scar on his left hand from the bullet that dug a ravine in its heel at Cynthiana nearly two years earlier. Nothing he could think of was left undone.

Then he noticed those below him closest to the scaffold shushing those behind. A bald little man wearing a green eye-shade held a pencil poised above a pad of foolscap. Prentice? He doubted it. Jarom turned his eyes from him, elevating his line of sight over their heads, nesting them in the top of a gigantic elm at the far end of the fairgrounds. The faintest breeze cooled the sweat runneling down his forehead. That same breeze thumbed the elm's willowy upper limbs, swaying its green-tipped branches, which seemed for an instant to be the only thing moving in that congestive place.

"Is there anything you would like to say?" Swope repeated, his tone this time immediate and palpable as a nudge.

A hush came over those close about, and Jarom heard himself effortlessly intoning, louder than he imagined he was able, the words he'd repeated over and over in his cell.

"I am a regular Confederate soldier and have served in the Confederate army four years. I fought under General Buckner at Fort Donelson and belonged to General Morgan's command when he entered Kentucky. I have assisted and taken many prisoners, and have always treated them kindly. I was wounded at Cynthiana and cut off from my command. I have been in Kentucky ever since. I could prove that I am a regular Confederate soldier. I am not guilty of the murders charged to me. I hate no one. I hope I will go to heaven. I hope in and die for the Confederate cause."

From behind he felt a hand remove his forage cap. Blinking, he tried to adjust to a new intensity in the sun. Then across the sea of faces he saw the elm transfused with a flood of pink light, tree and light dropping into darkness as someone lowered the hood over his head, the smarting in his eyes instantly soothed. He swallowed. And then he felt the noose, deftly but firmly tightened around his neck. As Swope began the counting, he felt the invisible observers suck in their collective breath and hold, his own breath held and shortened under the smothering veil.

"Lord, have mercy on my soul," he said. "Lord, have mercy on my soul."

EPILOGUE

As the procession was forming outside the military prison at Tenth and Broadway and before the guards brought Jarom from his cell, a tremendous bull suddenly appeared in the middle of Broadway. Apparently alarmed by the music, the throng of people in the street, and so much turbulent movement, the animal jumped its fence in a nearby field. According to a witness, the bull put his head down and pawed the earth with his forefeet, throwing clouds of dust over his shoulder. Fearing danger, some citizens in front, pushed forward by those behind, pulled out their pistols and fired at the bull. The wounds from the shots only inflamed the beast and made him furious, while the shots, "acting like an electric shock," as the witness described it, made every man in the crowd either run or draw his weapon. Finally, as the crowd pressed against his lowered horns, the bull fell dead. Those behind thought a riot was in progress or that remnants of Sue Mundy's band had arrived to cheat the hangman. People fled as the reserve inside the prison arrived with fixed bayonets, prepared to quell a riot. One commentator said the event engendered a black memory for the whole city. Had he heard the clamor outside, Jarom might have imagined the Berry brothers having arrived prematurely or perhaps on time to create a diversion of some kind.

Billy Magruder was not well enough to stand trial until September of 1865. During the proceedings, four guards carefully carried his cot into the courtroom each day. After a leisurely trial of thirteen days the commission pronounced him guilty and condemned him to hang. He received the sentence without any visible emotion, requesting only that he be executed in Bullitt County, a request the commission denied. Instead, a scaffold was set up in the prison yard. He was a smaller catch than Sue Mundy, and only about a thousand spectators were on hand. Five months after Appomattox, the political climate was changing, and there was less tolerance of military bloodletting. Like Clarke, Magruder often met with the Reverend Talbot, who, at Magruder's request, took down his confession. When the minister declined to have it published, Magruder persuaded Major Cyrus Wilson, his captor, to shepherd it into print. The result was *Three Years in the Saddle: The Life and Confession, Henry C. Magruder, the Original "Sue Munday," The Scourge of Kentucky, written by Himself.* Wilson said he agreed to publish the confession "for the moral effect it would have on young men." At the same time, with an eye to boosting sales, he misidentified Magruder as Sue Mundy. Praising Magruder's undying loyalty to his friends, the Reverend Talbot, later quoted in the newspaper, cited instances of noble actions on their behalf. His spiritual state, in Talbot's opinion, bespoke devotion to no higher being:

> He certainly had great tenacity for life both in terms of hope and physically. He has not made the preparation for dying that a man would naturally do who expected to die shortly. As his spiritual advisor, I have not attempted to teach him any further than the general truths of religion.

On October 20, his execution day, a priest, not Talbot, came to his cell and administered the last rites of the Roman Catholic Church. His mother, who came up from Bullitt County, was permitted to stand with him on the scaffold, where he made a request for a last smoke. After taking a few puffs, he passed her the butt and whispered goodbye just before they lowered the hood. He was suspended "between heaven and earth" a minute or two after four in the afternoon. When the body was cut down, it was loaded onto his mother's farm wagon and conveyed to Bullitt County, where his remains were buried on a hilltop near Lebanon Junction. Someone, probably a journalist, recorded his last public words: "Has anybody got a cigar?" For some reason, his comrade Henry Medkiff was released from custody after a stint in prison and allowed to go his way.

William C. Quantrill was not so lucky. On May 10, 1865, Edwin Terrell and his guerrilla hunters surrounded the barn of James H. Wakefield on Salt River in Spencer County. Quite by accident, Terrell and a party of thirty or so of his men had been passing along the roadway and spotted horse tracks leading to the Wakefield barn where Quantrill and his men had taken refuge after a terrific rainstorm. As Quantrill, alerted by Terrell's gunfire, was attempting to mount behind one of his men, the horse was shot from under them. Trying to pick himself up from the mud, he was hit by a Spencer ball that shattered his collarbone and ranged downward along the spine, paralyzing him from the chest down. A second freak shot took off his index finger, the trigger finger. Terrell had the wounded man loaded onto a wagon and driven to Louisville, where he died on June 6. In his last will and testament Quantrill left five hundred dollars to Kate King, known also as Kate Clarke, his common-law wife. With her legacy she went to St. Louis and opened what became one of the most famous whorehouses in the West.

Adam R. Johnson, blinded by his own men in a skirmish at Grubb's Crossroads in the Cumberland River country, was captured and sent to Fort Warren in Boston Harbor. Later exchanged, he refused a discharge, insisting on joining his old command in Mississippi. He reached Macon, Mississippi, just as news of Lee's surrender arrived at camp. He then returned to Texas, where he had settled before the war, and founded the town of Marble Falls, started a family, and also wrote a history of his war experiences, *The Partisan Rangers of the Confederate States Army* (1904). Born, like Patterson, in 1835, he died in 1922, aged eighty-eight.

In 1883 or 1884 a middle-aged resident of Webster County was arraigned in United States Court in Louisville on a charge of selling beer without a license. The illegal sales were made in a little saloon at Sebree Springs in western Kentucky. Called on to stand and make his plea, the defendant was assisted to his feet by a friend. Placing his cane before him, the man rose slowly and faced the direction from which the judge's voice had come. The prisoner's eyes were missing from their sockets.

"What is the matter with that man?" asked the Honorable John W. Barr, the judge presiding.

"He is blind, sir," answered the friend.

"How did he lose his eyes?" the judge asked.

"Had them shot out in the war."

"I don't care to go on with this case," said District Attorney George M. Thomas. "I cannot prosecute a man like that for a trivial offense like this."

And the prisoner, John L. Patterson, was released.

After the war ended, One-Armed Berry was arrested, tried by a military commission, found guilty on February 10, 1866, of eleven separate murders, and condemned to be hanged on March 3. As a result of appeals for clemency by Berry's relatives and friends, there came a siege of petitionary letters, including one from George D. Prentice, who described Berry as "the most humane and best of them all." John Palmer, still military commander of Kentucky, commuted the sentence to ten years of hard labor at Sing Sing Penitentiary in New York, where Berry died after serving seven years. Before being incarcerated, he married and had a son. He complained that he was the fourth-longest-serving inmate in the prison and the only Confederate still serving time. He also complained that during his imprisonment he never saw the light of day.

Thomas F. Berry was more fortunate. He survived his many war wounds, both real and imagined, and went on to fight as a mercenary in Mexico and in North Africa with the French army. Later, he set up a medical practice in Louisville and wrote an account of his wartime experiences, as much fiction as fact, *Four Years in the Saddle with Morgan and Forrest* (1914). He eventually moved west to Paul's Valley, Oklahoma, where he died peacefully in the second decade of the new century.

As mentioned, both of George D. Prentice's sons joined the Confederate army. Courtland was mortally wounded by a minie ball, mistakenly fired by a friend, during Morgan's fight at Augusta, Kentucky. After the death of Courtland in 1862, the father assuaged his grief by publicly professing his faith in the Divine Creator, being baptized December 7, 1862. In 1870, at the age of sixty-seven he quietly died of pneumonia, his last words being "I want to go. I want to go." After a speech in 1833, he had stated his hope that he might pass "the remnant of my years and finally . . . be gathered to the dust of Kentucky." And so it was. His surviving son, Clarence, ended the war with the rank of colonel. He was accused of murdering a fellow soldier. On the way to Richmond, Virginia, to attend his trial, editor Prentice stopped in Washington City for an interview with President Lincoln, who is supposed to have said, "Did you think I'd let them hang your boy? Sit down, Prentice, and tell me a good story."

There are two traditions about what became of Mollie Thomas. One is that, true to her sweetheart, she remained a spinster and was still living near Bloomfield, Kentucky, at the outbreak of World War I. The other is that she married a few years after Clarke's execution and was still living near Bloomfield, Kentucky, at the outbreak of World War I.

After the execution Jerome Clarke's remains were taken to the old Western Cemetery to be sent in care of his aunt, Nancy Bradshaw, by early train south to Franklin, Kentucky. Souvenir seekers had stolen his black velvet cap and cut the buttons from his dark cavalry coat as well as locks of his curly black hair. In 1914, nearly fifty years after his death, the Simpson County Chapter of the United Veterans of the Confederacy had the remains exhumed and moved to Green Lawn Cemetery to be buried among the Confederate dead. The transfer, which cost ten dollars and fifteen cents, was performed by L. L. House Mortuary in Franklin. One of the charges was for furnishing a coach, horsedrawn and seating eight, for the "Old Soldiers" who accompanied the remains on their journey—a kind of honor guard. When the coffin was opened to identify the body, House said that the skeleton contained the remnants of a Confederate uniform. The skull was nested in tangles of long black hair. The neck bones were broken.

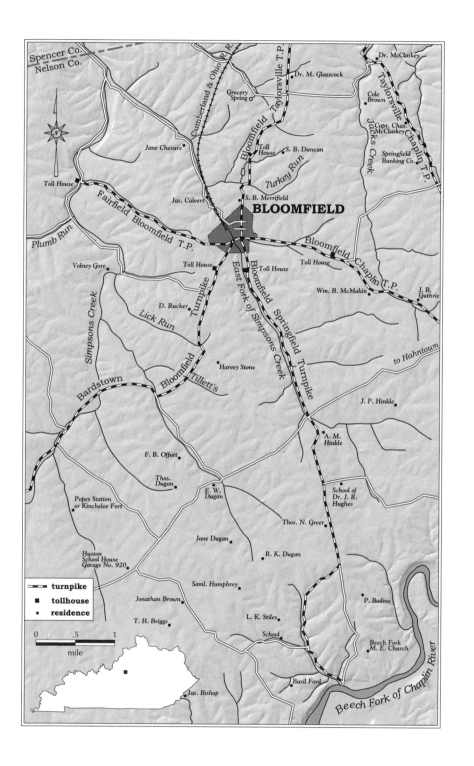

Spencer Co.
Nelson Co.

Cumberland & Ohio R.R.

Bloomfield Taylorsville T.P.

Dr. McClaskey

Dr. M. Glasscock

Grocery
Spring

Taylorsville Chaplin T.P.

Cole
Brown

Jacks Creek

Capt. Chas.
McClaskey

Jane Chesure

Bloomfield

Toll
House

S. B. Duncan

Springfield
Banking Co.

Turkey Run

Toll House

Jas. Calvert

S. B. Merrifield

BLOOMFIELD

Fairfield Bloomfield T.P.

Plumb Run

Bloomfield Chaplin T.P.

Toll House

Toll House

Toll House

Volney Gore

Bloomfield

Turnpike

Wm. B. McMakin

J. B.
Guthrie

D. Rucker

Lick Run

East Fork of Simpsons Creek

Bloomfield Springfield Turnpike

Simpsons Creek

Harvey Stone

to Hahntown

Bardstown

Bloomfield

Tillett's

J. P. Hinkle

A. M.
Hinkle

F. B. Offutt

Thos.
Dugan

E. W.
Dugan

School of
Dr. J. R.
Hughes

Popes Station
or Kincheloe Fort

Thos. N. Greer

Jane Dugan

R. K. Dugan

Huston
School House
Garage No. 920

Saml. Humphrey

P. Bodine

turnpike

tollhouse

residence

Jonathan Brown

T. H. Briggs

L. K. Stiles

School

Beech Fork
M. E. Church

0   .5   1

mile

Basil Ford

Beech Fork of Chaplin River

Jas. Bishop